Felicity at the Cross Hotel

HELENA FAIRFAX

ISBN 13: 978-0-9933615-9-3

To Joe
Wish you were here

ACKNOWLEDGMENTS

With grateful thanks to
Paul and Kath Renucci
and the divers of Penrith Divers' Club

Chapter One

Fliss

At last it had stopped raining. Fliss lowered the window of her old car, letting in the smell of damp asphalt and sodden leaves. A faint whiff of burning mingled with the earthier odours, and she cast an anxious glance at the bonnet.

'Don't give up on me here, Agnetha,' she pleaded. 'This is no place to break down.'

For the past three miles as she'd climbed the steep incline out of the valley, Fliss hadn't seen a soul. The village of Emmside, whose high street had provided her with the last latte of civilisation, now lay far below her. Here, high up on the fell, there was nothing but shadows and the dark, brooding branches of trees hanging over her head. It was enough to make a girl feel dismal.

Fliss, never one to remain downcast for long, switched on the radio to banish the silence, and soon the merry sound of her singing streamed down the hillside through her open window. She put the car into its lowest gear to round a sharp curve and slammed on the brakes.

'Wow. Look at that. This was worth the climb.'

Agnetha, Fliss's faithful car of many years' travel, rumbled and spluttered in agreement. The road had surfaced above the trees and far below was Lake Emmswater, shimmering green

3

and silver, like a scene from a fairy tale.

On an impulse, Fliss turned her car into a lay-by on the other side of the road, pulling up beside a dark four-by-four. There was a man standing by the dry stone wall that bounded the steep slope. He was gazing down at the lake, shoulders hunched, hands thrust deep in his jacket pockets. Apart from the light breeze ruffling his hair he could have been carved into the wall himself.

Fliss climbed out of her car and moved to stand beside him. The jagged mountains of the Lake District rose and fell in great dark peaks on the skyline, their sides flecked with splashes of bright, mossy green. Soft fields crept down into the valley, dotted with the fluffy white forms of sheep, and lying at the centre of it all was the gleaming lake.

Fliss took in a deep breath, letting the fresh air fill her lungs. 'What a magical place,' she said to the man standing next to her. 'All those gloomy trees – and now this.'

Her neighbour turned at the sound of her voice, moving slowly, as though surfacing from a dream. Fliss, who'd been too enthralled by the scene to pay him much attention, was taken aback to confront eyes as sombre as the trees behind them, and as cheerless. His complexion was browned by the sun, and his strong hands, which he'd removed from his pockets to rest on the wall, were weathered. Wherever he'd spent the past few years, it wasn't under these leaden skies. Something about his bearing made Fliss think of the sea. It was as though here, on dry land, he was lost and out of his element.

Fliss wasn't often given to fanciful thoughts. *If you see someone without a smile, give them one of your own.* It worked for Dolly Parton, and so Fliss smiled. The stranger blinked at the full wattage of her beam.

'I had to stop,' she told him. 'It was the view. And look, the sun's come out.' She held up a hand to the pale sky. 'Where I come from is so flat. I'm starting to get vertigo here, but in a really good way. Like being on the roller-coaster at Great Yarmouth fun fair.'

Her smile turned into a deep-throated chuckle.

The man in the walking jacket leaned back against the wall. Fliss was used to strangers being baffled by her chattiness and didn't usually let it deter her. Just now, though, something in this man's remote expression gave her the feeling she'd done something wrong, like laugh out loud at a funeral. Discomfited, she looked at her watch, and said in a rush, 'Oh Lord, I didn't realise how late it was. Time I drove on.'

'Have you far to go?' His voice, when he finally spoke, was surprisingly melodious. Despite his sun-tanned features, he had the soft Cumbrian accent of the Lakes. No romantic stranger, then, and obviously a local. Fliss smiled to herself at her wayward imagination.

'I'm heading for the Cross Hotel,' she told him. 'Do you know it?'

The stranger stretched out his hand. 'I should know it. I'm Patrick Cross.'

Finally he returned her smile, and his sombre features were transformed, like the lake appearing out of the gloom.

Fliss took his hand in hers and continued to smile up at him. 'Patrick Cross! Then you'll know who I am. Felicity Everdene. Good to meet you.' She registered his blank expression. 'Fliss Everdene,' she repeated. 'I've come to help out in the hotel?' Still no reaction except a small, baffled frown. 'Jilly Cross is expecting me,' she finished.

Patrick Cross let go of her hand, realisation dawning. 'Ah. Something my mother organised.'

'That's right.' Now it was Fliss's turn to be puzzled. 'Your mother and mine are old friends. It was arranged between them just a few days ago. Your mum hasn't mentioned my coming?'

'No.' Patrick cast an uncertain glance at Fliss's old car. 'My mother hasn't been herself recently. I expect you know my father died three months ago.'

The smile left Fliss's face. Of course. How stupid of her. Patrick Cross must be grieving, and there would be confusion in the hotel. 'I'm sorry,' she said. 'My mother told me. It must have been a terrible shock.'

Patrick shrugged. 'His death was quite sudden, but I suppose with his lifestyle and temperament, he was bound to have a heart attack.'

For once Fliss was speechless, silenced by the callousness of his reply.

Patrick's lips twisted under her scrutiny, and he added, 'I'm on my way back to the hotel now. Would you like me to lead the way?'

His offer was civil enough, but the chill in his expression made Fliss wonder what sort of welcome awaited her at the Cross Hotel, high on the hillside and miles from other people. She had to remind herself that Patrick was the son of one of her mother's friends, and hardly likely to be an axe-murderer.

'Thanks for the offer,' she said. 'My car's been playing up for the past few miles. It would be good to have an escort.'

Patrick threw another doubtful glance in Agnetha's direction, but said nothing, and merely headed for his Land Rover. He'd already climbed inside and had the engine running while Fliss was still fumbling with her car's door. The old catch continued to stick, no matter how many times she oiled it.

'Don't play up, Agnetha,' she murmured. 'We're being watched.'

Fliss was used to defending her car from criticism. Keeping Agnetha on the road was yet another of the "eccentricities" her father complained about.

'You're Operations Manager in the Everdene hotel chain,' he'd once said, exasperated. 'How do you expect staff to take you seriously if you arrive in that decrepit piece of junk?'

A sudden image of her father popped into her mind – white-faced and furious after their last row. Fliss hated conflict of any kind, and it was an image she'd been unable to shake off for the entire journey.

Feeling Patrick's eyes on her, she wrenched open the car door, and, once seated behind the wheel, jabbed her key in the ignition and turned it. The engine gave a whining screech, followed by an ominous whirr, and then silence. The lights on the dashboard winked reproachfully.

'I'm sorry, Agnetha!' Fliss turned the key again – using more care this time – but the car's old engine failed to respond.

In her rear view mirror Fliss could see Patrick climbing back out of his Land Rover. He began making his way towards her, a resigned expression on his face. She gave an inward groan and leaned her head out of the window as he approached.

'My car is just not used to the mountains,' she told him defensively. 'We were fine in Norfolk.'

The frown deepened on Patrick's brow. He was studying the exhaust, where a wisp of black smoke was slowly sinking onto the ground.

Fliss took a deep breath and swung open her door.

Patrick

Patrick could swear the engine carried on rattling, even as Fliss stepped out of the car. The look of dismay on her face was so comical he might have laughed, if the weight of his own worries hadn't been so oppressive. What on earth was his mother thinking, asking this eccentric young woman to stay? As if they didn't have enough problems, without giving free board to every waif and stray.

He cleared his throat and said stiffly, 'If you'd like to get your bags, I'll give you a lift. It's not far to the hotel. Our porter is good with engines. I'll ask him to pop down and take a look. Hopefully he'll be able to get her going again.' He checked himself, annoyed at having succumbed to giving the rust heap a personality. 'I mean "it", not "her". Your car.'

'Thank you.'

Fliss smiled. It was a nice smile, and Patrick couldn't help but soften a little, but as she picked her way towards the boot to retrieve her bag his attention was drawn by her shoes – shiny, pastel blue, and several inches high. How on earth had she managed to drive all the way from Norfolk? Then she lifted the boot door, revealing an astonishing array of random belongings wedged into the tiny space inside. Several items would have fallen out if Patrick hadn't darted forward. He caught hold of a bright red clutch bag in one hand and an empty cassette box in the other.

Patrick hadn't seen a mix tape in years. He turned the box over to examine the playlist and the urge to laugh returned, despite himself.

'I didn't take you for a Beastie Boys fan,' he said.

'It's my sister's favourite.' Fliss cast him a glance, as though about to say something else, but then added merely, 'Sometimes singing "You've Gotta Right (to Party!)" is the only thing to keep her happy on long journeys. Even our dad has been known to sing along.'

She pushed aside a couple more bags and dragged out her suitcase, which Patrick took from her, wincing under the weight of it.

'Thanks,' Fliss said. 'Just one more thing.' Leaning right into the car again, she began to rummage through the contents. 'It's in here somewhere.'

A bewildering selection of articles was stuffed in the tiny boot. Patrick noted a tennis racket, an inflatable dolphin (still only partly deflated), several battered paperbacks, and various other bits and pieces, all mingled together with a jumble of handbags and brightly-coloured berets.

'I'll have to leave all these here,' Fliss said, rooting through. 'I'll just get the essentials for now.' The muscles on her slender arms bulged as she gave a furious tug. 'There.' She stepped back in triumph. 'Got it.' She clutched a large stuffed giraffe to her, her face flushed with exertion. She caught the look on Patrick's face and raised her chin. 'It's one of my sister's. She wanted me to bring it.'

The blue of Fliss's eyes held a disconcerting amount of steel, as though challenging Patrick to comment.

'I see,' he said mildly. 'And how old's your sister?'

There was a short hesitation. 'Eighteen.'

Again the challenging look, as though Fliss were daring him to mock her sister's childlike enthusiasms. Unfortunately the effect was lessened by the fact that she was brandishing a stuffed giraffe. A giraffe with only one eye.

Patrick gave a genuine smile, for the first time since meeting her. For the first time in a long while, if truth be told. He bent to collect her wheeled case, noting as he did so the expensive logo. It was a brand well out of the reach of most hotel workers' pay packets. Fliss's luggage was probably worth twice as much as her car. Patrick's brows rose, but he said nothing, merely hoisted the case up, trying not to stagger under the weight of it, and made his way to the Land Rover. While he stowed the bag in the boot, Fliss climbed into the passenger seat.

Patrick opened his own door to get in the driver's side and found the giraffe wedged in the space between them. Its long neck slumped towards him as he climbed in. Fliss gave a throaty chuckle. Her hand brushed Patrick's leg as she righted the stuffed toy.

'Raffles could do with his own seatbelt,' she said.

Fliss launched into a stream of one-sided conversation that lasted all the way to the hotel. She told Patrick all about her journey from Norfolk and how she'd travelled the world, but had never been to the Lake District. She told him how magnificent the scenery was here, and how she couldn't believe she hadn't visited Emmside sooner, even though her mum and Patrick's mum were such good friends

Patrick let Fliss's easy flow of chat wash over him, his mind on several problems waiting for him back at the hotel. The list of his problems was long, and so it was a while before it dawned on him that there was something a little forced about Fliss's relentless cheer. He glanced in her direction. The ridiculous giraffe had flopped against her shoulder, and she had stopped talking briefly in order to right it. There was a small frown on her face as she patted the soft toy into place, as though she too had things on her mind.

They emerged from the overhanging branches of the single-track drive and into the hotel forecourt. The sun was falling on the whitewashed walls of the Tudor building. Fliss sat up straight. When Patrick looked her way again, he was astonished to find she was scrutinising the hotel's exterior, a shrewd expression on her face, for all the world as though she were an estate agent about to put in an offer.

Fliss noticed his attention on her and turned to him with a wide smile. 'What a lovely surprise after that dark approach. You can see right down into the valley from your terrace. And all those mullioned windows and the old oak beams. Your hotel must have been here for centuries. It's an amazing place.'

Patrick brought the car to a halt in the car park. The mullioned windows Fliss raved about were in need of repointing, and the oak beams badly needed coating before the autumn set in. Patrick thought of all the other jobs his father had left undone, and the money needed to pay for them. He found himself unable to reply, afraid of the bitterness that might creep into his voice.

There was a light touch on his arm. Fliss was studying him, full of sympathy.

'I expect this old building takes a lot to maintain,' she said. 'I can see why my mum thought I might be able to help.'

Patrick was speechless. He was unable to work out how this stuffed-toy wielding chatterbox could possibly be a help.

The giraffe slid sideways again, half-falling onto Patrick's lap. He pushed it aside and opened the car door.

'Let's go and find my mother,' he said gruffly. He leaned back in to add, with a confidence he was far from feeling, 'I'm sure she's expecting you.'

Chapter Two

Fliss

Fliss made her way over the gravel towards the hotel entrance, wondering if Patrick Cross was always this bad-tempered. There had been a ferocious scowl on his face as he'd stepped out of the car. Then she thought of the one time he'd smiled. The shadows had lifted, and his dark eyes had danced. He'd looked completely different. Fliss – always ready to see the best in people – reminded herself that Patrick had just lost his father. Underneath the irritable exterior there was probably a charming man lurking. Then he held the door wide for her, and she cast a glance at his stony face. The charm was obviously hidden quite deep.

Fliss stepped into the reception, taking in her surroundings with a quick, professional eye. With the light filtering through the mullioned windows and with the old oak beams giving it character, the reception at the Cross Hotel could have been delightful. Instead, the place was distinctly unwelcoming. It was hard to ignore the worn curtains, since their shade was a vile puce. A stiff row of chairs was ranged along one wall, and the stern notice stating "Lost Keys Must Be Paid For" did nothing to make guests feel at home.

A middle-aged woman stood behind the reception desk. She was wearing a pair of chic black-rimmed glasses, her hair swept back off her brow with an Alice band, and was flipping through some papers in a bewildered manner. She lifted her head at their entrance and straightened up, painting a bright smile of welcome onto her strained features.

'Hello,' she called out, looking at Fliss curiously.

Fliss tucked the giraffe under her arm and approached the desk, hand outstretched. 'You must be Jilly,' she said. 'You look just like your photos. Mum's told me so much about you. She said you were pretty, and you really are.'

A youthful blush rose to Jilly's face. She studied Fliss at a loss for a moment, and then her eyes widened. 'Oh darling, you must be Felicity.' She came out from behind the desk and gave Fliss a hug, the giraffe wedged between them, its one eye wide in surprise.

'Yes, that's me,' Fliss said. 'Only call me Fliss, please. Felicity is so worthy. Why my parents saddled me with such a name, I don't know. It doesn't suit me at all.' She stood back, taking in Jilly's pallor and the faint shadows under her eyes. Her smile faded. 'I was sorry when Mum told me,' she said. 'About your husband, I mean.'

'Thank you, darling.' The lines in Jilly's forehead deepened.

Fliss glanced at the papers littering the desk. 'Mum thought I could help. She would have come herself, only you know how it is…'

Jilly squeezed Fliss's hand. 'It's so like your mother, darling. We haven't seen each other in years – you know the ties of the hotel trade, more than anyone – but we've always kept in touch. Your mother's such a dear friend. It's good of her and your father to let you go. I'm sure they must need you far more than we do.'

'Not at all. Dad works me so hard, coming here will be like a holiday.' Fliss gave another of her cheerful laughs. Out of the corner of her eye, she thought she caught Patrick roll his eyes at her mention of a holiday, as though she were some sort of airhead. She shifted a little, so he was no longer in her line of vision.

Jilly held Fliss at arm's length to examine her. 'Well, I can't believe Helen has a grown-up daughter.'

'She has two,' Fliss reminded her with a smile. 'Minnie was really upset I've gone away again, so she gave me Raffles to look after me.' She waved the giraffe in front of Jilly's face.

Jilly laughed. 'Oh did she, the darling? Minnie must take after her mother, then. Always thinking of other people.' Her laughter died as quickly as it had come. 'I'm so glad you're here, Fliss. We're so busy at the moment, what with one thing and another. And now one of the staff has left us in the lurch. Although why Pauline had to go off like that, I don't know.' She cast a quick glance at Patrick, and Fliss noted a flicker of something pass between them. Jilly went on with forced brightness, 'I'm sure you must be dying to get to your room and unpack. And then perhaps you could start behind the bar this evening?'

'The bar?' Fliss faltered. This wasn't exactly what her mother had had in mind when she'd offered Fliss's expertise. 'Oh, I've never worked behind a bar. I thought – '

Behind her there was a muffled sigh from Patrick.

Jilly broke in swiftly. 'Really, darling? I could swear your mother said you'd run a bar. But we've been all at sixes and sevens these past few weeks. I daresay I got confused. Never mind, there's nothing to it. And if you get stuck, I'm sure Patrick will be happy to help.' She lifted her head in Patrick's direction, not quite meeting his eye. 'Won't you, darling? Now, I really must get back to these invoices.' She hurried back behind her desk. 'We must catch up when you're settled, Fliss. There's so much to talk about.'

'Yes, that would be lovely.' The brightness left Fliss's voice for a moment, but she squeezed the giraffe to her chest and treated Patrick to another wide smile. 'So, better show me the ropes.'

It was all very different from Fliss's usual hotel visits. When she arrived at an Everdene hotel in her capacity as Operations Manager, the staff would make sure she had the best room available. The manager would escort her to her room, where there would be flowers to welcome her, and soft, fluffy towels, and requests to phone reception if there was anything at all she needed.

Here, after showing Fliss the way up a couple of flights of stairs, Patrick deposited her case without ceremony in a bare bedroom. He proceeded to tell Fliss where to find the staff showers, that dinner for the staff was served at five pm, and that her first shift behind the bar started at six.

Then he added, 'If you give me your key I'll get our porter to drive down and take a look at your car. I'm pretty sure he'll be able to get it started. He'll at least get it back to the hotel until you have time to call a garage.'

Fliss smiled gratefully and fished her key out of her pocket. She was just reflecting that perhaps Patrick wasn't so bad after all, when she caught him frowning at her shoes. Patrick took the key from her and added, without sounding too hopeful about it, that he was sure Fliss had some sensible footwear, as she'd be on her feet for some time.

After Patrick had gone, Fliss flopped down onto the bed. After the unwelcoming atmosphere in reception, it was a pleasure to find her room so cosy. Everything was spotlessly clean, the linen on the bed crisp and white. Above her were the same wooden beams she'd noticed in the entrance, with its low ceiling and stone window arches. It was all a delicious change from the uniform bedrooms that were found in every Everdene Hotel.

Fliss smiled to herself, lifted Minnie's giraffe and stared into its one eye. 'We're a long way from Kansas, Raffles.'

Raffles didn't answer, and so Fliss sat up and placed him on the window ledge. It was then she noticed the view again. She opened the window and leaned out, breathing in a great gulp of wild, fresh air. The coppery smell of wet earth, the wild garlic beneath the trees, and the woody scent of yellow gorse filled her nostrils. The afternoon sky was palest blue over the mountains, growing ever paler until it became almost colourless on the horizon.

'Isn't this glorious?' she whispered. Raffles continued to

ignore her. She was just contemplating leaving her room to explore the hotel when there was a knock at her door.

'Hello-o-o,' came a male voice. 'Are you the new barmaid?'

Fliss pulled the window to. News of her arrival had spread, in that way it did in small hotels. And apparently she really was now a barmaid.

'I am,' she called.

A pale, handsome face appeared round the door, beneath a blond quiff. A pair of enquiring blue eyes met Fliss's, and the face split in a smile of intense relief.

'Thank God you're here.' The young man caught sight of Raffles, sitting at a drunken angle on the window ledge. Without waiting to be invited in, he made his way across the room and picked up the giraffe, waving it at Fliss. 'And who's this? Reinforcements?'

'That's Raffles, and my name's Fliss. I'd say come in, but you already are.'

The response was an unrepentant grin. 'My name's Johnny. I'm the head waiter. Or I was until our last barmaid left.' His smile vanished. 'No one's heard anything from Pauline except a scribbled note. I don't suppose you – ?'

Fliss shook her head. The mystery of the missing Pauline was beginning to intrigue her. 'I know nothing. I'm a total stranger here. And anyway, why would Pauline leaving mean you're not head waiter anymore?'

Johnny dropped onto the bed, clutching Raffles, his expression miserable. 'I've had to take over Pauline's shifts on the bar. That means Patrick's been doing front-of-house. God, everything in this place is just such a mess. Please tell me you're starting tonight.'

'Well, I am, but I can't promise I'll be much help. I've never worked behind a bar in my life, and all Patrick said was he didn't have time to show me, and I'd pick it up no problem.'

Johnny grunted. 'Typical. Patrick doesn't know his bum from a banana.' His forehead wrinkled. 'I thought Jilly Cross said you were some sort of hotel whizz kid.'

'Oh.' Fliss eyed Johnny's friendly countenance. How nice it

would be to enjoy an easy conversation with the staff for a while, without being associated with her father and the notorious Everdene Hotel chain. 'I've got a lot of experience working in hotels,' she said, which was the truth – although not all of it. 'And now I can add the bar to my CV.'

'Well, in that case you'll learn the ropes no problem. So, I'm guessing Patrick was too busy to show you around?'

Fliss nodded. 'I got the showers, and that's where my tour ended.'

'That sounds about right. Patrick never has time for anything.' Johnny stood, tossing Raffles back onto the window-ledge. 'Come on, I'll show you round.'

Fliss hadn't had much opportunity to examine the hotel during Patrick's hurried march to her room. Now, as she and Johnny came down the stairs in a more leisurely fashion, she noticed the sash window on the landing, and the way the wonderful view over the valley was spoiled by a pair of worn velvet curtains in the same hideous shade she'd seen in reception. Several prints of the Lake District, in heavy frames, lined the stairs. The pictures were fading, but all had been dusted, and the glass shone. The red floral carpet – an overpowering mass of swirls – was also clean and well swept. Everything was orderly, despite the signs of decay.

Fliss was surprised, and quite touched, to see Johnny's world-weary irony fall away as he surveyed the magnificent view from the window. She took in his rapt expression and asked, 'Have you worked here long?'

He turned to lead the way downstairs, the brightness fading. 'Since I left school.'

'The hotel can't be that bad a place.'

'I've had good times here.' The slump of his shoulders belied his words.

Goodness, what an unhappy hotel this seems to be, Fliss thought. She followed Johnny in silence until they reached the ground floor and the corridor leading to the reception. Here was another tall window, flanked by more of the ghastly curtains. Again Johnny was drawn to the view, and Fliss went to stand beside him. This time even the beauty of the scene outside failed to raise his spirits, and his mouth turned down. On one of Fliss's sudden impulses she decided to try and cheer him up. She reached forward to pull the curtain out of its brass holder and, draping it around herself, peered out at Johnny from beneath its fringe.

'My name is Felicity Charlotte Everdene.' Her voice vibrated with melodrama. 'You killed my father. Prepare to die.'

Johnny laughed. He had a high-pitched laugh, and the sound of it was incongruous coming from his smooth, handsome features. Fliss couldn't help but laugh as well. There was the noise of voices from a room along the corridor. She put her hand over her mouth to stifle her snorts. Johnny's shoulders shook, and although he pressed his lips together, his giggles continued to come out in a high wheeshing sound that made Fliss shake with the effort to control her laughter.

The sound of a male voice grew louder. Instantly Fliss tried to disengage herself from the curtain. Johnny was no help. He abandoned her, turning to the window, hands in his pockets, pretending to look out at the view. Only his shaking shoulders gave anything away. To her dismay, Fliss found her necklace had become snagged on the curtain's worn lining. She gave a couple of tugs and realised she couldn't extricate herself without ripping the tired fabric. She thought with panic of hiding herself completely behind the drape, but it was too late. Patrick came to a stop in front of them, an astonished expression on his face.

Patrick

Patrick glanced from Fliss to the head waiter, whose back was towards him, shoulders trembling with suppressed mirth. He might have known it. Johnny had been full of nothing but irony and facetious comments ever since Patrick arrived back at the hotel, and after Pauline's sudden departure his attitude had grown worse.

The fringe of those hideous curtains hung over Fliss's face, and she was peering out at him, full of remorse. If he hadn't been so full of irritation at Johnny, Patrick might have laughed.

'I was just looking out of the window, and I don't know what happened.' Fliss raised one arm, baffled. 'I seem to have got stuck in the curtain.' The drape slid further over her forehead, and she pushed it back. Johnny made a choking sound. Fliss's eyes brimmed with laughter. 'I'm sorry,' she said.

Patrick took a step towards her and gave the curtain a hefty tug, causing her to jerk forward, stumbling into him. He caught hold of her arms and saw that her necklace was fastened in the lining.

'Could you possibly leave the furnishings alone?' he said, exasperation finally getting the better of him. 'My mother's got enough to worry about, heaven knows, without replacing damaged curtains, or having guests think they've wandered into a kindergarten.'

He moved to release her, his hands brushing her skin as he worked the caught links free. Her face was close to his, and he had the fleeting impression of sun-warmed peaches, and a trace of some fresh scent, and then the curtain fell away. Fliss stepped back, running her fingers through her dishevelled hair. She had stopped laughing and was looking at him with a sober expression.

Patrick glanced up to find Johnny glowering in the window, and all his irritation returned.

'Just think next time, will you?'

He turned away. By the time he reached reception he was filled with remorse. He had a sudden vision of his dive school in the Caribbean – the crisp sand burning in the heat, the sun dancing on the clear water as he pushed out his boat. The yearning to escape the stifling confines of the Cross Hotel was sharp and fierce, and he was forced to quell it.

He pushed open the door to reception to find his mother in almost the same position he'd left her, sifting through a handful of brown envelopes. All thoughts of abandoning the hotel he'd inherited vanished. He came round to her side of the desk and gathered up the letters into a neat pile.

'Why don't you take a break for a while?' he said gently. 'I've finished in the office for the day. I can easily take over here.'

'I'm all right, Patrick.' The forced cheerfulness in her voice was painful to hear. 'We're not busy. And isn't it great that Felicity is here? I'm so glad her mother suggested her coming. I'm sure she'll be such a help, and now she's on the bar you won't have to work in the evenings, and Johnny can go back to his job waiting and perhaps he'll cheer up.'

'Mum.' Exhaustion took hold of Patrick like a physical thing. 'I'm sure your old friend meant well, it's just that – ' He spread his hands wide, not wanting to hurt his mother's feelings. 'I'm not convinced this Fliss, or whatever she's called, is really cut out for hotel work.'

'Not cut out for it?' His mother's eyes widened in astonishment. 'Whatever are you talking about, Patrick? She's Felicity Everdene. Her dad is James Everdene. Of Everdene Hotels. And she has some high-powered title, like Operations Manager, or some such. There was even an article about her last year in one of the Sunday papers. Her mum sent me the link.'

Patrick tried to fit this high-powered description with the young woman he'd found giggling like a schoolgirl in the corridor, and failed. Then he remembered the way she'd examined the outside of the hotel and the shrewd glance she'd given the reception room as they'd stepped through the door. His heart gave a dive so swift he was momentarily bereft of speech.

'You mean you've invited someone from Everdene Hotels to come and work here?'

The shock of his father's death, followed by his discovery of the terrible state of the hotel's finances, were all taking their toll. Patrick tried to remain calm, but he could feel his impatience swelling, along with a rush of anxiety. Of all the foolhardy things to do! He caught sight of his mother's worried expression and tried to damp down his response.

'I've been away from the hotel trade for years, Mum, but

even I've heard of James Everdene. He only needs a sniff of a hotel in financial trouble and he's straight in with his legal team. Next thing you know he's bought it up for his own blasted chain, and plastered the Everdene logo everywhere. If Fliss Everdene is James Everdene's daughter, then perhaps it's not such a good idea to have her working here.'

Jilly's eyes met his, wide and troubled. 'I'm sure my friend Helen would never be party to anything underhand. Not with me. I've known her for years.'

'And when did you last see her?'

His mother frowned, considering. 'It was when you and Fliss were toddlers.' She caught Patrick's exasperated expression and added quickly, 'Well, she lives so far away, and we're both busy. But that doesn't mean we haven't been in regular touch. I can't believe Fliss has any ulterior motive in coming here. Just the opposite. Between you and me – ' She lowered her voice. 'Helen told me there's been a lot of conflict recently between Fliss and her father. Apparently Fliss was supposed to be streamlining a new takeover in Sydney. I don't know what happened but it seems she didn't do whatever it was her dad wanted her to. When she got back from Australia there was a big row. Her mum thought Fliss might like to come here for a break for a while, that's all.'

Patrick digested this information in silence and then sighed. 'Well, we can hardly send her straight back to Norfolk. It's just as well you asked her to work on the bar. Hopefully that will keep her out of harm's way.'

Later, when Patrick was back in his office – having relieved Jilly of the bills on her desk – the sudden memory of Fliss's face close to his came back to him, her lively eyes peeping out from beneath the curtain. He thought of the easy-going way she'd accepted her tiny room and shared showers, even though she must be accustomed to having an entire suite to herself. He remembered how she'd raised her chin in defence of her sister's ridiculous giraffe. In different circumstances, Patrick might have looked forward to getting to know Fliss better.

His eye fell on the bills in front of him and he frowned.

With the way things were, having Felicity Everdene on the loose in the hotel was only adding to his worries. The sooner she left the Cross Hotel, the better.

Chapter Three

Fliss

'Actually, meals aren't too bad,' Johnny conceded grudgingly as he and Fliss continued their tour. He pushed open the door to the staff canteen. 'Tomasz is a good chef. Only don't tell him I said that, because his head's big enough already. Literally.'

They made their way to the serving hatch, behind which the kitchen staff were preparing the evening meal. There was the same atmosphere of suppressed urgency that Fliss had noted in umpteen similar establishments. A young man was bent over a table slicing vegetables with infinite care. An older woman threw ingredients into a massive pot simmering on a hob, whilst a girl scurried from the preparation table to the dish-washer and back. The kitchen at the Cross Hotel was clean and ordered, and the staff were working together in quick harmony. The quiet was broken by a jaunty whistle, the dish-washer rattled and emitted steam, and overall the delicious smell of garlic, rosemary, and roasting lamb wafted towards them.

'Seen Tomasz?' Johnny called.

'Who wants him?' An enormous head poked round the side of the dish-washer, followed by the chef's gargantuan frame. He waved a shining kitchen knife, clutched in a massive hand as round and pink as a joint of ham. 'Oh, it's you, Johnny.' His voice was a rumbling volcano. 'No food until dinner time. ' He caught sight of Fliss. 'And who is this?'

'Tomasz, this is Fliss, come to work on the bar. This is Tomasz, our head chef,' Johnny said. 'And no matter how hungry you get, he won't give you anything until meal-times. Guards his kitchen like a gorgon. Sometimes the bar staff are allowed in the inner-sanctum in the evening to make guests a snack, but only if the kitchen staff have gone home.'

Tomasz raised his monstrous fist and the knife glittered. 'Make sure you tell Fliss to tidy everything away. No strawberries dropped on my clean floor, no lids left off the ice-cream, everything melting, like that last girl Pauline. If she hadn't scarpered already I would chop her hands off.'

'Yes, chef.' Johnny was obviously not the slightest unnerved. It was evident there was little to be feared from Tomasz's threats of violence, despite his size. 'Put down your weapon. Fliss has been around hotels. She knows what she's doing.'

'Yeah?' Tomasz dropped the hand wielding a knife and regarded Fliss with new interest. 'Where've you worked, love?'

Fliss took a deep breath. It had been a refreshing change being accepted by Johnny as just another ordinary member of staff, but there was no point concealing her identity. In any case, she was far too honest.

'I work for Everdenes.'

There was a stifled gasp from Johnny.

Tomasz's dark eyes sharpened. 'The hotel chain?'

Before either the chef or Johnny could say anything derogatory they might regret, Fliss said, 'That's right. I'm Fliss Everdene. James Everdene's daughter.'

There was an astonished silence for a couple of seconds. Johnny turned his head to give Fliss a look of mingled ire and suspicion. Behind the hatch Tomasz whistled. Fliss's heart sank. If only her father realised just how much his business methods were despised in the trade. But then of course he did realise – he just didn't care what people thought of him, as long as Everdenes was making a profit. Fliss took in the hostility in Tomasz's expression and realised how tired she was of having to defend herself.

'My mum and Jilly Cross are old friends,' she explained. 'I've taken some time off work, and I'm here on a sabbatical from Everdene business. I'm just helping out until Patrick and Jilly have got things back on track.'

Tomasz and Johnny exchanged glances. It was a brief look, but Fliss gathered they would grudgingly accept her presence, for Jilly's sake. It was a start.

Fliss propped her elbows on the counter. 'Where did you work before, Tomasz?'

If she'd thought to bring the chef round, this was obviously the wrong question. His face darkened a shade.

'Florence, Genoa, Lyon. Along the Mediterranean coast.' He took in his kitchen with a disgruntled look. 'And now Emmside.'

'Tomasz's wife is a local,' Johnny explained. 'Isn't that right, Tomasz? You gave up the glamour of Monte Carlo for love?'

'Pfft,' said Tomasz.

'Wow, fancy working on the Côte d'Azur,' Fliss said. 'The beaches, the restaurants. Mmm, and the food! What a place to learn to cook.' She gave a low whistle. 'Your wife must be really something for you to give all that up.'

'Yes, she is.' Tomasz shuffled his feet. Fliss's comment brought the pink back to his features.

'Don't you like living here?' she went on. 'You might not have the weather, but the scenery is fabulous. And do you have to give up everything you learned in France, just because you're in the Lake District? Surely you can still make some of the same dishes.'

'Ha.' The chef's face fell, his great folds of flesh drooping. 'Sausage and mash. Steak and kidney pudding. Cauliflower cheese. Roast, roast, roast.'

'Don't listen to him, Fliss.' Johnny nudged her. 'Tomasz's cooking is awesome. One of the best things about working here.'

'Pfft.' Tomasz turned away with a final, irritated wave of the knife. 'Go away, now. Otherwise there'll be no liver and onions for dinner. Then heaven help us all.' He retreated to his counter and began slicing wafer thin pieces of liver with vicious dexterity.

Fliss turned to Johnny in dismay.

'Better leave him to it,' the waiter muttered.

He led the way back down the corridor to an uncarpeted flight of stairs that led to the basement. Fliss pondered Tomasz's comments about the menu. Yet another unhappy member of staff. There was more wrong at the Cross Hotel than a new barmaid and a change of décor could put right. Her professional curiosity was piqued.

'What was all that Tomasz meant about the menu?' she asked. 'I mean, I understand about the traditional English cuisine, and everything, and there's nothing wrong with that, but Tomasz is a skilled chef. Can't he even vary it just a little? Add something more modern?'

'Modern? Ha! Or as Tomasz would say, *pfft*.' Johnny gave an eloquent impression of Tomasz's shrug. 'Our menu's been pretty much the same since Patrick's granddad ran the place in the seventies. Then when Jonathan Cross took over – that's Patrick's dad – he refused to change it. Kept saying we're living in Cumbria, not with Johnny Foreigner, and we'll eat English food.' Johnny stopped at the bottom of the staircase and glanced round, making sure no one was within earshot. 'To be honest, Patrick's dad wasn't a very nice guy.'

Fliss opened her eyes wide. 'What do you mean?'

'A bit of a bully to work for. You know the type. Domineering. Didn't make many friends.'

Fliss opened her mouth to ask Johnny how Patrick had dealt with it. Had he stood up to his father in the family business? Patrick seemed to have a strong mind of his own, but he didn't appear the domineering type, despite his present irritability. She remembered the gentleness of his fingers as he'd freed her necklace, and the sudden warmth of his smile at the sight of her stuffed giraffe.

Johnny's eyes were on Fliss, as though sensing all the questions running through her head. She pursed her lips. She was dying to find out more about Patrick, but her conscience wouldn't let her gossip with his staff behind his back. Reluctantly she steered the subject away.

'Is this where they bury the bodies?' She examined the peeling walls in the basement corridor, the bare floor and dim lighting.

'I wouldn't be at all surprised.' Johnny's shoulders sagged once more as he set off towards a grubby door. The wood had swelled with damp, and it took a little effort for him to shove it wide. Fliss, peeping over his shoulder, gasped aloud. The mildewed door, with its scuffed paintwork, gave no indication at all of the magnificent room that lay beyond.

'Wow,' she breathed.

She stepped inside. The whole room was covered from floor to ceiling in the most wonderful 1950s tiles, illustrated with colourful wildlife. A host of owls, pheasants, badgers and foxes peered out playfully through the dust and cobwebs. Sunk in the middle of the room was a swimming-pool. Grimy and filled with abandoned junk, it was a long time since the pool had seen any water. An old parasol from a patio table, a couple of suitcases, a roll of bubble-wrap, a high-chair, a fold-up bed, a dralon-covered headboard, and various cloths and old curtains and rags, all jumbled up together, had been dumped in the empty pool and forgotten.

'How has everything been allowed to get in such a state?' Fliss took in the changing cabins ranged along one wall, and the flaking red paint of their doors. 'It must have looked magnificent in its day. Why don't they restore it?'

Johnny shrugged. 'Don't ask me. Not enough money, I expect.'

Fliss's mind ticked over rapidly. From what she'd seen so far, the Cross Hotel might have its problems, but a host of solutions and possibilities were opening themselves up to her. What a wonderful project this lovely hotel could be.

'I'd love to set this room to rights,' she said.

Johnny gave her a sceptical look. 'When you say "set to rights", do you mean rip it all out and put in some white tiles and the Everdene logo?'

'No, of course not.' She glared at Johnny, hurt, and felt obliged once again to defend her father's business. 'Look, I know all our hotels look the same, but "Everdenes" is a brand. Our hotels are for business travellers. The sort of guests who expect the same make of coffee with their breakfast, no matter where in the world they find themselves. This – ' She waved her arm, taking in the changing-rooms and the quirky tiles. 'This is completely different. It's a fabulous room in a lovely family hotel. I'd just like to see it back to its former glory, that's all.'

'Hmmph,' was all Johnny's reply. He paused as a thought struck him and gave Fliss a hesitant look. 'If you know so much about hotels, do you really think you could do something to rescue us?'

'Oh, I'd love to! I've got so many ideas already.' She pulled a face. 'Trouble is, I don't think Patrick and I got off to a very good start. At the moment he thinks I'm an eccentric chatterbox who can't even pull a pint. Still,' she took another look around the dilapidated room, and a surge of optimism swept through her. 'I'm here for two months. Plenty of time to show Patrick what I can really do.'

*

There was just time before the staff sat down to their evening meal for Johnny to show Fliss the dining-room – a characterless place, despite the crisp tablecloths and gleaming cutlery – and the lounge, which lay at the furthest point of the hotel's L-shape, looking onto the valley. The doors were thrown open, and a few afternoon visitors were taking tea and cake outdoors. The sky was a heavenly shade of blue, and the setting was magnificent.

Such a shame, then, about the lounge itself. Fliss examined the drab surroundings in silence. Again the puce curtains. What was it with this colour? Was there a time when this virulent shade had actually been fashionable, or had Patrick's granddad simply bought a job lot from a closing-down sale?

There was the sound of brisk footsteps behind them. Felicity turned to see a woman in a black skirt and top coming in from the dining-room, a crumpled table-cloth in her hand. The woman glanced at Fliss curiously.

'This is Jean,' Johnny told Fliss. 'She's our housekeeper, and she's been here forever. Jean, this is Fliss Everdene. As in

Everdene Hotels. Her dad owns the whole caboodle.'

The warmth in Jean's features chilled a degree but Fliss held out a hand, saying, in her usual friendly fashion, 'Good to meet you, Jean. My mum and Jilly were at uni together. Mum thought Jilly might use my help for a couple of months.'

The housekeeper's lined face softened. 'I expect Jilly will be glad to have you. Everything's all at sixes and sevens at the moment.' She folded the table-cloth over her arm, ready for a chat. 'So what will you be doing here, Fliss?'

'It's actually a bit of a baptism by fire. I'm working the bar tonight, since I heard Pauline left in a hurry.'

'That's right. Pauline left shortly after Patrick got back – ' Jean stopped short, and Fliss was surprised to see a faint colour come into her cheeks. 'I mean, not that Pauline rushing off like that was anything to do with Patrick coming home, of course.' She straightened up. 'Anyway, I need to change this table-cloth before dinner. Nice to meet you.' She waved and hurried away.

'What was all that about?' Fliss asked, turning to Johnny. 'Did Pauline leave because of Patrick? And has he been away?'

Johnny was staring at the carpet, a strange expression on his face, his shoulders stiff. He looked up. 'Don't you know? Patrick doesn't live here. He only came back when his father died. He lives in Dominica.'

'Dominica?' Fliss's eyes widened. She'd wondered about Patrick's deep tan, and the features lined by the sun. If he lived in the Caribbean, then that would explain it.

Johnny glanced round before adding quietly, 'You may as well know, because someone's bound to tell you. There was a tragedy here years ago, when Patrick was a teenager. He was supposed to be working in the hotel one afternoon but he sloped off to go diving with a mate in Emmswater. His friend drowned. Patrick's dad blamed him for it. Kept saying it would never have happened if Patrick had been working, like he was supposed to. After the accident, Patrick left and never came back. Apart from a few holidays, that is, and then it was only to see Jilly. Patrick and his dad never got on in the first place. And then when Patrick's friend died, well…' Johnny spread his hands, as though that explained everything.

'I had no idea!' Fliss turned Johnny's revelation over in her mind, confounded by it. Her mother had mentioned an old tragedy, but for some reason Fliss had taken it for ancient history. Now she felt the weight of the past bearing down on Patrick and the whole hotel. It was clear to her now just why Patrick had appeared so remote when she came across him staring down at the valley. The lake must be a constant reminder of his friend's tragic death. What a dreadful thing. 'But I still don't understand,' she went on. 'Why would Pauline want to leave just because Patrick came back?'

'Pauline is Jacob's sister. The friend who died.'

Fliss was struck dumb. She'd thought the hotel a troubled one, but never dreamed the roots of its unhappiness ran as deep as this.

Johnny must have seen the emotions chase each other across her features because he rushed to add, 'But that's not it.' He straightened up, his colour heightening. 'It was actually nothing to do with Patrick why Pauline left.'

Fliss was astonished to see the waiter's cheeks flush dark. He was obviously in the grip of some strong emotion. Fliss waited for him to explain himself but he turned abruptly.

'Right. Time to show you the bar before dinner.'

Fliss followed in silence, her mind reeling. What on earth had made Pauline rush off in a hurry? But there was no time to ponder the mystery. They reached the bar and Johnny began showing her round a bewildering array of bottles, optics and pumps. Fliss examined the cabinets full of bottled beer and the racks of wine in some trepidation.

'It won't take you long to find everything,' Johnny told her, offhand. 'And it's only dinner that's a bit of a rush. You won't have much to do after that. The evening drinkers are just a few old dears drinking Campari and soda in the lounge, and then everyone's in bed with their cocoa by ten thirty. We're not exactly the Lake District's centre for ravers.'

Patrick

'Two Margaritas, a Strawberry Daiquiri, two Mojitos …' Patrick dropped his tray on the counter with a weary clang. 'And a Horny Bull.'

It was Fliss's third evening behind the bar, and Patrick felt a stab of guilt at the look of dismay on her face. Although it was after midnight, the youthful party in the lounge showed no signs of wanting their cocoa. A whole coachload of fell walkers had stopped off at the hotel, tempted by the mild evening and the views from the terrace. One drink had turned into two, and then three, and then the party forgot to count and had settled in for the long haul.

Fliss shuffled from foot to foot, trying to pretend her heels weren't killing her.

'A Horny Bull?' She gave Patrick a suspicious look. 'Is this for real?'

Patrick pointed at the drinks menu. 'The ingredients are all here. Think you can manage?'

She lifted a brow and he held up his hands. 'OK.' There was another shout of laughter from the lounge, and he gave a grimace. 'I'll leave you to it.'

Patrick entered the lounge just as Johnny came in from the balcony, carrying a tray full of empties from the tables outside. It was long past time for the waiter to be heading for home, and he looked as tired as Patrick felt. Several of the women – by now in a thoroughly merry mood - greeted Johnny with loud cheers. He responded with an easy smile and the good-natured charm he showed everyone. Everyone except Patrick, that is.

'I've called last orders,' Patrick told Johnny as they passed each other. 'Fliss is making up the last round. There are just the empties to collect now.'

Johnny gave him an ironic nod and pushed the door to the bar open, the empty glasses rattling as he disappeared. Patrick repressed a sigh. He was fairly sure the head waiter's mutinous attitude was nothing to do with him personally. The negativity and flippant remarks had probably started under his father. He wouldn't be surprised if his dad had got Johnny's back up, same as he had with the chef. Johnny was an excellent sommelier and his talents were seriously underused.

Or maybe it was all down to Patrick, after all, and Johnny simply resented him giving orders because he knew he had no idea how to run a hotel. Patrick gave a wry shrug. He'd be right about that. Whatever the case, the waiter's attitude was all part of the general malaise of the place.

One of the women in the group lifted a hand, beckoning Patrick over to her table with a smile.

'You look like you're ready for bed.' The woman surveyed him through long lashes. The friend next to her giggled.

Patrick felt his cheeks redden. He'd come to realise just how good Johnny was at his job. He wished he had the head waiter's easy charm but dealing with drunken guests was beyond him. As he picked up the empty glasses from the table he had another vision of his boat, lying unused on a moonlit beach in Dominica, beside the clear, silent depths of the ocean. He tried to drive the image from his mind, concentrating instead on balancing the tray on the tips of his fingers without dropping it.

Johnny swept past him, the cocktails mixed by Fliss held expertly aloft. Patrick noted how the glasses were prettily frosted, and that Fliss had found a couple of ripe strawberries for the daiquiri. For someone who'd never worked on a bar, she'd proved remarkably quick on the uptake, and she only ever made a mistake once. On her first day she'd pulled a pint that was more foam than beer, added an olive instead of a Maraschino cherry to a Manhattan, and handed Patrick a glass of wine that was so corked you could have smelt it in the Caribbean. Just two days later and it was as though she'd been serving cocktails for years.

Fliss was studying the drinks menu as Patrick approached the bar. There was a small frown of concentration on her face that he'd come to recognise. Patrick guessed she was memorising the ingredients to a Horny Bull.

He placed his tray on the counter. 'I need a Pink Flamingo,

a White Russian, a white wine spritz – '

'You're joking!' A spasm of horror crossed her face.

Patrick broke into a grin. 'Yes, I am,' he confessed.

Fliss stared at Patrick blankly. The thought hit him that she probably hadn't seen him laugh since the day she'd arrived. What a curmudgeon she must think him. He loosened his bow-tie, fumbling with the unfamiliar stiff collar, and thought with longing of the shorts and shirt he normally wore on the beach.

'This thing's like a strait-jacket,' he told Fliss. 'Do waiters really need to wear a tux these days?'

Fliss cocked her head on one side, giving his question serious thought. 'Well, a lot of guests like the waiters to look formal. It adds to the experience of a night out. Besides,' she added, giving him a mischievous smile, 'women love a man in a suit. Just think how disappointed your guests would be if you weren't all dressed up.'

Patrick reddened. Was Fliss making fun of him? But when her eyes met his he found they were full of sympathetic teasing.

He gave a rueful grin. 'It's been a bit of a jungle out there this evening,' he confessed. 'I don't know how Johnny copes with it every night.'

'Oh, Johnny flirts with everyone. And anyway, women have to put up with this sort of harassment all the time. And at least you don't have to stick a rabbit's tail on your bum, like some waitresses do.'

Patrick burst out laughing. 'I can't picture the staff wearing that in Everdene Hotels. I didn't think that was your dad's style.'

'Oh heavens, no.' The smile left Fliss's face. 'Even my dad wouldn't stoop that low.'

She dropped her eyes. There was a second or two's silence. Patrick darted a curious glance at her bowed head. Did Fliss think James Everdene's practices were low? The silence became a little awkward.

'I'm sorry Mum asked you to work behind the bar,' Patrick

said, breaking the pause. 'If I'd realised straightaway who you were – '

Fliss waved a hand. 'Don't worry about it. I can't tell you how sick I get of the VIP treatment every time I visit a hotel. It's good to feel normal for once.'

He smiled. 'Well, I can see how the VIP treatment would be tiresome.'

Fliss continued to look at him curiously, as though she were unused to the side of Patrick that made jokes.

'Don't worry. I've managed,' she said. 'These blasted shoes haven't helped, though.' She gave a grimace of pain, slipping her feet out of her shoes and dropping a couple of inches in height as she did so. 'Tomorrow I'll drive down to the village. See if I can get something flat and sensible. And ugly,' she added ruefully.

Patrick undid his cuff buttons and shook his wrists. 'Well, don't drive in that death trap you came up in. Now our porter's managed to get it back to the hotel, you'd better leave it here until you can book it in to a garage. If you want to go to the village tomorrow, I'll give you a lift.'

He noticed the quick look of surprise Fliss gave him, as though she hadn't expected such a thoughtful offer. Was he really such a grump these days?

'That's really kind of you,' she said. 'I'd planned to get your porter a bottle of whisky in the village, too. I was so relieved he managed to start her again. Agnetha has seen better days but I can't bear to part with her. She's a brilliant car. I really don't know what I'll do when she finally has to go. It doesn't bear thinking about. I'll have to throw myself on top of her in the scrapyard, screaming.'

'Agnetha,' Patrick repeated.

'Yes. She's Swedish,' Fliss explained. 'That would be great if you could take me to Emmside.'

The swing door clattered open. Johnny dropped his tray on the bar. 'Did I hear you say you're going to Emmside tomorrow?'

'Yes. I'm sensible shoe shopping.'

He rolled his eyes. 'Fancy a pub lunch afterwards?'

Patrick couldn't help the irritation creeping back into his tone. 'Fliss won't have time for the pub,' he said. 'I'm taking her in my car, and then I need to get back here.'

'Not a problem,' Johnny said, without turning to look at him. 'I can give Fliss a lift back in my car.'

There was a stubborn set to the waiter's shoulders. Patrick's irritation deepened a couple of notches but before he could reply, Fliss intervened, saying quickly, 'Actually, lunch is a great idea, Johnny. I passed another hotel in the village on my way here. Perhaps we can go for lunch there.'

'The Lakeside?' Johnny recoiled. 'What on earth would you want to do that for?'

Patrick was curious, too. From what he'd heard of the Lakeside, it was all style and no warmth, with an over-priced, trendy menu.

Fliss rounded up the empty glasses and began loading them into the washer. 'I just thought it would be good to check out the competition.'

'Well, it's pricey,' Johnny said. 'You're not talking a ham sandwich and a bag of crisps with their menu.' He threw Patrick a sideways glance, part embarrassed, part challenge. 'I'm a bit short at the moment, until pay day.'

'That's OK,' Fliss said. 'My treat.'

'What?' His mouth dropped in astonishment.

Fliss's cheeks turned pink under Johnny's stare, and Patrick felt a twinge of sympathy for her. For the past three evenings they'd worked together as a team but Fliss's careless offer had just brought them all up hard against the truth. Fliss wasn't actually an ordinary hotel worker like the rest of them, and if they wanted, her parents could buy the whole Lakeside Hotel along with their starter.

Fliss said quickly, 'Can't a girl pay for a guy's lunch? And anyway, I owe you for all the help.'

Johnny gave a big grin. 'Well now you're talking. I look forward to it. See you tomorrow.'

He strode out, swinging the bar door shut behind him with

a nonchalant whistle. Patrick turned his attention to Fliss. She was busying herself wiping down the counter and didn't quite meet his gaze. There was something oddly vulnerable in the resolute way she carried on with her job. Patrick wondered just how difficult it must be for someone as sociable as Fliss to be constantly made to feel an outsider because she was rich.

'That's a great idea to check out the competition,' he told her. 'It's exactly the sort of thing my dad should have done when the Lakeside first opened. They've taken away quite a few of the casual guests we used to have.'

For a few minutes they chatted about the other hotels Fliss had passed on her journey through the Lake District, and the tourist trade in general, until Fliss dismissed Patrick with a wave of her hand.

'Well, anyway, I can see you're in a rush to be off,' she told him, 'so you get on and I'll tidy round here and lock up.'

Patrick stood for a moment, a wry smile on his lips, before bidding her goodnight.

He made his way to his suite of rooms on the top floor. As he stripped off his suit and tie, he remembered Fliss telling him to go, and he smiled to himself. After running his own business for several years, being told what to do was a novel experience. Then he remembered that Fliss was far more used to being in charge than taking orders. It was a sobering thought. When Patrick finally laid his exhausted head on the pillow, he had resolved to give Fliss Everdene no opportunity at all of taking the upper hand.

Chapter Four

Fliss

The clouds were thin wisps over the mountains when Fliss left the hotel the next morning, and the sky a dull grey. She glanced up. It wasn't raining yet, but she'd come prepared and was carrying her biscuit-coloured mac over one arm.

Patrick was already waiting for her and was leaning against his car, chatting to a large, balding man wearing blue overalls. Fliss guessed this must be Alan, the porter. Patrick straightened as she approached.

'Good morning,' she said cheerfully, before glancing towards the skyline. 'Although it's not looking a good morning is it? I wonder why everyone always says "Good morning", even when it isn't one.' She turned to the porter with a smile. 'Thanks so much for starting Agnetha. I was so anxious about her when we climbed up that hill. She was making a terrible racket, poor thing. It reminded me of the time her exhaust fell off in the middle of Birmingham. It was such a noise. Everyone was staring.'

Alan looked back at her blankly. Fliss opened her mouth to speak again, but before she could utter another word, Patrick took her arm and steered her to the passenger door.

'See you later, Alan. Any problems with that delivery, give me a ring.' And then to Fliss he added, 'Hop in.'

'Oh, thanks, it's very good of you to give me a lift, and to ask Alan – '

'No problem at all.'

There was a silence while Patrick manoeuvred the car out of the car park. Fliss took in the shadows under his eyes and the lines of strain. The more relaxed Patrick who'd appeared all too briefly the evening before had disappeared. Perhaps he was just a figment of her imagination.

In an attempt to lighten the atmosphere, Fliss launched into conversation. 'Do you know, my feet are so sore, anyone would think I'd been dancing the lead in Swan Lake all night.' Patrick didn't answer, so she went on, 'And talking about Swan Lake reminds me of the time I took my sister to see The Nutcracker. When it got to the bit with the Sugar Plum Fairy – you know the tune,' she hummed the opening bars, 'Minnie stood up on one of the seats and started dancing along. I was worried people might get cross, but after a couple of minutes everyone around us got up and started dancing as well.'

Fliss chuckled. It was a memory that never failed to make her smile.

Patrick had his eyes on the road ahead as it twisted and turned towards Emmside. The hollow look remained, and it was obvious his thoughts were miles away.

Fliss contemplated the handbag in her lap and began fiddling with the strap.

'I'm sorry about your dad,' she said, after a couple of seconds' silence. 'It must have been awful to find out so far from home. Did it come as a terrible shock?'

Patrick shot her a glance with something of surprise in it, along with another emotion she couldn't make out. He returned his attention to the road. There was a long pause, and Fliss began to wonder if he was ever going to speak at all, but then he said, 'Do you know, you're the first person to ask me how I feel about it. Ever since I heard the news I've been swamped with all the practicalities. The funeral service, the will, what's going to happen to the hotel.' His voice, with its mellow Cumbrian accent, harshened. 'To be brutally honest, the main thing I feel at the moment is angry. We didn't get on, and it's typical of him to leave things in such a blasted mess.'

Patrick caught Fliss's shocked expression and looked away, as though embarrassed at his outburst. 'My father wasn't the easiest person to get on with,' he went on. 'Perhaps you've guessed as much already, since the staff are bound to have talked to you. They'll tell you my dad wasn't popular, he was set in his ways, and he could be a bit of a bully. And all of that's true. But in spite of everything – ' He broke off, a muscle in his cheek tightening. 'You're right. It was very difficult hearing the news so far from home. All I could think about was how I didn't have the chance to say goodbye. And I'd let years go by without trying to put things right between us.'

Fliss wondered how on earth she would cope herself, if her own father died after one of their many disagreements, and before she had the chance to tell him just how much she loved him. When she glanced at Patrick, she found his mouth was set in a straight line, as though clamped down over the emotion that threatened to spill out. To give him a chance to compose himself, she turned the subject.

'It must be wonderful to live in the Caribbean. It's no wonder you've got such a tan. I'd been asking myself how you did that, with all the grey skies and mist here, and to be honest at first I thought it must all be sun-beds, until Johnny told me you lived in Dominica. What on earth do you do there? And doesn't your mum miss you, being so far away? I know you didn't get on with your dad, and everything, but it's obvious your mum adores you.'

Her tactics worked. The angular lines of Patrick's face softened a little, and he even gave her a small smile.

'Well, if you'd let me get a word in edgeways.' He shifted the gearstick. 'I run a dive school in Dominica. And my mum does miss me, but every year after Christmas, during the hotel's quiet season, she comes to stay with me. And I come home for a couple of weeks once a year, and we also Skype each other every week.'

They began to chat about life in Dominica and the diving to be had round the islands. Fliss had visited the Caribbean several times – both through her work at Everdene Hotels and on holiday with friends. She'd even dived there herself, but it soon became clear to her just what an expert Patrick was. He became much more animated when he spoke about his job, the wonderful sea life to be found in the crystal waters, the old wrecks he'd dived, and the pleasure he got from teaching others. When he told her diving was his passion, Fliss gave him a puzzled look.

'So I guess that means you'll be going back to Dominica,' she said. 'What will your mum do then? And what will happen to the hotel?'

Patrick slowed the car as they reached the final curve of the fellside. 'Well, those are big questions. To tell you the truth, when I found out my father had left the hotel to me and not my mother, it came as a bit of a surprise.' He pulled a face at the understatement. 'But during the past few months I've come to see how hard my mum would find it to run the place on her own. Perhaps my dad just thought I had a better head for business than my mum, and it would be better to entrust the hotel to me.' He paused, his face drawn. 'But I'll never really understand his reasons for leaving the will as he did, and now it's too late to ask him.'

The lake – heavy with rain – came into view between the trees. Patrick glanced at the water once. The abrupt way he looked away again reminded Fliss that Emmswater was the lake where he'd lost his teenage friend, Jacob. What a terribly unhappy place the valley was for him. Then Fliss thought about Jacob's sister Pauline leaving, and she felt swamped with the misery of it. Patrick must feel he'd driven Pauline away. The whole valley must be a constant reminder to him of the tragedy.

Fliss was just about to break the silence with some words of sympathy when Patrick spoke. 'I haven't thanked you properly for helping on the bar. It can't have been easy, being thrown in the deep end, but Johnny says you've already suggested some improvements with the stock control, and how the orders are handled.' His voice was expressionless. 'I can see how you must be an asset to Everdenes. Streamlining, and suchlike.'

Fliss stiffened. "Streamlining" was another way of saying "making redundancies" – something Everdenes were accused of doing after every takeover. She threw Patrick a suspicious glance.

He carried on, 'It's good of your father to let you leave work to come here and help. Some of the staff have been asking me why you're here, and if you're at the hotel on Everdene business.' His eyes met hers briefly. He changed gear and went on, 'I heard Everdenes bought out a hotel up the road in Kendal last year.'

Fliss felt a flash of anger as she took in his insinuation. Did Patrick seriously think Everdenes would buy out the Cross Hotel? For a moment she was tempted to reveal just how problematic she found it working for her father's business – the high turnover of staff, the corporate image that stamped out any individuality, their reputation for putting profit first, and the atmosphere of bitterness and distrust that surrounded her everywhere she went in the trade. But for Fliss to tell Patrick – a stranger – about her difficulties would be a betrayal of her father. Despite everything, her loyalty to her family ran deep.

She bit back her reply and tried to keep the anger from her voice. 'I can see how your staff might be concerned, but as I've told everyone several times, I'm not here on behalf of Everdenes. I'm here to help your mum until the hotel is back on its feet. And I had nothing to do with that takeover of the hotel in Kendal. It happened while I was abroad, working in one of our hotels in Sydney.'

They'd reached the bottom of the fell. Patrick flicked the indicator as they approached the junction.

'Oh yes, my mother told me you travel the world for your job. That sounds fun.'

Fliss whipped her head round at that. Patrick was looking the other way, concentrating on the traffic before making the turn. Her anger solidified. *Fun*? She thought of the hostility of the staff when she'd first arrived at the Sydney hotel, and how painful she'd found it to carry out her father's instructions.

Instead of making people redundant, Fliss had spent six weeks in the Australian hotel training the staff to work more efficiently, so that long-serving staff like the housekeeper and porter kept their jobs. Her father could have accepted this at a pinch, but Fliss had also allowed the hotel to retain its image. Sure, they'd had new menus printed up in the Everdene house colours, but the menu was completely different to what was served in the rest of the Everdene chain. The recipes had local colour. And instead of being furnished in Everdenes' white and navy, the bedrooms had homemade quilts and cushions, and aboriginal art decorating the walls. Apart from the discreet use of the new company logo, the hotel remained virtually unchanged.

When Fliss got back from Sydney, her father had been livid. He'd questioned her commitment to the family enterprise, and Fliss had retaliated by questioning his business ethics. Their row had been ferocious, and Fliss still hadn't got over her father's anger. And Patrick thought she travelled the world, taking advantage of free hotels, generally behaving like an airhead – and that her job was *fun*! He'd obviously made his mind up about her.

Fliss cast Patrick a sidelong glance. She decided to treat him to the sort of aimless, ditzy chatter she knew he found annoying. She began by telling him all about how much she was looking forward to lunch, moved on to the type of shoes she was going to buy, wondered aloud whether Emmside's shops stocked the fashions she was used to buying in London, and finished by asking whether there was a chemist's where she could get some plasters for her feet, which were still killing her.

'Oh, this is just like something from one of those old period dramas,' she exclaimed as they passed the old stone houses, the red telephone box, and the Post Office on the corner. 'Just so steeped in history. I know, it reminds me of *North and South*.' She chewed her lip. Elizabeth Gaskell's classic novel was the perfect allusion. A sideways glance at Patrick's expression revealed he was puzzling over her words. 'Although now I come to think of it,' she went on, 'it's not like *North and*

South, because we're in the countryside, and wasn't *North and South* all grimy and industrial, with mills and things?' She shot Patrick another look. 'Now, I wonder what made me think of that book? Hmm.' She considered for a moment. 'Well, whatever, now I've got the image of the hero, John Thornton, in my head.' She gave him another pointed glance. 'I seem to remember he was all dour and northern and grumpy.'

Patrick turned into the Pay & Display car park. By the time he'd found a parking spot, Fliss was busily looking through her handbag, checking she had everything with her.

'Well thanks so much for the lift,' she said. 'It's been lovely getting to know one another better.' She opened the car door and stepped out, leaning back in to add, 'And don't forget I'm coming back with Johnny. We're going for lunch. And fun.'

Patrick's eyes met hers. She was surprised to see a twinkle in them as she swung the door shut.

Patrick

Patrick watched Fliss stride away over the car park, her blue and white checked dress a splash of colour against the damp asphalt. He smiled to himself. "Northern and grumpy." Well, that was one in the eye for him. He got out of the car. By the time he reached the ticket-machine the smile had left his face, and he was thinking of the meeting that lay ahead. He'd had to get up early to go over his father's paperwork, and what he'd found there had given him a headache. It was no wonder Fliss thought he was grumpy.

Quarter of an hour later Patrick was sitting across the desk from his father's bank manager, a cup of tea and a plate of biscuits in front of him. Patrick knew Alison Travis from school. Although she was a couple of years older than he was, as teenagers they'd known each other well. Guy Travis, Alison's boyfriend at the time, was a keen diver and a member of Patrick's dive club. He and Patrick had often dived together. After university, Alison and Guy had gone on to marry.

Patrick spent a pleasant few minutes admiring photos of

Alison's and Guy's two children, and reminiscing about old times. He had come to the meeting in the hope their old friendship might weigh in his favour. Ultimately, though, their acquaintance only meant that Alison was more embarrassed than usual about having to turn down a request for a loan.

'Your dad came to see me about a loan six months before he died,' she told him. 'He'd already mortgaged the Cross Hotel to the max, and he had several other debts. He couldn't convince me he had the means to repay the bank if we loaned him any more money, and so I had to turn him down. I'm afraid, unless you can tell me the situation has changed since then, that position still stands.'

Patrick took a sip of his tea, but the liquid failed to ease the constriction in his throat. He was more and more convinced that the pressure of mounting debt had been a factor in his dad's fatal heart attack. If only he'd spoken to Patrick about his financial problems, maybe all this could have been avoided. But Jonathan Cross would have been too proud to admit failure, especially to his son.

Patrick replaced his cup on the table and drew out a document from the folder he'd brought with him. He passed it to Alison. 'If my dad was refused a loan by you, then that explains this. It's a loan agreement with a company called Cassh-Ex. Take a look at the figures. Their repayment terms are criminal.'

Alison registered the amount with shock. 'This is terrible, Patrick. I'm so sorry.' Her eyes met his, wide with sympathy. 'If there was anything I could do as a friend, I would. But this document only confirms that I can't possibly take a risk with the bank's money by giving you a loan.' She pushed the paper back over the table. 'I'm really sorry,' she repeated. She hesitated, then added, 'Patrick, even if you could raise the cash to pay off the debts, what then? The hotel needs more than an injection of money. It needs someone with the time and enthusiasm to rejuvenate it. Do you really have the heart to take it on?'

Patrick met his old friend's intelligent gaze and dropped his eyes to the cup in his hand. 'That's the question, Alison, isn't it? I've made a success of diving. I know how to run a dive school, but I know nothing about how to run a hotel. Personally, I don't want to take it on, but what's the alternative? The Cross Hotel is my mother's home, and it's been in my father's family for generations. My mother can't run it by herself. I've talked about selling, but she gets distressed at the very mention of it.'

'If there's anything I can do to help personally...'

Patrick gave a resigned shrug. 'Pray for a miracle. That might work.'

He lifted the remains of his tea and drained it. Alison continued to chat to him civilly, and by the end of their meeting she'd invited him round for dinner to meet up with Guy and talk about old times. Her final words to Patrick were that she'd given her professional opinion. Her opinion as an old friend was that Jonathan Cross had run the hotel's finances into the ground. Patrick had inherited a disaster.

Patrick left the bank head down. What on earth had his father been playing at in the last few years? When Patrick left, business had been fine. His parents weren't wealthy, by any means, but they were making a decent living. Of course the Lakeside had opened in the meantime, but another hotel in the area could be a good thing if used to advantage, bringing in new clientele. It seemed to Patrick his father had buried his head in the sand and refused to move with the times. The Cross Hotel was exactly the same as it was when Patrick left, even down to the blasted curtains. Nothing had changed, except to grow shabbier.

He manoeuvred his car out of the car park, feeling the weight of responsibility settle once more on his shoulders. As far as he could see, he had two options. He could have another attempt at persuading his mother to agree to him selling up, and try and get her to come and live with him in Dominica. He didn't hold out much hope of success. The few times he'd dropped a mild hint, his mother had only got flustered and changed the subject. Patrick could perfectly understand why.

Jilly Cross's family had been part of the fabric of the valley for centuries. All her loved ones, including her husband, were buried in the graveyard by the church on Crag Fell. How could she ever countenance leaving?

The other option would be to sell up his thriving business in Dominica and move back to Emmside. He remembered the chill that had settled on him as he'd driven past the lake with Fliss that morning, until her friendly chatter had lifted it. After Jacob died, he knew he could never dive Emmswater again.

But diving was his life.

With his circular thoughts oppressing him, Patrick made his way towards the tiny bridge over the river Emm. His window was down, and he heard their laughter before he saw them. Fliss and Johnny were standing by the bridge's stone parapet, throwing sticks into the water below. Fliss's blond bob was tousled by the wind, and the skirt of her checked dress clung to her legs as she leaned right out to watch her stick fall. She straightened and made to dart over the road, halting abruptly on the kerbside as she heard his car approach. Her smile widened as she caught sight of him. She lifted her hand in a small wave. Her figure, glowing with health and cheerfulness, was like a burst of sunlight breaking through Patrick's gloom. His heart did that strange small lift it had done that morning at the sight of her. He wanted to return her smile, but his troubles were foremost in his mind, and his temple throbbed. Then Johnny joined Fliss on the kerbside and placed a careless hand on her shoulder, and the moment was gone.

Patrick carried on over the bridge and up the hillside.

Chapter Five

Fliss

The shops in the village had provided a much-needed distraction for Fliss. By the time she met up with Johnny she'd bought some expensive shoes in sensible navy blue, and was pleased that they weren't too ugly. She'd gone on to buy a fleece for walking in the hills and a woolly sheep to send to Minnie, along with a postcard of some cartoon cows, which she'd addressed to *Miss Minerva Alice Everdene.* Minnie liked to see her full name on anything posted to her. It made her feel important. The thought of Minnie's pleasure had cheered Fliss enormously. When she'd bumped into Johnny crossing the bridge on the way to the Lakeside, she couldn't resist challenging him to a game of her sister's favourite Pooh-sticks.

Johnny had seemed downcast as she approached, but he'd brightened considerably.

'You're on,' he said.

They proceeded to throw stick after stick into the rushing brook below, with Johnny rushing ahead to cheat ever more outrageously.

Fliss was never one to be upset with someone for long, and so when Patrick drove past them on the bridge she gave him a friendly smile and a wave. She watched as his car disappeared up the hill, with Patrick frowning at the wheel.

'Does Patrick ever smile?' she asked Johnny.

She must have sounded hurt. Johnny put his arm around her shoulder and gave it a brief squeeze. 'He's like that with everyone. A miserable git. Come on, let's get some lunch.'

A few minutes later they were pushing open the glass doors of the Lakeside Hotel. Fliss cast an inquisitive glance around her. The windows let in a lot of light, and the lobby was bright, if a little soulless with its stainless steel furniture and black counter. She would have liked to have lingered a little longer on her spying mission, but Johnny was already heading into the restaurant, claiming he was starving. Fliss was about to follow when an exclamation stopped her.

'Fliss Everdene!'

She turned to find a suited man in his thirties bearing down on her, hand outstretched. Her heart sank as she recognised him, but she fixed on her best smile.

'Cameron! How nice to see you here.'

Cameron McIntyre took her hand in his, his owlish brown eyes alive with curiosity. 'Fliss. What a surprise. What on earth are you doing in this neck of the woods?'

'I'm staying at the Cross Hotel.' She indicated the hills above the Lakeside. 'Jilly Cross is an old family friend.'

'Busman's holiday?' His hand still clasped hers, a little too tightly. Cameron always did have a thing for Fliss. Or maybe he'd just fancied getting it on with the boss's daughter. His tone oozed sardonic flirtation.

Fliss pulled her hand away. 'Sort of. I'm helping Jilly in the hotel for a little while, after Jonathan's sudden death.'

Cameron murmured bland sympathies for Jilly Cross's loss.

'How about you?' Fliss continued. 'What are you doing here?'

'I'm the manager.' Cameron scowled, put out.

'Oh, of course,' she said quickly. 'I remember you were leaving Everdenes to manage somewhere else. I hadn't realised it was here.'

If she were perfectly honest, Fliss hadn't really wondered too much about what had happened to Cameron after he left Everdenes. He'd been running one of their hotels in the

Midlands, and the staff had been happy to see him go. He was a poor manager of people and inclined to take the easiest route whenever he could, sitting back to let others do his work for him. Morale in his hotel had been low, and his staff had breathed a sigh of relief when he left. Fliss wondered how he was getting on at the Lakeside.

'What a wonderful place to work,' she said, gesturing to the view of the lake through the wide windows. 'This is my first trip into Emmside. Such a beautiful location. You must get a lot of tourists?'

'Checking out the Cross Hotel's competition, Fliss?' he countered drily.

At that moment Johnny stepped back out of the restaurant, brandishing a menu. '*Pan-fried breaded cod goujons*? What the hell…?'

He stopped short, catching sight of Cameron. The manager of the Lakeside stiffened, his face taking on an even redder hue.

Johnny didn't trouble to hide his grin. 'Afternoon, Cameron,' he said breezily.

Cameron's eyes narrowed. 'Johnny.'

Keeping her pleasant smile in place, Fliss glanced from one to the other. It was obvious Johnny and Cameron were already acquainted, and that their dislike was mutual. She didn't quite trust Johnny not to try and get Cameron's back up.

'Cameron and I were just talking,' she told Johnny. 'We actually know each other. It was such a surprise to meet an old colleague. Cameron, I take it you know Johnny already? We've come to have lunch in your restaurant.'

Cameron gave a curt nod. 'Yes, I know Johnny. Looking for a new job, lad? It'll take more than buying the boss's daughter lunch to get a manager's job in Everdenes.'

Fliss began to propel Johnny towards the restaurant. 'Well, it's been such a lovely surprise seeing you here, Cameron. Johnny and I are about to have lunch, but we must meet up again. Catch up with all the gossip.' She gave Cameron a friendly wiggle of the fingers and headed determinedly away, hoping he wouldn't suggest joining them. That would be awkward.

Cameron hesitated, until professional pride must have caught up with him. 'I'll introduce you to our head waiter. Make sure he finds you a good table.' He gave Fliss a conscious smile as he fell into step beside her. On her other side, Johnny was smirking.

A few minutes later they were seated at the best table by the window, menus in hand. Cameron murmured something to the waiter as he left. Fliss had no doubt he was giving instructions that they were to receive every attention.

'Well,' she said, examining the menu cheerfully. 'Isn't this nice? And what shall we have to drink? Shame we can't have something alcoholic. I could murder a glass of Prosecco. Even two or three of them. But not if we've got to work this evening.' She chatted on like this for a while, exclaiming over the menu and the view, but Johnny wasn't to be headed off.

'So this is what it's like to be an Everdene,' he said, the first moment Fliss drew breath. He gave her a look of mingled disgust and admiration. 'The table in the window. The VIP treatment from the manager. I tell you what, if I had all your money I wouldn't be helping out behind a bar. What are you doing at a dump like the Cross Hotel? Are you really scouting the place, like Tomasz thinks?'

'No, of course not,' Fliss said crossly. Her irritation at Johnny's assumption was mixed with a good deal of anxiety. The hotel trade was a hotbed of rumour. Already people were stating as fact that her dad was going to buy out the Cross Hotel. Fliss remembered Patrick's dry comment about their buyout of the hotel in Kendal. Time to knock the gossip firmly on the head. 'How many times do I have to say this?' she went on. 'I'm only here because Jilly Cross is my mum's old friend. I came to help her out when Jonathan died, as a family favour, nothing else. And I'm only helping on the bar because Jilly asked me to, since Pauline's walked out.'

To her surprise, Johnny went red at this. 'What's Pauline got to do with it?'

'Nothing.' Now it was Fliss's turn to eye him in surprise. 'It's just that the bar was short-staffed.'

Johnny mumbled something Fliss didn't catch and picked up his menu.

Fliss continued to eye him curiously. She remembered the despondent look on his face as she met him on the bridge, before he was aware of her presence. She would have loved to have pressed him on just what Pauline's disappearance meant, but his usually open features had taken on a shuttered look. It was obvious he had no desire to confide in her.

She picked up her own menu to study it, thinking perhaps it would be tactful to change the subject. 'How do you and Cameron know each other?'

'Everyone knows everyone in this place. Joanne - the woman who manages the bar here – she used to go to my school. If it weren't for Joanne, the Lakeside would be in a right state. She does a lot more than run the bar, because Cameron's too bone idle to sort things out.' Johnny's face darkened. 'Every time I see Cameron, he always has something sarcastic to say about the Cross Hotel. And he's a bully. He sucked up to you, but he's not like that with his staff, I can tell you. Guy gives me the creeps.'

Fliss could only agree. There was something sycophantic about the way Cameron had spoken to her. She hadn't known he had a reputation for being a bully, though. It seemed Everdenes were well rid of him. She drew Johnny's attention to the menu, and for the next hour or so they chatted companionably about what the Lakeside had to offer.

It hadn't taken long for Fliss to realise Johnny's sardonic attitude towards work masked a surprising depth of knowledge, both in managing a restaurant and as a trained sommelier. His imaginative critique of the items on the menu also revealed hidden talents. So why did he give every appearance of being bored to death when he was at work? He was ironic and flippant, riling Patrick and flirting outrageously with the guests.

Fliss continued to ponder this as they ordered their dishes. Johnny enjoyed picking apart the chef's abilities and comparing him unfavourably with Tomasz. By the time they reached dessert, Fliss was dying to understand why he buried his talents under such a mask of indifference. She poured a helping of custard onto her apple crumble and picked up her spoon. 'You've learned a lot working for the Cross family.'

Johnny shrugged. 'Yeah, I've been with them a long time. Too long.'

There it was again – the weary boredom, as though he found everything about the Cross Hotel deathly dull. He began tucking into his cheesecake.

'So why stay?' Fliss went on.

'Born and raised up the road. My mum and dad still live here, and my sister and her kids live in Ambleside. The Lakes are in my roots. And you get to know people in that hotel. Once you've been there a while, they're like family.' He stopped, the spoon midway between plate and mouth. 'A dysfunctional family,' he added, meeting her gaze with a twisted smile.

Fliss thought of Patrick's rift with his father, his evident unhappiness at being back, and Jilly's perpetual vagueness. And then there was Tomasz's discontent and the mystery of Pauline suddenly leaving. There was definitely a lot wrong at the Cross family hotel.

'I heard Patrick's dad wasn't that easy to work for,' Fliss said diplomatically. 'But perhaps things might change now Patrick's back. I mean, I know there's a lot needs improving – '

Johnny snorted. 'Patrick won't stay here long. He's got his dive school. He's only come back for his mum's sake. He never could stand it here. Next thing you know he'll persuade his mum to let him sell up, and some blasted chain will take over.' He looked up quickly, remembering himself. 'No offence to Everdenes.'

But Fliss had stopped listening. She was thinking of the first time she met Patrick, on the bend in the road, surveying the valley with a look of desolation on his face. She'd thought he was grieving for his father, but all along he was thinking of his friend. On the surface, the old Tudor building appeared so tranquil, looking down from its vantage point on the fellside onto the soft beauty of the valley. But like the lake itself, it hid a wealth of tragedy beneath its calm surface.

*

When Fliss and Johnny arrived back at the hotel, they found Patrick's mother manning reception, another pile of letters on the desk in front of her. She was eyeing them as though they might transmit some terrible disease. Fliss noted the dark circles under her eyes. She looked wan and exhausted.

'All right, Mrs C?' Johnny, ever oblivious to the moods of others, waved a cheerful greeting and strode on through the lobby in the direction of the canteen, where he'd arranged to meet a couple of the other waiters before his shift started.

Fliss halted beside Jilly's desk. 'We've just been for lunch at the Lakeside,' she said brightly. 'It's a lovely menu, but we both agreed Tomasz could do much better. My gravy was too salty, and the custard was out of a packet. Tomasz would have a fit. But maybe you could come with us next time. It's fun lunching out in hotels when it's not your own business. And we could have a look round the shops, too. What do you think?'

There was a flicker of interest in Jilly's eyes, but the spark soon died. Close up, her complexion was an unhealthy grey. 'That's a lovely idea, darling, but I really don't know when I'll find the time. We seem to have so much to do. All these bills arriving since Jonathan...' She shifted the brown envelopes on the desk with the tip of one finger.

Fliss said gently, 'I'm good at paperwork. Why don't I take a look?'

'Yes, but there's Patrick...I mean, of course he'll deal with them, but he was busy with the bank this morning. And when he came out of the office just now he seemed very cross. He'd been talking to Cameron at the Lakeside. Well of course Cameron is enough to put anyone in a bad mood.'

Oh dear. The Lakeside's manager had obviously wasted no time in getting on the phone to Patrick to stir up trouble. Fliss wondered just what he'd been saying.

'And then I was going to ask Patrick about these,' Jilly continued, indicating the bills on the desk. 'But he went back to the office without saying a word. He looked so like he used to look when his dad was here. Oh, I do hope he won't leave again. I've no idea what I'd do without him.'

A surge of remorse ran through Fliss. 'Oh, I do hope I haven't upset him, too,' she exclaimed. 'It was kind of him to offer to drive me to Emmside, only I got in a bit of a huff, because – ' She broke off guiltily, realising she was on the verge of telling Jilly just how surly and awkward she thought her son could be.

'It's all right, darling.' Jilly blew into a handkerchief. 'I'm not surprised. We all know how Patrick's been. All he's ever lived for is diving. It's good of him to stay and try and sort things out.'

Fliss scooped the envelopes off the desk. 'I tell you what,' she said. 'Why don't I take these in to Patrick and offer to help him out? I've learned a lot from working for my dad. I'm sure between us we'll get it sorted.'

Jilly brightened a little. 'Thank you, Fliss. You're always so cheerful and pleasant. I did so want a daughter.'

'No problem.' Fliss, too, felt a little cheered. It felt good to be able to offer some real help at last.

Patrick

Patrick swivelled his chair round and stared out of the window of his office. This part of the hotel looked out directly onto the fellside. There was nothing in the view to hold his interest apart from the grey stones of the scree and a few shrubby bushes. A misty drizzle was falling. He thought of the view from his office back in Dominica – the rolling waves, the palm trees, the sunshine and the wet sand. He pressed his fingers to his forehead, massaging the dull throb in his temple. His head had been aching ever since he drove past the lake that morning with Fliss. He wondered if his reaction to the sight of Emmswater would ever change – the dryness in his throat, and the way his heart still pounded whenever the thought of his friend's last moments.

He sensed Fliss arrive before he heard her. She had a scent he'd come to recognise, like the sun on peach blossom. He turned to find her standing in the middle of the room, clutching a handful of brown envelopes. Her outing that morning had brought a healthy glow to her complexion.

Her bright gaze met his, and the wrinkle deepened on her forehead. 'Is everything all right?'

All the many ways in which things weren't all right passed through Patrick's mind. And now here was Fliss, to add to his list of uncertainties.

'I've just had a call from Cameron at the Lakeside,' he told her. 'He wanted to know why James Everdene's daughter was working behind the bar at the Cross Hotel. He insinuated that you'd rushed here because we're in financial trouble. He offered his sympathies, and then he had the gall to offer his assistance, because, in his words, "we small independents should stand up to the corporate giants."'

A flash of anger crossed Fliss's open features. Patrick was reminded once more of the steel that lay beneath her deceptively sunny disposition. The thought that Fliss was as strong-minded as her father did nothing to cheer him.

He went on, 'When I didn't to rise to Cameron's bait, he came right out and said he thought you were on a fact-finding mission, and that James Everdene was planning to buy out my hotel. Of course I dismissed it as rubbish, but he more or less told me I was an idiot.'

The flash of anger burst into flame. Fliss took a step forward, her blue eyes hot with ire. 'You mean he actually accused me of spying on you? I should sue him for slander. Everdenes would never – '

The furious retort died on her lips. Patrick watched the emotions chase each other across her face. He wondered how she would continue. It was one thing having lunch in a rival hotel in order to check out their menu. Planting employees in order to get insider knowledge was something else entirely. James Everdene had a reputation for such underhand tactics.

A conscious flush rose over Fliss's cheeks. 'That's not why I'm here,' she said. 'My mum was worried about Jilly. And besides, she thought I needed a break. We both agreed it would be good for me to spend some time away from Everdenes. It's nothing to do with buying out your hotel.' There was a momentary pause whilst she appeared to gather some resolve. She raised her chin. 'But I can see you don't trust me, and neither does anyone else.' Her flush deepened. 'If you'd prefer me to leave, I quite understand.'

Patrick stared at her, taken aback. The realisation hit him suddenly that he'd be very sorry if Fliss Everdene left his hotel. That if she did, he would never see her again. It was a revelation that cast him adrift momentarily.

He pulled open the drawer of his desk and drew out her car key.

'Alan's taken a look at your car,' he said. 'He thinks it's the catalytic converter and you'll have to get it replaced.' He added, with a glimmer of a smile, 'I don't want you to leave, but it seems you're stuck with us anyway, at least until your car is fixed.'

Fliss reached over and took the key. As she did so, his nostrils filled again with the scent of her. A tendril of her hair dropped forward as she bent towards him. Her eyes met his. She drew in a breath and stood back, her fingers around the key.

'Thank you,' she said. The colour remained high in her cheeks. 'I expect you think I'm a little eccentric keeping that car on, but I've had her since I was seventeen. She was my first car. We've been through everything together. I told you I'm not parting – '

'With Gudrun, I know,' he finished.

'Her name's Agnetha. I told you, she's Swedish. And since when was there a Gudrun in Abba?'

Patrick couldn't prevent a laugh escaping. Fliss smiled back spontaneously, and her constraint fell away. Her blue eyes brimmed. She waved the car key at him.

'You know, you look really nice when you smile,' she said. Then the pink in her cheeks returned. 'I mean, I'm not saying you look grumpy all the time. That's not what I mean at all. Or that you don't look nice, anyway.' She caught his astonishment and waved a hand. 'Oh, you know what I mean. I'm sorry we got off to a bad start.'

'So am I,' he said. 'And I'm sorry I let that idiot Cameron get to me. We could do with your help, so I hope this means you're going to stay.'

He didn't have to wait for an answer. Fliss beamed.

'I was happy to come and help out, when Mum asked me. But now I'm here, I can see how much needs doing in the hotel, and what a wonderful place it could be with the right work. And if you and Jilly want me to just work on the bar, then that's fine. But I've got a lot of experience in hotel management, and you might as well make full use of it.' She pushed the brown envelopes towards him over the desk. 'And quite frankly, I think a new barmaid is the least of your worries.'

Relief flooded through Patrick. In the months since his father's death he'd felt as though he were coping with everything single-handedly. If Fliss was actually as effective in business as Cameron said, then standing in front of him was the miracle he'd asked his bank manager to pray for. He felt a ridiculous urge to leap up from his desk and pull her into a hug.

'I don't know anything about how to run a hotel,' he told her. 'Teaching people to dive, yes. Organising laundries and chambermaids, no. But the Cross Hotel has been a big part of Emmside for more than a hundred years. As soon as I got back, I realised how impossible it was to sell it out of the family.'

As Patrick said the words, he understood for the first time that deep down he didn't actually *want* to sell. This hotel was part of his roots. His childhood had been spent here. He *belonged* here. He was so struck by this revelation, it was some while before he noted that Fliss, too, had fallen silent. Fliss not speaking was such an extraordinary occurrence, he sat up straight, sharpening his focus on her. She was staring at something a couple of feet to his right, just outside the window, her mind obviously elsewhere. She was chewing her lip in that way of hers he'd noticed, a little frown marring her brow. Patrick knew Fliss well enough by now to know that her quick mind was racing over everything he'd said.

When her eyes met his, they were glowing with excitement. 'I think I can help.'

'Fliss, the staff in the Cross Hotel are suffering from rock bottom morale. Everyone from my mother to the chambermaids is thoroughly depressed. And not only that, we need a massive injection of cash, and instead, all we have is crippling debts. It's going to take a miracle to do anything.'

She smiled a confident smile. 'I have an idea.'

'An idea,' he repeated. His tone was sceptical, but Fliss wasn't one to let scepticism stand in her way.

'I've a million ideas.' She spread her arms wide. 'This hotel has the potential to be a huge success, with people coming from miles around. It's in a stunning location, and it's a beautiful old building. You have great staff. You could have guests from literally all over the world.'

Patrick shook his head. It was all very well being enthusiastic, but ideas had to have some grounding in reality. 'All I see is an old house leaking money.' He pointed to the worn carpet in his office. 'Who'd want to stay in a place like this?' Fliss opened her mouth, but he carried on, 'And it's not just that. The locals think there's something wrong with the place. They say it's unlucky, and that it's seen too much tragedy. And now with my father dying…'

The cheerful light in Fliss's eyes died a little. Patrick hated himself for dampening her optimism, but he had to look at things realistically. It was going to take a lot of work to bring round the fortunes of the hotel, and there was more wrong with the business than just optimism could cure.

He might have known Fliss would refuse to be downcast. 'I know it's an unhappy place at the moment,' she admitted. 'I only have to see Jilly's face to understand that. But we can bring it round. Really.' When he didn't answer, she went on earnestly, 'If we try to make a change, even if we don't succeed, at least it will give Jilly something to focus on. It will give her a sense of purpose.'

Patrick thought this one over and had to admit the truth of it. He'd seen the way his mother's face lit up whenever Fliss appeared. Fliss seemed to have that effect on everybody. Since she'd arrived, Johnny wasn't quite as manic. Even Tomasz didn't seem as cantankerous.

Patrick took in Fliss's hopeful expression, her head cocked on one side, waiting for him to answer, and he couldn't help but feel his own spirits rise.

'So, what's your idea?' he asked. 'It has to be something that doesn't cost too much money, because to be perfectly honest, we don't have any.'

'The place to start is right here, with the people in the valley.' Her words came tumbling out, as though she'd been thinking them over for some time. 'Tourists and fell-walkers come and go with the seasons, but the locals are your regulars. We need to make local people forget they ever thought the Cross Hotel an unhappy place. We need to make sure when they think of the Cross Hotel, they think of fine dining, fine wines, a place where they'll be looked after and enjoy themselves. Once we've attracted the locals, the others will follow.'

Patrick turned over her suggestion and had to admit that what she said made sense. 'My dad tended to look down on the locals. Like they weren't worth bothering with. I can't remember the last time anyone from the village came into the restaurant.'

'Exactly. And your dad was missing a lot of good custom.' Fliss leaned forward, caught up in her own enthusiasm. 'The

Lakeside is your only real local competition, and Cameron's chef is nowhere near as good as Tomasz. You've got a great chef here, and he's just itching to be let loose on something more exciting than meat and two veg.'

Patrick shrugged. 'Fine, so we change the menu. It's still going to take a long time for people in the village to realise things have changed, and that we'll pull out all the stops for their custom. Unless…' He stopped, mulling over what Fliss had said. 'I suppose we could hold a launch party. Invite all the local bigwigs. Let them find out for themselves that we've turned over a new leaf and we mean business.'

'Yes, exactly.' Fliss grinned. 'We invite all the movers and shakers. Travel companies, the local council and businesses. Let's get the press in. And your local MP. Let's even invite Cameron.' She gave a wicked laugh. 'Why not? Let's show him he's got some competition.'

Patrick chuckled as a thought struck him. 'We could even invite my bank manager.'

'And here's something else that will definitely attract people. We make it a Tudor night. With a banquet and fancy dress.'

The smile died on Patrick's lips. A theme night. Everything his father would have hated. A party for the locals would have been bad enough for Jonathan Cross, but having to host it waving chicken drumsticks and wearing tights would have been his idea of hell.

Fliss was regarding him, eyes bright, waiting for his reaction in that way she had. Sensing his reluctance, she rushed on. 'This is a magnificent building with an ancient history. People locally have forgotten – even you and Jilly take it for granted, you've lived here so long – but as soon as I walked into the reception I knew this hotel had a unique atmosphere.'

Patrick thought it over. Perhaps she was right. Perhaps the tragic memories that clung to the place were all in Patrick's head. Maybe other people saw the place differently. To Patrick, the Cross Hotel was just his home – the scene of family arguments and unhappiness. But maybe the building did have charm beneath the decay. Fliss certainly seemed to think so. Perhaps a Tudor night would rekindle people's interest.

Fliss smiled, a wide smile that had an irresistible warmth to it. 'Why not just try it?' she asked him. 'You never know, it might even be fun.'

Patrick found himself smiling back. He realised if this was a taste of the Everdene ability to do business, he was lucky to have Fliss on his side.

Then he remembered Cameron's hints that the Everdenes were on no one's side but their own, and his smile wavered a little. But no doubt Cameron was just jealous. There was no reason at all not to trust Fliss Everdene completely.

Chapter Six

Fliss

Fliss had lots to tell her parents, but it wasn't until much later that afternoon that she had the opportunity to phone home. The mobile phone signal at the Cross Hotel, as in most of the Lake District, was patchy. She'd discovered the best reception could be found by leaning precariously out of the window in her bedroom. From here she could see far down into the valley, with the mountains ranged all around it, and the shining lake in its centre.

The terrace beneath her room was empty of guests. A soft rain was falling, and the tables had been stripped of their covers. Fliss pulled up the hood of her sweatshirt to keep the rain from her hair and pressed her mother's number.

'Hello Fliss, darling. Lovely to hear you. How are things at the Cross's?'

Fliss immediately registered the tension in her mother's voice, despite the cheerful question. What had been happening since she left home? Instead of replying, she said quickly, 'Is everything all right?'

Her mother began to protest that all was fine but gave up when Fliss insisted she could tell just from the sound of her voice that it wasn't.

'I didn't want to worry you.' Helen gave a sigh. 'It's just Minnie. Our trip to the residential home didn't go well.'

'Oh, no! What on earth went wrong? She was really excited about it.'

'Everything was OK when we got there. In fact it seemed like the perfect place for her. Not everyone in the school has Down's syndrome, but there were a few others like Minnie, and all the kids had learning difficulties of some sort. But honestly, Fliss, the work they do there is incredible. There's an indoor swimming pool and a gym for physio, they run a craft shop where they make all sorts of things from leather and fabrics, they keep a garden where they grow fruit and vegetables, and they even sell the produce in their own shop. Plus there's a kitchen where they can learn to cook. The staff were marvellous. Minnie seemed really happy and excited, playing computer games in the sitting room with some of the others. She didn't even want to leave when we said it was time to go. But on the way home, when we talked about her staying there, she got cold feet. She said she'd go there, but she wanted to come home every day and sleep in her own bed.' Helen drew in an audible breath and went on, 'We tried to point out to her that it was too far to come home every day, and how much you'd loved it having your own room at university with your new friends, but it was no good. There was one of her do's.'

Fliss groaned aloud. She could just picture the scene. Minnie's "do's", as her family had come to call them, were few and far between, but when they came they were memorable. Ordinarily, Minnie was the sunniest girl you could imagine, but sometimes she had difficulty controlling her emotions, especially if she was frightened about something. When she lost control, it was like a toddler having a tantrum, only ten times worse because the tantrum was going on in an adult's body.

'It was my fault for starting the conversation in the car,' Helen said. 'I could kick myself. She was so over-wrought your dad had to pull over. God knows what people thought.' Her voice quavered. 'Honestly, when she gets like this, people must think we're about to murder her. The only way we could get her to calm down was to promise to pick up a burger and chips on the way home. And she'd already had a big meal at the residential school. She's not supposed to over-eat, but I just couldn't think of anything else.'

'Oh, Mum. I'm so sorry.'

'Well, don't you be worrying about it, Fliss darling. I'm sure we'll bring her round eventually. We'll just have to keep taking her for visits, until she's really got used to the idea. Although how we're going to find the time, I don't know. There's a meeting of the directors next week, and I still have my report to finalise, and your father has the guys from Germany coming over.'

'I'll come back, Mum.'

'No.' Her mother's protest was sharp. 'No, there's no need for that, darling. You've only been gone a few days, and Jilly needs you. I spoke to her yesterday, and she was raving about what a delight you were, and how you'd cheered everyone up. And anyway, I don't want – ' Her mother broke off quickly.

'Oh, I'm sorry, Mum,' Fliss said, stricken. 'You mean you don't want Dad and me rowing and complicating things even more.'

'Well,' Helen flustered. 'It's these dealings with the German hotel. You didn't like how your dad went about it.'

Fliss felt again the physical queasiness she'd experienced after hearing how her father had pursued his latest acquisition. The hotel in Stuttgart was in financial difficulties, but Fliss was sure it could have survived on its own, if her dad had only allowed them time. But true to form, he'd moved in with ruthless speed and bought them out at a rock bottom price.

When Fliss failed to answer, her mother went on, 'This is how business is done, darling. And you know, everything your dad's done to build up Everdenes has been for you and Minnie. He wants to leave you both looked after.'

'I know, Mum.' Fliss didn't need to expand on her reply. Her father was anxious about the day when he and her mother were no longer able to look out for Minnie, and Fliss would be left to care for her. Sometimes Fliss thought her father was driven by a misguided sense of responsibility, expanding the business ever further, as though he felt the fact of Minnie's

Down's syndrome was somehow his fault, and he could make it up to her by accumulating wealth. There was no doubt he adored Minnie, and adored Fliss, too. Understanding her father's complex motives didn't mean Fliss condoned them. It just made her feel torn and distressed.

'Don't you be worrying about Minnie,' her mother repeated. 'One way or another, we'll find something that suits her when she leaves school. How are things in the Lakes?' she asked brightly. 'Is Jilly still having you rustling up cocktails?'

Fliss allowed herself to be diverted. She began to try and cheer her mother up by telling her about the previous evening, when a coach full of guests had turned up out of the blue, and she'd learned how to mix a Horny Bull. She went on to tell Helen about her conversation with Patrick, and her ideas for a Tudor night.

Helen listened with a professional ear, adding a few ideas of her own for the relaunch, before saying wistfully, 'Oh, it does seem a shame the hotel's so run down. I remember visiting Emmside when Jilly had just started seeing Jonathan. The hotel was a lovely place, then.'

'It still is, Mum.' Fliss surveyed the hills, where the late afternoon shadows were creeping down the valley. 'It's just so beautiful here. But it's not only the location. The staff in the hotel make the place seem like a home. Somewhere with a tradition. A place people care about. It's such a change to work in a hotel where everyone's known each other for years – even gone to school together, some of them. They're like a family. And I like Patrick and Jilly. I want to help them.' Fliss thought about Patrick, the way he'd looked at her when she'd enthused about the hotel, his rare smile transforming him. 'I feel as though I could really make a difference here.'

Helen was silent for a moment. Then she said quietly, 'Well, it's lovely to hear you talk like this, Felicity. It's a long time since you've been so enthusiastic about making a change in a hotel. I wish I could be there with you.'

Fliss felt a pang of guilt. Her mother was right; it was a long time since she'd shown any interest in her parents' business. A sudden idea struck her. 'Why don't you come and see for yourself, Mum? After the directors' meeting, you could come up for a weekend. I'm sure Jilly would love to see you again.'

Her mother's laughter gurgled. 'That's a lovely idea. The last time I saw Patrick, he was a little boy. I'm dying to meet him. If he's anything like his dad was as a young man, he'll be quite a looker.'

Fliss thought of her conversation with Patrick earlier, the energy that radiated from him, and the light in his eyes as they'd rested on her. Although not conventionally good-looking, as Johnny was with his blond hair and easy smile, underneath his troubled frown Patrick had a warmth that was surprisingly attractive.

There was a noise in the background. 'Oh, here's Minnie, back from school.' Helen's voice faded. 'Do you want to say hello to Fliss, darling?'

'Hiya!' Minnie's greeting was a cheerful burst.

'Hey, Minnie. What's up?'

'Whassu-u-up,' Minnie repeated loudly.

Fliss remembered how much she missed her sister's giggle.

'Are you still at Mum's friend's?' Minnie went on. 'When are you coming home?'

Fliss told her sister she'd be home in a few weeks, that Raffles was OK and was sitting on her window-ledge looking at the view. She told her there was a lake, and sheep, and how she'd been to the Post Office to post Minnie a present.

'Miss you.' Minnie drew out the words, making them sound forlorn.

'Miss you, too, Minnie. We'll talk again soon. Be good, honey bee.'

Minnie handed her back to their mum, and Fliss finished the conversation hurriedly. Her shift behind the bar was about to start, and she still had to change into her uniform.

'I'll talk again soon, Mum. Give my love to Dad. And I'm sorry about Minnie's residential school. If you want me to come back, just let me know.'

'Thanks, darling. I'm sure everything will be OK. Say hello to Jilly for me.'

Her mum had given her usual cheerful goodbye, but underneath the breezy farewell there was a definite hint of strain. Fliss frowned as she replaced her phone in her bag. At least there was still plenty of time before Minnie was due to start at her new place. If her mum and dad hadn't managed to bring Minnie round to the idea of leaving home by then, perhaps Fliss could try. She could tell Minnie that it would be an adventure, just as going away to university had been exciting for her.

But there was nothing that could be done for Minnie yet, and so Fliss hurried into her black skirt and white blouse and made her way downstairs to the bar, ready to begin her shift.

It was a quiet evening. No coach full of fell-walkers arrived to break the monotony. After serving dinner drinks, Fliss polished all the glasses, wiped clean the cabinets and restocked the optics. Pauline had left the bar in an excellent state, and it wasn't long before Fliss ran out of things to do. She thought wistfully of her one busy shift. Even throbbing feet were better than this boredom. There were a handful of guests in the lounge, lingering over coffee and wine. Nothing Johnny couldn't cope with. After dinner was cleared away, Patrick had left to go and work in his office. A notion struck Fliss that perhaps it was Patrick's absence that was causing the evening to drag. Then she rolled her eyes. She definitely must have too much time on her hands if she were missing Patrick.

Patrick

Patrick's office was a dingy room, stuck at the back of the hotel. When Fliss stepped through the door the next morning it was as though she brought the sun with her. She was dressed in a yellow-gold dress, patterned in tiny sprigs of bright flowers, and as usual she was smiling. Patrick's spirits lifted.

'What do you think of this?' He pushed the design he'd been working on across the desk towards her.

'Good morning.' She glanced at him quizzically and pulled out a chair. The smile continued to play on her lips, but Patrick couldn't work out if she was smiling at the abruptness of his question, or at some other secret thought. Fliss was always smiling. She picked up the mock-up Patrick had passed her and examined it.

Patrick had found some images of red roses which he'd printed around the margins of his design, and at the top he'd placed a Tudor cross. An elaborate, old-fashioned script declared, "*Mistress Jilly Cross and Patrick Cross, Esquire, do cordially invite you to an exclusive Tudor banquet at the sixteenth century Cross Hotel. Sumptuous meats, pastries, and all manner of fish and fowle will be served, as well as hearty ales and fine wine.*

Dress: in Tudor fancy dress or your finest twenty-first century garments."

Patrick had added the date and the price for the meal and then:

'*We await your courteous reply.*'

'I can't afford to pay a designer,' he said. When Fliss didn't answer immediately, he added, 'Do you think it's OK?'

'I love it.' She looked up with a grin.

Patrick was surprised to note how anxious he'd been for her opinion. He leaned back with relief. 'I googled some ideas. So you really like it?'

'I think it's perfect. I love the Tudor cross. It would make a great logo, and the cross symbol fits perfectly with the Cross Hotel. But the date you've given for the party is only four weeks away. That can't be right, surely? We'll never be ready in time.'

He took the print-out from her with a shrug. 'There's a lot to do, but I literally can't afford to wait. If I could bring the date even further forward, I would. I've already drawn up a list of people we should invite. My mum's offered to put together the mailing.'

'Well, you've certainly been busy. I'm starting to see why your dad thought you'd be the best person to run the hotel. And it's great your mum wants to be a part of it.'

'When I told her your idea, she was really excited about it. It's the first time I've seen her show any enthusiasm since I got home.'

'There,' Fliss's eyes lit up, 'What did I tell you? And I know you think a Tudor banquet is a totally tacky idea, but people will love it. Just wait and see.'

Patrick rolled his eyes. He wasn't looking forward to kitting himself out in fancy dress. On the other hand, even if the evening turned out to be a disaster, it had already been worth it to see his mother show the first spark of interest in a long while.

'I'm glad you like the Tudor cross,' he said. 'I thought we could revamp our image with it. We can get new stationery and menus printed up in time for the relaunch. We just need to run everything by Tomasz. If we're going to make big changes, he needs to know now. After all, the kitchen staff are going to bear the brunt of it.'

He'd barely finished speaking when there came the sound of laboured breathing and heavy footsteps in the corridor, followed by the appearance of Tomasz's enormous frame. He stood for a moment in the doorway, glancing from Fliss to Patrick, his fleshy face drawn and pale.

'So, the kitchen staff bear the brunt,' he said, the corners of his eyes drooping. 'I guessed this day would come.' He heaved his frame into the room. There were two beads of sweat glistening on his temple. 'How many have to go?'

'What?' Patrick looked up at him, nonplussed.

'How many staff do I have to let go?' he repeated, coming to a halt in front of Patrick's desk. 'I tell you I can't lose Maria. We won't find a better sous-chef. And we need Hal.' The chair groaned beneath his weight as he dropped into it. He mopped his forehead with a handkerchief. 'And Hannah. I need all of them.'

'Tomasz, we're not getting rid of anyone. Quite the opposite, I hope. Here.' Patrick pushed the mock-up invitation over the desk. 'Fliss has had an idea for an exclusive event to relaunch the hotel. What do you think? Any suggestions?'

The chef's great bulk spread over the edges of the chair as he settled himself. He reached into the pocket of his white jacket and pulled out a tiny pair of glasses which he perched on the end of his nose. Patrick's eyes met Fliss's above Tomasz's bowed head. Fliss grimaced. The harassed expression on Tomasz's face was painful to witness. It was distressing to see just how low morale in the hotel had sunk.

Tomasz examined the invitation in silence. The seconds stretched out, until Fliss could bear it no longer.

'What do you think?' she asked.

He replaced his glasses in his pocket slowly. When he looked up, his round face was filled with relief and surprise, and his colour had returned. 'I think this is a wonderful idea.' The heavy jowls and fleshy cheeks rearranged themselves in the nearest Tomasz ever came to a smile. 'A Tudor feast. I did something similar for a hotel in York. I'll pull out my old recipes. Venison, game pie, trout.' His black eyes gleamed. 'Some curd tarts and fresh strawberries.'

'Something to get your teeth into at last, Tomasz,' Patrick said. 'It's handy you've done something like this before. We've got four weeks to pull it off.'

'Four weeks?' The chef spluttered, and his features refolded themselves into a scowl. 'That's not enough time. Not to do it properly. If we're inviting the press, we need to source the best suppliers. The fish, for example, has to be of the freshest. That frozen stuff we buy is only fit for swine. We want everything to be the highest quality, and that takes time to source.'

'I agree,' Patrick said. 'Everything has to be fresh and local. Once you've decided exactly what you need, you can leave the rest to me.'

'Hmmph.' Tomasz eyed him doubtfully. 'There's a couple of dairy farmers over towards Windermere. And some seafood suppliers in Whitehaven. Your father would never let me approach them. He said why change what we had.'

'My father's not here now, Tomasz, and things are going to have to change, whether my dad would have liked it or not. And that brings me onto another thing. You'll be glad to know that after the Tudor night is out of the way you can change the menus for the restaurant.'

Tomasz's jaw dropped like a flounder fish. 'Change? You're kidding me.'

'I'm not kidding you.' Patrick indicated the Tudor cross design. 'We need the new menus printing up in time for the banquet, so our guests can see we mean business. I'll need you to cost up a few ideas and let me know your suggestions as soon as possible.'

'Pfffft.' Tomasz hauled himself up out of his chair. 'This is good news.' His hand engulfed Patrick's, and he shook it until Patrick's eyes watered. Then he turned to Fliss, and his small, sharp gaze fastened on hers. 'Seems there are going to be big changes here. Not too many, I hope.'

His beady eyes remained on Fliss for a little longer than necessary. Then he muttered something non-committal about being needed in the kitchen and made his way out.

Fliss looked to Patrick. 'What do I have to do to get people to trust me?'

Patrick thought of his own misgivings. Fliss was one thing. James Everdene was something else entirely, and an unknown quantity. He took in Fliss's despondent expression and said, with a confidence he was far from feeling, 'It's quite something to have a member of the Everdene family here, helping to turn the hotel around. And you know hotel gossip. In a few days' time they'll have forgotten all about where you come from, and we'll all be working together.'

Fliss nodded, but her hands were clenched a little too tightly in her lap. For an instant, Patrick felt an urge to reach out to her across the table.

Then she lifted her head and looked him in the eye. 'Well if they don't trust me, I'll just have to prove them all wrong, won't I?'

Chapter Seven

Fliss

The Cross Hotel was beginning to bubble with new life, like fresh water springing up in the dried bed of a lake. When Fliss started her shift that evening, she found Patrick and Johnny deep in animated conversation. She noted with amazement that Johnny was actually listening to what Patrick had to say. There was an intent expression on his face, and not a sneer to be seen.

'Look, we've already been through the wine cellar – ' Patrick was saying.

'Hmmph. What's left of it,' Johnny broke in. 'You saw for yourself there's hardly anything on the racks. And what we've got I wouldn't use as toilet cleaner. We can't serve that up to a roomful of posh guests. They'll be wanting their money back.'

Patrick picked up one of the hotel's battered menus. 'We're getting a whole new set of stationery printed up, and that includes this drinks menu. So now's the perfect time for you to replenish the cellar. You can decide on a whole new drinks list, while you're at it. Maybe get rid of the Horny Bulls,' he went on dryly. 'But I'll leave that up to you, along with anything else you'd like to try. Oh, and we'll need a special selection of drinks for the Tudor evening. Something authentic and original. Not just boring old mead.' He pulled a face at the thought. 'If you want to take a day off to go round some suppliers, let me know.'

Johnny nodded, trying to look as though all this was nothing special, but Fliss could see he was almost bursting with delight. It was probably the first time Johnny had been trusted with any responsibility in all his time at the hotel.

The guests began to sit down for their evening meal, and Patrick headed back to his office. The old Johnny would have whiled away the shift making sarcastic comments about the guests and casting sly digs at Patrick, or else driving Fliss crazy by endlessly whistling an inane tune. Now, whenever a lull arose, he pored over a wine catalogue. All his old sullen irony had vanished. It was a miracle.

With nothing much to do after dinner except serve the odd glass of port and lemon, and since Johnny was occupied, Fliss was glad she'd brought along a paperback. She kicked off her shoes and was fully immersed in the twists and turns of a grisly psychological thriller, when Johnny cleared his throat.

Fliss looked up to find him hovering.

'Tomasz thinks it's all down to you,' he said.

'All what?'

Johnny waved his hand. 'Tomasz thinks it's because of you Patrick's stopped being such a miserable grump. He says since you got here, everyone's changed. It's like we've suddenly got something to work towards.'

Fliss felt her cheeks go pink. Whenever she visited an Everdene Hotel she was treated like an outsider, imposing an unwanted regime on resentful staff. For the first time in her career, she felt a sense of belonging. She was touched to find Tomasz had such a high opinion of her.

'Well, the Tudor party was my idea,' she admitted, 'but it's Patrick who's seeing it all through. Ever since I mentioned having a relaunch, there's been no stopping him. I can see how he's made a success of his business in Dominica.'

Johnny cast her a quick, speculative glance and looked away again. 'Yeah, well. You and Patrick make a good team.'

It was so unusual for Johnny to compliment Patrick on anything that for once, Fliss was speechless.

'I don't suppose you'd think of staying?' he went on.

Fliss stared at him. Remain at the Cross Hotel and not go back? The thought hadn't occurred to her. For a moment she allowed herself to imagine staying in this wonderful hotel in the mountains forever, with the staff she'd already come to see as friends. She thought of working with Patrick every day, and watching the hotel thrive.

She picked up a cloth and began wiping the gleaming counter with brisk movements. 'I wish it was as easy as that, Johnny.'

'Can't you just hand in your notice? Your parents would be able to cope without you, surely.'

'My dad would be devastated if I went to work in another hotel. In fact, he'd be really hurt.' Fliss put down the cloth. 'But it's not just my dad. My mum wants to spend more time with my sister, Minnie. Most children grow up and leave home, and they need their parents less and less, but with my sister it's different. She has Down's Syndrome. In a way she needs my parents even more now than she did when she was little. That's why I've taken on more of my mum's responsibilities in the business. Everdenes is a global chain, but we're a family, too. I'd feel terrible if I just walked away.'

Johnny's face fell. She gave him a small smile. 'Perhaps I can come back as a guest next year. I'll sit in the lounge with my feet up, ordering Horny Bulls and Wah Wah Shooters and trying to get Patrick riled.'

This made Johnny laugh, but later that night, as Fliss lay in bed staring at the starry sky through her window, she couldn't help turning over in her mind the thought of staying. A crescent moon began to edge its way over the dark outline of the mountains, silhouetting Raffles' familiar shape in its silvery light. The sight of the giraffe's head drooping on his long neck made Fliss think of Minnie and her parents, and she turned restlessly in her narrow bed. The Everdene chain would always cope without Fliss Everdene. After all, no one was indispensable. Perhaps if she spoke to her dad...

Then she sighed and turned over to face the wall. As she did so she had an image of Patrick sitting behind his desk, his reserve evaporating as they discussed her ideas in his office. He'd even smiled a couple of times. He had nice eyes when he smiled. The thought gave her a comforting feeling, far more pleasant than dwelling on her problems working for her father, and it wasn't long before she was drifting off to sleep, the image of Patrick's rare smile in front of her.

*

Jilly was on reception the next morning. She raised her head as Fliss passed through, and Fliss was struck by the fresh colour in her cheeks.

'Morning, Jilly,' she said. 'I'm going down to the village. Want to come with me?' She came to a halt by the desk. 'We could go for a coffee.'

Jilly put her head on one side for a couple of seconds to consider it, then said regretfully, 'I'd love to, darling, but I've so much to do.'

The stack of dull brown bills was gone from her desk. In its place was a pile of cheerful envelopes, in bright colours ranging from purple to green to orange.

'I've got the invitations for the Tudor party to post,' she explained. 'And then I need to speak to the housekeeper about cleaning up the lounge.'

Fliss picked up an envelope. 'Love the colours.'

Jilly had printed the address labels on gold paper, with a cartoon Henry VIII in one corner. They certainly looked arresting.

'What a great idea,' Fliss went on. 'These will really get us noticed.'

Jilly gave a relieved smile. 'I'm glad you like them. I thought they'd stand out. And of course the Tudors loved bold colours, so they're quite appropriate. Although I'm sure Patrick thinks they're tacky.' Her smile turned down. 'Honestly, he's so like his father sometimes, even though he'd hate me for saying so.'

'Well I love them.' Fliss grinned. 'And so will everyone else. Never mind what Patrick thinks.'

Patrick

Patrick was making his way down the corridor from his office. He came out into the reception hall to find Fliss standing by his mother's desk, clutching one of the invitations. She turned at the sound of his footsteps and must have realised he'd heard her last words. She had the grace to look a little self-conscious as she saw him approach

'I'm just admiring Jilly's invitations.' She lifted her chin. 'Aren't they fabulous?'

Patrick didn't think they were fabulous. If he were quite honest, he thought the envelopes were garish, but his mother was delighted with them, and that was what counted. He gave a resigned shrug. His mother caught Fliss's eye and they both burst out laughing.

Fliss tapped him on the arm with an envelope. 'Don't be so stuffy. Everyone will be dying to know what's inside.' She turned to Jilly. 'I could take these down to the village Post Office, if you like. I've got my car booked in for its repairs at the garage this morning.'

'Maybe I'd better follow you,' Patrick said. 'Just in case Gudrun finally falls to bits on the way down the hill.'

Fliss rolled her eyes.

'What a good idea,' Jilly said. 'I'd hate to think of you broken down alone on the hillside, Fliss. If you could post some of these invitations while you're in the village, that would be perfect.'

As it turned out, it was just as well Patrick had offered to go with Fliss. He followed her slow descent of the fellside, listening to her car thundering, and wondered how on earth she'd made the long trip from Norfolk without being pulled over by the police. The noise from the engine was deafening. It was just as well the hotel lay in a remote spot, otherwise the residents would think an army of tanks had invaded. Luckily the garage was situated on the outskirts of the village, where there was no chance of disturbing the peace.

When Fliss drew up in the forecourt, Patrick got out of his car to join her. She looked a little embarrassed as he approached.

'Thanks for the escort.' She cast a worried glance at her car. 'She wasn't like this on the trip up, honestly. I think the final climb to the hotel must have done for her.' She bit her lip. 'Anyway, no point worrying just yet. I'll see what the mechanics can do.'

Fliss stood there, obviously expecting Patrick to go, but something made him say, 'It's going to take a while for them to fix it. Why don't we head off somewhere while you wait? We can take a walk by the lake, until it's ready.'

A look of astonishment crossed Fliss's face, and Patrick was taken aback himself at his own suggestion. He had so much to do back at the hotel, and now here he was, asking Fliss if she'd like to spend some time with him. And what devil had made him suggest going to the lake? There were days when he was overwhelmed with dread at the very mention of Emmswater.

Yet now, when Fliss nodded unexpectedly, giving him one of her smiles, Patrick felt a stab of pleasure.

'Thanks. That's a lovely idea.' She beamed. 'I wanted to explore the lake last time I was in the village, only there wasn't time. And anyway, I was with Johnny, and he turned his nose up at going for a walk, so we just came back to the hotel. I'll speak to the mechanics, and then we can be off.'

She tripped lightly up the steps to the reception, dangling her car key in her hand.

Patrick leaned back against Fliss's car to wait. If anyone had told him only last week he'd be looking forward to spending a morning walking round Lake Emmswater, he'd have said they were crazy. But when Fliss came back down the steps, still smiling at him, he actually smiled back.

'They're going to phone me when they've had a look at her,' she said, a little breathlessly. 'I'm looking forward to a walk.' She giggled. 'This feels like playing truant. Only it doesn't matter, because I think you could do with a morning off, for once. It would do you good. And look.' She waved a hand at the sky, where threatening clouds loomed over the edge of the mountains. 'It's not even raining yet. So let's make the most of it.'

'Come on.' Patrick ushered her towards his car. 'We can take a drive right up to the top of the lake. There's a shingle beach and a path we can walk on.'

Fliss hopped up into the passenger seat, and Patrick climbed in beside her. As he turned the key in the engine, he glanced down at her shoes. 'It's quite pebbly by the lake. Will you be all right in those?'

Fliss lifted a foot to examine her white wedged heels. 'Oh, it'll be OK,' she said. 'I knew white would get ruined in no time, so I bought three pairs. I've got a couple more the same at home.'

She turned to fasten her seat belt, missing the look of amazement on Patrick's face. There weren't many people who would be so relaxed about ruining an expensive pair of shoes, and Patrick had never met anyone before who thought nothing of buying three identical pairs at once. He reflected on how rarely Fliss showed just how wealthy she really was. For someone who'd had everything she'd ever wanted handed to her, she was remarkably down to earth. She'd taken to working behind the bar as though she'd done it forever, standing for hours on unsuitable shoes without complaining, putting up with Patrick's grumpiness and chatting cheerfully with the guests. It wasn't surprising that several of the regulars had taken a real shine to her.

Patrick found himself curious to discover more about Fliss's home life. He was just about to ask her a question, when Fliss – never silent for long – began to chat away of her own accord.

'Oh, look at those flowers,' she exclaimed, indicating one of the houses in a terrace as they drove past. Every window ledge had a box from which white and purple petunias tumbled in glorious splendour. 'How pretty is that! Is it like that every year?' Then she glanced across at Patrick, remembering. 'Oh of course, you wouldn't know, would you? I forgot you've been away. It seems to me like you've always been at the Cross Hotel, for years and years. It must be strange to be back here.'

Patrick turned his head to examine the flower-bedecked house as they passed. 'That place has been the same every summer for as long as I can remember. Always petunias. I know I've been away a long time, but it's funny – every time I come home it's as though I've never left. The lady who lives in that house used to be our school dinner lady. She's retired now.'

'How wonderful to know everyone.' This set Fliss off on another train of thought, and she proceeded to ask Patrick about every person they passed on the street, becoming excited if he knew them, and wanting to know all about their personalities and what they did. As he answered her questions, Patrick's years in Dominica fell away, making him feel like a local again. He realised how much he felt at home here, despite the long absence, and was surprised at how welcome the feeling was.

Once out of the village, Patrick drove down an incline off the main road and onto a narrow, winding track that ran beside the lake. There were hardly any cars here, and the edge of the lake was only a stone's throw away. He slid his gaze to where the water lay and swallowed the hard lump in his throat. Fliss continued to make small talk, but Patrick's answers grew less and less frequent as they approached the northern end of the lake. Eventually the dirt car park he was aiming for appeared on their right. The entrance was exactly the same as when he'd parked there with Jacob all those years ago. He made the turn into the narrow opening and brought his car to a halt under the branches of a birch tree. His fingers tightened on the wheel for a moment before he reached for the ignition and cut the engine. His mouth was dry.

Fliss was telling him how much bigger the lake was than she imagined, and how sometimes it appeared a lovely soft blue from her bedroom window, but now she saw it close up it was actually more of a muddy green. Patrick had never felt more glad of her bright company. The hedges were overgrown since the last time he'd been here, the trees taller. And they'd laid asphalt over the dirt. It was strange, but now he'd arrived, the realisation that this spot had changed since the day he last saw it was incredibly painful. Strange, too, how he could be so wounded by such a thing. As though he expected the lakeside to remain forever the same, frozen in time with Jacob's death. He took a deep breath.

'Is everything OK?' Fliss's eyes were on his, curious and watchful.

Patrick realised she'd long since stopped speaking. He nodded and smiled at her. 'Let's take a walk.'

He swung open the car door and moved round to Fliss's side, helping her to alight from the high passenger seat. The fresh scent of her hair caught in his nostrils as he guided her down, and her hands were warm on his. Her slight body was real and alive, banishing the ghostly memories that clung to him.

There was a small frown on Fliss's brow when she glanced at him. She was swift to grasp the feelings of others, but Patrick had no desire to let his own dark train of thought cloud her day.

'Come on,' he said. 'Let's go and chuck a few rocks in the water.'

Fliss nodded and looked away. Patrick wondered if she felt rebuffed – if maybe she'd guessed he was shutting her out of his painful memories – but then she began to chat about the fens near her home in Norfolk, and how different they were from the Lakes, and how she wished she could bring her sister here, because nothing made Minnie happier than throwing all sorts of objects into water, with the bigger the splash, the better.

They made their way down the earth track to the lake's edge. The small shingle beach was unchanged. Fliss started towards the water. Patrick would have followed her, but at the final moment he found that, after all, he couldn't bring himself to stand on the spot where Jacob had last stood. He turned away abruptly to take a narrower path leading to a different inlet. Fliss left the shingle without comment and followed him.

A group of ducks was basking on the rocks. They raised themselves huffily as Fliss and Patrick approached, waddling into the water in a dignified fashion. Fliss crunched over the stones, heedless of the scuff marks marring her shoes. She bent to pick up a small, flat pebble and, with an adroit flick of the wrist, sent it skimming over the water. The pebble bounced a few times before plunging below the surface.

She raised her hands and did a graceful skip. 'Bet you can't beat that.'

Patrick cast an expert eye over the stones before choosing a flat rock. He stepped a little nearer the water and moved his arm back, releasing the rock with a swift flick of his fingers. It bounced six times with a slapping sound before disappearing.

He gave Fliss a satisfied grin. 'Beat that.'

'I certainly will.'

For a while they took it in turns, each trying to outdo the other. It was a long while before Fliss gave up, but eventually she had to concede defeat.

'It's only because you've had more practice,' she said grudgingly.

'We used to play at skimming stones a lot. We called it Ducks and Drakes.' Patrick checked the sky, which still showed the odd patch of blue. 'Shall we walk a little further up the lake? Looks like the rain's holding off.'

They made their way over the rocks until they reached a rutted footpath, where they ambled side by side for a while. Patrick glanced at the water. It hadn't been as traumatic as he'd expected, returning to this spot. There was still that uncomfortable sensation in his chest – a fluttering and bubbling in his veins, as though something terrible were about to happen – but his anxiety remained subdued and manageable. With practice, he thought, and with more trips to the lake, maybe the feeling of dread might disappear altogether. Although the effect of the trauma might become easier to bear, he knew he would never forget Jacob.

Fliss said carefully, her attention on the path ahead, 'You must think about your friend a lot.'

Patrick turned his head to her in swift surprise. Could she read his mind?

'Johnny told me about the accident.' Fliss glanced at him hesitantly. 'I hope you don't mind me mentioning it. I guessed you must have skimmed stones here with your friend, and that's how you got so good at it.'

Patrick remembered how as a boy Jacob would comb the rocks for the best stones, stock-piling them out of Patrick's reach. He gave a small smile. 'We were both quite competitive,' he told her.

The track narrowed, becoming too tight for them both to walk abreast. Fliss ambled ahead, her hands in the pockets of her mac. There was a graceful sway to her walk.

'Did you compete over girls?' she asked over her shoulder.

He laughed. 'No. But Jacob was a good-looker. He had loads of girls swooning over him at school.'

'Don't tell me the girls weren't all over you at school, as well.' She threw him a brief glance, cheeks dimpling.

He shook his head. 'If they were, I didn't notice. To be honest, we were neither of us interested in girls in those days. All we cared about was diving. That all changed when Jacob went off to university. We both changed then.'

A breeze sprang up, ruffling Fliss's hair. She pushed the strands away from her face. Patrick checked the sky again. The dark clouds had come in off the horizon and were now beginning to roll over their heads.

'We'd better get back to the car,' he said. 'Looks like the rain's going to come down.'

Fliss stopped and turned. Her eyes were serious on his. Patrick knew it was important to tell her just how much it had meant to him to have her company at the lake, before the moment to do so passed. He opened his mouth to speak, but the next minute fat drops of rain were bursting on the stones. Fliss lifted her face to look at the sky and blinked as the rain fell on her.

He caught hold of her hand. 'Come on. Let's go, before you get soaked.'

They both began to run, laughing and gasping as the rain turned to torrential sheets.

Chapter Eight

Fliss

The stones quickly became slick with wet. Fliss stumbled as she hurried along the path. Patrick caught hold of her hand to steady her. They rushed back the way they'd come, breathless, the lake a sheet of rippling silver on their right. When they reached the car, Patrick held her door for her. The rain plastered his dark hair to his head and moulded his shirt to his chest. The muscles in his arms tensed as he swung the door shut after Fliss.

She shivered, wrapping her arms around herself. Patrick slid into the seat beside her. Water glittered in droplets on his bare forearms. He reached into the back seat and drew out a towel, offering it to Fliss.

Fliss's mac had protected her from the worst of the rain, but there were cold drops running down her hair and onto her face, and sliding down her collar. She dried herself as best she could before passing the towel to Patrick, who began to rub his head vigorously.

Fliss tore her gaze away and reached for her mobile phone, to check if the garage had rung. The signal was almost non-existent in the mountains, but the mechanic had managed to get through to her voicemail. She listened in silence, chewing the side of her thumb.

'Bad news?'

She pulled a face as she cut the call. 'They're keeping her in until tomorrow. The part she needs has to be ordered, and apparently there are one or two other things to look at. Basically there's even more wrong with her than I'd thought.'

Patrick lowered his towel. After all his ironic comments about Agnetha, his expression was surprisingly sympathetic. 'She's not going to last for ever.'

'I know.' Fliss sighed and returned her mobile to her bag. 'I just thought I could keep her going for a little while longer.'

He turned the key in the engine. 'No matter how attached you are to that car, you still need to get rid of it. She could be a death trap.'

'Not if they fix her,' Fliss said stubbornly.

Patrick grunted and shifted the gear into reverse.

'And you just called her "she",' Fliss added, casting him a sidelong glance. 'I think secretly you love her as much as I do.'

He laughed. It was a warm sound. Fliss didn't think she'd heard Patrick laugh properly before. He was reversing the car, and his head was turned towards her. His teeth showed white against his tan, and his cheeks dimpled attractively. It was such a transformation from his usual strained and solemn expression, Fliss felt her insides flutter.

'I suppose now you'll need a lift back to the hotel,' he said, teasing her. He guided the car out onto the road. 'We'll call in at the Post Office and mail my mother's invitations first. Perhaps it's just as well she chose such neon colours. At least we know they're not going to get lost in the post.'

Patrick

There was a long queue at the counter in the Post Office. The room was warm, and steam rose gently from various macs and anoraks. Several heads turned as Patrick entered with Fliss, and a few people nodded in greeting.

An elderly woman in a rainproof cape was studying the rack of birthday cards. She looked up as they approached. 'Hello, Patrick, love.'

Mrs Blake was the grandmother of one of Patrick's old school friends. Her attention flicked from Patrick to Fliss. There was no appearing in the village without people wanting to know who you were with and why. Patrick made the introductions, and Fliss tagged on to the tail end of the queue.

Silence fell, and Patrick began to feel all the usual awkwardness of appearing in Emmside. The last time he'd seen Mrs Blake had been at Jacob's funeral. Perhaps this had occurred to her, too. Instead of plying Patrick with friendly questions, as she would have done in years gone by, Mrs Blake shuffled her feet and returned to her examination of the greetings cards, as though they were of the greatest interest.

The silence would have gone on, until Fliss spoke up.

'What a day,' she remarked, to no one in particular. 'Is it always like this in the Lakes?'

'You not from round here, love?' The old man in front of her turned, and in no time at all Fliss was telling him all about life in Norfolk and how it compared to Emmside, and wondering whether it really did rain more in the west than the east, and how this was her first time in the Lake District. Soon all the locals were advising her on the best places to visit, and everyone seemed on the road to becoming firm friends. Then Mrs Blake joined in, and Patrick added a few comments of his own, and people he didn't even know began chiming in with advice and arguing amiably amongst themselves about the best local attractions. As the conversation around Fliss grew more animated, Patrick leaned against the wall next to a display of leaflets, a quiet smile on his lips, his previous feeling of awkwardness gone.

The queue inched forwards slowly. Outside, the rain showed no sign of letting up. Then the door opened with a nervous jangle, and a gust of cold wind eddied around Patrick's feet. Everyone stopped talking to see who else had come in, and there was the manager of the Lakeside Hotel in the doorway, shaking water from his umbrella.

Cameron stopped short at the sight of Patrick. Then he glanced over to where Fliss was approaching the counter. His lips twitched.

'Is she sending a telegram?' There was a smug tone to Cameron's question.

Patrick frowned.

Cameron jerked a thumb in Fliss's direction. 'I thought she might be sending her dad some urgent support.'

Fliss was now at the head of the queue. People began to turn their attention to Patrick's conversation, seeking fresh entertainment. Patrick had no idea what Cameron was talking about, but he didn't like the self-satisfied look on his face. It was the same look Patrick had seen in his rugby-playing days, when a player brought down a rival in the mud and stood gloating over him. He wanted to cut short the conversation and leave, but Fliss was still at the counter.

Cameron's smirk intensified. 'You mean you haven't heard?'

Just inside the doorway was a shelf of newspapers. Cameron bent to pick up one of the broadsheets. He leafed through it until he came to the business section and held it up to Patrick's view.

With a sinking feeling, Patrick took in the headline: "Stuttgart Hotel says *Nein Danke*. Legal Action Threat after Everdene Takeover." There was a photo of a short, stocky man with dark brows, above the caption "James Everdene". In the background was a hotel emblazoned with the famous Everdene logo.

Patrick ran his eye over the article with mounting unease. It seemed the Everdene chain had stirred up real problems with yet another aggressive takeover. A smaller photo showed a grim-faced couple standing on the steps of a solicitor's office. The caption told readers that these were the former owners of the hotel, and they were about to take James Everdene to court.

Patrick kept his expression neutral. He wouldn't give Cameron the satisfaction of knowing he'd needled him. Besides, he could feel several pairs of eyes on them. He was conscious of the urge to protect Fliss from malicious gossip. Patrick could hear her chatting happily to the man behind the counter. He willed her to stop talking for once and to let them get out of the shop.

But there was no halting Cameron now he'd started. 'So I guess you don't know what's happened?'

By now they'd attracted the attention of almost everyone in the Post Office. Most people in the queue weren't even bothering to hide the fact they were listening avidly. Patrick handed the newspaper back to Cameron, who held it up, as though deliberately showing everyone the headline. Patrick moved in front of him - not that there was much point trying to hide the news. Cameron would delight in spreading the gossip far and wide as soon as Fliss had left the shop.

'Looks like James Everdene has finally broken the law,' Cameron said loudly. 'He may actually be in trouble this time.'

Patrick became aware of Fliss's presence by his side. He glanced down and was shocked by the icy anger in her face. When she made to speak, he took her arm and gripped it warningly.

'Thanks for passing on the gossip, Cameron,' he said. 'Great talking to you, as usual.'

He ushered Fliss towards the door, but the show still wasn't over. The man behind the counter called out, 'Hang on a minute, mate. Are you going to pay for that?' He indicated the newspaper, sodden at the edges where their wet fingers had touched it.

'Don't worry, I'll get this.' Cameron pressed the newspaper into Fliss's hands, and turned to Patrick. 'It's good to have friends in high places,' he told him. He slid his eyes towards Fliss. 'Until they turn out to be not such good friends, that is.'

Patrick pushed opened the door and propelled Fliss out before she could vent the anger he sensed was ready to burst. Outside, the rain continued to come down in sheets.

'Come on,' he murmured. 'Let's go.'

The door jangled shut behind them. As they hurried down the wet street, Patrick became aware that Fliss had changed from the carefree, chatty companion of the morning into a completely different person. She was striding along, head erect, barely noticing the rain coursing down. There was an air of determination about her that Patrick had noticed before on occasion, but never with such force. Cameron's warning words rang in his head. In the ruthless world Fliss's father moved in, friends could quickly become enemies.

A burst of thunder rolled over their heads. He took Fliss's arm, and they began to run.

Chapter Nine

Fliss

The newspaper article lay open on Fliss's knee, the pages lifting gently in the warm air blasting from Patrick's car heaters. Rain dripped from her hair, blotting the newsprint until the words spread and merged.

Fliss's father was surrounded by the best in the legal profession, and his actions were always within the law. This time, though, it appeared he'd trodden very close to the limit of what was legal, and his takeover had ruined a family of hoteliers. A quote from the hotel's previous owner made Fliss's blood run cold.

"James Everdene is notorious in the hotel industry. He doesn't like to be beaten, and he usually gets his way. He attacks underperforming hotels in an aggressive and hostile fashion."

Fliss shivered, her fingers gripping the damp edges of the paper. If her mother hadn't suggested she come to the Lakes, Fliss might right now be at the Stockmann Hotel in Stuttgart, implementing the Everdene chain's strategy. She would be caught in a maelstrom of bad feeling, trying to turn around a workforce who bitterly resented her. How far could her loyalty to her father take her? To riding roughshod over other people? To gaining the same reputation he had for ruthlessness?

She lifted her head to look out of the rain-spattered windscreen. She was surprised to find they were climbing the fellside already, on the narrow road back to the Cross Hotel. The trees above them were black and shaking violently in the wind. Patrick concentrated on the tight turns, made treacherous in the wet. Since leaving the Post Office, he'd said nothing at all. Fliss was grateful for his calm handling of Cameron, but she wondered just what he made of the article. It painted her father in the worst possible light.

'Sometimes I wish I could run a small family hotel,' she told Patrick on impulse. 'Something like yours. Somewhere where the staff actually enjoy working for me. Somewhere I can really make a difference in people's lives, for the good.'

Patrick said nothing. He kept his eyes on the road ahead.

Fliss took his silence for scepticism. 'I mean it,' she said. 'OK, so at the moment your hotel has some money problems - but nothing that's insurmountable. It can all be turned around, and it would be a challenge doing it.' She surveyed the darkening fell, which was majestic, even in the torrential rain. 'If I could just buy a small hotel in a lovely spot like this and build it up, I'm sure it would be…' She tailed off. Cold rain trickled down her collar. She bent her head, and her eyes fell on the photo of her father, whose imposing features had been photo-shopped in front of the German hotel. She abandoned her train of thought and gave a sigh. 'I don't know how my parents' business got so out of hand.'

Her last words weren't quite the truth. Most people didn't see the real person behind the driven image in the press. To outsiders, James Everdene appeared merciless in his ambition for his company. But there was a lot more behind her father's apparently brutal expansion plans than appeared on the surface. It wasn't until Minnie was born that Fliss's father had begun to build up the Everdene chain in a relentless and determined fashion. It was ironic that his love for his daughters made him such a monstrous person in business.

To Fliss's dismay, she felt the prickle of tears. She reached into the pocket of her mac for her tissues.

Patrick brought the car to a halt in the forecourt of the hotel and switched off the engine. He shifted in his seat and turned towards her. 'I know I've spoken before about selling up this hotel,' he said. His voice was quiet, but the hard edge to it caused Fliss to tense. 'And I know I told you I wanted to go back to the Caribbean. The thing is, I still haven't decided what I'm going to do. One thing I do know. I'd never sell to a chain like Everdenes.'

Fliss whirled round, aghast. 'Of course not! That's not what I meant at all. When I said I'd like to run a small place, I wasn't talking about buying you out. This is your mother's home.'

There was a chill in the dark eyes on hers. Did Patrick really think her capable of plotting, like her father? Fliss felt a stab of pain at the thought and tried to harden herself. She sat upright, ramrod stiff.

'There are plenty of other hotels in the country you could buy up,' Patrick continued.

It was too much. Fliss forgot her distress, her pain turning to swift, hot anger. She thrust her face towards Patrick's. 'How dare you? I've come here as a favour to Jilly, to try and rescue the hotel your dad's done his best to drag to the ground. You've said yourself you know nothing about the hotel business. And Jilly's in no fit state to run it.' She jabbed a finger. 'But if you'd like me to leave, just say the word. My mum needs me at home. You can sort out your dad's mess yourself.'

She drew back, snatching her bag up, and made to open the car door.

'I'm sorry,' Patrick said, pre-empting her. 'I spoke out of turn.'

Fliss gave a scornful snort.

Patrick rubbed his face. 'I'm grateful for all your help. I really am. It's just that I worry about going back to the Caribbean and leaving my mother alone. One of the things I worry about is that if I leave she'll let herself be bought out by someone unscrupulous.'

'Someone like my father, you mean,' Fliss said, without looking at him.

Patrick didn't reply. Fliss turned her head and saw how his jaw was set. The signs of strain that had disappeared so briefly that morning by the lake had returned in force.

'If you worry about leaving your mother in charge, then have you thought about staying permanently at the Cross Hotel?'

His hands clenched. 'Of course I have. It's not as simple as that. I already have a successful business. And diving is my life.'

She indicated the valley below them. 'But you can dive here.'

His face whitened. For a couple of seconds he said nothing. Then he said, through stiff lips, 'I haven't been able to dive in Emmswater since Jacob drowned.'

Of course. How stupid of her! Fliss opened her mouth to speak, but Patrick pressed the latch on his car door and swung himself out, letting in a gust of rain. He hunched his head against the downpour. By the time he'd reached Fliss's side of the car, he was dripping with rain. He opened her door as another roll of thunder rumbled over the hills.

'I didn't realise,' Fliss said over the sound. She laid a hand on Patrick's, feeling the warmth of his fingers. Then she swung herself out of the high side of the vehicle, half falling, until his hand steadied her. A blast of wind caught them, and Fliss's teeth chattered. She looked up into his stark features. 'When we were at the lake, this morning, is that the first time you've been back?'

Patrick nodded. The rain ran down his face and over his pale lips.

'I had no idea. I'm sorry.' She looked back the way they'd come, as the rain streamed in rivulets down the fellside. 'I'm so sorry, Patrick. What a terrible thing.' She pressed her fingers on his. 'If you want someone to go there with you again, any time …'

He returned the clasp of her fingers. Then he glanced up at the sky.

'Let's get inside.' He pushed the car door shut behind her and together they ran through the rain to the hotel.

Jilly greeted them with dismay as they stood dripping in the doorway. 'Oh, you poor darlings. You got caught in the rain.'

She rushed round the desk towards them, stopping when she caught sight of Patrick's expression. 'Whatever's the matter?'

Patrick ran a hand through his wet hair. 'We're fine. We just got soaked.' He set off for the hallway and his rooms. 'The invitations are posted. I'm going to get dry.'

The light left Jilly's expression as she watched him stride out.

'We went for a walk by the lake,' Fliss said. 'It was Patrick's idea.'

Jilly turned quickly. 'You went to the lake? How was he?'

Fliss thought of how Patrick had caught hold of her hand, his laughing eyes as he'd urged her to run faster in the rain. 'He was fine.' She glanced guiltily at Jilly, remembering her angry words in the car. 'Really. It wasn't until we got back here…'

To Fliss's surprise, there was a small smile on Jilly's lips, and a speculative light in her eyes. 'Patrick's avoided the lake ever since the accident,' she said. 'I'm so happy he went there with you, Fliss. And this is the first morning he's taken off work since he got back from Dominica. I think you're doing him good.'

Fliss didn't think she and Patrick had been doing each other any good at all, but she didn't have the heart to contradict her. She thought of Patrick's insinuation that her father might stoop to buying out the Cross Hotel. Try as she might, she couldn't put the hurt behind her. Patrick was under a lot of strain, and his bitterness was excusable. But even after Fliss had showered and changed into dry clothes, there was still a chill lodged within her.

Patrick

The rain poured down all afternoon. Patrick stood in the empty lounge, arms folded, watching the water gather in great dark puddles on the flags of the terrace. Ten years ago he'd been clearing the tables on that very same spot when Jacob had called. Patrick had gone over their conversation in his mind over and over again since then. He'd told Jacob he shouldn't go out diving alone – that he'd leave work and go with him. The real truth was that the lure of the lake, shimmering in the sun, had proved too hard to resist. Patrick hadn't needed much persuading.

If he could turn back time, and do everything differently…

He pressed his forehead to the cold glass of the window. The stony beach where he'd taken Fliss that morning hadn't changed at all. He remembered finding Jacob sitting on an old tree-stump, trying to wrestle himself into his cumbersome dry-suit. Patrick had taken one look at Jacob's pale face and puffy eyes and realised his friend was hungover. They should have gone home.

Patrick had fetched a bottle of water out of his rucksack.

'Here,' he'd told Jacob. 'Rehydrate yourself. You look like death.'

'I'm not hungover.' Jacob had almost snatched the bottle out of Patrick's hand and taken a few greedy gulps.

'Listen, mate, this is a bad idea. You're not fit, and look at those clouds.'

The lake shone in the sunlight, but the sight was deceiving. At the far end of Emmswater valley great, threatening clouds were rolling over the hills. A breeze ruffled the lake's surface in jerky bursts.

Jacob threw the plastic bottle on the pebbles and returned to struggling with his suit.

'You're being a wuss,' he said. 'A bit of rain never stopped us before. Anyway, we're here now, we might as well go in.'

Patrick folded his arms.

'Fine.' Jacob gave another grunt, tugging at his zip before finally hauling it up over his belly, grown soft from his time at college. He reached for his belt of weights. 'You go home then, Paddy. I'll go in by myself.'

Patrick had examined the mulish set of Jacob's lips and ticked over the alternatives. He could stand his ground, but he knew how stubborn his friend could be. He thought about walking away, but the dive club had drilled into them that they should never dive alone. What if he left now, and something happened to his friend? He'd never forgive himself.

'If I come with you, we don't go over the ledge.'

There was a ledge of rock beneath the lake's surface, sloping gently for a distance before ending in an abrupt, plunging drop. Novice divers – and those who were unfit or out of practice, as Jacob was – stayed in the area of the ledge. Only experienced divers went down into deeper waters, where the temperature was colder, the water pressure stronger, and visibility poor.

Jacob eyed Patrick in disgust. 'Stay on the ledge?'

'I mean it, Jake.' Patrick stood unmoving, arms folded. 'We go out to the end of the ledge together, then along to the rock face, turn back, and when I give the signal, we come up. Got it?'

Jacob shrugged.

'I said did you get it?'

'OK, OK.' Jacob snapped his computer band around his wrist. 'We stick to the ledge.'

Patrick glanced over at the clouds, which seemed to have advanced several feet towards them. 'Come on then, let's get going, before this lot bursts over us.'

They finished kitting up in silence. Patrick checked the computer on his wristband before motioning Jacob to show him his. Jacob held his arm out. He'd grown unfit while he was away at college, but at least he'd kept his kit in good order. The dial showed plenty of air in his cylinder. Patrick would insist on checking it again when they were underway. Their dials would tell them the depth and water temperature, and would predict how slowly they should ascend, in order to avoid decompression sickness. Patrick took one look at his friend's sweating face and had no intention of descending deep enough to run the risk of the bends.

They put on their fins and began to edge sideways over the shingle and into the water. Patrick was filled with a rush of anticipation. No matter how many times he dived this lake, each time was like entering a new and secret world. He looked at Jacob and saw the same light of anticipation in the eyes that met his through the mask.

The water on the surface was choppy, but not so much that it would cause them a problem once they were below. Patrick took slow breaths in and out as the lake rose to his chest. Then the cold waters swirled over their heads, the hills and the lowering sky above them vanished, and their weights carried them downwards.

Patrick had dived in locations around the world since then, but there was nothing quite like the still green waters of his home valley. Entering Emmswater was like stepping into a mystical country, where everything was tinged with green, and the bubbles rose in silvery threads to the surface. A couple of perch swam past them as they levelled out, looks of surprise on their faces, their scales flashing green as they darted by. Patrick turned to Jacob, who held one thumb aloft, eyes bright.

It was inevitable, this close to the ledge, that they would leave a trail of thick cloud behind them, muddying the green water with chalky white. In order to avoid each other's trail, Patrick and Jacob finned along side by side. Occasionally they pointed things out to one another. Here was the fallen tree trunk Patrick had encountered on his first dive in the lake. Who knew how long it had lain on the ledge, the colour slowly bleaching from it? Here was the narrow fissure running crosswise, where the rock had split centuries since. A few small fish flashed out from inside and swam rapidly away. This split in the rock was Patrick's point of reference. As they passed over it, he knew they were only a few metres from where the ledge ended and the lake plunged away. He lifted his wrist to check his computer, as he always did at this point. They had been underwater for quarter of an hour. Jacob raised his arm so that Patrick could check his dial. Patrick frowned as he examined the reading. His friend was using up air more rapidly than he should. Another sign he was unfit. But there was no need to be anxious. They were now approaching the end of the ledge, where the inviting green of the water faded into dense black. Patrick lifted his gloved hand in front of Jacob's face, indicating they should go right to avoid the drop and begin their return to shore. They turned, leaving a cloud of silt behind them, and made their way along the outer edge of the ledge towards the place where the rock face lifted sheer above them and out of the water.

It was Patrick's intention to head towards this vertical rock, and from there turn right again, keeping close to the wall and following the ledge as it rose back towards the shingle beach. Jacob had dropped a little behind him and was still close to the rim, where the lake plunged away. As they approached the rock face, Patrick indicated right with a movement of his hand. There was no response from Jacob. He was looking to his left, to where the green waters of the lake disappeared into murky darkness. Patrick reached over and tapped him on the shoulder.

Jacob gave a flick of his head. For years afterwards, Patrick would try to interpret this gesture, slowed and distorted by the water around them. What had his friend meant by it? Agreement? Refusal to come back with him? All chance of understanding was lost when Jacob made a rapid movement, hitting the ledge with one of his fins and releasing a great cloud of silt that enveloped Patrick and left him sightless.

For a couple of seconds Patrick had remained frozen, marooned in the disorienting chalky fog that enveloped him. His heart lurched wildly, and he took a deliberate slow breath on his air tube, trying to regulate his pulse and slow the whirl of thoughts that threatened to impair his judgement. Then he rose steadily, inching upwards to escape the blinding white water, and to see if he could find his friend's trail.

The rock wall loomed out of the murky cloud to his right, grey and familiar. Patrick put his hand to the stone with relief. At least now he could orientate himself. He finned along the top of the trail Jacob had left behind. The muddy, worked up waters led back to the shore. Had Jacob headed homewards already, or was that just the same trail they'd made as they advanced? He turned back, looking from side to side, trying to catch even a glimpse of movement other than swirling silt. The motion of a fin, a hand lifted above the murky cloud –

anything to show him the whereabouts of his friend. His heart began to beat uncomfortably fast again, and he took a couple more slow breaths from his cylinder, releasing the air in a long stream of crystal bubbles.

By now, he'd left the security of the ledge. Below him the water plunged away to thirty metres. There was no sign of Jacob. He shouldn't have disappeared so suddenly. The thought struck Patrick that Jacob had scraped the bottom of the lake on purpose, in a deliberate attempt to raise a silt cloud and shake him off. The fear knotted inside him was replaced by irritation. Jacob was too unfit and too out of practice to play stupid tricks.

For a minute more, Patrick continued to head away from the ledge, searching for some sign. His heart thrummed in his chest, and he began to feel light-headed. The waters of the lake, so familiar to him, began to seem like a treacherous and threatening host. He glanced at his wristband. He knew the drill. If you lost your dive buddy, you searched for one minute, and then surfaced. One minute, and no more. Jacob, too, was well aware of the procedure. Perhaps he'd already surfaced and was even now waiting for Patrick to join him.

Somehow Patrick doubted it.

Another couple of slow, steadying breaths through his apparatus while he turned over all the options. If he surfaced now and Jacob wasn't there waiting for him, he wouldn't be able to dive down again a second time. To dive down again so soon was dangerous and could cause an attack of decompression sickness, which would only hinder both of them. If Jacob had deliberately thrown Patrick off the scent, perhaps the best course of action was to remain searching below.

On the other hand, Jacob could have stirred up the cloud of silt by accident. He could have followed procedures after all and might already be at the surface, waiting. In which case, he would be getting anxious, scanning the water for Patrick's return.

Patrick took in another deep intake of air, releasing the

bubbles in a steadying stream that helped to concentrate his mind. Then he made the most reasonable decision he could in the circumstances. There was no sign of Jacob. He could be searching fruitlessly for a long time. He would follow safety procedures – follow the training that had been drummed into him – and head for the surface.

It was a decision, like many others he made that day, that he would bitterly regret.

With the fear tightening in his chest, he made a turn, thrusting downwards with his legs and at the same time pressing the button on his suit to add buoyancy. It seemed to take forever to reach the surface. When his head finally shot out of the water, he saw to his horror that the storm clouds that had been a threatening presence on the hills had now burst directly overhead. Great drops of rain were drumming on the surface of the lake, and the waves lapped up into his face, obscuring his vision. He thrust himself upwards to scan the surface. No sign of his friend. The water reflected the black of the sky. He was alone.

Ever afterwards Patrick would wonder how it was possible that two conflicting parts of his brain could be active at one and the same time. His heart pounded as though it might burst out of his chest. A terrified voice in one part of his head was shouting at him above the sound of the torrential rain, telling him to strike out for the safety of the shore. The other part of his brain was making a cold, reasoned assessment of his situation.

Patrick checked the time on the computer strapped to his wrist. How long had they been underwater? Twenty minutes or so. He read the air level on his cylinder. That part of his mind that was logical and unafraid began to make some rapid mathematical calculations. Jacob was unfit and would run out of air much sooner than Patrick. He glanced again at his dial and made the assumption that his friend's air would last another twenty-five minutes. No need yet to become anxious.

He turned his head and was hit by a small wave that caused him to choke. With his face this close to the water, it was impossible to see if Jacob had surfaced. He went into the manoeuvre he'd practised so often with his dive club and never imagined he would ever need. Thrusting his feet downwards, he levered himself clear of the surface, so that the water lapped at his chest. His thighs were strong, and he held position for several seconds as he made a rapid scan of the lake.

Nothing.

He headed further away from the shore and tried again, calling Jacob's name, the rain dashing into his face. He called again in another location, and again and again, until the muscles in his legs were on fire with effort. Still no sign, and with the wind tearing at him, his calls were whipped away.

He checked the time. A part of him was now icy with terror and exhaustion. The other part told him to gather his strength and head for shore, where he could see more easily. He finned over the surface, urgency giving power to his weary muscles, and hauled himself onto the rocky beach. Quickly, with fingers shaking despite the heat generated by his thick suit, he divested himself of his weights and buoyancy jacket. He tore off his fins and, ignoring the sharp stones cutting into his feet, ran along the side of the lake to where a rise of higher ground gave him a vantage point. Panting, he reached the top and began to call again.

'Jacob! Jacob!' His voice was hoarse and spent. He ran his eyes across the water, trying to slow himself, to make a methodical scan for tell-tale bubbles. With a heart heavy with dread, he found no sign. He checked the time again. Thirty minutes now since he'd lost him. With his pulse thudding in his throat and his feet burning on the stony ground, he made his way swiftly up the shoreline, calling Jacob's name repeatedly, checking each nook and inlet.

Then, under the dark afternoon sky, he made out a pair of headlights from a lone car making its way along the side of the lake. Patrick threw himself up the steep bank, clutching at the dry tufts of grass, and hauled himself out into the road. He could lose precious time by making his way back to his own car, where his mobile phone lay useless, the signal deadened by the surrounding hills, or hope that this passing stranger would stop and drive him on to the village, where he could use a phone box.

He stood in the middle of the road, a dark figure in his diver's suit, the rain streaming down his face and plastering his hair to his head.

The headlights approached, and the car braked to a stop. Patrick ran, thrusting his hands out to the window. An elderly woman stared at him in astonishment.

'Help!' he rasped, his voice hoarse from calling Jacob's name. 'Please. I need to phone the coastguard.'

He pulled open the passenger door and collapsed into the seat, his diver's suit soaking the upholstery, and stumbled out his story.

The driver pressed her foot to the accelerator and they shot away, the lake – wild with rain and wind – receding behind them.

A week later Jacob's body was found, washed up in an inlet half a mile from where he'd entered the water.

Patrick never dived Emmswater again.

Chapter Ten

Fliss

Fliss was still feeling low as evening approached. Johnny gave her a cheerful wave as she entered the canteen, and her spirits rose a little at the sight of him. They rose another notch at the mouthwatering display of food at the serving-hatch. Tomasz's cooking could tempt even the most depressed. She filled her plate with lasagne and fresh green salad, and took her tray over to where Johnny was sitting.

'Take a look at this,' he said as she sat down. He pushed a crumpled sheet of paper towards her. 'I made a list of drinks for the Tudor night.'

He carried on tucking in to Tomasz's lasagne, as though Fliss's opinion was the least important thing in the world to him. Fliss knew him well enough by now to know deep down he was anxious and impatient to hear exactly what she thought.

Fliss frowned over his handwriting. 'Has a spider run over this?'

'Haha.'

She gave him a grin and ran her eye down his list of Tudor-style drinks. Johnny had chosen some English ales – sourced from local breweries – plus a selection of French wines and clarets. He'd also included the "boring old mead" Patrick had suggested. But what surprised Fliss, and gave the selection a completely new twist, was Johnny's inventive set of cocktails. Besides a Bloody Mary, there was a Virgin Queen, a Saucy

Anne, a Gin and Tudor, a Horny Henry, and half a dozen other Tudor-themed mixes of Johnny's own devising. Fliss guessed Patrick would think the names were tawdry, but the spiced drinks were original and fitted the theme perfectly. Besides, the relaunch was all about bringing in money, and she knew the guests would put their hands in their pockets and shell out the extra for cocktails like these. It was a great list.

'I love them,' she said, passing back the tattered scrap of paper.

Johnny gave up pretending to be nonchalant and turned pink with pleasure. 'So you think this is OK to give Patrick?'

'Yes.' She turned back to her meal and added, 'And tell him I think they're brilliant.'

Fliss remembered Patrick's doubts about the whole idea of a themed evening. Perhaps he thought Tudor nights were a gimmick, and typical of the Everdene style. The thought of Everdenes and her father's recent actions in Germany, never far from Fliss's mind, caused the mouthful she'd just taken to stick in her throat. She took a sip of water, but suddenly even Tomasz's delicious concoction no longer appealed to her. She swallowed a few more desultory mouthfuls and placed her fork back down on her plate.

'Better not let Tomasz see you're leaving that,' Johnny said. 'He'll have one of his meltdowns.' He reached over and took her plate from her. 'I'll help you hide the evidence.' He began tucking in. 'Just to keep the peace, of course.'

'Feel free.' Fliss stood, pushing her chair back. 'I'm just going to phone home before we start work.'

She made her way through the lounge and out onto the terrace to try out the mobile phone signal. The rain had finally stopped, but the outdoor tables remained deserted. Great pools of water had collected in the hollows where the old flagstones were worn away, and the wooden tables were dark with wet. The sky was still sullen, despite the sun's attempts to break through.

Fliss pressed her mother's number and looked down at the lake as she waited for her to answer. Its surface was an unbroken sheet of silver, vaguely threatening in the early evening light. She thought of Patrick's friend and Patrick's stark expression as he'd stood beside her in the downfall, and a shiver prickled the back of her neck.

'Fliss, darling.'

Her mother's rather breathless voice brought Fliss back to the present with a start.

'Mum, I've been dying to speak to you. I read the paper. I was in the village and that odious Cameron McIntyre couldn't wait to point it out. Oh, Mum. What's been going on? Are you all right? And Dad?'

'Fliss, I'm so sorry you found out this way. I tried to phone you this morning as soon as we heard it was in the press, but your line was dead. And then ever since everything's just been manic.'

There was an unusually high-pitched quality to her mother's voice.

Fliss drew in a breath. 'Sorry, Mum. I was out with Patrick by the lake. You can never get any signal down in the valley. On the way back, we called in at the Post Office to send off some invitations for the Tudor event, and that's when we bumped into Cameron. Of course he had to tell Patrick all about it.'

Fliss's anger fired up again as she thought of the expression on Patrick's face as he'd stood there with the newspaper in his hands. She took another slow breath. Losing her temper wouldn't help her mother in any way at all.

'So what happens now?' she went on. 'Will there be a court case? And how's Dad taking it?'

'Oh, you know your father. He won't back down, no matter what happens. He's been through everything again and again with his lawyers. Nothing he's done is against the law.'

There was a short silence. The two women both knew that while not exactly breaking the law, James Everdene's actions had been morally questionable.

Fliss was the first to speak. 'I think it's time for me to come home, Mum. You can't carry on like this.'

Fliss heard her mother's breathing as she mulled things over. 'It's good of you to offer, darling, but there's really no need. Jilly needs you at the Cross Hotel for the moment. She's relying on you to at least help oversee her Tudor event. And in any case, your father has everything in hand. Actually, there's something we're going to propose to the Board of Directors in a few weeks that will put an end to all this bad feeling. Something we've been thinking about for a while, even before all this blew up.'

'Oh?' Fliss stood by the railing of the terrace, her hand on the wet iron trellis work. 'What are you planning?'

'We're still not sure how it will all work out, darling. When we've finalised the details, I'll phone you straight away. I'm sorry not to be more forthcoming, but your dad wants to think a few things over before we go ahead. It'll mean a totally new direction for us if it all goes through, but it's something I'm sure you'll be happy with.'

Fliss realised how tightly she was clutching the iron bar of the railing and lifted her hand, absently noting the flecks of rust mingled with water on her palm. Her mother's air of mystery was doing nothing to reassure her. Why all the secrecy? Was this going to be another one of her father's decisions that she'd bitterly disagree with?

Her mother changed the subject, saying brightly, 'And how about you? How is everything at the Cross Hotel?'

Fliss turned to look at the hotel. She'd been going to talk about her trip to the lake with Patrick, and how he was still coming to terms with his friend's death, even after all these years. But then she thought of how her mother had enough worries of her own, without adding to them. Instead, Fliss contemplated the lovely old building, the charming lines of the old roof and the chimney-pots, and said, 'Mum, don't you think it would be wonderful to own a small hotel?'

As soon as she'd ask the question, Fliss realised she was echoing the words she'd used to Patrick earlier. The thought of owning her own hotel must be constantly bubbling away in her subconscious, without her realising it.

There was a small silence at the end of the phone, then her mother said, 'Is that what you'd like, Fliss?'

Fliss shrugged. 'Oh, I don't mean anything by it. I just love it here at the Cross Hotel. I feel like I'm making a genuine difference.' She turned and caught sight of a ray of sun, lighting up the tips of the mountains. 'And the views are magical. Some days I feel I could live here for ever.'

It was an unusually dramatic statement for Fliss. She realised how close she'd come to saying she didn't want to go back to work at Everdenes. The last thing she wanted to do was upset her mother.

She swallowed and gave a short laugh. 'But don't take any notice of me, Mum. Maybe I've been working too hard recently. And talking of work –' she glanced at her watch. 'I'd better get started on my shift. Don't want to be in trouble with Patrick. He can be a bit of a grump.'

Her mother laughed. 'I hope you're not giving Jilly's son any trouble, Fliss. I know how stubborn you can be.'

Fliss thought of her heated conversation with Patrick in the rain that morning, and felt a stab of guilt.

'All Patrick wants to do is go back to the Caribbean,' she said. 'Perhaps it would be better if someone did buy him out, then all his problems would be solved.'

There was a movement on the path below the terrace. A dark figure was making his way from the rear of the kitchen round the side of the building to the car park. It was Patrick.

Fliss frowned. Sound carried up here on the fellside. Had he overheard her conversation? She thought back over what she'd said, and could find nothing incriminating, except that she'd called him a grump. She felt a little bad about that one. Still, eavesdroppers never heard good about themselves. She and her mother said their goodbyes, and Fliss turned on her heel to make her way to her room to change.

Patrick

The next morning, Patrick glanced up at the sky as he left the hotel and shook his head at the fickleness of the weather. A soft yellow sun was spreading its rays over the slopes, with a promise of warmth to come. It was as though the valley was sorry for the previous day's storm and was offering a present to make up for it.

The door opened behind him and Fliss stepped out into the sunshine. She was dressed in dark cotton trousers and a thin cream sweater. Although she greeted Patrick with one of her usual smiles, her blue eyes held a hint of wariness. Patrick felt a wave of remorse. There had been a strained atmosphere as they'd worked together the previous evening. Then when Johnny had brought out his list of drinks for the Tudor party, Patrick had said something dismissive about the cocktail names. He'd regretted it straightaway and could have bitten off his tongue, but it was too late. Johnny had got in a huff, and it had taken all Patrick's diplomacy to bring him round.

After that, Johnny had been his usual talkative self, until Fliss had asked Patrick whether he'd started to look for a permanent barmaid.

'He can't do that,' Johnny had said quickly, sliding his empty glasses onto the bar. 'Pauline might still come back.'

Patrick had turned aside and began straightening the drinks menus on the wall.

'Actually, Pauline's not coming back,' he'd said quietly. 'I got a letter from her today. She said she had her reasons for not wanting to work at the Cross Hotel, and she was sending her formal notice to quit.'

Although Pauline hadn't stated her reasons, Patrick could well imagine what they were. It was obvious Jacob's sister didn't want to work for him.

There was a silence behind him for an instant, and then a ringing clang that made Patrick jump. He wheeled round to find Johnny crouching down to pick up his tray. Patrick stared at him in astonishment. Johnny was never clumsy, and it was unheard of for him to drop anything.

Johnny gave a choked grunt and stood up, his face dark red, before making a hasty exit for the lounge.

After that, the evening had deteriorated further. Johnny had become almost manic, striding into the bar, collecting his drinks with a relentlessly cheerful whistle that drove Patrick to distraction.

All in all it had been a trying evening. It was a pleasure to wake up to a sunny day – and to be greeted by Fliss's smile.

Patrick waved in the direction of the sun-tinged slopes. 'I was just thinking how much I miss the sunshine in Dominica, and then I come out this morning to one of the most glorious views on earth. After the storm yesterday, it's like the mountains are on their best behaviour.'

The constraint left Fliss's expression and she smiled. 'Well they can't fool me.' She opened her bag to show Patrick the umbrella and fold-up mac inside. 'I'm armed for the worst.'

She took a step forward, and Patrick's attention was caught by her feet. Fliss was wearing a pair of dainty kitten heels, in a fetching lilac.

'You're never thinking of walking down to the village in those,' he said.

A car crunched up the pebbly path and into the hotel car park. Fliss lifted a hand to wave to the driver.

'I'm not walking. Thanks for asking, but Johnny's taking me.'

Patrick glanced behind him to see Johnny's car pulling into an empty space.

'I'd have been happy to give you a lift,' he told Fliss. 'There was no need for Johnny to come all the way up here.'

Fliss gave him a quick, unreadable glance. She twisted the strap of her bag in an unusually awkward gesture. 'I thought you might be busy. Johnny's taking me to pick up a hire car, so now you won't have to drive me round.'

'It was no problem.' He hesitated. Feeling guilty for their strained conversation of the day before, and wanting to make things perfectly clear, he added, 'Actually, I enjoyed driving you round.'

'Really?' The leather strap slipped through Fliss's fingers and her bag landed with a soft thud on the gravel. They both bent to pick it up, but Patrick reached it first. His head was close to hers.

'I'm sorry.' They both spoke together. Patrick caught Fliss's light, warm scent, and her breath fluttered against his cheek. For an instant their eyes locked. Then Johnny leaned out of his window and gave a piercing whistle. Patrick passed Fliss her bag.

'OK, OK,' she called to Johnny. She cast Patrick a smile filled with apology before making her way to the waiting car, her heels crunching lightly on the gravel.

Chapter Eleven

Fliss

Johnny drove out of the hotel car park at a speed that was far more headlong than dashing. The gravel sprayed from under his wheels.

Fliss clutched the side of her seat. 'Are we in a hurry?' she asked mildly.

'What?' Johnny gave her a puzzled look, taking his eye off the road.

'Nothing,' she cried, pressing her brake foot to the floor in a pointless reflex action. 'Only watch the road.'

'Fine. Keep your hair on.'

He slowed down a little. Fliss got through the rest of the journey by keeping her eyes on the bag on her knees and not on the fellside hurtling past the window. When Johnny finally brought the car to a lurching halt in the pay and display car park, she breathed a sigh of relief.

'Is everything all right, Johnny?'

Johnny had his hands on the steering wheel still and was frowning out of the window. He turned a darkling look in Fliss's direction. 'Of course. Why shouldn't it be?'

Fliss held up her hands. 'No reason. Thanks for the lift. Let me pay for the car park ticket.'

Johnny grunted. As they approached the ticket machine, a couple of women stepped out of a saloon car. One of them bent back inside to release a toddler from his baby seat. The other woman caught sight of Johnny and called out to him.

'Hey, Johnners!'

Johnny rolled his eyes without turning round. The woman called again and came running over the car park to join them, her trainers thumping the asphalt.

'Johnny,' she said breathlessly.

He finally stopped in his tracks and turned to glare at her. 'Fliss, this is Georgia, Georgia, this is Fliss. Fliss is working behind the bar at the hotel, I'm giving her a lift, and no, she's not my girlfriend. Curiosity satisfied?' He folded his arms.

Georgia's cheeks went pink. 'What's up with you, grumpy bollocks?'

Fliss stopped to look at Johnny's acquaintance with respect. It was a question she'd been dying to know the answer to herself, ever since they'd shot off down the hill in Johnny's car.

Johnny merely grunted again and added in an aside to Fliss, 'Georgia was at school with me.'

'Nice to meet you,' Fliss offered politely.

The young woman gave her a frigid smile and continued to address Johnny. 'We were wondering what's happened to Pauline. Me and Rachel haven't heard a thing. Tried texting, DM-ing, even tweeted her, and nothing. What's up? Her mum says she's all right, but we just want to talk to her.'

'Well if her mum says she's all right, she must be, mustn't she? But if you're so desperate to know, she's gone to her aunt's. Somewhere in the Midlands. Satisfied?'

Georgia continued to regard Johnny in a belligerent way, but he shrugged and turned away huffily. 'And now if you don't mind, Fliss and I have some things to do.'

Georgia's chilly gaze met Fliss's. Fliss held her hands up. 'I just work on the bar,' she repeated. Georgia stood looking at her sharply for a minute or two longer, before turning to rejoin her friend.

'Tell Pauline we're asking after her,' she threw over her shoulder.

Fliss put her money in the machine. As the ticket printed out, Johnny shifted from foot to foot, agitation radiating from him in waves. Fliss said nothing, and in silence they fixed the ticket to the windscreen of Johnny's car and made their way out of the car park and over the stone bridge.

It was finally too much. 'Look, Johnny, I know this is none of my business – '

'No it isn't,' Johnny said crossly.

'OK.' Fliss came to a halt on the bridge. 'I just want you to know that if you want to talk about anything, I'm happy to listen. I know everyone knows everyone in this place – ' Yet another grunt from Johnny, hands in his pockets. Fliss ignored him and carried on. 'But I'm not from round here, and I'll be going home in a few weeks. If you're looking for an impartial ear, I'm happy to listen.'

Johnny shrugged his shoulders.

Fliss added, 'Believe it or not, I can keep quiet and listen for more than a minute.'

This finally forced a short laugh. Johnny's innate good humour was never far from the surface. He hesitated, before blurting out, 'How would you like to go for a drink?' He caught Fliss's eye and reddened a little. 'I mean, nothing in it, just a drink and a chat. Tonight's our night off. Do you fancy going to the pub?'

Fliss cocked her head on one side. 'I'd love to.'

Johnny breathed out in relief. 'Great. That's a date.' Then he straightened up and added quickly, 'But not in that way.'

It was finally too much for Fliss. She laughed out loud. 'You really know how to flatter a girl, Johnny. Just for that, the first round's on you. And I'm having the most expensive cocktail on the menu.'

After that, they both went their separate ways – Fliss to pick up her hire car, and Johnny to meet up with some of his friends. He invited Fliss to come with him, but since he was planning to play computer games and his invitation was obviously half-hearted, Fliss had no trouble declining. In any case, she had promised Jilly she'd join her back at the hotel, to discuss how to refurbish the dining-room for the relaunch party.

So Fliss drove her hire car home alone, and an hour later she was standing beside Patrick's mum, studying the lounge. The walls were covered in a clashing mish-mash of faded photos and canvases. Fliss glanced at Jilly, who was peering over her glasses at a 1980s print of a technicolor sunset. Fliss wondered if all these pictures were actually in Patrick's mum's taste. She was trying to come up with a way to suggest a clean sweep, when to her relief, Jilly spoke first.

'How about we just throw everything out and start again?'

'Hmm.' Fliss put her head on one side, pretending to give it some thought.

Jilly patted her arm. 'No need to be tactful, darling. Jonathan bought half these pictures as job lots in auction houses. What he was thinking, I don't know. And the rest belonged to his grandmother. She's not here now to get upset if we get rid of the lot.'

Fliss relaxed with a grin. 'Oh, I'm so glad. I've been absolutely itching to take everything down, ever since I first got here. I've had a few ideas for items we could put up in their place, if you're interested. We could maybe keep one or two of the nicer frames, and just take the old prints out and put something fresh in. That should give the room an immediate lift, without costing too much money.'

She surveyed the rest of the room. The mid-morning light was streaming through the windows leading onto the terrace, illuminating the drab lounge and the shabby wallpaper. It was well overdue for complete redecoration.

Jilly sighed, guessing at her thoughts. 'Of course I'd love to give the whole place a total revamp. But Jonathan and I never had the time to get to grips with it. Or the money,' she added sadly. 'Completely redecorating this room would mean closing the restaurant until it was finished. There's never been a time when we could afford it.'

'Well, we only have a short time until the Tudor event, but there are a few things we could do.' Fliss outlined some suggestions that wouldn't cost a great deal, such as removing the clutter of ornaments from around the fireplace. They could have the chimney swept and a log fire made up in the grate. New table-cloths would brighten the dining tables. The sofas and chairs in the lounge were arranged in a rigid way, and not close enough for people to chat comfortably. Fliss asked Jilly whether she thought they could run to a couple more coffee tables, and maybe some new cushions to brighten the furniture. If they made the lounge more attractive for guests, people would stay and linger after dinner, rather than going down to the village.

'Would it be OK to get rid of the plastic flowers, too?' Fliss asked.

'Oh, heavens,' Jilly said. 'They are quite ghastly, aren't they? It's funny, but when you see something every day, you just get used to it. I don't know what possessed us to start using them. I suppose it was just easier than getting fresh flowers every day.'

Fliss gave a sigh of relief. Jilly seemed as keen as she was to start afresh, so Fliss asked the question that had been eating away at her ever since she first arrived. 'What about the curtains?'

For the first time, Jilly seemed taken aback at her suggestion. 'Don't you like them? I can't remember where we got them now. I suppose they have been up for a long while. Oh, dear.' She twisted her hands together. 'I don't know what Patrick would say if we suggested replacing them. He's putting up the money for the party out of his own pocket. I hate to keep mentioning things we need to include. I think maybe the curtains would be a step too far.'

Fliss pursed her lips thoughtfully. New curtains would certainly be an expense, but the old ones were shabby and hideous. And because the windows were so long, there seemed to be just so *much* of them. They dominated the room. Even after the refurbishment, they would continue to hold sway, in all their alarming puce-ness. She considered them in silence for a moment, her brain ticking over. Then she said, 'Is Patrick in this morning? Perhaps I could see what he thinks. You never know.' She gave Jilly a grin. 'Perhaps new curtains are the first thing on his shopping list.'

'Well, you can try asking him.' Jilly looked worn again. 'I expect he'll be at his desk, worrying over some spreadsheet or other. I'll ask our housekeeper to organise a day when we can all muck in and do a clean-up, and then we can start by taking some of these pictures down.' She brightened a little at the thought. 'I must say, I'm looking forward to the party. It was such a lovely idea of yours, Fliss.'

Patrick

Patrick pulled open a drawer in his desk, looking for a pencil to make some notes on his spreadsheet. For a second or two he halted, disorientated. The contents of the drawer belonged to his father, and it was a stark reminder that the office had been his. Patrick had moved his father's desk so that the light from the window fell on it as he was working. Unlike his father, he always left the door to the office open, so that the staff could come and see him whenever they needed. He'd put up some photos on the wall - his business partner Oscar, smiling wide, carrying his new-born baby in their dive school in Dominica, and one of Oscar's photos of the sun setting over the Caribbean. The office was beginning to feel like Patrick's own, but with this sudden reminder of his father he felt like an interloper. There was a pad in the drawer with a note about wine, scribbled in his father's hand, and one of his father's fishing-hooks, lying on top of an old catalogue.

Patrick thought of all the changes he'd planned for the hotel. Would his father have approved? Although it was useless now to dwell on their uneasy relationship, he couldn't help his thoughts turning once more to the past and his regrets, and so it was a welcome relief to hear Fliss's footsteps in the corridor.

She popped her head around the door. 'Are you busy?'

Fliss's clear gaze met his, bright and cheerful. Patrick stood to greet her. 'Just looking at the books,' he said. 'Come in. How was your trip to the village? I saw your hire car in the car park. Bit of a difference from Agnetha.'

'Isn't it just? I decided to copy everyone else who lives round here and get myself a 4-by-4.' Fliss gave an airy wave. 'Drove back feeling queen of the road.'

Patrick gave her a lop-sided grin. 'Agnetha will be getting jealous.'

This made Fliss laugh. 'See, I knew you'd start talking about her that way. My hire car is a soulless robot compared to Agnetha. She has a personality all her own.'

Patrick was about to laugh, too, until he remembered the last time they'd driven out together, and their heated conversation in the pouring rain.

'Look, about the other day, I've been meaning to tell you - '

'It's OK,' Fliss countered. 'I don't tell many people this but… ' She breathed out heavily. 'Well, between you and me, I don't find my dad the easiest person to work with, either. So there's no need to apologise. If anyone should be sorry, it's me. I shouldn't have asked you about diving here. It was thoughtless of me. '

Patrick brushed her apology away. 'Don't worry about it. Johnny tells me I need to lighten up. I hate to admit Johnny's right about anything, but I think in this case he is.'

'Well.' Fliss held out her hand. 'Truce?'

'Truce.' Patrick took her hand in his and smiled. 'Here, sit down.' He pulled out a chair for her before sitting down himself. 'Did you want to see me about something? Oh,' he added, picking up the list the chef had given him. 'Before you start, what do you think to this? It's what Tomasz has come up with for the Tudor dinner.'

He passed her the sheet of paper. Unlike Johnny's scrawled drinks list, Tomasz's menu was neatly typed up and annotated with suppliers and likely cost.

CROSS HOTEL TUDOR FEAST

Leg of lamb with gallandine sauce
Chicken stuffed with leek
Whole baked halibut with lemon and herbs
Wild rabbit and morel stew…

The chef's suggested meal ended with a selection of spiced pastries and cream, followed by local cheeses and fresh plums.

'Wow,' Fliss said. 'I knew Tomasz was bursting to try something different. This all sounds delicious.'

Patrick frowned. If only it was a simple as just drawing up a list.

'Is something wrong with it?' she went on. 'I know you didn't much like Johnny's cocktail names, but you can't object to this, surely?'

'No, of course not. It's not that.' He drew his spreadsheet in front of him. 'I'm just trying to work out the costings. With everything Tomasz wants, the profit margins are way lower than they should be.'

'Oh.' Fliss bit her lip. 'Then I suppose now isn't a good time to talk about new curtains for the lounge.'

'No.' He gave an amazed laugh. 'New curtains are the last things we should be talking about.'

Fliss reached across the table and touched his hand. 'You're going to pull this off, you know.'

'I wish I shared your confidence. From where I'm sitting, we've a very, very long way to go.'

'So, it's going to be hard work. But it could be fun, as well.' She gave him one of her irrepressible smiles. 'What's not to like about a party? And if it's the last party the Cross Hotel ever has, at least you can say you went down having fun.'

Her eyes twinkled. She radiated such optimism, Patrick couldn't help but smile back

'If I'm ever on a sinking ship,' he said, 'I hope you'll be on board.' Then he added quickly, 'Well, not literally, obviously. I'd just love to see you persuading the crew they should be enjoying the moment as we plunge into the water.'

Fliss chuckled, and Patrick reflected again on just what an easy person she was to be around. An idea came to him.

'So, talking about enjoying the moment,' he said. 'Tomasz left me a list of suppliers to go with the menu.' He indicated the pile of papers on his desk. 'How would you like to take a drive to the coast this afternoon and check out fish?'

There was a short silence. Patrick added awkwardly, 'I mean, today's your day off. If you haven't anything else planned, I thought you might like a trip out. I suppose a fishmonger isn't an exciting prospect, but Whitehaven is a great place. You could take a walk on the prom, or down on the beach. Afterwards I thought maybe we could try one of the seafood restaurants.'

'I'd love a trip to the coast. And I'd love to try out one of the restaurants, too. It's just that – well, I have to get back this evening. I promised Johnny I'd go for a drink.'

Patrick dropped his eyes to the table for a moment. Johnny again. Then he said evenly, 'That's a shame about the restaurant. But we could still make it to the coast this afternoon to visit the supplier. I could bring you back in plenty of time to go out with Johnny. That is, if you'd like to come?'

Fliss beamed. 'Yes, I'd love to.'

Patrick shuffled the papers on his desk. He had something else on his mind that he felt he ought to tell her, even though he felt awkward bringing it up. He waited for a Fliss to finish speaking – she was speculating on whether they could get a discount for their first order, and whether the supplier might drop the price for a bulk delivery. She was just about to launch into an account about an unscrupulous trader who once supplied Everdenes when Patrick cleared his throat.

'Listen,' he said. 'I thought perhaps I'd mention that Johnny isn't a great person to go out for a drink with.'

'What?' Fliss stared at him.

He twisted his pen in his fingers. 'I hope you don't think I'm interfering – '

'Well I do.'

The stubborn look had come over Fliss that Patrick recognised. He dropped his pen on the table. 'Fine. I just thought I'd give you a friendly warning.' He stood abruptly. 'If you'd sooner find out for yourself, go ahead.'

'I will.' Fliss pushed back her chair. 'I really don't know what you've got against Johnny. He's been bending over backwards ever since you asked him to help out with this

Tudor event. It's no wonder he's demoralised at work. All you do is criticise him.'

'That is absolutely not true.'

Perhaps Fliss realised she'd overstepped the mark, and that Patrick had been encouraging Johnny to take more responsibility. She put up a hand, as though about to apologise, but some devil made Patrick continue, 'Johnny talks too much when he should be working. Anyway, his work ethic isn't the point – '

Fliss didn't let him finish. She drew herself up, saying, in a chilly tone, 'So Johnny *talks too much*. It's better than going round with his lips zipped together. And anyway, the guests all love him. Anyone would think you were jealous.'

'*Jealous*?'

For a second or two there was complete silence in the room as they eyed one another. Then the atmosphere shifted. The stillness became charged with something electric; with an emotion far removed from anger, but equally intense. Fliss's clear features were raised to his, her lips parted, the blue of her eyes darkened to an indigo that swam before him.

One of the chambermaids passed by in the corridor, her trolley rattling. The tension was dispelled.

'I'm sorry – ' They both spoke together, in a rush of words. Then they looked at one another awkwardly. Something was different. For once, Fliss actually seemed hesitant to speak.

Patrick's lips lifted in a small smile. 'Let's not argue any more. I'm not very good at it.'

She gave a shaky laugh. 'Me, neither. I hate arguments.'

Patrick held out his hand. 'We broke the truce,' he said. 'Now we'll have to make another pledge.' Her warm fingers met his, and he pressed them lightly before releasing them. 'Please come with me to the coast. I won't disagree with you about a single thing.'

'Thanks. I'd like that.'

Fliss's smile returned, and Patrick's heart lifted. He almost embarrassed himself by lifting his hand to caress her cheek. Luckily, he came to his senses.

'I'm setting off in half an hour,' he said. 'Can you be ready by then?'

'Yes, I can.' Fliss glanced at the window, where the sunlight was creeping round the side of the fell. 'Ready and waiting with my mac and umbrella.'

She lifted her hand in a wave.

After she'd gone, Patrick shifted the papers in front of him without really noticing what he was doing. What on earth had just happened? One minute he'd been furious. There was a stubbornness about Fliss that could goad him beyond endurance. The single-mindedness, the way she questioned everything he said. And then he'd tried to give her a hint about Johnny, and she'd refused to listen to him, blowing up and accusing him of being jealous.

He leaned back in his chair, rubbing a hand over his face. *Jealous.* That was it. That was the trigger. Even during the heat of the argument, he'd tried to listen objectively. When Fliss told him he was jealous, he realised she was right – only not in the way she imagined. Patrick wasn't jealous because Johnny was more popular than him with the guests. He was jealous because Fliss was going to spend an evening alone with him

As soon as that realisation hit him, a lot of other things did, too. He finally understood how much he'd grown to love having Fliss around, and how much he loved seeing her walk into a room and light the place up. He realised a lot of things all at once, but most overwhelming of all, he realised just how much he wanted to kiss her.

He swivelled his chair round to survey the sun-tinged scree outside his window. What a massive mistake kissing her would have been. He could just imagine the look of horror on Fliss's face if he'd taken her in his arms. The embarrassing scene afterwards. The thought made his skin burn. He screwed up his eyes.

Get a hold of yourself, he told himself. *You don't even know if you can trust her yet.*

What on earth was he thinking, anyway, getting involved with a member of the Everdene family? Cameron was right to warn him. A family like that would eat him up for breakfast and spit out his bones.

Patrick hadn't forgotten how he'd been passing the hotel terrace on his way to the wine-cellar, when he'd overheard Fliss talking into her mobile.

"Perhaps it would be better if someone did buy him out," she'd said. "Then all his problems would be solved."

Icy fingers clutched at his chest. Her words had carried clearly as he'd passed beneath her. Fliss was a godsend at the moment, but would that turn? Whatever happened, it wouldn't do to let Fliss Everdene gain too strong a hold.

Whether he meant a hold on the hotel, or on himself, Patrick didn't question too deeply.

Chapter Twelve

Fliss

Patrick drove upwards away from the hotel. To the right of them the steep slope of the fell dropped away, down and down until it reached the lake, while they climbed up, aiming away from Emmside, to take the winding road over the top. It was a slower route to the coast than the main road, Patrick had told Fliss, but he thought she'd enjoy the views.

The hills were completely empty. Not a car or a cyclist, or a walker on the fells; not even a shepherd's hut on the slopes. Centuries-old stone walls criss-crossed the hillside, tumbling down in places, the stones spilling onto the bracken. Occasionally Fliss would catch a glimpse of the valley below them, bathed in sunlight, before the trees that were clustered on the roadside rushed to block her view, and they were once more enveloped in shadow.

Fliss was reminded of the day she'd first arrived in Emmside and had driven up through the overhanging trees towards the Cross Hotel. Then, she had switched on her radio for company. Now, here was Patrick beside her at the wheel, but despite their recent truce, he appeared to have withdrawn into himself.

She cast a sideways glance at him. His tanned hands rested lightly on the wheel. His frown had disappeared, but he was distant, his mind obviously elsewhere. Fliss wondered if he was thinking about problems at the hotel, or whether being back at Emmswater meant his friend's death was constantly on his mind. Wherever you rested your eyes in this landscape, there was no escaping the presence of the lake in the centre of the valley, a dark mirror where it appeared between the trees.

Patrick dropped a wry look in her direction. 'You've been quiet ever since we left the hotel.'

'I do occasionally have moments of quiet contemplation,' Fliss responded primly. 'And I thought you'd appreciate some time to think. Anyway,' she added, spoiling her answer, 'we only left the hotel five minutes ago.'

He laughed, and the distance vanished, just like that. 'A whole five minutes and you haven't said a word. I thought you might be sickening for something.'

'I was just admiring the view.'

At that moment the lake appeared again between the trees. The road curved, giving them full sight of it. Strange that when Fliss first looked down on the lake, the day she'd stood next to Patrick by the dry stone wall, she'd thought it magical. Like something from a fairy-tale. Now the water stretched beneath them with an air of menace, like a dark eye staring upwards. She shivered.

Patrick slowed on the corner. When he'd rounded the curve, he said, 'I'll tell you about it, if you want.' Fliss turned her head, and his eyes met hers briefly before returning to the road ahead. 'If you want to know about Jacob, I mean.'

Fliss wondered at the way their thoughts had begun to mesh. She'd been asking herself whether Patrick was thinking of his friend, and then he invited her to ask him outright.

'I'd like to know about Jacob,' she said. 'I'd like to know what he was like, and why you were such good friends. And maybe if you told me about that day he died, it might help you. Sometimes things can stay trapped in your head for too long.' She looked at his stark profile, his eyes fixed on the road. 'But not if it's too painful.'

'It will always be painful.' He felt for the gear lever, slowing the car once more for a twist in the road. 'What did I like about Jacob?' He gave a small, downturned smile. 'We were mates from day one, after I watched him scale the wall apparatus to get away from Mrs Hobson. He didn't want to go to school, and he ran out of the class and into the gym. He got to the top of the apparatus and just sat there, arms folded, refusing to come down.'

'Poor Mrs Hobson.' Fliss laughed. 'How old were you?'

'I can't remember. Five years old, I suppose.'

She whistled. 'Friends since then. He sounds a proper rebel.'

'You could say that. Really, he was just full of life. He didn't like being cooped up. As he grew older, the teachers found it harder to deal with him.'

He proceeded to tell Fliss how he and Jacob had become diving buddies as teenagers, and how they'd both joined a dive club at the same time. Jacob's zest for life often crossed the line into hot-headedness, and his parents reasoned that the discipline involved in training with a professional dive club would be good for him. It was safer than letting him hang-glide from the fells, they'd joked.

Patrick drove on in silence for a while, the irony of that last statement hanging heavy in the air.

'And you?' Fliss prompted. 'Why did you take it up?'

Patrick gave a wry grimace. 'To get away from the hotel. Now I look back on it, I think my dad was struggling to keep the hotel afloat, even then. But I didn't realise it as a teenager. All I understood was my dad constantly bawling me out, telling me I didn't help out enough in the business, and that I was bone idle. During the busy seasons, my schoolwork suffered. I was always washing up pots in the kitchen, or helping clean out the bedrooms. When I went diving, it was like escaping to freedom. The first time I dived under the surface of Emmswater...well, it was an incredible feeling. Everything so quiet and still. Just our breathing, and the bubbles drifting upwards. It was like being in a totally different country.' He turned to look at her. 'Like the Emerald City in the land of Oz. Everything in Emmswater is tinged with green. After that, I was hooked.'

'And Jacob? Did he feel the same?'

Patrick shrugged, eyes back on the road. 'In his own way, I guess he did. But he was much more impatient than me. We were taught discipline at the dive club, and the importance of taking precautions. I never, ever dived alone at that age, but if Jacob couldn't find anyone to go with, he sometimes went off by himself. I tried to tell him how dangerous that was, but he wouldn't listen. By the time he went to uni he said he'd dived Emmswater a hundred times, and I should stop being an old woman.'

'He sounds impetuous.'

'He was, but mainly he was just really good fun. It wasn't until he went to uni that all that began to change.' Patrick's lips twisted. 'I suppose that was inevitable. He'd grown up, moved on, while I was still at home helping my parents in the hotel. As far as Jacob was concerned, he'd left me behind.'

Fliss digested this in silence for a couple of seconds. Then she asked, 'How about you? Didn't you want to go to university? Did you feel as though you really were left behind?'

He glanced down at her, surprised. 'Not for a minute. I didn't want to be stuck in a lecture theatre, listening to someone droning on. When Jacob told me about it, he was always moaning how boring it was. His main occupations seemed to be drinking and shagging.'

Fliss giggled, and Patrick gave a wry smile. 'I don't think I was cut out for an academic life. To be honest, in a lot of ways I enjoyed working in the hotel. And my free time was totally given over to diving. After a while I became a mentor in the dive club, and I enjoyed teaching people. When Jacob came home, I felt as though he'd stayed a teenager, and it was me who'd grown up. If it wasn't for my dad… ' He shrugged. 'As I grew older, I found it more and more of a strain working for him. I realised how he was making mistakes. Upsetting the staff and wasting money. But I was still young, and maybe I rubbed him up the wrong way, too,' he added, with characteristic honesty. 'Perhaps if it hadn't been for Jacob's accident – perhaps if I'd stayed – we could have learned to work together. But all that ended the day Jacob and I went diving.'

Fliss listened as Patrick told her about that terrible morning – how he should have been working in the hotel, but had been tempted by Jacob to go for a dive, even though he knew the clouds were gathering; how they'd argued on the shoreline, and how he'd lost Jacob in a cloud of silt as they prepared to head for shore. He related the story with an unnatural calm, as though it was something that had happened to someone else. There was his desperate journey to the village to phone the coastguard, and then the hours of fruitless searching with the rescuers.

Fliss sat straight-backed in her seat, frowning out at the road ahead, her fingers twisted together on her lap.

'You were both so young. I'm so sorry, Patrick.'

Patrick's eyes were dark when they met hers. 'I tried to dive the lake again after that, but it wasn't the place I remembered. As soon as the waters closed over me, everything was threatening. My heart started pounding, and I couldn't regulate my breathing. It was like I was in some sort of horror film.'

'And is that why you left Emmside? Because you couldn't dive here anymore?'

He shook his head. 'I would have coped with not being able to dive. It hadn't become my way of life, like it is now. If my dad had wanted me to stay, I would have. But he didn't.'

Fliss flinched at the harshness in his voice.

Patrick went on, 'My dad blamed me for the accident. I should have been helping in the hotel that day, not diving with my friend, especially when there was a storm brewing. According to my dad, I was not only lazy, I was stupid as well. He told everyone in the village how sorry he was I'd caused Jacob's death. Soon they all believed it, too. No one said it outright, but I could tell that's what they were thinking.'

'No,' Fliss cried. 'I don't believe it. It was wrong of your dad to blame you. You tried your best to look after Jacob that day.' Patrick made to interrupt, but she insisted. 'You could have left him to go alone, and if you had, he would very likely have died, anyway. You went with him to try and keep him safe. You followed all the right procedures, and Jacob didn't. Your dad should have stood by you, instead of making you feel ashamed.'

Patrick

Patrick took in Fliss's raised chin and the faint flush on her cheeks. He was touched by her vehement defence.

'Thank you. I wish I could have felt the same then. Even now there are times when I go over and over that day in my mind, thinking of all the things I should have done differently. It was easy to accept that everyone blamed me, because I blamed myself.'

'What about Jilly? Surely she didn't blame you?'

'No. No, she didn't, not deep down. But my mum is a gentle person, and my dad could be quite overbearing. In the end, the atmosphere at home became unbearable. When I told them I'd applied for a job in a dive school in Dominica, I think it came as a relief all round.'

There was silence after that. Fliss stared straight ahead, still frowning. Patrick knew her well enough by now to know she'd be revolving what he'd said in her mind, trying to piece everything together. He had come to recognise just how thoughtful Fliss was underneath the lighthearted chatter.

Then he thought of something his friend had said that day – something that had stayed with him.

'You know, when Jacob and I drove down to the lake, he was in really high spirits. He was talking non-stop.' He gave Fliss a grin. 'He could easily have given you a run for your money when he got going.'

Fliss stuck her tongue out at him, but her eyes remained fixed on his..

'Jacob could be really witty sometimes,' Patrick went on. 'He was a great mimic. He started telling me about the night before, when he'd been in the Black Bull. There was a group of girls in there – fell-walkers on holiday – and he was trying to chat one of them up. The trouble is, it's hard to get romantic in a pub full of lads you went to school with. Jacob told me he'd had his arm round this girl, and Bob said, "Don't be going home with him, love. He never changes his underkeks."'

'Ugh!' Fliss pulled a face.

'Bob was the landlord at the Black Bull. In fact, he still works there now. He was a few years above us at school, and he used to make our lives there a misery. I started laughing when Jacob told me about it, but he said to me, "I don't know how you put up with it, living here, Paddy." He wasn't laughing, he was deadly serious. I can still see his expression.' Patrick's hands tightened on the wheel. 'He told me he was sick to death of feeling stifled in the village. He said, "There's a damn sight more to life than Emmside, and I intend to get out of here and grab hold of it. And when I do, I'm going to live it to the full."'

Patrick ran his tongue over his lips a couple of times, his throat dry. Beside him, Fliss was completely still.

'I've never forgotten that look of determination on Jacob's face,' Patrick said. 'He was always in a hurry for everything. It didn't matter what. To rush out of the classroom, to get to the pub, to go diving, to explore the world. He just couldn't wait to embrace life.'

Patrick's voice shook, despite himself. He pressed his lips together.

They drove in silence for a short while, until Fliss said, without turning her face from the window, 'What did you say to him?'

'I don't know. Made some joke, I expect. It wasn't like Jacob to come out with deep comments. Anyway, next thing we were getting into our dry-suits.'

'That must have been one of the last things your friend ever said.'

Patrick nodded.

The road undulated in front of them, twisting round and down until it reached the bottom of the fell. Fliss uncurled the fingers in her lap and reached across to touch his knee. For the briefest of seconds her hand rested there, warm and easy. Then she drew her hand away, and they were on the main road into Whitehaven. The clouds that hung over the fells were behind them. In front were just a few streaks of white and oyster grey, rolling in on the horizon. The rest of the sky was a clear, wondrous blue.

Chapter Thirteen

Fliss

They were nearing the sea. The air was filled with the delicious, fresh smell of the English coast. There were low white houses lining the road, and the fields were dotted with buttercups. Fliss wondered how it was that a day could be so perfect and yet carry the undercurrent of so much pain and loss, how a hotel as splendid as the Cross Hotel could be home to so much sadness. Fliss was used to using her imagination to try and solve a problem, but not all her resourcefulness could wind back time and wipe out the pain of Patrick's grief.

Patrick broke in on her thoughts. 'There's nothing anyone can do to change that day. It's done and gone.'

Fliss turned to look at him. Once again, Patrick had guessed what was going through Fliss's mind.

They drew up at a set of traffic lights. Patrick took one hand from the wheel and touched her hand briefly. 'Thanks for listening to me. It's been years since I talked to anyone about Jacob. Today he seems more alive. Like he still matters to people.' The lights changed, and he shifted the gears, his concentration back on the road. 'You're a good listener.' He glanced sideways at her, a smile on his lips. 'For a chatterbox.'

Fliss lifted her nose in the air. 'Right, that's it. I've a good mind to spend the rest of this trip in stony silence.'

The road rose upwards, and as they crested the brow the sea came into view, shining silver and blue.

'Oh, look,' Fliss cried, forgetting her threat to stop talking. 'Isn't it funny how it's always so exciting to see the sea? I love going to the Norfolk coast. Minnie and I had some brilliant holidays there when we were little. We always took our dog Lexi, bless her. She loved the beach so much, she used to run mad as soon as we let her off the lead, barking and barking until she was literally sick with excitement.'

Fliss's stream of reminiscences continued until they were on the outskirts of the town. Patrick listened without speaking, glancing across at her once or twice, a quiet smile on his lips, until they entered Whitehaven.

The fish merchants were based in a low grey building directly on the shore, near the marina. Patrick manoeuvred the car along the concrete entrance road and into the visitors' car park. Fliss couldn't wait to open her door.

'Mmm, smell that fresh sea air,' she cried.

Patrick wrinkled his nose. 'Smells distinctly of fish.'

A fresh breeze whipped in off the sea, lifting Fliss's hair from her head as she stepped out of the car. She breathed in deeply. 'Rubbish. It's invigorating. I love the seaside. Thanks so much for asking me.'

Patrick smiled down at her. 'You don't have to come in with me. Go for a walk along the bay, if you like.'

'Of course not. I'll come in and give you some support. That's why I came.' She looked up at him and added, 'That is, if you'd like me to?'

'I'd love you to. Last time I bought fish it was wrapped up in newspaper with some chips and a dollop of mushy peas. I've never ordered it in hotel quantities. I'd be very glad of your support.'

As it turned out, Fliss soon realised Patrick had no need of any assistance from her whatsoever. For someone who'd spent the last ten years away from the hotel trade, he had a remarkably good idea of what was required. Tomasz had asked him to order fresh halibut, but the fishmonger – a portly, grey-haired man called Martin – told Patrick halibut was unavailable, due to the unseasonal warmth of the sea. He suggested whole red sea bream might make a good alternative. Patrick took a couple of minutes out to consult with Tomasz by phone, and then proceeded to negotiate a price. Fliss was surprised to find how charming and positively chatty Patrick could be when the circumstances required. His conversation with Martin moved on from fish prices to a discussion about the local rugby team, and then to diving off the coast, and the local tourist trade. In fact, the only thing that marred the encounter was Fliss's presence.

As they were leaving, Martin rose to shake her hand. 'Felicity Everdene,' he said, fixing her with his round, rather protuberant eyes. 'Would you be anything to do with the Everdenes who own Everdene Hotels?'

Fliss went into her usual reply, informing Martin that yes, she did indeed work for the Everdene chain, but that she was in the Lakes on holiday. She explained how she was taking some time away from her own job to help Jilly Cross.

The fishmonger dropped her hand with a grunt. 'We did a lot of business with a hotel in Kendal a few years back. Then we lost it all when the hotel was bought out by Everdenes. The chain didn't want local suppliers any more, seemingly.'

The amiability he had shown when speaking to Patrick had gone. His fleshy mouth was a cold, straight line.

Fliss felt the chill in his expression seep into her. She was used to defending the practices of the Everdene chain – in fact she was beginning to think public relations was the main purpose of her job. She felt Patrick's eyes on her and put on her best professional manner.

'I'm sorry you've lost business with a local hotel. Everdenes already has an existing network of suppliers, who we have good relations with. It's always a difficult decision when we acquire a new hotel, but in the end we have to think of our loyalty to the suppliers we already work with.'

Loyalty. Even as Fliss said the word, she sensed its hollowness. She wasn't surprised to see the fishmonger's lip curl.

'Aye, so I've heard,' he said. 'Loyal as long as they're giving you rock bottom prices.'

'We try to negotiate the best deals, it's true.' Fliss tried to ignore the merchant's snort. 'Just as you and Patrick have negotiated on price. It's exactly the same.'

'Maybe. And maybe there's a difference between negotiation and bullying. The big fish always eat the little ones.'

'I'm sorry to hear Everdenes has a reputation for swallowing up little fish.' Fliss gave him a warm smile she was far from feeling. 'I'm not making any promises, but perhaps if you'd like to give me your catalogue and a card, I'll pass them on to the staff in Kendal and ask them to get in touch.'

Martin brightened at this and busied himself getting some documents together for Fliss to take back with her. By the time they said their goodbyes, Fliss had managed to win him round. He ushered her to the door with many cordial invitations to visit again and next time take a tour of their premises.

When Fliss and Patrick finally exited the building, the sun had disappeared behind a cloud. The breeze had dropped, leaving the air sultry, with the smell of fish even more noticeable. Patrick cast a glance at the sky and began making his way back to the car. There was a grim line to his mouth. When he opened Fliss's door for her, his eyes fell on the catalogue Martin had given her.

'You're good at this, aren't you?' he said. 'Is the mighty Everdene chain really going to do business with a local fishmonger's? Or were you just going through the motions as part of the PR machine? Getting the locals on side, without actually doing anything for them?'

Fliss felt the heat rise in her cheeks, and anger mingled with hurt. 'How dare you criticise my parents' business?'

It was very rare indeed for Fliss to lose her temper with anyone. It was such a rare occurrence that on the occasions she did react, people would recognise that they'd overstepped the mark and would invariably back down. It appeared Patrick wasn't one of those people. He stood his ground, glaring down at her.

'You don't understand anything about this business,' Fliss told him. 'People who stay the night in an Everdene Hotel aren't interested in fine dining. All they want is a cheap place to stay. Our guests understand that you can't have it both ways.'

Patrick glowered. He seemed all set to counter her argument, but some of Fliss's pain must have shown in her face.

'I'm sorry,' he said. 'You're right. Your parents' business is no concern of mine.'

Fliss was far too good-natured to remain angry for long. She was never one to cry, either. She blinked, but it was no use. She turned her head aside.

Patrick reached out and caught her arms. 'I'm sorry,' he said again. 'I could cut off my tongue sometimes.'

Patrick

Fliss's lips were trembling. She looked away, with a tight little shrug. 'It's not your fault. It's just complicated, that's all.'

Patrick remembered everything his mother had told him about the rows Fliss and her father had been having, and how this trip to Emmside was meant to be a break for her. It was easy to assume Fliss was happy. She was always so cheerful, and her smile alone could make an entire room light up. Patrick was filled with remorse. He realised how selfish he'd been, and how wrapped up in his own problems. He remembered the first time he'd met Fliss, and how he'd had a feeling that underneath her brightness she was actually deeply troubled.

'Do you want to take a walk and talk about it?' he asked.

Fliss cast him a doubtful, sideways glance

Patrick added swiftly, 'It's OK. I know the hotel trade is rife with gossip, but if you've got problems, I'm not about to share them with anyone else. Everything you say about your parents' business will be in complete confidence.' When Fliss didn't answer, he gave her a small, teasing smile. 'I've just offered to listen to you talking. I can't believe you're going to turn down a golden invitation like this. It might never happen again.'

He was relieved to feel the tension in her arms ebb away. She smiled back at him. 'You're right. I'd be mad not to bend your ear back.'

Patrick took her papers from her and placed them in the car's glove box. Then he closed the door and locked it. 'Let's take a walk along the harbour wall. There's no one about. It'll be nice and quiet.'

Somehow it felt completely natural to take her hand in his. They made their way to the sea.

The harbour walls at Whitehaven spread in an arc of weathered brown stone into the sea, protecting the moored fishing boats from the worst of the swell. The turning tide slapped at the wall's base. Patrick helped Fliss up onto the wide walkway, which was damp underfoot with spray, and they began to make their way towards the lighthouse at the furthest point of the harbour. Apart from a few seagulls, wheeling and crying their sharp-tongued cries, they were entirely alone.

Fliss kept her eyes on the horizon as they made their way, saying nothing until they reached the very end of the wall. Her hand remained clasped in Patrick's, and he waited patiently.

'You know,' she began, 'when my dad took us to the coast in Norfolk, I used to think he was powerful as a king. I would build a sandcastle on the beach, and he'd stand on the shoreline, pretending to order the waves back, so my sandcastle didn't get washed away. He's not tall, but he had something imposing about him. He still does.' She looked out at the gently rolling sea. 'I have a vivid memory of him, standing broad and proud, one hand held up, commanding the waters. And slowly, slowly, the waves drew back and left my sandcastle alone, just as he told them. I thought it was absolutely magical. Of course what I didn't know was he'd guessed exactly where the high tide line was, and he knew when the tide was about to turn. It wasn't magic, at all.' She kicked at a small pebble, watching it roll over the edge of the wall and hit the sea below. 'When you grow up, you realise your parents don't have the answer to everything. Sometimes they make mistakes.' She paused for a moment, and added, 'Sometimes they might not even be very nice people.'

Patrick took in her hunched shoulders. It struck him how few people Fliss must have to talk to about her job. To outsiders Fliss appeared to have the perfect life – travelling the world, staying in the best rooms in the hotel, and earning a good salary. There were plenty of people who would give their right arms to swap places. Patrick realised it wasn't as simple as that. There was no freedom in being under someone's shadow, no matter how gilded the cage.

He pressed Fliss's hand. 'I used to argue with my dad a lot as a teenager,' he said. 'But it wasn't until I started working in the hotel that our relationship really went downhill. I knew by then he was making mistakes in the running of the business, but he was far too proud to admit it, especially to me. In the end, maybe it's for the best I left. We would never have got on if we'd tried to work together, and our relationship was only upsetting my mother.' He paused for a moment, his eyes on the sea below them. 'It's hard, because I loved him, in spite of everything.'

Fliss lifted her head at that. 'That's exactly it,' she said, her voice animated. 'That's exactly how I feel about my own dad. When he's not at work, he's the most generous, most affectionate person in the world, and I love him to bits. But in business he makes so many enemies. I feel sure something's going to happen that will land the company in serious trouble. I wish I could persuade him to work differently. I'm in a situation where I can't leave, and I just can't stay any longer.' Her voice rose. 'I just don't know what to do.'

A seagull cried overhead, and a wave curled over and hit the wall beneath them with a great slapping sound. A few drops of spray shot up. Patrick put his arm around Fliss's shoulders and drew her back from the water's edge.

He turned to face her, his hands lightly clasping her shoulders. 'You've got such a gift for the hotel business. I can see that from the difference you've made at the Cross Hotel, and you've only been here a short time. You said once how good it would be to own your own place. A small family-run hotel like mine, in a nice location. Do you think you'll ever go through with it?'

She looked away. 'Of course, that would be a dream come true. But it's not likely to happen, is it?'

'No?' He continued to regard her for a moment or two, remembering how he'd overheard her telling someone – perhaps her father? - that it would be better if someone did buy up the Cross Hotel, and that all Patrick's own problems would then be solved. Had it really not crossed her mind that Everdenes could easily be the business to take him over? That if they did, she'd have the small family hotel of her dreams?

There was a faint flush on Fliss's cheeks, and she was looking over his shoulder, as though not wanting to look him in the eye. Patrick dropped his hands to his sides, suddenly filled with unease. And then a rogue wave hit the wall, the spray towering above them, and Fliss let out a cry as the cold droplets rained down on them.

Patrick took her arm. 'Come on,' he said. 'Let's go into the town and find a café. I think we need a coffee before we head home.'

After a hot cup of coffee – and a large vanilla slice each – they spent a pleasant half hour wandering along the front, where Fliss bought her sister some seaside rock and another postcard. Their conversation was perfectly amicable, but a constraint had arisen between them that depressed Patrick's spirits and did nothing to lift his nagging anxiety. When he caught Fliss looking at her watch, he said, his voice over-bright, 'Of course. You need to get back for your night out with Johnny. Let's start heading for home.'

'There's no rush,' she protested. 'We're only going to the pub in the village. It's not a date, or anything.'

Patrick didn't answer. The day had been heavy work, one way or another. Somehow he felt sure Fliss would prefer Johnny's uncomplicated company to his own, and the thought did nothing to cheer him up.

Chapter Fourteen

Fliss

Johnny had promised to drive up to the Cross Hotel to pick Fliss up. He was twenty minutes late. Fliss glanced at her watch as she waited in reception. She was beginning to think it was all very well Johnny being easy-going, but sometimes it was possible to be just a little bit too relaxed.

She was passing the time chatting to Jilly about the lounge refurbishment, when her mobile rang. Johnny's name appeared on the screen

'Flish?' he said.

Flish?

Fliss's eyes opened wide. 'Of course it's me. Where are you?'

'I'm in the pub. Listen, I bumped into a couple of guys from school, and one thing led to another. Do you mind getting a taxi down? I've had one too many to drive.'

Fliss groaned. If Johnny was with a group of mates – and they'd all started drinking already – it didn't bode well for the rest of the evening. Her voice was a little tart when she answered. 'Look, if you're with some friends, why don't we call it off? We could go out another time.'

'No,' he protested. 'They've gone now, and anyway, I wanted to chat, somewhere away from the hotel. It's fine, I've just had a couple of pints, that's all. I'll pay for the taxi.'

There was that faint hint of desperation in Johnny's voice that Fliss remembered from their last meeting. Out of kindness, she relented. Out of curiosity, too, if she were perfectly honest. What on earth was he so keen to talk about?

'Don't worry,' she told him. 'I'll pay for my own taxi. Only do me a favour and drink lemonade until I get there. Otherwise I'm going to have a lot of catching up to do.'

She clicked off and turned round to find Patrick standing right behind her. His arms were folded, and there was a frown on his face. Fliss could well understand why Johnny was so keen to talk away from his work-place. There was no keeping any secrets in a hotel.

'I take it Johnny's been drinking,' Patrick said.

Fliss raised her brows at his tone. She was annoyed, too, but Patrick's comment made her leap to Johnny's defence. 'It's his night off. He's entitled to spend it how he likes.'

'Yes, and having a drink is usually how Johnny spends his free evenings. And now you need a lift. I'll drive you down to the village.'

'Oh, for goodness' sake. I'm perfectly capable of ordering a taxi.'

'It's no problem.' He reached into his pocket for his car key.

Fliss would have loved nothing better than to dig in her heels and insist on taking a cab, but unfortunately Patrick's mother had been hanging on to every word of the conversation.

'Patrick's right, Fliss, darling. You don't want to be waiting here for a taxi. There's only Doug who drives one in the village, and he could be ages at this time of night. Let Patrick take you.'

Fliss tried to think of a way of refusing that wouldn't appear childish and stubborn, and failed. She forced out a stiff, 'Thank you.'

Patrick nodded equally stiffly. There was nothing for Fliss to do except bid Jilly a civil good evening and make her way out in as dignified a fashion as possible. But as she pushed open the hotel door, and the fresh night air enveloped her, her chagrin dissipated. The sight outside swept everything else from her mind, and she gave a gasp of wonder. The night sky was clear above the trees, and to the west, where the fellside dipped down to the valley, the heavens fell away in a sheet of black, sprinkled with a thousand stars, so close, she could be walking through them.

'Will you take a look at that?' She stepped forwards over the gravel and made her way to the terrace, where the stars swung down. The sky was deepest black, and the Milky Way floated high, high above them, in a swirl of fabulous glory. Fliss rested her hands on the railing, her head tilted up to the sky.

Patrick moved to stand beside her. The starlight cast a white glow over his features, deepening the lines on his face. His mouth was a straight line, and his eyes glittered. Fliss turned her head to look at him. His gaze was fixed on the firmament. Then his eyes met hers.

'It's even more spectacular in the Caribbean,' he said. 'On a calm night, when you come up from a dive, you could be alone in the universe, floating along, with the stars a golden cloak above you.'

'That sounds amazing. I can see how you must miss it.'

He hesitated, before saying, 'I don't miss it as much as I did.'

The breeze in the trees stilled. Fliss heard the sound of Patrick's breathing. Then an owl broke the silence, bursting out of the wood on the hillside below them with a great sweep of its wings. Fliss gave a startled gasp. Patrick placed his hand on her arm, his breath quickening with hers. At his touch, Fliss's heart leapt. His eyes were bright on hers, his lips parted. For a wild moment she thought he was about to kiss her. She waited, heart thudding, a thousand emotions clamouring within her. He bent his head to hers, and for a couple of seconds they stood perfectly still, their quick breath intermingling.

Then Fliss's phone beeped, the sound discordant and jarring in the quiet. Patrick dropped his hand. Fliss took a swift step back.

'I'm sorry,' she said. She wondered how Patrick would take her apology. That she was sorry her mobile sounded just as he was about to kiss her? That she was sorry for wanting to kiss him? Fliss herself had no idea what she'd meant by it. She fumbled for her phone, but Patrick was already turning, making his way over the forecourt to where his car was parked.

The phone's screen spelled out a message. "*Bored of lemonade. Where u?*"

Fliss tapped in a quick reply – "*On my way*" – and strode in Patrick's wake.

They journeyed down the hillside in silence, their brief intimacy dispelled. Patrick was concentrating on the dark road ahead. The glorious night sky was hidden from them as they passed beneath the trees, and the bright white of the car's headlights lit everything in a harsh glare. If there really had been anything between them just now – if Patrick really had been on the verge of kissing her – he appeared to have completely forgotten it. Either that, or he was thinking of his lucky escape.

Fliss sighed and turned to the window. 'What do you think you'll do?' she asked, breaking the silence. 'About staying on here, I mean. You said you didn't miss the Caribbean now, as much as you did. Does that mean you're getting used to being back in the Lakes? That you'll stay?'

Her question must have jolted Patrick out of his reverie. He changed gears with a clumsy clunking sound. He muttered to himself before answering, 'No. I won't be staying. If I can get the hotel back on track financially, I'll leave it in the hands of a manager and persuade my mum to come back with me to the Caribbean. That's always been my plan, and I can't see any reason to change it. If Mum won't come permanently, then I hope she will stay with me at least for the winter months.'

Fliss fixed her eyes on the tree trunks drifting past, their branches dark and sombre. The thought of Patrick returning to Dominica filled her with dismay, which was ridiculous. Even if he did decide to stay, Fliss would be leaving herself in a few weeks, to go back to her job at Everdenes – a job that involved endless travelling. After her stay at the Cross Hotel, it was highly unlikely that she and Patrick would ever cross paths again, except perhaps occasionally through Jilly. Fliss was surprised at how despondent that thought made her.

Patrick cleared his throat. 'What about you? After you told me you weren't looking forward to going back to work for your father …' He hesitated, before continuing, 'Well, I wondered if you'd like to stay on longer at the Cross Hotel. You'd be welcome.' He glanced across at her, a small smile on his lips. 'It will be very quiet when you've gone.'

Fliss was touched by his offer. Her heart soared for a moment. Remaining in the Lakes, in this amazing old hotel, would be like a wonderful dream come true. Then cold reality hit. Leaving would be painful, but she had to harden herself. She thought of her mother dealing with all the flak from the Stuttgart takeover, and of how her parents were worried about Minnie, and knew it would be wrong to stay.

She shook her head. 'That's kind of you, but I don't think my dad would be happy if I extended my leave. He's expecting me back, and my mum misses me, too.'

'Well,' Patrick said quietly, his eyes once more on the road ahead. 'The offer's there if you change your mind.'

They had reached the village, and the streets were eerily quiet. A string of white fairy lights shone from the roof of The Lakeside as they passed. They could see into the bar, which was thronged with people. Someone was doing great business in Emmside, even if it wasn't the Cross Hotel.

They carried on, over the stone bridge. The Black Bull was on the outskirts of the village, in a row of shabby terraces, well away from the picturesque setting of the lake. The street was dark when they turned into it, but the sound of pounding music and shouted conversations spilled out of the pub's open window. A few locals were huddled in the doorway, drawing on their cigarettes under a sullen pall of smoke.

Patrick cast a glance in Fliss's direction and said dryly, 'I expect this isn't your usual scene.'

Fliss shrugged. 'It's not that. It's – ' She broke off. She'd been about to say that a noisy pub hardly seemed the place to have a quiet chat, but then she remembered Johnny wanted to keep the conversation private. 'Oh, never mind,' she went on, reaching for the car door.

Patrick surprised her by placing a hand on her arm. 'Listen, if you have any problems, just give me a ring. I can come and pick you up. It doesn't matter what time it is. You've got my mobile number, haven't you? And the hotel's number?'

'Yes, but – ' She turned her eyes on him. 'I mean, I really can't see it coming to that. We're just going to have a chat.'

'Johnny's chats tend to get out of hand when there's alcohol involved.'

'Oh, I'm sure you're worrying over nothing.' She put Patrick's comment down to jealousy. Honestly, Johnny was one of the most hard-working people in the hotel, and one of the most reliable. She pushed open her door and stepped out, leaning back in to add, 'It'll be fine. I'll phone Doug the taxi.' Patrick looked so serious, she couldn't resist adding cheekily, 'Don't wait up for me, darling.'

She swung the door shut and made her way across the road to the pub doorway. Behind her Patrick's car moved off. Despite the confidence of her parting words, she felt a sudden sensation of abandonment.

'Don't be silly,' she told herself. 'What could possibly go wrong?'

As she approached the pub door, one of the youths pulled it open for her, cigarette dangling from his fingers. The smoke wafted into her eyes.

'Evening,' he said.

Fliss gave him a friendly nod and passed inside, where the racket was unbelievable. She glanced around, ignoring the curious looks in her direction, searching in vain for Johnny. He wasn't among the group at the bar, who were shouting to make themselves heard above the music. He wasn't one of the people playing pool, either, or one of the lads at the dart board, who were focused on the game in silent concentration, despite the din. Fliss turned her attention to the groups sitting at the tables, and it was then that she noticed one of the women staring at her. It wasn't a particularly friendly stare, either. Then she remembered the two young women who had chased after Johnny in the car park. This had to be Pauline's friend, Georgia. Fliss hadn't recognised her at first. She was all dressed up for a night out. The puffa jacket and trainers were gone, and she had on a lace top and skin-tight trousers. Her hair was swept up in an elaborate do, and her pale face carefully made up. She rose to her feet when Fliss noticed her, muttering something to her friends. Fliss watched her approach with a sinking heart.

Georgia came to a halt, both hands on her hips. Fliss had only ever seen people stand like this in cartoons, and she had to bite her lip.

'Looking for somebody?' Georgia said.

'Yes.' Fliss spoke as mildly as she could over the bumping bass. 'I'm looking for Johnny. Have you seen him?'

Georgia gave a tell-tale glance towards the door of the snug. 'He's not here.'

'Oh? What a shame. Well, never mind, I'll go and see if I can find anyone I know in the snug.'

Fliss turned on her heel. As soon as she pushed open the door to the snug, she knew meeting Johnny in the pub was a big mistake. He was sitting at one of the rickety tables, his hand wrapped round a pint of lager, with what looked like an empty whisky chaser next to it. Pauline's friend number two was bending over him, wagging a finger in his face. Fliss was on the verge of beating a cowardly retreat – even texting Patrick to admit he was right had to be better than this – when Johnny caught sight of her and stood, swaying slightly.

'Flish. Where've you been?'

Friend number two whirled round and pointed at Fliss. 'What's she doing here?'

Pointing fingers, hands on hips. It was obviously a place for body language clichés. Fliss decided to join in by folding her arms.

'I've come to have a chat with Johnny,' she said. 'We're not on a date. It's a quiet chat between friends.' She tried a smile. 'Nice to see you again. Can I get you a drink?'

The girl dropped her finger, looking a little nonplussed. 'Well, I – yes, I'll have a vodka and coke, since you're offering.'

'No, you won't,' Johnny said. 'I want to have a talk with Fliss. In *private*. Bugger off back to Georgia and leave us alone.'

The girl rolled her eyes and stalked to the door. 'Suit yourself. But I haven't finished yet. Pauline's a mate, and mates stick together.'

'Yeah, right,' Johnny muttered as the door shut behind her. 'What would you know?'

He slumped back into his seat and took a long pull on his lager. Fliss pulled out the chair opposite his. At least in the snug the noise levels were several decibels below ear-damaging, and it was possible to have a conversation. She looked pointedly at the glass Johnny was lifting to his lips.

'Sorry,' he said, replacing it on the table and swaying once more to his feet. 'What are you drinking?'

Fliss thought longingly of a large glass of red wine, but decided against it. Better for at least one of them to remain sober.

'I'll have a lime and soda, thanks.'

Johnny stumbled his way to the bar, leaving Fliss in no doubt that he'd long since given up drinking lemonade. When he returned, he was carrying her glass, another pint of lager and a whiskey chaser. At least his years of training as a waiter meant that despite his inebriation, he didn't spill a drop. He ranged the drinks carefully on the table and sank back into his seat.

'Cheers.' Fliss lifted her glass with a cheerful smile, and Johnny returned her salute. 'So,' she went on, 'let me guess what you'd like to talk about.' She took a sip of her drink, wrinkling her brow as she pretended to mull it over. 'This is a wild guess, but could it be anything to do with Pauline leaving the Cross Hotel?'

Johnny sat bolt upright. 'How did you know?' he said. 'What have you heard?'

'Nothing. But it doesn't take a mind reader to work it out. Every time anyone mentions her name, you go bright red. And you're being stalked by her two best mates.' She leaned forward, regarding him earnestly. 'Listen, Johnny, what's up? Have you two had some sort of tiff? Is that why Pauline left?'

Johnny pushed his empty pint glass aside, picked up the full one, and took a long swig. 'Something like that,' he muttered.

'Oh. Then what I don't get is why the big secret? Why are we talking here and not at the hotel? And another thing – if you and Pauline have had some sort of row, don't you think it's time to tell Patrick that's why she's gone? You know why he thinks she left, don't you? He thinks it's all his fault, and Pauline hasn't forgiven him for her brother dying.'

'I know, I know.' Johnny hung his head. 'Don't think I don't know it. I've wanted to tell him. Not that he's the easiest person to talk to – wandering round the place scowling all the time. Enough to make anyone depressed. Christ, it's no wonder they call it the Cross Hotel. Everybody's permanently in a bad mood.' He took another long swig.

'Then tell him Pauline left because of you,' Fliss insisted. 'Because if you won't, I will.'

'No! It's not as simple as that. Pauline doesn't want me to tell anyone.'

'Why on earth not?'

'Because she's pregnant,' he burst out. He gave a hasty glance round the room, before leaning towards her over the table. 'She's pregnant,' he said again in a loud whisper.

Fliss's jaw dropped wide. 'You? You're the father?'

'Of course I'm the father. Who else would be? We've been together for two years. What sort of person do you think she is?'

'Just checking,' Fliss said hastily. 'No offence.'

To her horror, Johnny's cheeks became mottled with colour, and his eyes glistened. 'Yeah, well, now you know. And she's run off to her auntie's. I thought she'd have come back by now, but she won't answer any more of my calls or texts.'

Fliss took in his distress, puzzled. 'I still don't really understand, Johnny. Why would she run off because she's pregnant? And why hasn't she told her friends?'

Johnny shrugged. 'You've seen what her mates are like. They're all right deep down, but they're a bit overpowering. It's not just them – this whole village is a hotbed of gossip. Pauline wanted to get her head wrapped round the whole baby thing in peace and quiet. Make her own mind up about the future before she tells everyone.'

'But aren't you part of her future? Why won't she talk to you?'

His colour heightened. He put his head in his hands again. 'I made a mistake. When she told me she was pregnant, I said I didn't want it.'

Fliss stared at him. 'Oh, Johnny.'

'It was just a reflex. Course I'd do anything for her! I mean I was just worried, that's all, and I wish I'd never said it. But now she's stormed off. She said if I don't want the baby, that's fine, because I'd be a useless dad anyway. She said I was wasting my life, and I wasn't going to waste hers and her kid's. She told me if I wasn't going to support her decision, never to bother her again.'

Fliss felt her own eyes fill with tears. She could have kicked herself for not seeing the signs of his anguish earlier. 'Are you saying you want her to keep the baby, after all?' she asked.

'Yes, of course. The more I think about it, the more I'd love it. And I want her back. But I keep thinking of our baby, and every time I think of it, I think she's right. What have I got to offer her?' Johnny looked round the dingy pub in disgust. 'I mean, is this it?'

Fliss reached over the table and took his hand. 'You've got plenty to offer her,' she assured him. 'And I think you'd be a brilliant dad. We'll think of something.'

Patrick

Patrick made his way back to the hotel, following each bend and twist of the road on auto-pilot. The journey into the pitch black tunnel produced by the overhanging trees was so familiar he could almost drive it blindfold, which was just as well, since his attention was wandering like the devil. He dipped his lights as a car came towards him, then pulled into a stopping-place to let the other vehicle pass by. The car disappeared with a grateful flash of its lights and was swallowed up by the bend below him, but Patrick sat there still, the engine idling, his hands resting loosely on the steering-wheel and his thoughts down in the village, with Fliss.

When she'd said goodbye with that mocking, "Don't wait up, darling," he'd barely noticed the irony in her voice. All he could think of was the swell of her breasts as she'd leaned into the car, the diamond on her necklace falling forward, gleaming softly in the gloom. He'd been consumed with the same desire for her he'd felt as she stood beside him on the terrace, gazing out at the night sky.

"You must miss it," she'd said about his home in Dominica. It was true, he did miss his old home, but if anyone had asked him to change places then, to step away from her side, he'd have resisted with every breath in his body.

He raised a hand, rubbing the lines that were deepening on his forehead, a habit of his when he was at a stand. He'd only known Fliss a few weeks, but already he was looking forward with dread to the day of her departure. Once she'd gone back to her job at Everdenes, and after Patrick had returned to Dominica, he'd never see her again.

And then he realised something else. That evening, looking down at the starlit valley with Fliss beside him, was the first time he'd looked on that view since his return, and not thought of Jacob. He'd thought of nothing else but Fliss's wonder in the scene around her. And then when she'd turned to him, her eyes wide and glowing, her smile a flash of joy in the dark, all he'd wanted to do was kiss her. And what an idiot he'd have made of himself if he'd tried.

He shook his head as he manoeuvred his car back onto the road. When he turned in to the Cross Hotel and came to halt on the gravel, the light from the reception spilled out onto the forecourt. He pushed open the door to find his mother behind the desk, studying some papers. She glanced up and gave him a warm smile when she saw who it was. Patrick noted how the harsh lines of strain had begun to leave her features, leaving her softer, more like the woman he remembered before his father had died. Another result of Fliss's presence in the hotel.

Sure enough, Jilly held up the print-outs she was studying. 'Fliss downloaded all these for me,' she said. 'Isn't she a darling?'

Patrick took the colour photos from her hand and examined them.

'It's to give me some ideas for refurbishing the lounge,' Jilly explained. 'See, look.' She pointed to one of the sheets of paper. 'These are all similar hotels to us, but in the Highlands. They're all reasonably priced, like us, and they have the same sort of clientele – a mixture of outdoor types and older people looking for a quiet retreat. Fliss wanted to show me how their dining areas were furnished. Just to show we can refurbish to make the place look much nicer, without spending too much money.'

There was a swatch of fabrics on Jilly's desk, too, beside her notebook. Patrick eyed it suspiciously.

'Without spending too much money,' he repeated. 'Fliss has been on and on about getting new curtains. I think her idea of spending and mine are a little bit different.'

'Nonsense.' Jilly pushed the swatch aside hastily. 'Fliss is very sensible. She's been around the hotel business forever, and you can't deny the Everdene family knows how to handle money.'

Patrick bit back a retort. He didn't want to upset his mother by saying anything derogatory about her old friends, but there was a huge difference between being good with money and the rapacious way James Everdene went about expanding his business. He was about to mention the dubious takeover in

Stuttgart, and to give his mother a gentle hint that perhaps all was not sweetness and light in her friends' business, but his mum spoke first.

'You know,' she told Patrick, 'before Felicity came here I'm ashamed to say I'd given up hope in the Cross Hotel. Without your dad, and with you not interested, there didn't seem much point continuing. But Felicity has made me see this place with fresh eyes.'

Patrick followed her gaze as she studied the shabby lobby. The rug had seen better days and needed replacing, and the light-fittings were old-fashioned and cumbersome, but he had to admit that the room itself could be welcoming and airy, especially when the hideous curtains were drawn back.

'Felicity has made me see how beautiful this old building is,' his mum continued. 'And she's made me realise how lucky we are to have such loyal staff. She's managed something I thought would be impossible only a few weeks ago, and that is to renew my enthusiasm. I wondered if – ' She looked up at Patrick hesitantly. 'Well, I wondered if the hotel starts doing well, maybe you might think about coming back. About staying on here.'

'Mum.' Patrick took in his mother's hopeful expression, the brightness in the eyes that had been dull for so long, and said gently, 'We've been through this, Mum. I've got my own business, and I've made a success of it. I don't know enough about the hotel trade. Fliss is the one who's come up with all the ideas.' The light left his mother's features. Patrick had to steel himself to continue. 'We'll still see each other lots if we stick to our plan. We can get the hotel back on track, and then I'll get a manager in. Then in the winter months you come and stay with me, and when diving tails off in monsoon season, I'll come here to stay with you. That way we'll see each other most of the year.'

Jilly's head drooped. Her eyes fell on the print-outs and she moved them absently. Then a thought struck her, and she straightened up. 'You're right, Felicity is the one who has had all the ideas. And I've seen the way she gets on with everyone.

150

Even Tomasz has a smile for her. She told me herself she'll miss us all when she goes. Why don't we offer her the job of manager? Then she can stay here forever.'

Patrick stiffened. His mother's eyes were eager on his, and she seemed to think she'd solved all their problems at one stroke. Did she really not understand why that would be a dangerous thing to do?

'Anyone can see what a massive difference Fliss has made here already,' he said. 'She'd be absolutely the perfect person, if it wasn't for the fact she doesn't come alone. She's part of the Everdene chain. Fliss has made it very clear to me that that's where her loyalty lies. And you know how the Everdenes operate in business.'

The way his mother's face fell told Patrick all he needed to know. She understood exactly what he was hinting at. The Cross Hotel was a minnow compared to the great shark that was the Everdene chain. If Fliss got a toe-hold in the hotel, could they really trust her father not to take advantage of their precarious financial position?

Jilly gave a defeated shrug. 'Perhaps you're right. The last thing we want to do is put poor Felicity in an awkward position. Her father can be quite single-minded in business. Helen's told me such things – ' She drew herself up and added, 'Oh well, that's by the by. I'm sure James has built up a wonderful inheritance for his daughters. He does it all for them, you know.'

Patrick drew in his breath to make a curt reply, but his mother was looking at him so defensively he swallowed his answer and glanced down again at the papers on the desk. 'Can I do anything to help you with your plans?'

His change of subject had the desired effect. Jilly brightened. 'That's very kind of you, but I think between us Felicity and I have everything covered. I'm so looking forward to the Tudor party. And the whole lounge is going to look fabulous.'

'Apart from the curtains,' Patrick finished.

'Oh, no, that's – ' Jilly broke off quickly and pushed the swatch to one side, avoiding Patrick's eye. 'What I mean is, that's not important, is it? What's important is making people feel welcome and providing delicious food and drink.'

'Quite.' Patrick eyed her in silence for a while, but decided whatever she'd been about to say, it wasn't worth pressing her. 'Well, if you're sure there's nothing I can do, I'll be in my office.'

'All right, darling. Don't be up too late.'

Patrick couldn't resist a smile as he made his way down the corridor. He'd left home a decade ago, and his mother still thought he was incapable of deciding on his own bedtime. He switched on the light and examined the notes on his desk. He'd much prefer to be staying up past his bedtime with Fliss, instead of stuck indoors with his spreadsheets, but he sat down and switched on his laptop. For the next couple of hours he immersed himself in his new projections for Alison at the bank, wrestling with the figures, trying to turn the red bottom line into a black one. If Fliss's Tudor nights were carried out on a regular basis and drew in the clientele they predicted, and if Tomasz's more upmarket offerings were priced accordingly, the balance could gradually be tipped in the hotel's favour.

Occasionally, in between staring at his screen, Patrick got up from his desk and visited the lounge, where all was quiet. Another waiter stood in for Johnny on his nights off. There was the usual handful of guests that evening, and the waiter seemed to be coping perfectly well, so after a while Patrick left him to it. Eventually, so engrossed did he become in his paperwork, it wasn't until he heard the last guests leaving the lounge and making their way to bed that he realised Fliss wasn't home yet.

"*Don't wait up for me, darling.*" He remembered her mocking look but couldn't resist a glance at his watch. Surely she should be home by now? Unless…He lifted his head, a thought stabbing him in the gut. Unless Fliss had left the pub and gone back with Johnny to his house in the village.

'If she has, that's her business,' he told himself, but the jealous thought refused to go away. He stood and made his way down the corridor into the reception. His mother had gone to bed, and the hotel door was locked. The only light was the muted lamp left on for late returners, who would let themselves in with their own key. Perhaps Fliss was already back? But surely he would have heard her come in. And if she'd made out the light in his office, he knew she would have stopped by to say good night.

He looked at his watch again. What if she hadn't managed to get Doug's taxi service, and had set off to walk? It would be just like Johnny not to make sure she was OK. Other guests had made this mistake in the past, misjudging the distance and failing to realise just how dark it was on the fellside without a car's headlights to illuminate it.

He began to feel anxious. Perhaps he should drive down to the pub and rouse Bob, the landlord. He was turning everything over in his mind when the phone on the reception desk sprang to life with a shrill ring, making him jump out of his skin.

He picked it up. 'Cross Hotel.'

'Hello? Patrick?'

It was Fliss, after all. His pulse rate subsided, and even as it did so, he registered a relief on hearing her voice that was out of all proportion.

Annoyed with himself, he said crossly, 'Where are you?'

'Well, don't get mad, but I'm at the police station. You said I could phone if I needed help, and so...'

Her voice trailed off, and Patrick rolled his eyes. Now all became clear. 'I hope Johnny hasn't gone and got himself arrested for being drunk and disorderly.'

'No, it's not that. It's me. I'm the one who's been arrested. Sort of.'

'What?' He snatched up his car key from the desk. 'I'm on my way.'

Chapter Fifteen

Fliss

Sergeant Willis was a large, balding man in his late forties, with the hang-dog face of a person who'd seen everything. He was the father of three teenage girls, two of them twins, he confided to Fliss, in a weary fashion that elicited her sympathy. They were sitting together companionably in the cramped office of the police station, drinking strong tea and eating their way through the sponge cake his oldest daughter had baked for him.

'This is delicious,' Fliss mumbled with her mouth full. She waved her cake in Sergeant Willis's direction. 'I can't believe she baked this herself. Has she thought of taking it up professionally?'

'I wish. Nice steady job as a baker would be grand. But that's not what she wants. She's on and on about being a scientist. Wants to join forensics. I keep telling her it's no job for a young girl, but she won't have it.'

Fliss swallowed the last mouthful and licked her fingers. 'Well, I can see that would be a worry. It would be a great career if she could get into it, but she'd witness some terrible things.'

'I've told her all that. Told her there's things she'd see as would turn anyone's stomach. Things that stay printed on your skull so you can't sleep nights. She won't listen to me, though. She's watched too many police dramas, that's what it is.'

Fliss felt for his dilemma. The stresses of her own job seemed suddenly as nothing compared to the stress of being a parent.

'Is she good at science?' she asked, looking hopefully at the rest of the cake.

The sergeant brightened. 'Straight As. I can't knock her for not working at it.'

He pushed the tin towards her, and Fliss cut herself another slice, watching with relish as the jam oozed out.

'Well,' she said. 'If that's what she's set her heart on, then perhaps you'll have to let her go her own way. It's better for her to have the career she wants than to be miserable.'

The sergeant was about to answer when a flash of headlights caught the window, and a car rolled into the car park.

'That'll be your white horse,' he said.

Fliss glanced down with regret at her uneaten slice, and he passed her a napkin.

'Here, wrap it up if you like.'

The buzzer on the police station door gave a short rasp, and Sergeant Willis heaved himself to his feet. 'No rest for the wicked.'

He made his way to the front desk, and, after wrapping her cake as best she could and placing it in her handbag, Fliss followed.

On the other side of the grille stood Patrick, a look of mingled anxiety and temper on his face. Fliss bit back a smile. It was quite good fun being on this side of the policeman's window. She hadn't known it was possible to shake your head and roll your eyes simultaneously until she saw Patrick do it.

'What's going on, Willy?' Patrick's gaze flicked from the sergeant to Fliss, whose giggle finally escaped her. *Willy*? How on earth could anyone keep law and order with a nickname like that?

'All right, Paddy. Something and nothing.' Sergeant Willis pressed in a code on the door and gave Fliss a nod. 'Good to meet you, Miss Everdene. But don't make a habit of practising your jiu-jitsu in pub toilets. Next time you might not get off so easily. '

'Have you been fighting?' The look of censure on Patrick's face had a sobering effect.

Fliss lifted her chin. 'It wasn't like that. I wasn't drunk. And it wasn't my fault. She started it.'

'Aye, they all say that,' Sergeant Willis muttered.

Fliss took no notice. 'It's been a pleasure to meet you, Sergeant Willis. Did you know the Cross Hotel is having a party? We're holding a Tudor night in a few weeks. It would be lovely if you and your wife and daughters could come along.'

For the first time what could almost pass for a smile crossed Sergeant Willis's long-suffering features. 'Well, that's very kind of you,' he said. 'I'll have to speak to the missus. Thanks for the kind thought.'

'No problem. I'd love to meet the girl responsible for the delicious cake. I'll ask Jilly to add you to the invitation list.'

After a few more pleasantries and a handshake from Sergeant Willis, Fliss left in Patrick's company.

'Thank you *so much*,' she said, heaving a heartfelt sigh of relief. 'What a terrible evening. I thought it was all going to end in total disaster, but Sergeant Willis turned out to be a total sweetie. Just as well, since Johnny was no help at all.'

They were halfway to the car. Patrick stopped and turned. 'And just where *is* Johnny? I can't believe he's left you like this.'

Even in the dark, Fliss could see the lines of anger deepening on his forehead. It didn't bode well for Johnny when he came in to work the next day. Fliss tried desperately to think of something that might work in Johnny's defence, but it was difficult without giving away the fact that Pauline was pregnant – something she'd promised to keep secret.

'Johnny had a bit to drink,' she said finally. This was an understatement, but there was no need to go into details. 'So

156

when the constable told me to get into the patrol car, Georgia and I thought it was probably better if she walked Johnny home.'

'Georgia?' Patrick repeated, bewildered. 'Georgia Riley?'

'I don't know what her surname is. Small girl. Dark hair. Friend of Pauline's.' Fliss put her hand to her cheekbone and winced. 'Packs a mean punch.'

'Is that who you were fighting with?' Patrick's tone was incredulous. Somewhere inside the police station a light came on. The glow fell across Fliss's upper body, and Patrick's eyes widened in amazement. 'Good God. Is that blood?'

Fliss followed his gaze to the red stain on the lapel of her mac. She scraped at it with the tip of her finger. 'No, of course not,' she said. 'It's jam. Sergeant Willis's daughter baked him a cake. It was absolutely delicious. In fact, I said to him she should consider baking as a career, only he said – '

'Oh, for heaven's sake. Stop talking and get in the car.'

'OK.' Fliss followed him meekly. 'I'm very grateful to you for coming.' Patrick held the door for her, and she carried on, 'I would have called Doug, only by the time Sergeant Willis had told Constable Hield there was no need to arrest me it was getting late. The sergeant said Doug would be in bed on a week night, and it seemed a shame to wake him. And since Constable Hield needed the patrol car – '

Patrick shut her door, cutting her off in mid-flow. He came round to his side and slid into his seat. 'Do you think you could start the whole story from the beginning, without rambling? Why were you fighting with Georgia?'

Fliss drew in a deep breath.

*

There hadn't been many people in the snug that evening, which made it all the more difficult to ignore Georgia. Every time Fliss went up to order a drink, there she was, in the tap room on the other side of the bar, scowling at her. Georgia was drinking some sort of hideous blue cocktail, and the more of them she knocked back, the more ferocious her expression became. Once, when Fliss was ordering a round for herself and

Johnny, she happened to catch Georgia's eye despite herself, and the girl jutted her chin aggressively. After that, Fliss was too intimidated to leave the table, and she sent Johnny to buy their drinks. As long as she stayed in the snug and Georgia remained in the tap room, she was hoping to get though the evening without any sort of confrontation.

Unfortunately, Johnny wasn't much help, and in retrospect, Fliss wasn't surprised at Georgia's attitude. From a distance it could easily have seemed as though she and Johnny were whispering sweet nothings over the table to each other. For a large part of the evening Johnny had clutched Fliss's hand, his eyes soulful with love. What Georgia hadn't guessed was that Johnny had been talking of nothing else except Pauline – how he wasn't good enough for her, and what did Fliss think he ought to do, and how he missed Pauline so much it hurt, and so on and so on, until his speech became more and more slurred.

Finally, Fliss had managed to persuade Johnny that it was time to go. While he fumbled with his phone to call Doug, Fliss had gone to the ladies. She was in the loo when to her dismay she heard the door to the ladies open, and footsteps outside her cubicle. She held her breath, hoping whoever it was wasn't Georgia.

'No use hiding in there.' Georgia's voice was slurred and belligerent. Fliss gave a deep sigh. The perfect end to a trying evening. She glanced at the window. Just her luck. Far too small for her to crawl through. There was nothing for it but to put on a dignified front and to try and persuade Pauline's by now very drunken friend that they were actually on the same side, and that Fliss was not – and never would be – Johnny's girlfriend.

Fliss opened the cubicle door, pasting a friendly smile on her face. For the first time Dolly Parton's advice failed her. Georgia took her smile entirely the wrong way.

'Do you think this is funny? Pauline's effing heart-broken.' Georgia balled her hand into a fist and swung it at Fliss's face. If Fliss hadn't been so tired by then she'd have dealt with it more neatly. She'd had lessons in self-defence for years, at her father's suggestion. When she first began travelling abroad for the Everdene chain, her dad had worried about her travelling alone. He'd thought a set of jiu-jitsu classes would help her look after herself. Fliss had much enjoyed her lessons and continued to practise whenever she could. Although she'd travelled round the world, luckily she'd never been called on to use her skills in real life. Not until confronted by a drunken friend of Pauline's in a pub in Emmside.

Fliss leaned aside just a little too late, and Georgia's fist managed a glancing blow along her cheekbone which smarted. Luckily Georgia was the worse for drink. She carried on lunging long after the blow had landed. It was easy enough for Fliss to catch hold of the other woman's arm, lock it and swing her round until she landed with an *ooomph* on the tiled floor. Georgia let out a scream, more in anger than in pain, but unfortunately another young woman chose that very moment to walk in. She found Fliss standing over Georgia, holding her arm in a lock, one kitten-heeled foot pressed on her shoulder to keep her down.

It only took Georgia's cry of, "Get her off me!" for the other woman to start screaming as well. Next minute the ladies was full of people, and someone was phoning the police.

*

'So that's how it all got out of hand,' Fliss told Patrick. 'And when Constable Hield arrived in the patrol car, he told me he was only a special constable, not a real policeman, and last time he arrested someone Sergeant Willis was very annoyed. He seemed a bit worried, so I said why don't we go down to the police station and ask the sergeant what to do? Constable Hield seemed to think that was a great idea, so that's how I ended up getting in the patrol car with him.'

'For goodness sake.' Patrick rolled his eyes. 'And that's when Johnny sloped off home, I take it.'

'It wasn't exactly sloping,' Fliss said defensively. 'I persuaded Georgia it would be better if she set off home with Johnny, before the police turned up.'

'Don't tell me. You and Georgia are now fast friends.'

'Well, she apologised for screaming. Said it hadn't hurt really, but I'd taken her by surprise. And then we were both quite cross about the other girl bursting in and screaming for no reason, and Georgia explained that this was one of her cousins, and she'd always been a drama queen, ever since she was a baby. After that, we got on quite well. Georgia said she hadn't thought I'd have it in me to floor her. Then she admired my shoes. She told me she hadn't noticed them until I stood on her shoulder, and she recognised the designer name on the sole. So I said I've got another pair the same, hardly worn, and said she might as well have them if she liked them. And then Georgia said – '

'OK, OK.'

They were now nearing the hotel. Patrick slowed down to take the turn into the driveway and added in a mutter, 'Poor old Willy. What a night for him.'

Fliss chuckled. 'What a nickname for a policeman. It must be hard being a copper in the town you grew up in. Did you call him Willy at school?'

'At school?' Patrick was thunderstruck. 'Of course not. Willy's way older than I am. He'd left school before I even started.'

'Oh, of course. He said he'd – ' Fliss broke off abruptly. They reached the hotel forecourt, and Patrick cut the engine.

'Said he'd what?' His eyes met hers. The forecourt was plunged in darkness. Without the sound of the engine, the silence outside pressed against the windows like a physical being.

Fliss hesitated only a fraction before saying squarely. 'Sergeant Willis said he'd been on duty the day they found Jacob's body. He was the one called out.'

Patrick stiffened. 'I don't remember.'

'He said he was only a constable at the time, but even then he thought it was a shame your dad blamed you. Everyone knew Jacob was always rushing into things, and that you were always the sensible one.'

Patrick's profile was a pale, stiff white. 'I see,' he said. 'Sergeant Willis had a lot to say for himself. I'm surprised he got a word in edgeways.'

'I hope you don't mind my mentioning it. I thought it might help.'

'Help what?' Patrick turned his head towards her. 'My friend drowned, and I couldn't save him. My life changed forever, and he's never coming back. In what way does that help?'

Fliss refused to back down. Despite Patrick's anger, it was important to say what she knew in her heart was true. 'Everyone knows you weren't to blame, no matter what your dad said afterwards. It wasn't your fault.'

Fliss wanted to add that Patrick's return wasn't the reason Jacob's sister had left the hotel in such a hurry, despite what he thought. She wanted to tell him his feelings of guilt had blinded him to what was going on around him. The truth about the real reason Pauline had left hovered on her tongue, but she pressed her lips together, mindful that this wasn't her secret to tell.

Patrick clenched his jaw for a second or two. Then he let out a breath. 'You never give up, do you?'

Fliss darted him a glance. There was a grim smile on his face, and she felt a stab of relief. 'Ever since I arrived here,' she told him, 'I see how much people like you and trust you. I hate to see you carry such a feeling of guilt around. I thought if even the police don't think it was your fault – well, I thought that might change how you see things.'

There was a short silence, and Fliss waited. But Patrick said nothing. Eventually, he made to open his door. Fliss resisted the urge to put a hand on his arm, to force him to listen until he'd seen reason. She knew it would take more than a few words from her. Patrick had carried a sense of responsibility for ten years. It wasn't something he'd be able to shake off lightly.

His footsteps sounded on the gravel, and then he was opening her door. The night air was chill, and she shivered.

'Come on,' he said wearily. 'Let's get to bed.'

She placed her hand in his and leaned on his arm as he helped her down from the high vehicle.

'Thank you,' she said. She looked up at him, her hand still in his. 'For coming to the police station, I mean. And for being so understanding about everything. I'm sorry to cause so much trouble.'

She stood on the tips of her toes, intending to press a kiss on his cheek, but Patrick dropped her hand and moved his head a little, and somehow she ended up planting a kiss on his lips. His mouth was warm under hers. She made to break away, startled, but then his arms were around her and he was pulling her to him, and his kiss deepened so that her heart gave a lurch against her chest, slamming against her rib-cage with an intensity that knocked the breath out of her.

Instantly, Patrick relaxed his hold and broke away. His breathing, too, came in short bursts, and his eyes were dark on hers. The stars shimmered behind him in Fliss's unfocused gaze. He dropped his hands to his sides, and the chill of the night air whispered its way between them. They stood in silence. Fliss wanted to say something flippant, something to shift the sudden intensity, but for once the words dried in her throat. The longing for him to kiss her again was overwhelming, and so intense was the feeling, she pressed her fingers into the folds of her dress, to prevent herself reaching for him and suffering the hurt of being rebuffed.

Patrick's eyes dropped to her mouth. His hands clenched at his sides.

'I'm sorry,' he said abruptly. 'I shouldn't have kissed you.'

'I see.' Fliss's voice held no warmth in it, or understanding. She didn't see at all. She gave a tiny, hurt shrug. 'It doesn't matter. It was just a kiss.'

Patrick

Patrick sat in his office in the yellow glare of his lamp, tidying away his papers. He shifted the documents around with mechanical movements, eventually ceasing altogether as the thought struck him that Fliss was preparing for bed above him. He thought of the warmth of her mouth on his, the way her body had moulded itself to him, soft and yielding. The urge to climb the stairs and take her in his arms again was overwhelming.

He pressed his hands to his eyes. *Get a grip, man.* He'd spent more than a decade building a life for himself in Dominica, and he fully intended to return. And Fliss would soon be going back to her family and her job. Getting involved at this stage had no part in either of their plans. And on top of everything, hadn't he just told his mother it would be a big mistake to let a member of the Everdene family into their lives?

He scooped his papers into a jumbled heap, switched off his lamp and pushed back his chair. For a second he wished his mother had never invited Felicity Everdene to stay at the hotel, but that thought was banished immediately by a hundred others crowding his mind. The image of Fliss bending into her car the day she arrived to pull out a stuffed giraffe, her determined frown as she mastered the cocktail list, the cheeky grin she flashed at Tomasz as she filled her tray in the canteen, her smile of triumph as she'd flicked stones into the lake…

The lake. Patrick stopped short as he left his office. That was another thing. He'd stopped dwelling so much on the accident. On previous visits home, thoughts of Jacob had never been far from his mind. He'd wake up thinking that Jacob was gone from Emmside, and every view down into the valley reminded him of it. And whenever he forgot, there was always something or someone in the village to bring it all back. Jacob's sister Pauline, who had her brother's brown eyes and quick smile; their English teacher passing by in the street, who said hello without meeting his eyes; a class-mate they'd played rugby with, who'd studiously avoided talking about their school days; the lake itself…

He remembered the way Fliss had repeated Sergeant Willis's words, in that half-hesitant, half-determined way she had some times. "Everyone knows you weren't to blame, no matter what your dad said afterwards."

He tested the words on his tongue, anticipating all the feelings of shame and guilt he associated with that day to come flooding back to him. He waited. Nothing. He repeated the words again in his head. *"You weren't to blame."* For the first time since that terrible day, the weight of responsibility slid from his shoulders like a physical thing, vanishing into the earth beneath him. He let the words run through his mind one more time, trying out the feel of them. *"You weren't to blame."* He almost stood straighter. And as if she were really beside him, he sensed Fliss's eyes light up.

He flicked off the overhead light and made for the hotel annexe and his rooms. For the first time since he was a teenager, he was actually looking forward to waking up to another day at the Cross Hotel.

Chapter Sixteen

Fliss

Fliss glanced at the enormous bacon sandwich on Johnny's tray. His lunch was a sure sign he was hungover. When he looked up, his pale face and shadowed eyes confirmed it.

'How's your head?' she asked.

'Nothing a cheese and bacon butty won't cure.' He dribbled a generous amount of brown sauce on the contents. 'How was prison?'

'I got time off for good behaviour. And Sergeant Willis is coming to the Tudor night.'

'So all's well that ends well.' Johnny picked up his sandwich and took a large bite.

Fliss didn't answer immediately. She thought of the way the evening had actually ended, with Patrick's kiss-that-wasn't-a-kiss. She lowered her eyes to her bowl of soup and gave a non-committal shrug. 'I suppose so.'

With all the single-mindedness of a man who had no other concerns except his own, Johnny patted her hand. 'Don't sound so down,' he said. 'I've thought of a way to get Pauline back. And it's all thanks to you.'

'Oh?' She picked up her slice of bread and dipped it in her soup. 'I can't think I did anything helpful last night.'

'Well, you did. You made me see everything from Pauline's point of view. You said what she was looking for now was a boyfriend who'd be a good dad and not just a good laugh. It made me think a bit. It's time I stopped messing around and applied myself to my job here. Patrick's already given me more to do, and I've got some ideas for how I can take on more responsibility and bring in extra money for the hotel at the same time.' He took another large bite of his sandwich and mumbled through the crumbs. 'Hopefully get myself a rise and a lot more tips, too.'

'All these ideas on a hangover? I'm impressed.'

Johnny wiped his hands on his napkin. 'They are brilliant ideas,' he said modestly. 'But it was mainly down to you.'

Out of the corner of her eye Fliss noticed Patrick enter the canteen. He was making a beeline in their direction. She dropped her eyes to her bowl, annoyed with herself for the flush she could feel rising on her cheeks. With a few strides, Patrick stood beside their table. He greeted Fliss briefly, his face empty of expression, then turned to Johnny.

'Could I have a word when you've finished?' he asked. 'In my office?'

Johnny gave him a look of surprise. 'Yeah, of course. There's something I wanted to talk to you about, anyway.'

'Good.' Patrick gave them both a curt nod and left.

'That's a coincidence,' Johnny said cheerfully. 'Now I can tell him what my plans are.'

Fliss put her head in her hands. 'Johnny, don't go blundering into it like a bull in a china shop. I don't think Patrick's in a very good mood.'

'Oh?'

Johnny's puzzled expression almost caused Fliss to laugh, despite herself. Did he really have so little idea of what was going on around him? 'No,' she said. 'I don't think he is. He wasn't very happy that you went home and left me alone at the police station. So listen to what he's going to say first, before you leap in with what you want.'

Johnny continued to look a bit nonplussed. 'OK. But I don't know why he'd be so annoyed. Seems to me you had everything under control.' He rose to his feet, and would have picked up his tray, but Fliss placed a hand over his.

'And Johnny, tell him about Pauline,' she added. Johnny gave a vehement shake of his head, but Fliss pressed his fingers. 'Tell him, Johnny. I know she wants to keep it to herself for now, but Patrick won't tell anyone else if you ask him not to. And it's for the best. Believe me.'

Patrick

Fliss was behind the bar and didn't hear Patrick come in. She was reaching up to replace one of the optics, humming a tune to herself. For a second or two Patrick revelled in the luxury of watching her. Her head was tilted up, and her slim arm outstretched. She was giving the job the same attention she gave everything. When the bottle of cognac was positioned to her satisfaction, she took a step back.

'There,' she said, wiping her hands on her apron.

Patrick cleared his throat and she whirled round.

'For goodness' sake. You gave me the fright of my life.'

'You look well.' He put his head on one side. 'For someone who spent the night drinking and brawling.'

She touched a hand to her cheek, looking a little sheepish. 'Thanks. I don't feel too bad. Just a small bruise. I slathered it in concealer so as not to frighten the guests.'

He stepped forward. 'You're bruised? Why didn't you say?' He reached out a hand to touch her face, and she flinched. Patrick dropped his arm, feeling his colour heightening. 'I didn't realise you'd been hurt.'

'It's nothing,' Fliss said, at almost the same time.

They stood and looked at one another awkwardly. Then Patrick went on, 'I spoke to Johnny after lunch. About what happened last night. I was pretty annoyed about him going home and leaving you. I don't think he could see what the problem was. I'm sure you know by now sometimes Johnny can be a bit single-minded, but at least I tried.'

Fliss gave him a small smile. 'Good of you to look out for me.'

'No problem.'

There was another awkward silence. Patrick tugged on the bow tie of his maître d' suit. The truth was he'd had an intense conversation with Johnny after lunch, in which Johnny had been singing Fliss's praises, telling him how she had restored his faith in the hotel – restored his faith in himself, even. It was unusual for Johnny to be so earnest, and Patrick had actually been quite moved. He wanted to tell Fliss just how much her presence in the hotel meant to everyone – how much she meant to him – and was about to speak when Fliss rushed in first.

'I spoke to my mum this afternoon,' she said, 'and I'll have to be getting back home soon.'

Patrick swallowed. Of course he'd always known Fliss would go home sooner or later. The thought of her absence left a chill. His next words sounded far more stiff than he'd intended.

'You've already been more than generous with your time,' he said. 'I hope everything's OK at home?'

She gave a small shrug, her face clouding. 'To be honest, I don't know. My mum says everything's fine, but I can tell something's on her mind. It could be this legal action in Germany – although my dad says there's nothing at all to worry about. Or it could be – ' She frowned. 'I know they've been having a few problems with my sister. She's refusing to go to residential school. But when I asked my mum about it, she just laughed. She said it was all fine and they were looking at some other options, and for me not to worry about it. I'd really like to stay for the Tudor night, after all the planning we've put in. But after that…'

Her voice trailed off, and Patrick said quickly, 'Of course, you must be needed at home.' He paused. 'You'll be missed.'

Fliss concentrated on arranging the glasses on the bar. 'I suppose you'll miss my chatter when I'm gone,' she said, her attention on her task.

'Not just that.'

She raised her head. Her blue eyes were hazy. Patrick felt a lump in his throat. What he'd give to beg her not to go.

Instead, he made a ridiculous attempt at humour. 'That's not the only thing I'll miss,' he said. 'After you've gone, I'll have to get another barmaid, at least until Pauline's decided whether she wants to come back to work. Apparently she's pregnant.'

A burst of conversation in the lounge signalled the arrival of the first guests. Patrick picked up his tray. He hovered with it for a second or two, wanting to add something more, but could think of nothing else to say.

He made his way into the lounge, greeting the guests with a smile that felt false.

Chapter Seventeen

Fliss

The next morning Fliss told Jilly of her plans to leave after the Tudor party. Jilly's brave attempt to hide her disappointment was almost too much to bear. She had begun to unfurl out of her depression since Fliss's arrival. Her face had more colour to it, and there was a briskness of purpose about her that was in stark contrast to her previous lethargy. Instead of listlessly following Patrick's directions, she now had ideas of her own for the hotel, and she'd begun to look forward to the future with enthusiasm.

'So soon? Oh, well, of course you can't stay here for ever.' Her forced cheeriness made Fliss feel even worse. 'Your father must need you back by now, and we've taken advantage of you for far too long. It would be selfish of me to try and stop you. It's just that you've made such a difference here, darling, and Patrick – well,' she went on, her voice trembling. 'I haven't seen such a difference in Patrick for years.'

It was then her face crumpled.

Fliss took her hand. The mention of Patrick brought a lump to her own throat. She squeezed Jilly's fingers. 'Patrick seems better to me, too. When I first arrived, he seemed quite withdrawn. Now he's actually started fighting for the hotel. He's like a different person.'

'It's not just the hotel. Patrick has so much more time for other people since you've been here. He doesn't do all that brooding. Oh, dear.' Jilly brought out a tissue from her sleeve

170

and dabbed at her nose. 'And after you've gone, next thing he'll put the hotel in the hands of a manager and go back to Dominica anyway, and neither of you will ever see each other again.'

Fliss regarded Patrick's mother in astonishment. What on earth did it matter to Jilly that she and Patrick wouldn't see each other again? She tried to think of an answer, but failed. Since arriving at the Cross Hotel, she thought wryly, being reduced to silence was becoming a regular occurrence.

At that moment the housekeeper, Jean, pushed open the door of the lounge, closely followed by two of the chambermaids. Fliss was saved the necessity of trying to think of a reply. Jilly made one last dab at her eyes and straightened herself. This was the day they'd put aside for the refurbishment of the lounge, and they had only a short time to do it. Everything had to be ready and in place for the guests' breakfast the following morning, which meant they had twenty-four hours. The dining-room would be out of bounds to guests for the evening meal, but as the weather was set to be fine, Tomasz had suggested providing a barbecue for everyone outside. His idea had proved so popular all the guests had signed up, along with quite a few locals from the village. Heaters and screens had been set up on the terrace, and everyone hoped the evening would stay mild enough to be a success.

With the dinner arrangements in Tomasz's and Patrick's capable hands, and breakfast cleared away, Jilly and Fliss had time to concentrate on getting the lounge made over at record speed.

'First thing is to get these curtains down.' The look on Fliss's face as she surveyed the offending drapes caused Jilly to chuckle, despite her unhappiness. Fliss put a finger to her lips, adding in a mock whisper, 'But not a word to Patrick, don't forget.'

Jean and the chambermaids, Sarah and Clare, nodded in unison.

'Mum's the word,' Jean said, with a grin.

After that, Fliss and Sarah made their way to the basement to fetch a couple of step-ladders. It was the first time Fliss had visited this room since she'd been down here with Johnny on the day of her arrival. Once again she was struck by the unique beauty of the tiled walls. She couldn't help wondering if Patrick had anything in mind for the magnificent swimming-pool, and if he intended to reopen it at some stage. Then she remembered with a wrench that in just a few weeks Patrick's plans would be none of her business. The thought was thoroughly depressing. She hoisted her ladder onto her shoulder and made her way back up the stairs.

Luckily, there was plenty of work to be done in the lounge, and more than enough to keep Fliss from dwelling on her own miserable thoughts. In less than an hour, they'd taken down all the curtains, letting in a glorious burst of soft light. They removed the fading and dated canvases and prints from the walls, leaving rectangles of pale colour behind them, and pushed all the furniture back to so that they could give the carpet a thorough clean. There were dust-sheets over everything and several pots of paint stood in one corner, ready to give the walls a fresh coat.

'There.' Fliss stood back. 'Now we can really start to make a difference.'

Jilly's distress of the morning was momentarily forgotten. Her expression was bright as she joined Fliss in examining the room. 'Wonderful. And now how about if I get on with taking down the curtains in the rest of the hotel? Do you think you can manage here for a while?'

Fliss assured her she could. Jean announced that she was "far too old to be running up and down ladders with a paintbrush" and followed in Jilly's wake, leaving Sarah and Clare to collect a paint pot each and start work.

Patrick

When Patrick entered the lounge he found Fliss at the top of a ladder, head tilted right back as she painted the ceiling, her blond hair wrapped in a scarf. Sarah and Clare stood on either side of the room, rollers in hand, tackling the walls. All three of them were painting in time to the music belting out of a radio positioned in the middle of the floor. They were singing along to an R&B track. The loudest and most tuneless voice of all belonged to Fliss.

For a couple of seconds Patrick stood in the doorway, listening to Fliss's enthusiastic singing with a downturned smile on his face. When she put down her brush and climbed down a couple of rungs, he realised her slim legs were spattered with tiny flecks of paint. Her feet were bare. She was wearing a pair of shorts that just skimmed the tops of her thighs.

Patrick cleared his throat. The music boomed on. 'Anyone home?' he called.

Fliss let out an unladylike oath and grabbed hold of the top of her step-ladder. She turned precariously and looked down at him. 'Can you not creep up on people?'

She made her way down all the rungs to the floor, where she stood gazing up at him. With her scarf wrapped round her hair, despite the paint spatters she glowed with life, like a poster for a 1950s film star.

'What do you think of the colour?' She indicated the walls, where the chambermaids were applying a delicate shade of blue. 'Jilly and I chose it. I think it looks just like the sky when it touches the hills.' She turned slightly, surveying the sky visible through the open door to the terrace. 'I'd never seen a blue like it until I came to the Lakes. This shade's exactly right. Once everything's back in place, it will look stunning.'

Patrick examined the spread of colour without answering.

'Don't you like it?' She waited, head on one side, anxious for his reaction.

'No, it's not that.' Interior design wasn't a subject Patrick knew a great deal about. He spent most of his working life in a boat or under water. Now he examined the walls doubtfully. 'I just wondered – I mean, won't that blue clash with the curtains?'

To his surprise, Fliss glanced away, and her cheeks became a little pink. 'It'll dry a different colour,' she told him, a little too quickly. One of the chambermaids stifled a giggle.

Something wasn't quite right. Patrick frowned. 'Do you happen to know why my mother and Jean are taking down all the curtains in the hotel?'

'Didn't they tell you? They're taking them for cleaning.'

Fliss looked for all the world like a child caught chewing gum in class. She was a hopeless dissembler. There was the sound of footsteps in the corridor mingled with Jilly's laughter, and then his mother and Jean were in the room.

'Patrick, what do you think?' Jilly spread her arms wide, indicating the new paint. 'Doesn't it look wonderful? So clever of Fliss to choose this colour.'

Patrick registered the enthusiasm in his mother's voice and the lightness to her step. Not for the first time he noted how Fliss seemed to cheer people around her with effortless ease. She was looking up at him with an anxious expression, and he couldn't help feeling like a grumpy old man for questioning her.

Jilly, too, was looking at him expectantly. He smiled at them both. 'It's going to look great. I just came to see if there's anything I can do, but it looks like you have everything under control.'

'Thanks for the offer, darling, but I think we can manage. Don't you, Fliss?'

Fliss nodded and began to climb back up her step-ladder. Patrick kept his eyes from following her bare legs.

'In that case,' he told Jilly, 'I'll go and help Johnny set up a beer barrel outside.'

He made for the door. As he left the room, someone turned up the music to its previous volume, and Fliss began a rendition of *All the Single Ladies* that held more in enthusiasm than it did in tunefulness. For the rest of the afternoon, the song remained stuck in Patrick's brain.

Chapter Eighteen

Fliss

The sound of the guests arriving filtered through the terrace door, along with the delicious smell of Tomasz's spiced lamb, roasting on the barbecue. Fliss's stomach rumbled. The sun was hanging just above the fells, warm and golden, and long shadows were creeping down the valley. Jean and the chambermaids had long since gone home.

Tired and grimy, Fliss surveyed the lounge with satisfaction. The carpet was clean and all the furniture moved back into position. The chairs and sofas had been angled closer together than previously, to make the room more cosy. The cushions had new cream covers, and the plastic flowers were gone. In their place were some sprigs of lilac plucked from the shrubs lining the terrace. The fireplace was bare of all its clutter, and the grate and tiles had been polished.

The last remaining job was to hang the artwork. It had taken two coats of paint to cover the previous shade, and the walls still glistened wet in patches. Fliss made her way to where a group of framed paintings were ranged in a line against one wall, ready for hanging. The artwork had been provided by a local arts class. It had been Jilly's idea, and the class members had been delighted to offer their paintings for sale. It was the perfect arrangement – the artists had an outlet for their work, and the Cross Hotel strengthened its ties with the local community.

Fliss planned to get up first thing the next day, so that she and Jilly could have all the artwork hung before the guests came down for breakfast. Now she examined the line of sketches and watercolours, and once more her eye was drawn to a particular oil painting. She'd been much struck with the work when Jilly first brought it in. She picked it up to examine it more closely. The painting showed a view of the lake, taken, Fliss was sure, from the same spot where she'd first met Patrick as he leaned against the stone wall, looking down into the valley. It was a simple but arresting image. The mountains were a soft meld of greys and greens, with the blue of the sky the only other colour. In the centre lay the lake, a subtle, glowing green, like a living creature.

Fliss was tilting the painting, absorbed, when Patrick came in through the open terrace door.

'I came to see if you'd like something to eat,' he said. 'And I brought you this.'

He held a glass of beer in each hand. He'd left off his waiter's jacket and bow-tie for the barbecue and was dressed casually in black jeans and a white T-shirt. His arms were dark against the white of his shirt, and his tan was another reminder that Patrick's home wasn't actually here in the Lakes, but in the Caribbean.

'I thought you might need a drink, after all your hard work.'

They touched glasses, and Fliss took a few thirsty sips while Patrick inspected the lounge in amazement.

'What an incredible amount you've done. I can hardly believe it's the same room.'

There was a burst of laughter from the group outside. Jilly's bright laugh was recognisable amongst the others. Patrick turned his head at the sound. 'And my mum is a different person, too,' he went on. 'She'll be very sorry when you leave.' There was a pause, and then he added, 'And so will I.'

Patrick's eyes were on hers, waiting, and she wondered what he was thinking – if he were genuinely sad she was going, or only unhappy because after she'd gone he would lose all her help and advice. She scanned his features for any clue, but there was nothing to be gleaned from the dark eyes and slightly downturned mouth. The fact that he gave nothing away caused her unhappiness to deepen. To change the subject, she placed her glass on a table and bent down to retrieve the oil painting.

She held the scene up for his inspection. 'Don't you just love this? It looked exactly like this the day we first met.' She glanced up at him quickly, aware she'd imbued her statement with a romantic meaning she hadn't intended. 'I mean, it looks just like that day we looked down the valley. It was my first introduction to Emmswater. I thought it was magical.'

Patrick's face was a total blank apart from two small white lines etched either side of his nostrils. Only the hand on his beer glass, gripping it a little too tightly as he studied the painting, gave anything away.

'The colours are excellent,' he said. 'That's exactly how I remember it.'

Fliss tilted the painting towards her, and as she did so, noticed something extraordinary. At first sight, the lake was a shimmering green, but an element of darkest grey – almost black – in the brushstrokes meant that it could also appear a dark, threatening shadow, brooding amongst the splendour of the hills. Your view of it depended on the angle you held the painting to the light.

Fliss remembered too late how the sight of Emmswater must still affect Patrick. 'I'm sorry,' she said quickly. 'Of course a view of the lake wouldn't have the same happy memories for you.'

He smiled, the warmth seeping back into his features. 'It's a beautiful painting. You mustn't think I'm still haunted by Jacob's accident. When you held up that picture, I saw the lake in the same way you might see it. As a powerful thing, and a thing of beauty. For years I've associated the sight of that stretch of water with death. Now when I look at it, it doesn't seem as threatening as it once did.'

Fliss felt a surge of happiness at his answer. It surprised her how relieved she felt, as though she'd been bearing the weight of his grief herself.

'I don't suppose – ' She bit her lip, wondering if she might be taking a step too far, but then decided to risk the question she was burning to ask. 'I don't suppose you'd consider diving in the lake again, whilst you're back?'

He looked down at the beer in his glass. 'I've thought about it.' He swirled the liquid slowly and then looked up, his mouth lifted at the corners. 'You don't give up, do you?'

She smiled back at him. 'That's great you've thought about it. I hope you think about it some more.'

There was the sound of laughter outside. Tomasz's loud voice carried through the open door, calling impatiently for Johnny.

'I'd better go,' Patrick said. 'I've left Johnny for too long. Are you coming?'

She nodded. 'I'll get a shower and change. Don't let all Tomasz's lamb get eaten before I'm back.'

Later, Fliss sat on the terrace with a plate of the chef's mouth-watering barbecue and a glass of red wine. Darkness had fallen quickly, but the shawl around her shoulders and the warmth from the heaters were enough to keep off the evening chill. The guests around her were chatting, voices raised, and Johnny and Patrick were busily weaving between the tables with drinks and desserts. Jilly was deep in animated conversation at another table with one of her friends from the village. Fliss turned her head to look down into the valley, where the lights at the water's edge glittered yellow and orange against the black expanse of the lake. There was a sliver of moon reflected in the water, and she glanced up and saw a patch of stars peeping through where the clouds had parted.

She took a sip of her wine. It was a perfect evening. Perfect in everything, apart from the fact that soon she would be leaving, and that she was thoroughly miserable.

Patrick

The balmy night of the barbecue signalled the beginning of a rare heatwave in the Lake District. For the next few days a sultry sun glowered down on Emmswater, causing the lake's surface to glitter like tin foil. The lush fields flanking the hills began to turn dry and yellow, and at noon the sheep clustered below the dry stone walls, wilting in their shade.

Since his return from the Caribbean Patrick had almost forgotten what it was like to feel the sun scorch his skin. Every morning during the week following the barbecue he brought his laptop and paperwork out onto the terrace and would sit there, a steaming cup of coffee beside him, as the heat beat down and warmed his bones. From his vantage point, on several mornings he would see Fliss leave the hotel as she headed out on one of her excursions, dressed in her shorts and walking boots. Her car was back from the mechanics, its engine expensively restored. Agnetha lacked the luxury of air-conditioning, but the heat of the roads didn't seem to bother Fliss in the slightest. She would open her capacious boot and throw in a rug, some guide books, and a tote bag containing a lunch lovingly prepared by Tomasz's own hands. Then she'd put on her sunglasses, glance over at the terrace to give Patrick a smile and a wave, and off she'd go, driving over to Keswick or Ambleside or as far as the sea, or else merely down into the valley to sit and read at the water's edge.

Patrick waved her off one morning and watched her disappear down the hill, all her windows down and her music drifting in her wake, and thought wistfully of her freedom. What he'd give to be driving with Fliss through the Lake District, stopping off wherever they pleased to eat their lunch, or to climb one of the fells, or take a boat out on a lake. With preparations for the Tudor night in hand, and with her part soon to be played out, Fliss was enjoying the chance to go exploring before she left for home. For Patrick, though, even when the Tudor Night was finished his future in the hotel would still stretch ahead of him, and there was plenty to worry about.

One particularly hot morning, after Fliss had waved a cheery goodbye, Patrick gave a deep sigh and forced his attention back to his list of things that needed attention. Number one on his notepad stated: *Hire a barmaid.* With Fliss leaving and Pauline not coming back for the foreseeable future, this was one of his more pressing items, but since Jilly had offered to interview applicants, Patrick was able to tick this one off and move onto the next.

Number two: *wine-tasting evenings*?? This was the idea Johnny had been so eager to tell Patrick about. Apparently the sessions would be a "sure-fire money-spinner" for the hotel. Johnny had tried to convince Patrick that he had the knowledge and drive to see his scheme through. Since this was the very day after Johnny had got blind drunk and abandoned Fliss at a police station, Patrick wasn't in the best of moods to take him seriously.

'So what are you suggesting?' he'd asked him dryly. 'Get out a few bottles of plonk and ask the guests to play guess the wine?'

Johnny had appeared momentarily ruffled, but he hadn't let Patrick's sarcasm dampen his enthusiasm. In fact, to be fair to him he'd gone on to display an astute knowledge of wines, and of the potential market for wine-tasting evenings.

'We could have it all tie in with the Tudor theme, with French clarets and wine from Bordeaux. And I've been in touch with a merchant who's willing to supply us at a discount in exchange for us stocking his wines. I'm convinced something like this could work. There's nothing else like it in our area, and Cameron at the Lakeside doesn't even have a decent wine list.'

There was an eagerness in Johnny's voice that Patrick hadn't heard before. He thought how different Johnny looked when he was fired up about something, and without his perpetual half-sneer. It went against the grain to put a damper on his project, but with the present state of the hotel's finances, he couldn't afford to take risks.

'Have you really thought this through, Johnny?' he asked. 'Bear in mind we're up the side of a mountain. It will be difficult to attract the locals to a wine-tasting, because they won't be able to drink and drive home. And can we persuade staying guests to come all the way to the Lakes to taste wine? It's not exactly what people come here for.'

'No, but I've thought of that,' Johnny countered quickly. 'We have a buffet serving local cheeses and meats, so guests get to sample the produce from local farms at the same time, and they'll be able to buy it to take home. And if they make a weekend of it, they can go walking in the day or take a trip on the lake, or whatever else they want to do.' He waved his hand in the direction of window, dismissing the splendour of the Lake District scenery with all the familiarity of someone who'd lived there all his life.

Johnny's enthusiasm caught Patrick, and he began to give his suggestion serious consideration. Johnny was certainly knowledgeable enough about wine, and his ideas for the hotel's new drinks menu were inspired …but was he reliable? Nothing else the waiter had done so far in the hotel had convinced Patrick that he was. He'd turned up for work hungover on too many occasions, and most days he went about his job with a hangdog look, as though he were doing everyone else a favour by turning up. Patrick suspected his zeal for the project might be more hot air than action.

He took in Johnny's hopeful expression and relented. 'I tell you what,' he'd said, without much hope. 'If you bring me some proper research – and I mean working out a costing, written figures from suppliers, a plan for advertising, the whole works – and show me a way to turn this into more than just an evening's fun, I'll promise to take a look at it.'

Johnny opened his mouth to speak, and Patrick thought for a moment he was about to argue. He was pleasantly surprised when the waiter bit back his retort, drew himself up and nodded. 'You got it.'

Since their conversation, Patrick had heard nothing more. He had written it off as just a whim, one that would blow over as soon as Johnny was required to put any effort into it. He wondered how much longer he should leave the scheme on his list of items requiring attention, and for a moment his pen hovered over it, ready to cross it out, but then he decided a week wasn't really that long. He left *Wine-tasting?* on his list, and moved on to the next item.

The third thing on his list was the swimming-pool. Something Fliss had said about the disused basement had sparked an idea in Patrick's mind which, when it first came to him, he'd put to one side as unthinkable. For the past few days, though, the idea had begun to resurface in his thoughts more and more often. Now it nagged so insistently that in the end he'd given in and written it down on his to-do list. *The swimming-pool?*

He was lost in thought, doodling some fish swimming round the words jotted in his notebook, when he heard the sound of a car draw up in front of the hotel. He glanced over to see Johnny's blond head emerge. Patrick looked at his watch. It was still much too soon for the afternoon shift, which meant Johnny was probably here early to browbeat him again about his idea. Patrick swallowed the dregs of his coffee. He didn't hold out much hope that Johnny would have done anything concrete. Then he noticed the yellow document wallet the waiter was carrying under his arm as he made his way up the stairs of the terrace. He raised his eyebrows.

Johnny came to a halt beside his table and said, without preamble, 'Have you got a minute?'

There was a look of determination on his face. Was he actually going to prove Patrick wrong, after all?

'I'm all yours.' Patrick pushed away his coffee cup and hooked out a chair.

'You asked me to do some research,' Johnny said, dropping into the proffered chair and tapping the folder in front of him. 'And I have. First of all, you told me you didn't want just an evening's entertainment.' He eyed Patrick with a flash of his old challenge. 'Or a night playing "guess the wine," was I think how you phrased it.'

Patrick accepted his comment with a good-natured smile. 'So what have you got?'

He leaned back in his chair, curious, and was pleasantly astonished when Johnny opened the wallet and drew out a series of type-written notes, brochures and leaflets.

'I had a long hard think about what you said, and I realised we could make it more educational. Still a fun weekend, but with the emphasis on really learning about wine. We could run different sessions, some tailored for beginners, some for French wines, wines around the world, etc.'

He pushed one of the brochures in Patrick's direction. 'See, take a look at this. There's a hotel in Yorkshire that does something similar. I checked their online bookings, and all their courses are sold out for months. If they can get people interested, I don't see why we can't.'

Patrick took up the document and flicked through it. 'Looks good. Do you really think you can pull off something similar? I mean you've got the knowledge, I don't doubt that, but what about suppliers? Who do we go to? And, more important,' he pushed the brochure back towards Johnny, 'can it make any money? Because quite honestly, we have to turn things around here. If we don't...'

He gave a shrug, and Johnny's answering nod seemed to mark a shift in the relationship between them. For perhaps the first time, they regarded one another as equals in the fortunes of the hotel, and not just two people at loggerheads.

'There are several suppliers I could use,' Johnny told him. 'I've checked out a few places, and this one stands out.' He pulled out one of the leaflets from his wallet. 'It's not one your dad ever went to when he was here, but to be honest, your dad stuck with the same supplier for years, and they charged him over the odds because they knew he wouldn't go anywhere else. Basically, he was being ripped off. I tried to discuss it with him, but – ' He lifted his shoulders in a shrug. 'Your dad always thought if it was good enough ten years ago, why change now?'

Patrick could picture the scene: Johnny, the young, enthusiastic waiter he once must have been, with bright ideas for the future, and his dad stamping down on those ideas at every turn. Patrick had been just such a young man as Johnny himself once, and his father's attitude had irked him beyond bearing. Now, with the advantage of a few more years' maturity, he looked back on the past and wondered if his father had been frightened of change. Perhaps that's why he'd clung so desperately to the old ways. Another stab of intense regret ran through him. He would never know, now, or be in a position to help his father see change as an exciting step into the future, and not something to be terrified of.

'I can guess what it must have been like,' he said. 'I'm sorry.'

'Don't be sorry, mate. It wasn't your fault.'

Patrick let Johnny's words settle in his mind. *Not his fault.* Ever since he'd inherited the hotel and become aware of its precarious state, he'd wondered what would have happened if Jacob's accident had never been. If he'd stayed in Emmside, could he have prevailed on his father to alter the path he was going down? Could he have made a difference? Then he thought of the difficulties Fliss was having with her own father, and realised every family had its problems. Family dynamics were a difficult thing. Nothing was ever straightforward. For the second time recently, he felt some of the weight of responsibility slip away from him.

He was so wrapped up in this thought, that it was a while before he realised Johnny was still speaking.

'I'm sorry I was a bit of an arse when you first took over here,' Johnny said, eying him frankly. 'To be honest, I thought you didn't really care about the place and were going to sell up.'

Patrick met his gaze with a rueful grin. 'Ditto. I thought you were a waste of space. I had no idea you were actually so interested in your job.' His smile widened. 'Or is it just the thought of approaching fatherhood that's changed you?'

Johnny shuffled in his seat. 'Well, I've got to think of all our futures now. That's if Pauline will still have me.' The eagerness in his expression vanished momentarily. He shifted his gaze to the view over Patrick's shoulder, where the lake shone blinding white in the sun. 'I'm trying to persuade Pauline to come back here and live with me. I love it here. I've lived here all my life, and I don't want to live anywhere else. But you know, if you really love someone, you'll do anything for them. If Pauline said she wanted me to go and live with her in Birmingham, that's what I'd do if it meant not losing her.' He turned bright eyes on Patrick. 'Do you know what I mean?'

A few weeks ago Patrick would have said no, he had no idea what that felt like. Now his heart gave a lurch, but he said nothing. A couple of awkward seconds passed between them, in that way it did when two men who've never spoken honestly to one another before suddenly open up.

Then Patrick indicated the document wallet lying on the table. 'I tell you what,' he said. 'Why don't we give this a trial run? Let's set a date for it. See if you can get the suppliers to give us an introductory discount. Oh, and ask my mum about organising the advertising. She'll love it.'

Johnny's eyes lit up like a beacon, and to Patrick's surprise a great wave of colour spread over his face. 'Thanks,' he spluttered. 'You won't regret it.' He stood, pushing back his chair and collecting all his papers together, and added, 'You know, ever since Fliss got here everything in this place has been so much better. Jilly's stopped being so tearful, you're not so grumpy, even Tomasz has got a nice word to say from time to time.' He picked up his wallet and looked down at Patrick. 'It's a shame she's got to go.'

Patrick felt again that stab of something sharp in his rib-cage. He swallowed. 'I know. I asked her to stay, but she can't. She has family commitments.'

Johnny nodded. 'She told me.' He hesitated before adding in a rush, 'But how about you? Do you think you might stay now?'

Patrick's to-do list lay in front of him where he'd pushed it to one side, with the third item neatly written in his hand: *swimming-pool?* He studied it for several long seconds without answering.

Then he said, without looking up, 'I don't know. Maybe.'

Chapter Nineteen

Fliss

Fliss was tidying up behind the bar as the last of the guests finished their drinks, while Johnny regaled her yet again with his plans to restore the hotel single-handedly, and at the same time win back Pauline.

'So in the end, Patrick was well impressed,' he told her. 'He said I could get some advertising going with Jilly and give it a shot.'

'Yes, you told me,' Fliss said, polishing a glass and replacing it on the shelf. 'You've only mentioned it around half a dozen times.'

'And anyway,' Johnny went on, oblivious, 'I told him it was good to see a buzz about the place at last. I said a lot of that is down to you. Everything seems different since you got here.'

'Is that what you said?' Fliss turned round at that, forgetting the dish-cloth in her hand. 'And what was Patrick's answer?'

'Oh, I don't know. Nothing much. I can't remember.'

'Oh.' Fliss dropped her gaze. *Nothing much.*

Johnny went on, 'I asked Patrick if he could try and persuade you to stay, but he said you were determined to leave.'

'Oh, well, you know I can't stay here, Johnny.' Fliss turned back and began lining up the glasses on the shelves at random. 'I don't work here. I've already got a job, remember.'

'Yes, well never mind all that,' Johnny said, dismissing Fliss's future with an airy wave. 'You know how Patrick kept on saying he's going to go back to his dive school in Dominica. Going to hire a hotel manager to take his place here when he goes?'

'That seems to be his plan.' Fliss wiped away a speck of dust.

'Well maybe not.'

She stopped messing around with the wine-glasses and stilled. 'What do you mean, maybe not?'

'I mean Patrick's done a great job so far – better than I ever thought he would,' Johnny said generously, 'And so I asked him if he'd thought of staying.'

'And what did he say?'

'He didn't say anything for a bit. Just stared at some doodling on a piece of paper in front of him. And then he said, "Maybe."'

'"Maybe"?' Fliss turned and stared at Johnny.

'That's what I said. He said, "Maybe."'

They both pondered Patrick's words in silence. "*Maybe,*" Fliss thought, in growing wonder. Maybe he might stay! It was incredible how that single word changed everything. From dreading leaving, she now began to turn over in her mind how she might be able to come back and visit, perhaps for weekends – for whole weeks at a time, if she wanted to. Patrick's answer put a totally different complexion on things.

"*Maybe.*"

Fliss smiled broadly. The future lit up with more hope than she'd felt in weeks.

Patrick

The next day Fliss's spark of happiness was blown out, before it could ever become a flame.

Patrick left the hotel early. For days he'd been turning his plans for the swimming-pool round and round in his head, with a mixture of optimism and anxiety. He'd thought about his idea so long, he could no longer decide if it were just a fantasy or could actually be achievable. What he needed was someone impartial to discuss it with. It was impossible to bring up the subject with his mother. She would be wild with joy and eager for him to press ahead, no matter what the risks. And what was worse, if his plan came to nothing she would be plunged back into despair.

And so he'd made another appointment to speak with his bank manager. When he pushed open the door to Alison's office, his old school friend looked up at him warily. Patrick gave her a wry smile.

'Don't worry,' he told her. 'I'm not here for a loan.'

Alison stood to shake Patrick's hand. 'I'm sorry. You know if it were my decision...' She spread her hands helplessly.

He nodded. 'I know, and I appreciate it. But actually, I'm just after your advice.'

'Really?' Alison was curious now, and within a short space of time, Patrick had spread his folders over the desk, and they were going through them. Patrick had some photos on his tablet of the hotel's swimming-pool and basement, and as he flicked through them to show Alison what he intended, the bank manager's curiosity changed to surprise.

She raised her head and looked Patrick in the eye. 'You know, I always knew you had it in you to turn this place around, Patrick. If I could have lent you the money you needed out of my own pocket, I would have done. I'm not sure why you need my advice. You've got all the experience, and it seems to me you've thought all this through. This could actually be a real go-er.'

Patrick leaned back in his chair, relieved to have Alison's approval. He hadn't realised how much he needed someone else's independent validation.

'Thanks. I got the idea from something Fliss said about restoring the basement. I guess I just needed someone to bounce my thoughts off. I've been going over the plans in my mind so long, I'd stopped knowing if they made sense or not.'

Alison laughed. 'Yeah, I guess that can happen. And what does Fliss think to it?'

Patrick gave a non-committal shrug.

'I mean, surely you've asked her?' she pressed him. 'She's an expert in the hotel trade. She seems the ideal person to discuss it with.'

'Actually, I haven't mentioned it to her. To be honest – ' Patrick halted, wondering how much he should reveal, and then decided he could trust his old friend. 'I can't tell you how much Fliss has done for us in the short time she's been here. The idea for the Tudor Night was all hers. I hope you and Guy are coming to that, by the way?'

Alison told him Guy wouldn't miss it, and that they'd already picked out their costumes.

'That's great. The Tudor Night has given my mother a new lease of life. And you won't recognise what's been done in the lounge. Fliss was the force behind getting it all spruced up. It looks a different room.'

'Sounds like she's transformed the place. So what's the problem?'

'It's not Fliss.' Patrick's lips twisted. 'Does it sound suspicious if I say I don't trust her father?'

'Ah.' Alison frowned. 'I see.'

'I mean Fliss has been absolutely brilliant,' Patrick added quickly. 'I honestly don't know what we'd have done without her in the past few weeks. But the thing is, the hotel's vulnerable. We're still in a lot of debt. I need time to fix it. If James Everdene cottons on to how profitable we could be, and gets an idea into his head that we'd actually be a good addition to his portfolio instead of a liability – well, as things stand at the moment, I don't know if I'd be able to fend him off.'

'No.' Alison tapped her fingers together thoughtfully. 'I certainly wouldn't like to tangle with James Everdene. As your bank manager, I'd have to agree, discretion is the best policy.' She was quiet for a moment or two, and then she looked up sympathetically. 'As a friend, though, I'd have to say it's a pity. I've met Fliss a couple of times in the village, and I've heard a lot about her. Willy thinks she's the bee's knees, and there aren't many people Willy takes to. It does seem a shame not to take her into your confidence.'

'Perhaps you're right. The thought of the hotel drifting out of my family's hands and becoming part of the Everdene chain, though...' He shook his head. 'Well, it's something I can't contemplate.'

Alison was forced to agree. After that, their conversation wandered away from the hotel business. They chatted for a while about Patrick's time in the Caribbean, Alison's children and her husband Guy, and then they shook hands with promises to talk again at the Tudor night.

Alison's endorsement of his project had raised Patrick's spirits, and when he arrived back at the hotel he entered the reception feeling a lot more light-hearted than he had done when he left. His relaxed mood wasn't to last. He did a double-take as he walked through the door. Something was different. The old cork board with its messy display of leaflets was gone, but he'd already noticed that. His mother and Jean had taken it down when they refurbished the lounge. They'd also taken away the row of stiff-backed chairs that had been ranged against the wall, and in their place they'd moved in a comfy sofa and some scatter cushions. All this had been done several days ago. So what was new?

And then Patrick noticed the light, slanting in a haze across the tiled floor. He turned to face the window. Where once the ageing puce velvet had hung, there was now a beautiful blue damask silk, draped loosely over a gold hook. He made his way to the window and fingered the fabric in astonishment.

One of the chambermaids was manning the reception desk. He sensed her watching him covertly for his reaction, and he dropped the fabric back into its hook and turned to face her.

'Who put this up, Sarah?' he asked

Sarah gave a small, knowing smile, as though she were privy to a secret Patrick knew nothing about. 'Some guys came today to hang them all,' she told him.

'*All?* Do you mean there are more?'

He tried his best to keep the rising anger from his voice, but something of it must have shown in his expression. The smile vanished from Sarah's face and she gave him an uncertain nod.

Patrick objected to secrets being kept from him in his own hotel. He'd also specifically said – several times – that the accounts couldn't run to the expense of new curtains. But Sarah was looking at him anxiously, and so he merely asked her if she knew where he could find Jilly.

'She's upstairs. With Jean.'

Patrick nodded his thanks and made his way through the lounge – where a stunning series of drapes in the same blue silk was now hanging at the windows – along the corridor and up the staircase. At every window he passed, the stately fabric fell in expensive folds. They transformed the hotel from a shabby place into something extraordinary, drawing the eye to the windows and the view beyond, but as Patrick mounted the stairs a sick feeling ran through him. Surely his mother couldn't have lavished a fortune on new curtains, despite everything he'd said? How on earth did she think they were going to pay for them? He knew she'd been vague since his father had died, but he'd never imagined her capable of such extravagance. He reached the top of the stairs, his anger mingling with concern, and paused to take a couple of deep breaths.

Jilly and Jean stood beside the linen cupboard, each holding the end of a white sheet, which they'd opened out between them. Jilly was examining the fabric, a frown marring her brow. When she heard Patrick approach, she looked up, and her frown immediately became a smile. Instead of assuaging his anger, her cheerfulness only fanned the flames.

His mother held up the sheet for his inspection. 'Jean and I were just going through some of the linen. Some of it's getting quite worn in places. We were wondering if the accounts might run to half a dozen new sheets.'

'New sheets? Why not? Our finances appear to be a bottomless pit. I tell you what, let's redecorate all the bedrooms, too. And while we're about it, how about Prada uniforms for the chambermaids?'

Patrick heard the sarcasm in his voice, and hated himself for it. His mother stared up at him, bewildered.

'It's a few sheets, Patrick. Whatever's the matter?'

He pointed down the corridor, to where the sun was filtering through the windows. 'The curtains. Where the hell did they come from? Didn't I say we couldn't afford to replace them?'

'Oh, that.' His mother looked up at him, relieved. 'Don't they look fabulous? It's a surprise. We thought you'd be pleased. And there's no need whatsoever to worry about the cost. Fliss paid for them.'

For full thirty seconds Patrick was thunderstruck. He stared down at his mother, speechless. His expression must have revealed his emotions all too clearly. The housekeeper decided to beat a discreet retreat. She took the sheet from Jilly's hands.

'I tell you what, Jilly, why don't I take these downstairs and put them with the others. I'll wait to hear what you decide.'

Patrick hardly noticed Jean disappear down the corridor. He tried – and failed — to keep the anger from his voice. 'You mean Fliss, without consulting me, has bought new curtains and hung them in my hotel?'

Jilly's shoulders sagged. 'Oh dear, it's all my fault. She knew how much I loved the fabric when I saw it in the swatch. I said you didn't want to pay for new curtains, and she said it was no problem at all. She said she'd buy it for us, only not to tell you, and to let it be a surprise.'

Not to tell him. Patrick breathed out slowly. 'It's not your fault, Mum, of course it isn't. I'm sure Fliss meant it for the best.' He wasn't sure of this at all, but he kept that opinion to himself. 'I'm sorry I got so annoyed. It came as a bit of a shock.' He glanced over to where the curtains hung in all their splendour. God knew how much it must have cost. Far too extravagant for a gift, surely? He shook his head, anxiety gripping him again. 'Where is Fliss?'

'She went out half an hour ago, down to the village.' Jilly put her hand on his arm. 'Patrick, you're not really cross with her, are you? She only did it to please me.'

'If you're happy, I'm happy.' Patrick attempted a smile. 'If you see Fliss before I do, could you ask her to come and see me? I'll be in my office.'

'Yes, of course. Although I'm sure she'll come and see you, anyway. We've all had some exciting news this morning while you were out.'

'Oh?' Another bad feeling ran through Patrick. He wasn't sure how much more excitement he could take.

'Yes, Helen Everdene phoned.' Jilly almost bounced on her toes with excitement. 'She and James are coming to stay with us the weekend after the Tudor Night. And they're bringing Minnie with them. Isn't that wonderful?'

Patrick closed his eyes. He had a vision of everything he'd been working for sliding just out of his grasp. And at the same time he finally realised - with all the certainty that had been lacking up to this point - just how much holding on to the Cross Hotel meant to him.

Chapter Twenty

Fliss

An hour later Fliss trod lightly into the hotel's reception, in her arms a bunch of blue and white freesias she'd bought for Jilly at the market in the village. Their scent was delicious, and in a vase on the desk in reception they'd look just right against the new curtains. She glanced round with a happy smile as the door to the hotel swung shut behind her. Everything appeared so much more welcoming in the entrance than the day she'd first arrived. The difference was amazing, if she said so herself. Her stay at the Cross Hotel had given her new confidence. Working in the hotel trade was what she was good at, and, in the right circumstances, she loved it. She was excited, too, that her parents would be coming to visit – although when she'd first taken the call from her mum, she'd been taken aback, and more than a little worried. Her parents never took an impromptu break from work. Their holidays were scheduled in with all the precision of a military manoeuvre. And for her father to leave the business for a whole weekend on a whim was unheard of.

'Yes, of course we're fine, darling,' her mother had reassured her. 'Don't sound so surprised. We've heard so much from you about the Cross Hotel, we just wanted to see it for ourselves. And Minnie's missing you like mad. We all are. We thought we could have a weekend up there with you, and then all travel home together.'

Travel home. Even those words didn't make Fliss as sad as they had done. Not now she knew Patrick might be staying.

Already, she was thinking up reasons to come back and visit.

'Hi Sarah,' she said. 'Is Jilly around? I bought her these.' Fliss held out the flowers to the girl on reception. 'Don't they smell gorgeous? I'm going to find a vase for them. They'll just go with the new curtains. What do you think?'

Sarah's smile at the sight of Fliss faltered at the mention of the curtains. 'Patrick asked me to tell you to go and see him in his office when you came in.'

'Oh.' Suddenly, all Fliss's cheerfulness drained away. Sarah was looking at her with a mixture of sympathy and trepidation. Fliss took in the windows, where the silk curtains were hanging. She'd wanted to make Jilly happy, but now the thought struck her that maybe Patrick might not look at it in quite that light.

She clutched the bunch of flowers to her and made her way down the corridor to Patrick's office. With every step her nerves increased. Fliss was very seldom called to account for her actions, and when she was, she found it a very unpleasant experience. She remembered the day she and her best friend had been summoned to the headmistress's office at boarding school and asked to explain how the entire netball team's pristine white kit was now an eye-catching shade of fuchsia pink. Fliss had thought dyeing their shorts and shirts would improve team morale. Mrs Chadwick hadn't agreed. The telling-off Fliss received had stayed in her mind for a long time. Mrs Chadwick – or "Chadders", as she was known - had informed Fliss she was "well-meaning, but far too inclined to go her own way," and had muttered something about her being her father's daughter, which Fliss had taken exception to. A row had broken out. When Fliss's parents were told, her dad had laughed. He'd given the school enough money to buy new kit for several netball teams. The only lesson Fliss had learned from the experience was the value of family loyalty, and that her father would always back her up if she was in trouble.

She arrived outside Patrick's office to find his door shut. Her unease grew. The closed door was an ominous sign. It was most unlike Patrick to shut himself away. She knocked, and his voice filtered through. He sounded unusually abrupt. Fliss pushed the door open and put her head round.

'Did you want to see me?'

Patrick

Everywhere Patrick looked there was blue silk. It was as if his hotel had been taken over by a stranger. And now James Everdene was on his way. Patrick felt cold tentacles reaching out to clutch at him. Just when he'd resolved to put his plans for the hotel into place and could actually see a future in Emmside, was this the beginning of everything slipping away from him? He had a terrible fear that he'd left everything too late.

When Fliss put her head round the door, clutching a bunch of blue flowers, the look of guilt on her open features did nothing to relieve his anger.

'Take a seat,' he said.

There was a coldness in his voice he didn't recognise. Fliss heard it and flinched, but then her head went up, and that stubborn look crossed her features. Fliss probably wasn't used to being summoned to someone's office, Patrick thought, or to being told what to do, but this was his hotel. He sat perfectly still, his eyes fixed on hers.

After a moment's hesitation, Fliss drew out the chair opposite and sat down, resting the flowers on her lap. She gave Patrick one of her bright smiles.

'It's about the curtains, isn't it? I bought them as a gift for Jilly. I noticed her looking through a swatch of fabrics, and it was the first time I'd seen her actually look interested in anything, up to that point, and so we got chatting, and I could tell she'd really love to be able to replace your curtains, if she had the money, although of course she didn't say anything outright – '

'I understand all that.' Patrick didn't smile back. 'You do realise this hotel actually belongs to me? And I'd like to know why you've contacted suppliers and had curtains made up and installed in my hotel without asking me first?'

A wave of painful colour suffused Fliss's face. She opened her mouth to speak, but Patrick didn't give her the chance.

'I can guess why you didn't mention it.' His voice was taut with anger. 'It's because you knew I wouldn't agree. So you thought you'd just go ahead and do it anyway.'

'I wanted to do something to cheer Jilly up. I thought once you saw how happy she was – '

'That I wouldn't be able to say no,' Patrick finished for her.

'That's not how it was. ' The flowers on her lap trembled, shedding a few petals to the floor.

Patrick swept on, his voice icy. 'I can guess how it was. I know you're accustomed to taking over hotels and running them the way you want – '

'*What?*' She sat up straight, with a gasp.

'But this is actually my hotel. It belongs to me. It hasn't been taken over by the Everdene chain, and while I'm in charge it will be run as I see fit.'

'As you see fit? If it weren't for me you'd be selling this place up and hightailing it back to the Caribbean.' Fliss jabbed a finger at him. 'You told me you had no intention of staying. So don't come all high and mighty now about the place belonging to you. It might in theory, but in practice you couldn't care less about it.'

Patrick's chair scraped harshly against the floor as he rose to his feet. 'I think you'd better leave.'

Fliss stood too, the bunch of flowers falling from her lap to the floor, unheeded. Her face was white.

'I'm sorry I made you angry,' she said, her eyes overbright. 'But try and remember how the hotel was when I first got here. How defeated Jilly looked.' She clasped her fingers together. 'You must see how it's changed. Everywhere you go people are cheerful. They're enthusiastic about working here. They can see a future, and they have some hope in it.'

Patrick heard the truth in what Fliss was saying. Her eyes were fastened on his, wide and shining. The anger he'd felt ebbed away, and he was left with just the nagging unease. He came round to the front of his desk and picked up her fallen flowers, placing them carefully on the desk.

'You mustn't think I'm not grateful for everything you've done,' he said quietly. 'And I don't just mean the hotel. Since you arrived, my mother is a different person. You've changed us. You've changed things for me, too,' he added, with a rush of honesty. 'But this is my hotel. The Cross family hotel. And I'm the one who will be looking after its future.'

Fliss nodded. 'I understand. I'm sorry I acted without telling you. I'll go and pack my bags.'

'What?' Patrick caught her hand and gave an astounded oath. 'I didn't mean you to leave the hotel. I just meant – well, I lost my temper. I wanted you to leave my office, that's all.' He gave her a twisted smile. 'The last thing I want is for you to leave us. I'm sorry I was so angry. You've made my mum – all of us – very happy.'

Fliss turned her fingers in his so that she was returning the clasp of his hand.

'I'm sorry,' she said. 'I should have told you. And you're right, I'm too used to organising things the way I'd like.' She gave a rueful laugh. 'Perhaps you'll be glad to know I'll be leaving soon. My parents are coming the weekend after the Tudor party. I'll be going home with them.'

Patrick dropped Fliss's hand. 'My mother told me they were visiting us,' he said. 'I look forward to meeting them.'

Fliss heard the stiffness in his voice and cast him a doubtful glance. 'They're looking forward to meeting you, too. I've told them all about how much I've loved my stay here. They can't wait to see the hotel.'

Patrick gave a curt nod. 'I'm pleased to hear it.'

She continued to study him, puzzled, and then she gave a small, uncertain smile and held out her hand. 'Are we still friends?'

Patrick took her hand in his and leaned forward to place a soft kiss on her cheek. 'I'd hate to think we'd ever be anything else, whatever happens.'

After Fliss had gone, Patrick sat back at his desk. *Whatever happens.* He had a terrible feeling his words were about to be put to the test. There was only one person who could wreck their friendship, and that was James Everdene.

Chapter Twenty-One

Fliss

Fliss had worked in enough hotels to know you couldn't even blow your nose without all the staff knowing about it. Word spread like wildfire around the hotel that Patrick had been in a towering rage when he discovered the new curtains. When Fliss eventually made her way to the canteen for lunch, Tomasz took in her unhappy expression and knew what was troubling her at once. He brought out a slice of the raspberry cheesecake he normally reserved for guests only.

'Here. Don't tell the others,' he said gruffly.

His sympathy only made Fliss feel worse. When even Johnny patted her on the shoulder as she took a seat next to him, she had to school her chin not to wobble. Patrick's icy expression, and his claim that she was "too used to running things how she wanted", had gone round and round in her mind ever since she'd left his office.

She forced down a few mouthfuls of her healthy bowl of soup and took a desultory spoonful of the cheesecake, but even Tomasz's melt-in-the-mouth dessert failed to make her feel any better.

'Come on, Fliss.' Johnny glanced up at her, concerned. 'It's not like you to be down in the dumps. Take no notice of Patrick. He's a miserable old grump.' A thought occurred to him, and he chuckled. 'Remember that day you arrived, and your necklace got stuck in those horrible old curtains? The look on Patrick's face.' He continued to laugh, with the same high wheeshing noise he'd let out on that day.

Fliss picked up another spoonful of cheesecake and put it back on her plate. The event didn't bring back any happy memories for her. All she could think of was the strain in Patrick's eyes the day she'd met him, and the surprising gentleness in his fingers as he released her necklace.

Johnny eyed her cheesecake. 'Are you not going to eat that?'

She pushed the plate towards him. 'Go ahead.'

His eyes lit up. Taking a large spoonful, he mumbled with his mouth full, 'Well, at least you've got the Tudor Night to look forward to. I can't wait. Got my costume all sorted, and I look amazing, even if I say it myself. Like Henry VIII.' He swallowed his mouthful and added, 'Obviously I mean a young Henry VIII. Before he got fat and beady-eyed.'

His chatter finally forced a smile from Fliss. It was good to see Johnny looking so happy for a change. His plans for getting back together with Pauline must be going well. Fliss was about to quiz him on it when she remembered something else. The smile slipped from her face abruptly. She, too, had ordered a costume, and it was now hanging up in its plastic cover, waiting for her in her room. She'd persuaded Jilly to come with her on one of her recent excursions, and together they'd driven over to a theatre in Keswick that hired out fancy dress. It had been a fun morning. They hadn't been able to resist trying on lots of different costumes from the theatre's extensive collection. They'd taken a few selfies and giggled their way through some of the more outrageous outfits, before picking out something suitable. Then they'd still had time to spare, and so they'd strolled round the shops before going for lunch. Afterwards, they'd packed their costumes in Fliss's old car and driven round the lake, admiring the scenery. It could have been a perfect day, except for Patrick's reaction when they got back. They'd picked him out an outfit at the same time. Fliss had known full well he'd be reluctant to wear it, and she'd been right. He hadn't protested too much, to give him credit, merely rolled his eyes at the sight of the black leggings, feathered hat and heavy cloak. Now Fliss wondered if he'd been thinking she was "running things how she wanted" again.

She sighed and rubbed her temple. 'I think I'll go for a walk, Johnny. Clear my head before our shift starts.'

Johnny nodded at her, distracted by what one of the other waiters had stopped by to tell him, and he turned away to discuss the week's football.

Fliss was making her way through the lounge when she came across Jilly, standing motionless at the window leading onto the terrace. Fliss stopped in her tracks.

'Is everything all right, Jilly?'

Jilly turned, and Fliss was taken aback to see her eyes were full of tears.

'What's happened?' Fliss started forwards.

Patrick's mother gave her a tremulous smile. 'It's nothing. I was just thinking how wonderful this room looks, and how Patrick's father would have been so happy to see how it's been transformed. And so pleased with how Patrick's handling everything, too.'

Fliss squeezed her hand. 'I know. I'm sure Patrick's dad would have loved it.' She looked around at their transformation with a smile, until one of the curtains shifted in the breeze from the window and caught her eye. The silk shimmered in the afternoon sun, and her smile vanished at the sight of it. 'I'm not sure Patrick's so happy about it himself, though,' she added sadly.

Jilly followed her gaze to the curtains. 'No, he seemed very cross to me, darling.'

To Fliss's surprise, instead of appearing cast down at the thought, Jilly's expression brightened. She was looking at Fliss in a thoughtful way.

'Between you and me,' Jilly said, 'I think Patrick's always been a little too used to getting his own way. He can be very strong-willed. When I look back, of course it's no wonder he and his dad didn't get on. And now Patrick runs his own business, well, there's no one to check him at all.' She patted Fliss's hand. 'Not until you came.'

Fliss's mouth fell open, but she had no time to ponder her

words, because Jilly leaned forward conspiratorially and added, 'And I've had some more good news today. I put an advertisement in the local paper for a barmaid, and guess who answered it?' Fliss shook her head, and Jilly said dramatically, 'Joanne from The Lakeside.'

Fliss gave a small gasp. This was dramatic news indeed. Joanne was the old school friend Johnny had mentioned when they had lunch at the Lakeside. She was the one who managed the bar, and by all accounts could take a lot of the credit for turning the hotel into a thriving venue. If Joanne came to work for the Cross Hotel, it would be a fantastic move for them. She was sure to be an asset, and, best of all, might even bring some of the Lakeside's customers with her.

'That's brilliant news.' Fliss beamed. 'So have you interviewed her?'

'Not yet.' Jilly glanced at her watch. 'She's due here in an hour.'

'Wow. If you give her the job today, she might even be with us in time for the Tudor Night.'

'Yes.' Jilly's smile widened. 'And Cameron's invited, too. That should make an interesting evening.'

It was a wicked thought, but Fliss couldn't resist sharing Jilly's amusement. There was something underhand about Cameron, and she hadn't forgotten Johnny's revelation that he was rumoured to be a bully. Besides, it pleased Fliss enormously to see Jilly so diverted.

She pressed Jilly's hand. 'Good luck with the interview. I can't wait to welcome Joanne behind the bar.'

Patrick

Two days after his talk with Fliss, Patrick left the hotel for the lake. He sat down on a damp stone at one end of the shingle beach, in the shade cast by the rock face, and prepared to wait. The air was hot and humid, and several fat flies hovered over the pebbles. Beside him he'd placed a dry-suit and a pair of scuffed, well-worn fins. The sun beat down on the valley, and the green lake shone, the glare on the water so intense it hurt to stare too long. Patrick raised his hand to shade his eyes and looked around him. This was the beach where he'd last kitted up with Jacob, but the summer sun cast it in a completely different light to that day, making it appear another place altogether. On the afternoon Patrick lost his friend there had been clouds over the valley, and the lake had rippled with short, choppy waves.

Patrick took up a pebble as he waited in the hot sun and began to toss it from hand to hand. It was strange how, since he'd returned to the Lake District, all the old, painful memories of this beach were becoming overlaid with bright images of Fliss. Now when he thought of the lake's edge, an image of Fliss came to mind, throwing stones into the water and laughing up at him, eyes shining; Fliss catching hold of his hand in the rain as she ran over the rocks.

He dropped the pebble he was holding, hearing it clatter on the stony beach, and opened his palm, trying to banish his old memories even further by imagining the feel of Fliss's warm fingers on his as she'd pressed his hand. He remembered the sweet sensation of her soft mouth so briefly under his that night on the forecourt outside the hotel. He curled his fingers over, clenching them onto his palm so tightly the nails left an imprint on his hard flesh.

A crunch of feet on the shingle brought Patrick back to his surroundings. He looked up to see Guy Travis making his way towards him. The sight of Alison's husband – his old dive buddy, steady and reliable – eased the tension in Patrick's shoulders. He rose to his feet.

'Long time no see, Paddy.'

Guy's soft Carlisle accent, the humour in his eyes and the wiry strength in his body were just as Patrick remembered. His hair had receded, leaving a long, smooth brow, and the sun had etched several more lines on his face. Patrick noted the changes as they shook hands, and wondered what differences his old dive buddy was finding in him, too, after all these years. Guy's shrewd eyes met his, but he must have been content with what he saw, because he let Patrick's hand fall with a satisfied nod.

'A long time since we last dived Emmswater together.' Guy cast a glance behind him at the lake, whose glassy surface was perfectly still in the sun. 'Bit different from the Caribbean, eh? When was the last time you wore a dry-suit?'

Patrick bent down and picked up the suit, feeling the weight of it in his hands. Unlike wet-suits, dry-suits were insulated and kept cold water out. The suit was heavy and cumbersome. The equipment Patrick had borrowed for diving in an English freshwater lake was far different from what he wore in the warm seas around Dominica.

'I took a trip to the States recently,' he told Guy. 'Dived a few lakes in Michigan with some friends, and then on to Canada.'

Guy gave a whistle. 'That sounds quite a trip. Alison has family in Canada. She's always wanted to go.'

For the next few minutes they fell into a technical discussion on the water temperatures Patrick had experienced in the Great Lakes, depths dived down, and how it compared to lakes in Austria, where Guy and Alison had recently been on holiday with the children.

And then Guy said, 'And now you're home. And you've not dived Emmswater since that last day with Jacob.'

Guy was regarding Patrick in an appraising way, as though trying to guess how much the events of that day were likely to affect him during their dive.

Patrick swallowed, easing the dryness in his throat. 'It's not been easy coming back here, Guy, I admit. But I want to do it.' He thought of his plans for the hotel, the whole future of which hung on his willingness to dive the lake again. He thought of Fliss, who he'd never see again if he left Emmside. He added firmly, 'I *have* to do it.'

Guy nodded, pleased. 'We'll take it nice and steady. Any time you want to come back up, you just give the signal.'

Patrick felt a measure of relief. Guy was the perfect partner for his first dive in Emmswater. Calm and phlegmatic, he was a steadying presence. The terror that hovered like a ghostly presence retreated a little.

They began to kit up, Guy keeping up a low-voiced conversation, his northern accent gently lilting as they pulled on their heavy suits and adjusted the weights on their belts. They checked the computer dials on each other's wrist bands with the efficiency of many years' practice. The dials told them that their cylinders were full. They would indicate the divers' depth and the water temperature once they entered the lake.

Another memory flashed through Patrick's mind – the sour smell on Jacob's breath as he'd examined his dial, and Patrick's suspicion that his friend was hungover.

"OK. But if I come in with you, we don't go over the ledge."

Their last conversation rang in his ears – every word as clear as though it had just been spoken. But now Guy was picking up his fins beside him. He touched Patrick's arm, and together they made their way across that same shingle to the lake where the water lay flat and still. All those years ago, when Patrick had advanced into the water with Jacob as a teenager, a threatening bank of purple cloud had loomed over the far side of the valley. Today the sky was pure blue, and the sun shone bright and golden. Within minutes Patrick felt a trickle of sweat run down his back. His reaction was not just due to the heat of his thick suit. The palms of his hands were sticky inside his gloves. He dropped them into the water in an attempt to cool off as they edged further into the lake.

A dozen or more sideways steps and then Guy and Patrick were under the surface …and nothing, nothing had changed. The cold, green waters closed over Patrick's head. For a terrifying moment he was back, diving with Jacob, all those years ago. Again the sensation of dread and that terrible racing of his pulse, pounding in his ears. Patrick exhaled too rapidly, the bubbles rushing to the surface. Guy finned a little closer to him, his thin brows raised in query. Patrick took a slow breath from his cylinder and expelled it. He raised his hand, index finger and thumb joined in the signal that all was OK.

They began to fin steadily, their outbreaths rising in the familiar silvery, green-tinged bubbles. They passed the fallen tree trunk, still lying on the lake bottom after all this time. A couple of pale fish darted into its shelter as they glided by. When Patrick turned to look behind him, the water was already obscured by their twin trails of silt. Again the memory of that day slammed into him. He turned his attention to the water in front of him, breathing slowly. By his side, Guy was taking in their surroundings, occasionally reaching down to the ledge beneath them to pick up and examine an odd-shaped rock or an old coin lost years since.

In this way they made their way to the rim of the ledge, to where the water plunged away. The nearer they grew to it, the stronger Patrick's heart beat. It was here – right here, where the ledge ended and the rock face climbed out of the water on his right – that Jacob had disappeared, and Patrick's life had changed forever.

He tried to regulate his breathing, taking a few slow pulls on his air tube as he floated beside Guy. The expelled air drifted upwards in a long, gentle stream of bubbles. It was time to decide whether to carry on with Guy, out over the ledge to explore the deeper waters, or to ask him to make the turn and head back for the shore. Guy slowed almost to a halt. He turned his head towards Patrick, a question in his eyes, but Patrick froze, unable to respond. He felt an irresistible urge to stay where they were, hovering over the ledge. It was as though if they just waited here a little longer, Jacob would come swimming up towards them out of the green depths, his eyes wide and mocking, finger and thumb pressed together.

Finally the full force of that terrible day and all its horror washed over Patrick. Today the water was clear for quite some distance, the green stretching ahead as the sun penetrated it, but he felt marooned in the chalky fog that Jacob had stirred up, unable to see a thing before him. His heart lurched wildly as he remembered the cloud of silt that had disorientated him, and how he'd risen above it, casting about in frantic circles for a sight of his friend.

Patrick was jolted from his horror by a sharp tap on the shoulder from Guy. His dive buddy was hovering beside him, an anxious look on his face as he examined Patrick's features. Guy indicated with his thumb in the direction of the rock face. It was time to return to shore. Patrick lifted his own thumb in acknowledgement, and they made the turn, keeping the rock face on their left.

As they passed the wall of rock, Patrick noticed a piece of green glass glinting in a cleft in the stone. He slowed to examine it. It seemed to have been caught in the rock for many years. Its edges were worn smooth by the water. After a couple of attempts, Patrick managed to dislodge it. He scooped it up into his gloved palm. It was a thick chunk, half the size of his palm, worn into the perfect shape of a heart. The glass shimmered in his hand, as though he was holding a piece of warm, green, breathing lake water. How strange to find such a token here, in this very spot where he had lost his friend. If he were given to such fancies, he could almost take it as a token from the lake itself. He slipped the smooth glass into his pouch. It occurred to him that his find was the sort of thing Fliss would love.

As soon as the thought of Fliss entered Patrick's mind, all the horror of his memories vanished. Fliss was real and in the present and totally full of life, far removed from the spot that had been the source of nightmares for years.

As Patrick floated beside Guy, lingering beneath the surface, letting the nitrogen slowly leave his body before they made their final assent, he had plenty of time to reflect. His thoughts led him away from the past and towards the future. With his dive in the lake with Guy, Patrick had laid the first building-block of a new life in Emmside. But life at the Cross Hotel without Fliss would be empty beyond words. The question of whether he could persuade her to stay – and what role the Everdene family would play in their future – was as murky as the silt clouds he'd left on the lake's bottom.

Chapter Twenty-Two

Fliss

'So you see, you should never put the nozzle into the beer glass. It causes cross-contamination. Hold the glass like so,' Joanne tilted the beaker in Fliss's hands to an angle of forty-five degrees, 'and keep your hand at the bottom of the glass, so it won't warm the beer. There.' She gave a smile of satisfaction as Fliss lifted the foaming drink. 'The perfect pint.'

At her interview, Joanne and Jilly had got on brilliantly – so well that Joanne had gone straight back down to the Lakeside to tell Cameron she'd accepted a job at the Cross Hotel. What followed was no surprise to anyone. Cameron had been so incensed he'd told Joanne to pick up her pay slip and leave immediately. So now here she was, teaching Fliss the best way to pour a pint without it frothing over, advising her on how to tell a Shiraz from a Rioja, and how to top an Irish coffee with the perfect layer of cream. Joanne was capable and friendly, and the perfect addition to the staff. The thought should have cheered Fliss, but instead she secretly felt miserable and redundant.

Another result of Joanne's presence was that Patrick was no longer needed to help out with the evening shift. He told Johnny he had a lot to organise with his business partner in Dominica, and, because of the time difference, the evenings were best for them to talk. In the days leading up to the Tudor night, Patrick spent a lot of time glued to the phone in his office. Fliss began to wonder if he were making arrangements to go back to the Caribbean permanently. Whatever was going through his mind, ever since their heated words regarding the new curtains they'd barely spoken to one another.

All in all, it was a lowering few days for Fliss. Several times she wondered if she might as well pack her bags and return home to Norfolk early. It was only Jilly's excitement and enthusiasm for the Tudor party, and the thought of her disappointment if Fliss weren't there to share it, that prevented her.

When the afternoon of the party finally came around, Fliss stood in the dining-room surveying the transformation. The dining-tables had been pushed together to form three long tables, each covered with a dark blue tablecloth that matched the curtains. A separate table was set crossways at their head for Patrick and Jilly and special guests. There were fat white candles running the length of each table, and every setting had been neatly laid by Johnny and the waiting staff. Crystal goblets sparkled beside the cutlery, and on each plate was a folded napkin, on top of which sat a red apple. This final touch gave a cheerful, rustic look to the scene. It was something Tomasz had seen at a country wedding in France.

Fliss stepped forward to make a tiny adjustment to one of the candles.

'Looks splendid, doesn't it?'

She jumped at the sound of Patrick's voice and whirled round. He was standing in the doorway. Fliss was struck by a difference in him. The sunny weather of the past few days had deepened his tan and brought the freshness of the outdoors, but it was more than that. He seemed alive with new vigour, and the shadows on his features were gone.

'Tomasz told me I could find you here,' he said, stepping inside. 'I wanted to speak to you before everyone arrives tonight – to thank you for everything you've done.' He put a hand in his pocket. 'For everything you've done in the hotel, and especially for the way you've raised my mum's spirits. And mine.' He drew out his hand. In his palm was a small package wrapped in tissue paper. 'I thought you might like this.'

Fliss took the package from him in surprise, feeling her

cheeks turn pink with pleasure. 'You shouldn't have, really. I've loved being here. More than I can say.' She held the present to her, feeling the warmth of it from his pocket.

His eyes twinkled. 'Aren't you going to open it?'

Fliss undid the slim green ribbon holding the package together. Inside was a heart-shaped piece of green glass, attached to a gold chain. She placed the glass in her palm, letting the chain fall through her fingers.

'I found the heart at the bottom of the lake,' Patrick said. 'It was lodged in a crack in a rock and must have been there for years. I have an old school-friend in the village who makes jewellery. I asked her to polish it smooth and fasten it to the chain.'

'You found it at the bottom of the lake?' Fliss looked up, eyes wide. 'You mean Emmswater? Does that mean you've been diving here again?'

'Yes.' Patrick reached out a finger to touch the heart in her palm. 'I didn't tell anyone my plans, in case I bottled it. To be honest, I had a few sleepless nights. But it helped that I was going with an old dive buddy. I've known Guy for years. In fact, he's coming here tonight. He's married to my bank manager, Alison. He's a quiet bloke, and he kept me steady. Or he tried to. When we dived under – ' Patrick's jaw clenched. 'When the waters closed over my head, I wasn't terrified for myself. I was terrified of something happening to Guy. We dived down for ten minutes or so, but it was no good. Everything felt claustrophobic, and my heart was racing. Guy must have realised it was getting to me. He gave the signal to turn back, and I can't tell you how relieved I was. I couldn't wait to get out of there. And that's when I came across this piece of glass. It was caught on a ledge, at just the same spot where I'd last seen Jacob. As soon as I held it in my hand I thought of you, and how you might like it. And that's the really strange thing.' He gave her a small, puzzled smile. 'That's when all the horror just vanished. The lake was the magical place I remembered.'

'Patrick, that's wonderful that you dived again.' Fliss held the heart up to the window, where the sun caught it. The green glass flashed in the light, the same colour as the surface of Emmswater on a fine day. 'And finding this heart…It's almost as though the lake left you a sign. As though you were meant to find it.'

Patrick smiled, shaking his head. 'Maybe. But what's certain is, I can dive in Emmswater again.'

Fliss continued to examine the glass heart in the window. What an amazing thing to find. Mistaking her silence, Patrick added diffidently, 'It's not an expensive present – I mean it doesn't come near what we owe you for everything – but I thought you might like it.'

'I love it.' She raised her eyes to his. 'It's beautiful. Thank you.'

She stepped forward and hugged him, placing her arms around his neck and burying her face in his chest. The warm scent of him enveloped her.

And then Patrick's arms were around her waist, pulling her close. 'I'll miss you,' he said.

Fliss's face was pressed close to the warm, tanned skin at the base of his neck. His words vibrated in his solid chest. Her eyes filled with tears, and she pressed herself nearer to hide them.

'I'll miss you, too.'

Patrick's strong heart was beating, firm and steady, through the fabric of his shirt. His clasp around her waist tightened, and his heartbeat quickened.

'Fliss,' he said softly.

He reached a hand to her face and lifted her chin, forcing her to look at him. Her eyes swam.

There was a light footstep in the doorway. Patrick took a quick step back as Jilly stepped in, carrying a vase full of roses. Jilly glanced between the two of them, her expression alive with speculation.

Patrick cleared his throat and made his excuses, saying he had a lot to do before the party started. He made an abrupt exit, leaving Fliss and Jilly alone.

Jilly's eyes flew to the gold chain trailing from Fliss's fingers. 'What have you got there, Felicity? Is that a present from Patrick?'

Fliss uncurled her hand to display the glass pendant. 'He found it while diving in Emmswater.'

The flowers in her Jilly's vase trembled. She raised wide eyes to Fliss's. 'He's finally dived in the lake?'

Jilly began to speculate on what this might mean, and whether Patrick was now thinking of staying, and how like him it was not to breathe a word until he'd made his mind up about something.

'Diving in the lake was the one thing that was stopping Patrick staying,' she said. 'But now there's nothing stopping him at all. Oh, I do wish he'd confide his plans.' Her gaze was full of hope. 'But perhaps he's told you …?'

'Me? Why ever would he tell me?'

Jilly said nothing, her attention turning once more to the pendant. There was a smile on her face as she asked Fliss if she could take a look at it. She proceeded to enthuse over how beautiful it was, and how thoughtful it was of Patrick to give Fliss such a lovely present, until Fliss eventually managed to make her excuses and get away.

When she finally reached her room, Fliss took Raffles down from his look-out post at the window and hugged him to her.

'Honestly, Raffles,' she told him. 'Now it's going to be all round the hotel that Patrick's dived the lake and that he's given me a heart pendant. From the way Jilly was admiring it, anyone would think it was an engagement ring or something.'

She buried her face in the giraffe's squashy shape and worn fur. The smell of him was comforting and reminded her of home, until that thought reminded her that soon she would be leaving the Cross Hotel. She put Raffles back on the window-ledge with a heavy heart and opened the door to her wardrobe, where her Elizabethan dress was hanging.

Time to dress for the party.

Patrick

Patrick made his way downstairs to reception, feeling a little ridiculous. He had on a black leather doublet over a black silk shirt. His legs were encased in dark tights which he'd struggled to put on without ripping a hole in them (how on earth did women manage it?) and black knee-length boots. The white cuffs and the stiff white ruff around his neck had taken him ages to fasten. The ruff scratched uncomfortably. Fliss had managed to persuade him he ought to wear it, despite his protests. Fliss was very good at persuading people.

When Patrick rounded the stairs, there she was below him, standing by the window with her back to him, looking out at the view. She was in the same spot he'd found her on the day of her arrival, the day she'd caught her necklace in the curtains. He had a sudden vivid memory of her flushed face tilted up to his, her laughing eyes, and the scent of warm peaches.

She turned at the sound of his approach. She was wearing a dress of cream damask which fell to the floor in stiff folds, as though she'd just stepped out of a painting. In the low cut bodice her breasts were round and white, and around her neck was the green heart Patrick had given her. A pearly headdress framed her pale, serious face. She looked lovely.

Patrick descended the last few steps and stood in front of her. For once, Fliss failed to greet him with a smile. Her eyes were dark and serious. She reached out a hand to touch his cheek, where his skin was smooth and freshly-shaven.

'You look like a Spanish king.' She dropped her hand to her side and gave a small smile. 'All you need is a sword.'

He leaned forward and kissed her cheek. 'You look beautiful.'

For a heart-stopping moment, Fliss leaned in to his touch, then she drew back to smooth down her dress in a quick, awkward movement. 'Perhaps I shouldn't have chosen this colour. It will be ruined if I spill wine on it. And if I'm carrying trays, someone's bound to knock over a glass.'

'Carrying trays?' Patrick said in surprise. 'Of course not. You're not working tonight. I've set aside a place for you at my table. And I was expecting you to help me greet the guests.'

'Oh! But what about Johnny?'

'Johnny will cope just fine. We've got Joanne to help, and there are plenty of other waiters for him to order around.' He smiled. 'So, Mistress Everdene.' He tucked her hand under his arm. 'There's no excuse for you not to come and help me make conversation with all those guests.'

Fliss looked up at him through her lashes. 'I see what it is. You don't like talking to people, so you want me to do it for you.'

He pressed her hand. 'Of course. You do talking so well.'

She laughed outright, the seriousness of her expression banished, and Patrick thought what a lovely sound her laughter was.

As they came into the reception his mother looked up from her desk. 'Oh, how wonderful you look, Felicity darling. Doesn't she, Patrick?' Before he could answer, she rushed on, 'And your pendant goes perfectly. Look how well it suits you.'

'You look *fabulous*, Jilly,' Fliss said, eyes round in amazement.

Patrick watched his mother turn a shade of pink. She was wearing the costume she and Fliss must have chosen together on their trip to Keswick. It was a dark red brocade, with the skirt opening in a vee at the front above a cream underskirt. Her hair was pinned up under a red headdress, revealing pearl-earrings, and she'd removed her glasses. Perhaps it was the flush of excitement – and her enjoyment in the evening – but Patrick thought she looked years younger. How right Fliss had been about this party. Even if nothing came of their relaunch, it was worth going to all this trouble just to see his mother looking so radiant.

'Fliss and I are going through to the kitchen,' he told her. 'I expect Tomasz will tell us we're in the way, but the kitchen staff asked if they could see us in our costumes before the guests arrive.'

Fliss's long skirts rustled as they made their way down the narrow corridor towards the canteen. There was an unconscious regality to her walk. Her shoulders were straight, and her head held high in her headdress. Patrick held the door wide for her. Inside the canteen, the waiters were milling about in the lull before the guests arrived. There was an atmosphere of excitement in the place, and they were snapping photos of one another on their phones. Johnny was at the centre of the group, looking resplendent in a bright blue tunic. When he saw Patrick and Fliss, he took off his feathered cap and performed a sweeping bow.

'You look very dashing, Johnny,' Fliss said, admiring his doublet. 'And even better in tights than I do.'

One glance at Johnny's face was enough to show Patrick that the waiter's laughter was forced. His eyes glittered unnaturally, and his complexion showed an unhealthy pallor. For a horrifying minute Patrick wondered if he might be drunk.

Fliss, too, must have noticed something was wrong. She stepped forward to catch Johnny's arm. 'What on earth's happened?' she exclaimed. 'Is it Pauline? Is she all right?'

'Sssh.' Johnny glanced round. 'For goodness sake,' he added in a low voice. 'What did I tell you about her not wanting gossip?'

'Sorry,' she whispered. She cast Patrick a worried glance. 'Do you mind if Johnny and I go into the bar to talk for a minute? There's no one there yet.'

Patrick nodded. It was obvious now that Johnny's high spirits were a desperate attempt to mask some unhappiness. He just hoped that whatever it was that was troubling him, Fliss would be able to calm the waiter down. He watched her leave, her hand on Johnny's arm, and realised how much he'd come to rely on her calm good sense and small acts of kindness.

The hatch to the kitchen slid open abruptly. Tomasz's round, scowling face appeared. Instantly the waiters fell silent.

Tomasz took in the scene with a terrifying glare. 'Get out, all of you, and let my staff get on in peace of quiet. Some of us have no time to be prancing around in fancy dress.'

He slid the hatch shut again with a bang. The waiters began

to shuffle out. Patrick gave them a sympathetic grin and rolled his eyes, before making his way into the kitchen to appease Tomasz. The kitchen door opened on a scene of controlled feverishness. The staff were madly chopping herbs for the sea bream, lining up tiny pastries on trays, and stirring great pans on the oven. The pleasant smell of cinnamon and apples hung over all.

The Tudor feast was about to begin.

Chapter Twenty-Three

Fliss

Fliss slid behind the bar and began to heat up some water while Johnny slumped onto a stool. She gave him another worried look.

'Let's have a nice cup of tea.' She turned to open a cupboard. 'I'm glad to hear Pauline's alright. I was beginning to think something terrible had happened.'

'Something terrible *has* happened,' he said, without raising his head. 'She's seeing someone else.'

'What?' Fliss spun round, clutching the tea cups. 'Oh, Johnny! How did you find out?'

'Got an email from her aunt last night. She said Pauline didn't have the heart to tell me herself, so she would.'

'That's awful!' Fliss stared at him. No wonder he was distraught. 'Pauline should have had the guts to tell you. She can't just let someone else do her dirty work. In fact, I can't believe she has. Have you actually spoken to her?'

'I tried all morning. Same old story. Her phone just goes to voicemail. Might as well face it, it's over, and she doesn't want to see me.' He put his head in his hands. 'Looks like I've blown it for good. And now someone else is going to be my child's dad.'

The swing door to the bar opened and Joanne appeared. Unlike the others, she wasn't in costume. She'd started work at the Cross Hotel too late to organise a dress, but she was looking very cool and efficient in her black skirt and blouse and a pair of stylish flat shoes. She looked from Fliss to Johnny and then at the cups.

'Has someone got a hangover?' she asked.

'Of course not,' Johnny said, drawing himself up. He pushed back his bar stool and rose to his feet. 'I haven't had a drop of alcohol for days. And I'm perfectly capable of doing my job. And even if I weren't, Fliss is here to help, so what does it matter?'

'Actually, Johnny, I'm not working today,' Fliss confessed, feeling a little sheepish. 'Patrick asked me to sit at the top table with him and the guests.'

'Oh, did he?'

Fliss felt herself redden. She would have let Johnny's ironic scrutiny pass without comment, but when he and Joanne exchanged knowing glances, it was too much.

'Yes, he did,' she said. 'And why not? It makes sense for me to help him socialise.'

'Right. Nothing to do with Patrick having the hots for you.'

'What? He doesn't!'

Johnny looked at Joanne again and shook his head in disbelief. 'Anyone can tell he does.' He made for the door, stopping on the way to adjust his cap, whose feather had fallen over his brow and ruined his dignified exit.

'Looks like it could be an eventful night,' Joanne murmured, watching him go. She turned away and began to set out the beer glasses, ready for the first drinks orders.

Later, as Fliss stood in the doorway to the lounge helping Patrick greet the guests, she couldn't help watching him surreptitiously as he shook hands with everyone. Whatever the signs were of someone "having the hots," Patrick didn't seem to show any of them.

'Is there something wrong?' he asked eventually.

'I'm sorry?'

He tugged on the ruff around his neck. 'I mean, I know I'm looking a bit of a twit. Is that why you keep looking at me?'

'No, you look fabulous.' He threw her a disbelieving glance, and she couldn't help but laugh. 'You do, honestly. I've never seen anyone carry off a pair of tights quite so well.'

It was true. Patrick's legs did look superb. Hard and muscular.

And then it hit Fliss with a rush. *She* was the one with the hots! How could she only just have realised? All of a sudden her senses began to make themselves loud and clear, as though they were making up for lost time. She became aware of Patrick to the exclusion of everyone else in the room, and her nerve-endings buzzed like bees in a meadow. The sleeve of his dark jacket brushed against her arm, causing an intense thrill to course through her entire body. When he turned his head to face the door, his tanned profile appeared in startling clarity, with his strong neck, and the dark hair beneath his cap. In his Tudor outfit he was alive with masculine vitality.

Patrick's eyes were on the entrance to the reception. She followed the direction of his gaze and stiffened. The arrival of Cameron McIntyre was like a bucket of cold water on her turbulent emotions.

'Welcome to the Cross Hotel, Cameron.' Patrick held out his hand. 'Good of you to come.'

There was no corresponding civility from the Lakeside's manager. It was obvious he wasn't taking Joanne's defection well. His lip curled as he glanced around the refurbished lounge.

'I see there have been some changes since your father's time, Patrick.' There was a malicious glint in Cameron's eyes as they fell on Fliss. 'New curtains? They must have set you back.'

Everyone in the Cross Hotel knew how furious Patrick had been when Fliss ordered the curtains. And from the Cross Hotel to the Lakeside was only a couple of gossipy conversations away. Cameron must know perfectly well he was stirring up trouble.

'They're magnificent, aren't they?' Patrick said evenly. 'A generous present from Fliss to Jilly.'

Fliss threw Patrick a grateful look. Unfortunately, Cameron still hadn't finished.

'Generosity from the Everdenes?' His eyes widened as though such a thing were incredible. 'Good to see you're not worried about the Everdene family making changes to a hotel they don't even own.' He added, with another cold glance in Fliss's direction, 'They don't own it yet, anyway.'

Fliss was stunned. Even from Cameron, the remark was offensive. She drew in a breath to make a heated retort, but Patrick took her hand in his, pressing it with his cool fingers. His courteous smile remained fixed in place.

'Fliss has been very generous with her time, Cameron.'

To Fliss's intense relief, there was the welcome noise of new arrivals in reception. Patrick waved Cameron on into the lounge. 'Please help yourself to a free drink. You know Johnny, don't you? And of course you know Joanne. If you want to go through to the bar to say hello, then make yourself at home.'

Cameron's colour heightened at this mention of Joanne. He grunted a reply and stalked off, just as Sergeant Willis and his family appeared.

Patrick's hand still covered Fliss's. She turned to murmur a quick thanks, but was chilled by his unsmiling expression. Surely he didn't believe Cameron's slurs about Everdenes buying his hotel? But there was no time to question him, because there was Sergeant Willis, looking resplendent in a burgundy gown and flat cloth hat. He was a welcome sight, and Fliss took his outstretched hand with pleasure. She was so relieved to see his friendly face, she cried out, 'Willy!'

A burst of giggles from his daughters reminded her where she was, and she blushed. 'I mean, good to see you, Sergeant Willis.'

'Good to see you, too, Fliss. How well you look.' The sergeant beckoned forward his wife and three daughters. The women had all come dressed as maids, in fetching skirts and aprons.

'Oh, you all look lovely,' Fliss said. 'I'm so glad you've come. Which one of you made the delicious cake?'

Her question provoked a burst of chatter and loud laughter. Fliss finally discovered what had driven Sergeant Willis to become so taciturn. Even she struggled to get a word in edgeways. Finally Mrs Willis, or Sandra, as she insisted Fliss call her, said, 'You must come round to our house for tea some day, Fliss. Emma loves any excuse to bake a cake.'

'Oh, that would have been wonderful. I so wish I could. But I'm leaving Emmside in a few days. Next weekend, actually.'

The girls fell quiet. Sandra looked from Fliss to Patrick.

'Oh, we thought you and Patrick – '

Sergeant Willis took hold of his wife's arm and pressed it warningly. 'Come on, love. Time for a drink.'

Sandra moved away, looking flustered. 'Of course. Come on, girls.'

They made their way into the growing crowd, and for a second or two Patrick and Fliss were alone.

'You've made a hit with them,' Patrick said.

Fliss noticed he still wasn't smiling, but again she was unable to reply because after that Jilly came in with the reporters from the Cumberland Herald who had just arrived, and from then on, the guests began to pour in thick and fast.

Patrick

The noise in the dining-room was tremendous. From his position at the top table, with Fliss at his side, Patrick could survey the whole room. He was immensely relieved to see everyone enjoying themselves. Everyone except Johnny, that is. The head waiter and his team had brought out Tomasz's first course right on cue – tiny bowls of potted duck and slices of crusty bread, with a delicious home-made cranberry sauce, and little cheese tartlets that melted in the mouth. When Johnny appeared at Patrick's side to take his empty plate, Patrick tried to thank him. Johnny responded with a grunt and walked off, a gloomy set to his mouth. There was none of his usual banter with the guests, either. It was fortunate everyone was too busy tucking in to notice his drawn face.

'Did you find out what's wrong with Johnny?' Patrick asked Fliss. 'He looks like he's at a funeral.'

Fliss watched Johnny go, a worried frown on her brow. 'Things have got a bit complicated with Pauline. It can't be easy with them being separated like this.'

Patrick picked up his wine glass and took a hefty swig. 'I feel for the guy.'

Fliss gave him a swift, unreadable glance, but the local councillor, sitting on her other side, drew her attention with a comment about a recent holiday in Norfolk, and with her usual courtesy, Fliss turned away to speak to him.

On Patrick's right, his mother was deep in conversation with their local MP, David Barker. The Member of Parliament responsible for Emmside was a good-looking man in his sixties. His trim beard fitted well with his flamboyant Tudor costume. He appeared to be flirting with Jilly outrageously. Patrick smiled quietly to himself. He hadn't seen his mother look so sparkling since...well, since longer than he could remember.

The doors to the kitchen opened and the waiters arrived, bearing the next course. Despite Johnny's bleak expression he seemed to be keeping everyone on track. Patrick breathed an inward sigh of relief. Then he caught sight of Cameron, sitting further down the room, and his eyes narrowed. Surely this wasn't how his mother had organised the seating plan. The sly so-and-so must have swapped seats so he could sit next to one of the reporters from the *Cumberland Herald*. The young woman had her notebook out beside her plate and was making furious notes, avidly lapping up everything Cameron was telling her. The Lakeside's manager glanced in Fliss's direction and Patrick felt her stiffen beside him. Cameron smiled at Fliss – a bland lift of the lips – and raised his glass in a supercilious toast.

Fliss lifted her glass and returned the salute with a gracious smile of her own. Patrick admired her panache.

'What's that guy playing at?' he asked in an undertone.

'I don't know.' Fliss returned her glass to the table. She still had a smile on her face for Cameron's benefit, but Patrick could sense her underlying tension. 'I don't know why but I have an awful feeling something's going to go wrong.' She looked around the wooden-beamed dining-room, at the vibrant colours, the guests and waiters resplendent in their costumes. 'All this Tudor history is enough to make anyone feel on edge,' she went on. 'I can't help thinking about all those beheadings and skullduggery in the King's court.' She glanced down at her dress. 'The last person to wear this costume was acting the part of Anne Boleyn, and look what happened to her. Perhaps I shouldn't have chosen it. It feels like a bad omen.'

Patrick tore his gaze away from where her soft breasts were tantalisingly close and took a sip of his wine. 'If you ask my opinion, wearing Anne Boleyn's dress was very definitely a good idea.'

Fliss caught his eye and turned pink. At that moment, one of the waiters placed a plate of mouth-watering sea bream in front of her, topped with three round slices of lemon and garnished with fresh parsley. Fliss examined the dish with delight. 'Not that anything could ever put me off Tomasz's cooking. I must have put on pounds since I got here. I'm sure Anne Boleyn never had to weld herself into her bodice the way I did.'

She began to tuck in. Patrick ignored the meal in front of him. He was picturing Fliss squeezing herself into her bodice. The thought so occupied his mind it was a while before he realised his mother had left the table to see to something in the kitchen, and that David Barker was leaning across to ask Fliss a question.

'Jilly tells me your parents own Everdene Hotels, Felicity. Have they been to visit you at the Cross Hotel yet?'

Patrick had come to recognise the cautious look that crossed Fliss's face whenever someone mentioned her father's business. She answered politely, 'My parents are visiting next weekend, and they're bringing my sister. I'm sure they'll be interested to see the changes Patrick and Jilly have put in place.'

'Aye, I'm sure they will.'

It was a sardonic reply. Fliss raised her head. The MP went on, 'Everdenes already own a couple of hotels in Cumbria. Didn't you buy out a family business recently, over in Kendal?'

Fliss's hand tightened on the knife she was holding. 'That's right. We bought out the Borough Hotel. It was about to go bankrupt and we rescued it.'

'Rescued. Aye, that's one way of putting it.'

There was a momentary pause. Patrick was sure Fliss's head drooped for an instant – how on earth did she cope with the constant criticism? But then the next moment her shoulders went back and she raised her chin, saying, with admirable restraint, 'I expect you've heard about the hotel we bought in Germany. There has been a lot of negative reporting about it in the press. But being taken over by Everdenes isn't necessarily a bad thing. We've saved jobs, and as a matter of fact we created more jobs in the Kendal hotel we bought last year. We gave work to people and rejuvenated the business.'

Patrick never, ever thought he'd speak in James Everdene's defence, but Fliss's flushed features caused him to step in on her behalf.

'Take a look around, David,' he said, indicating the bustling dining-room. 'Remember how this room looked last time you visited? And now look at it. You're witnessing the Everdene magic in action. This hotel has been transformed, and I don't just mean the furnishings. I've never seen so many guests in the dining-room in the entire time I've lived here. If our relaunch takes off, we'll need to take on more staff. And if the evening's a success, it's down to Fliss. The whole thing was her idea.'

David Barker was forced to agree that it was wonderful to see the hotel looking so lively. They spoke for a while longer about the hospitality industry and its importance to the region, until Jilly returned and took her seat.

Fliss gave Patrick a wide smile. 'Thanks,' she murmured.

After that, the evening went better than Patrick's wildest expectations. Fliss's feelings of foreboding seemed to have deserted her. She contemplated Tomasz's dessert of apple tarts and cream happily and exclaimed over the amazing marzipan mice he'd made to go with their twenty-first century coffees. Only Johnny's hangdog face as he trailed from table to kitchen put a damper on things, but the guests were having such a great time Patrick could only hope that none of them noticed.

After the meal was finished and the waiters had left everyone with more coffee and liqueurs, Patrick rose to his feet. He tapped on his empty wine glass for quiet. The chatter, which had been fuelled all evening by Johnny's carefully-chosen wines and cocktails, took a while to die down, but eventually almost everyone's eyes were on him.

Patrick glanced around. There was still just the faintest murmur in the room and the occasional stifled laugh.

'Where's Mrs Grimshaw when you need her?' he asked loudly, spreading his hands wide.

This made everyone laugh out loud and finally got their attention. Most people in the room remembered their former dinner lady. Mrs Grimshaw could bring silence to the dining-room at their local primary school with just a stare. A few people heckled Patrick, reminding him of times he'd been in trouble with Mrs Grimshaw himself for talking, and then the room finally went quiet.

Patrick had been looking forward to this part of the evening. He, Fliss and Jilly had organised a surprise "thank you" for the staff. When Patrick called Johnny's name, the misery that had dogged the waiter all evening vanished momentarily, replaced by a look of gratified surprise. He stepped forward to accept his present – a bottle of good French wine – and the guests who actually knew Johnny gave an ironic cheer. Johnny took off his feather cap and bowed.

After that, Patrick presented an enormous bouquet of flowers to his mother, who flushed pink with happiness when he hugged her. And then Tomasz – purple in the face and sweating profusely – entered the dining-room to a resounding round of applause. Some of the guests even rose to their feet, including Fliss, who pushed back her chair and beamed at him. Tomasz accepted his bottle of malt whisky, shook Patrick's hand, and gave both Fliss and Jilly a smacking kiss on the cheek.

Once Tomasz was back in the kitchen, Fliss sank back

down, expecting Patrick's speech to be coming to a close. She had just taken a sip of her coffee when he said her name. She spluttered in surprise. Patrick reached for her hand and drew her to her feet.

'This wasn't in our plan,' she said, blushing as the room erupted into laughter.

Patrick kept her hand in his until he was sure he had everyone's attention.

'Most of you know I came back to Emmside a few months ago to a sad welcome. My father had just died, the hotel was in mourning, and many of us wondered if the Cross Hotel had a future. It was a very, very difficult time for all of us. And then Fliss arrived.' His clasp on her hand tightened. 'It's no exaggeration to say Fliss has transformed the Cross Hotel. Without her this evening wouldn't have happened. Mind you, you'd all have been spared the sight of me and Johnny in tights.'

There were some wolf-whistles from the guests, but these died down when Patrick reached under the table and brought out a small painting, wrapped in tissue paper. Fliss gave a gasp of surprise.

'My mother and I wanted to get you a memento of your stay here. Something to remind you of Emmside.' Patrick took off the tissue paper to reveal an exquisite oil painting of the valley – the one Fliss had admired so much when she was repainting the lounge.

Fliss's hands flew to her mouth.

'Don't tell me you're speechless,' he said.

'Thank you.' She dropped her hands, eyes shining. 'Thank you. I love it.'

She reached up and kissed his cheek, and for the briefest of moments he pulled her to him. There was her warm scent that had become so familiar, and then she stepped back, and everyone was clapping, and cameras were flashing. Her eyes met his briefly, wide with happiness.

Chapter Twenty-Four

Fliss

When Fliss sat down, her ears were filled with a strange roaring noise, like the sea off the coast at Norfolk. The colours on the painting swam in front of her. Beside her Patrick was finishing his speech by inviting the guests to take their drinks into the lounge, or out onto the terrace as the evening was so mild.

"A memento of Emmside", Patrick had called the painting. As though Fliss was never coming back. As though they were never going to see one another again.

The guests rose to their feet with a buzz of noise. Fliss picked up her precious painting from the table.

'I'll take this up to my room,' she told Patrick. 'I'd hate anything to happen to it.'

He pulled back her chair for her, bending to help her manoeuvre her stiff skirts free. She stood, and he gave her his attractive smile. In his black outfit he looked dark and handsome, like a sort of Tudor pirate. Behind her she heard the MP murmur to Jilly, 'They make a beautiful couple.'

Fliss cast a quick glance at Patrick to see if he, too, had heard the comment, but one of the guests approached their table, wanting to congratulate him on the evening, and his attention was occupied.

There was a hubbub of high-spirited laughter and chatter as the dining-room began to empty. Fliss held up her skirts with

228

one hand. She found leaving the dining-room was a slower process than she'd anticipated. Everyone was eager to speak to her as she made her way out, and she was forced to stop several times to offer her painting for guests to admire. Their friendly enquiries into how she'd been enjoying her stay in the Lakes, and how long she planned to remain in Emmside, kept her occupied for some time.

Fliss was just explaining to one of Patrick's old school-friends how much she would have loved to stay at the Cross Hotel if only her father didn't need her back at work, when she caught sight of Cameron. He was sitting at his table still, a smirk on his face. To Fliss's dismay, the journalist had left his side and was making her steely way towards her through the departing guests, notepad in hand. Something about the look of cold determination on the young woman's face made Fliss decide that perhaps she'd be able to face the interview better if she could just have a few minutes alone in her bedroom. She made her craven excuses, turned, and beat a swift retreat, through the reception and up the silent stairs to the quiet of her own room. She leaned back against the door, her eyes closed.

She'd left her bedroom window ajar to let in the fresh evening air, and now the sound of the guests gathering outside on the terrace drifted upwards. Fliss righted herself and propped her painting against the wall. Then she sat on the bed, head on one side, to admire it again. She was just remembering the first time she'd met Patrick – and trying not to be tearful at the thought she would soon be leaving – when she realised that the noise of the guests outside had quietened all of a sudden. There were now only two voices speaking. Two voices raised in anger.

Fliss lifted her skirts and stood on the bed to lean out through the window. The sun was setting over the mountains, and the terrace was illuminated by fairy lights strung along the railing. Several candles flickered in glass jars on the tables. The terrace was shadowy, but not so dark that she couldn't make out Johnny's back to her, and Cameron, edged against the railing, glaring up at him in fearful defiance. Johnny's hand was clenched in a fist at his side.

All Fliss's feelings of foreboding returned in force. She scanned the heads on the terrace, looking for Patrick, or even Sergeant Willis, but neither of them were there. With a cry she leapt from the bed, gathering up the skirts that threatened to impede her progress, and ran from the room.

Patrick

Patrick had seen Fliss rush out of the dining-room, holding her painting carefully in front of her, and guessed the reason for her hurry. The journalist who'd been so deep in conversation with Cameron had obviously decided to make Fliss Everdene the focus of her story, and not the Cross Hotel. Patrick was ticking over in his mind what he could do to head the woman off for the rest of the evening – he hated to see Fliss harried and hassled – when his phone buzzed in the pocket of his doublet. He fished it out and a text flashed up on the screen.

Got a minute, mate? Need to talk as soon as.

Something urgent must have come up. Patrick's business partner never summoned him in this way. It was bad timing, but Patrick made his excuses to Jilly, telling her he'd be back as soon as he could. He made his way to his office, where he clicked the green button on his laptop to put through a call.

His partner's beaming face appeared on screen. It was still daylight in the Caribbean, and their office was flooded with light. It didn't look like the scene of a disaster.

'Oscar, what's up?'

Oscar did a double-take at the sight of Patrick and burst out laughing. 'Dunno, Queen Elizabeth. You tell me.'

Patrick caught sight of himself in the webcam's screen. He gave a sheepish grin. 'It's a Tudor party. We're relaunching the hotel. Everyone's come in costume.'

Oscar shook with laughter. 'This is hilarious. I'm so saving this shot.'

There was no point protesting. Patrick's face, framed by a ridiculous white ruff, would soon be tweeted to all Oscar's friends, and there would be no living it down. He should just thank his lucky stars his tights were out of sight under the table. He let Oscar rib him for a couple more minutes, and then his partner finally got to the point. He held up some papers to the webcam.

'Sorry to disturb you at your party. Maybe good news, I don't know. Good news for you, but not for me.'

His huge grin faded to a wistful smile.

Patrick leaned forward. 'Tell me.'

He soon became so engrossed in what Oscar was telling him, he lost track of time. A quick five minute call stretched into quarter of an hour. Patrick glanced at the clock at the bottom of the screen and told Oscar reluctantly that he needed to be getting back to his guests.

'I'll text you my flight details,' he told him.

Oscar nodded. 'You take care, Your Majesty. Hope they let you through customs.' He cut the call with a wink.

Patrick swung round in his chair. His heart was beating rapidly with a mixture of nerves and excitement. At last his plans were coming to fruition. He couldn't wait to tell Fliss. He thought of how she would soon be leaving, and then – with a shock – he remembered her parents' impending visit. What if he'd left everything too late?

The door of his office burst open. His mother stood in the doorway, a bright flush on her face.

'Oh, Patrick, there you are, thank goodness,' she cried. 'It's Johnny. There's been a terrible row outside, and now he's squaring up to Cameron. Come quickly.'

Patrick leapt out of his chair, all thoughts of Dominica fleeing from his head. In Johnny's present state it wouldn't take much for Cameron to goad him into losing his temper. And to have Johnny lose the plot in front of VIP guests and journalists – not to mention a policeman – could ruin everything, besides getting the waiter into serious trouble.

Patrick raced through the cluster of guests still remaining in the lounge as fast as a person could without seeming to run. He nodded and smiled, but didn't stop long enough to speak to those who tried to greet him. As he strode towards the doors to the terrace he almost bumped into Fliss, who was headed in the same direction, her heavy skirts raised high so as not to slow her swift march.

'I hope Johnny hasn't been drinking,' Patrick murmured as they approached the doors.

'Of course not! He's sober as a judge. It's Cameron. He's enough to rile a saint.'

'Tell me about it. I've a good mind to punch Cameron myself.'

They burst on to the terrace together. By now the guests were listening in a mixture of stunned horror and amusement to the diatribe Johnny was inflicting on Cameron. Cameron's features were pale in the glow of the candles, and he was backed up against the railing, but there was a smug look on his face that told Patrick everything. He'd obviously goaded Johnny on purpose.

Patrick glanced to his right and his heart sank. The journalist from the Cumberland Herald was standing by the railing, notepad in hand, and, even worse, the press photographer was right next to her, camera clicking away like a machine-gun.

'Johnny!' Fliss called.

But Johnny was deaf to everything around him. He raised his fist. Patrick leapt forward. Out of the corner of his eye he saw Willy erupt onto the terrace, moving at surprising speed for someone so portly, and they both dived as one. Their actions deflected Johnny's aim, and his punch became a slight glancing blow. Cameron staggered back theatrically.

'Did you see that, Willis?' he cried. 'That's assault, that is.'

'Don't be such a bloody idiot,' growled the sergeant in a low voice. 'Or I'll show you what assault really looks like.'

'Willy. Johnny!' Fliss was standing behind the pair of them, a look of complete consternation on her face. Patrick had never seen anyone wring their hands before, but Fliss was managing it very well. In the flickering candlelight, pale and beautiful in her Tudor costume, she was attracting as much attention from the photographer as Johnny was. Patrick dropped Johnny's sleeve, which he'd been gripping to restrain him, and Johnny shrugged himself clear. It was obvious his grievance was still not settled.

'Never mind assault, Willy,' he said fiercely. 'You should hear what that slimy git said about Fliss. He should be up for slander. I don't know why you're not arresting him right now.'

Fliss's complexion, already pale, whitened. 'Leave it, Johnny.'

Patrick caught her hand in his and pressed it, intending to lead her back inside and leave Sergeant Willis to deal with Cameron, but the journalist stepped forward, a look of mock concern on her face. Patrick pulled Fliss to him, placing his arm around her waist in a protective gesture.

'Caroline Morton from the *Cumberland Herald.*' There was sympathy in her voice, but her eyes were hard and watchful. 'That's quite a story Cameron's told us.'

Fliss looked at her uncertainly. Patrick tightened his arm around her.

The journalist added helpfully, 'Apparently you pretended to be a barmaid when you first arrived at the Cross Hotel. Is that right?' She looked from Fliss to Patrick, eyes wide and innocent. 'It seems an odd thing to do. Cameron seems to think your father sent you undercover to check out the Cross family's business. Surely that's a little underhand. Are the Everdenes about to buy out the Cross Hotel? And where will Jilly live then? Do you have any comment to make?'

Fliss's body was rigid under Patrick's hand. When she didn't answer, he spoke for her, with a calmness he was very far from feeling. 'I'm sure you know better than to print gossip, Caroline. Fliss has been the impetus in turning round the fortunes of my family's hotel. She's been very generous with her time'

Caroline cast a sceptical glance in Fliss's direction. 'That's very unselfish of you to leave your own business for so long, Fliss.' She left a beat before adding, 'I'm sure you can't be surprised if people wonder whether there might be an ulterior motive behind your generosity.'

By now all the guests had assembled on the terrace. It was like a free gladiatorial performance, surrounded by candles in the gathering dusk, only Fliss was the one being thrown to the lions. Patrick could sense her quick mind turning over an answer. He guessed from the stiffness of her shoulders pressed against his that she was struggling. It had been a long evening, and now this.

He pressed her waist and felt her respond, and then, in a flash of impulsiveness he could later hardly believe of himself, he said the first thing that came into his mind. 'Actually, you're quite right. Fliss did have an ulterior motive behind giving up her time.' A hundred pairs of eyes, including Fliss's, turned to look at him in surprise. Patrick drew Fliss closer. 'We wanted to wait a while before announcing it, but you might as well know now. We're getting married.'

The assembled guests drew in a collective breath. Then everyone began speaking at once, and the journalist took a step forward, a look of sly delight on her face at this scoop. But Patrick had no eyes or ears for anyone – not Cameron, not the photographer, not even Jilly, who was pressing her way through the crowd. He glanced down at Fliss and found her clear eyes fixed on his, her lips parted, and a look of bewilderment on her face.

He bent to whisper in her ear, 'Stick with it.'

And then he pulled her closer and kissed her, in what was meant to be a brief touch of the lips for the benefit of the camera, until he found himself kissing her properly. His heart thudded as her lips parted under his. Her hands moved to his shoulders, and she was actually kissing him back. Fliss's soft body clung to him, and Patrick realised this – here and now – was the one thing he'd wanted ever since Fliss stood beside him by that dry stone wall and beamed her smile at him. He'd wanted to hold her in his arms. Suddenly, after months of feeling adrift, everything felt *right*.

Raised voices and laughter from the guests finally impeded on Patrick's senses, and he and Fliss broke apart. She looked up at him with a shy, stunned expression, and then everyone surrounded them. Sergeant Willis shook Patrick's hand, the journalist offered her congratulations in a cool voice, Cameron stared at them wild-eyed. And then there was his mother, standing in front of them both with tears in her eyes, and it was only then that Patrick felt the enormity of his declaration. He opened his mouth to speak, to try to hint to Jilly that it was all a ruse – a device to throw the journalist off the scent – but he found himself incapable of saying the words.

From behind him came Johnny's ragged voice, raised once more in altercation, and Cameron's scornful reply. Patrick whirled round to find the Lakeside's manager pressed once more against the railing, with Johnny gripping his lapel.

'Call him off, for God's sake!' Cameron cried.

Patrick was about to dart forward, when a woman's voice carried on the air, clear and brisk. 'Johnny, what the hell do you think you're playing at?'

Everyone turned. There, standing at the top of the steps to the car park, her belly showing round and soft through the fabric of her tee-shirt, was Pauline. She put a hand on her hip as she moved her head to survey the guests. 'Well, if I'd known it was fancy dress I'd have worn my catwoman outfit.'

Johnny dropped his grip and turned. 'Pauline!'

In his blue brocade jacket and cloth cap, and with his legs showing long and muscular beneath his breeches, and most of all, with his face suffused with a glow of joy, Johnny made a handsome and arresting sight. Pauline stood transfixed for several seconds, and then the waiter rushed forward, and next minute they were in each other's arms.

'Well, that's a sight for sore eyes,' said Sergeant Willis. He turned to grip Patrick's hand, and then Fliss's. He chuckled. 'It's better than one of Shakespeare's plays, is all this. I don't know when I've been to a better do.'

There was an enormous grin on his face, and when Patrick looked round, he realised every single person on the terrace was sporting the same wide smile. It seemed despite all the drama – or maybe because of it – the evening had turned into a wild success. Patrick still had his hand around Fliss's waist, unable to let her go. He looked down at her pale, uncertain features, and wished they could be alone somewhere to talk – there was so much he wanted to tell her – but they were surrounded by people all speaking at once and wanting to congratulate them both.

A camera flashed, right in front of them. Fliss slipped out of Patrick's grasp, looking up at him, wide-eyed. 'What have you done?' she asked.

'It was for the best,' Patrick told her. 'And it will all turn out all right. You'll see.'

Chapter Twenty-Five

Fliss

Fliss lay in bed the morning after the Tudor party, staring up at the ancient beams in the ceiling above her head. Outside, the sky was turning creamy white as the sun neared the horizon. The noise of birds tweeting and calling to one another in pre-dawn excitement could be heard through her open window. What a din. Fliss turned on her side, wondering why on earth she'd ever thought this part of the Lake District was peaceful. It was a hotbed of emotion and drama. Even the birds were in on it. Finally she sat up, giving up on any hope of catching more sleep. It had been a fitful night's rest, with images of the evening drifting in and out of her dreams, so that she could hardly tell real life from fantasy.

After Patrick's dramatic statement to the press that they were going to get married – married, for goodness sake! – Fliss had hardly had a chance to speak to him. Luckily Pauline's equally theatrical return had thrust Johnny into the limelight. Everyone forgot Patrick's announcement and crowded round the waiter, wanting to congratulate him on his impending fatherhood. And then, just when Fliss finally got the chance to ask Patrick what on earth he meant by telling everyone they were engaged, he'd told her he needed to get back to his office to arrange an urgent flight to Dominica, and then he was going to pack.

'You're leaving?' she'd asked wildly. 'How long for?' Later she couldn't believe how much emotion she'd injected into the question. Almost as though they actually *were* engaged, which was ridiculous.

The noise of chirruping intensified outside. Fliss inched her way along the bed on her knees and threw the window wide, letting the birdsong flood in. A peachy glow had infused the cream of the sky, spreading warmth down the mountains, gently waking everything in its path. Fliss breathed in the heady air for a few moments, hoping it might clear the fuzziness in her brain. Down below on the terrace the candles had long since guttered out, and the tables were all askew. It was too early even for Jean and the chambermaids to have started work clearing up. The fresh morning air was bracing, and Fliss was just contemplating getting dressed and going downstairs to start putting things to rights, when out of the corner of her eye she caught movement in the car park. She craned her neck. The edge of the car park was just visible beyond the terrace, but she could see nothing except an elongated shadow weaving about. She stood on the bed to lean right out. It was Patrick, loading a suitcase into his car. Fliss gasped and toppled backwards. Then, like a whirlwind, she leapt for the dressing-gown hanging on a hook, tugged open her bedroom door and went running down the corridor in her bare feet, shrugging her arms into her sleeves as she went.

The hotel was still in shadow, but when Fliss raced into the reception she found the front door had been propped open, and the dawn light was spreading across the floor. A light breeze had blown in the petals from the rose bushes outside, and they clung to Fliss's feet as she passed. She ran outside, wincing as her bare feet hit the gravel.

'Patrick!'

He was leaning into his car, placing a holdall on the back seat. He straightened when he saw Fliss. A smile lit his face.

'You're awake,' he said foolishly. 'I was going to come and knock on your door when I'd finished loading up.' He glanced down at her feet, where the rose petals clung, red and white. His eyes twinkled. 'Don't tell me you've run out of shoes.'

'I wanted to talk to you before you left.' Fliss tugged on the belt of her dressing-gown, suddenly conscious that she must look dishevelled and possibly a little deranged, but it couldn't be helped. 'What on earth am I supposed to tell people while you're away? About us getting married, I mean?'

He looked up from his interested study of her toes. To her dismay, he seemed not the slightest bit concerned. 'Don't worry about it. Everybody loves a wedding, and we've given the journalist a much more interesting story to run with than all Cameron's digs about Everdenes. In any case, I'll only be gone a week. If everyone's gossiping, I'll take care of it when I get back.'

'But what about all the people we know? Your mum looked elated. When you said we were getting married, I thought she might even start crying. If we tell her the wedding's off already before we've even set a date, she'll be devastated!'

Patrick had the grace to look a tiny bit abashed. 'I told her last night it was all a ploy. Although to be honest, I don't think she believed me.'

'You see,' Fliss cried. 'The whole thing's got out of hand!'

'Don't worry about it,' he repeated. 'I just have to sort out this business in Dominica. Then when I get back, there's something I'd like to discuss with you. A proposal.'

'A what?' Fliss said. 'A proposal?' She stared at him in amazement.

'Not that sort of thing.' His tanned features turned a shade of pink. 'It's something I'd actually really like. I mean, not that I wouldn't like – ' The pink deepened to red, and he broke off with a strangled laugh. 'I'm making a complete mess of this.'

He looked so discomfited Fliss was forced to laugh, too, and for a couple of seconds they giggled at one another. Then the smile left Patrick's face. He lifted his wrist to look at his watch. 'Look, we'll talk when I get back. I need to get off now if I'm to get this flight.'

Fliss's laughter died abruptly. She thought about how much she'd miss him, and for a moment felt her eyes might fill with tears. She dropped her gaze to her feet, which were tingling with cold on the gravel, and blinked a few times. When she looked up, Patrick's eyes were wide and dark on hers. Then he surprised her by taking one of her hands in his.

'I'll really miss you,' he said, echoing her own thoughts. He pulled her towards him gently, and then his mouth was on hers again, as it had been the evening before, only this time his arms tightened fiercely around her. Fliss clung to him, returning the pressure of his kiss, her arms around his strong neck. The morning air around them grew still, as if there were only the two of them in the world. Fliss's heart beat wildly. She pressed herself closer, until Patrick broke away with a groan, resting his forehead against hers.

'I'll miss you, too,' Fliss whispered. She gave him another brief, tight hug and stepped back. 'Have a safe journey. Let me know when you get there.'

He caressed her cheek. 'I will. Don't get engaged to anyone else while I'm gone.'

He opened the door of his car and climbed inside, giving her a brief wave. Fliss stood watching, her arms wrapped around herself, until the Land Rover had disappeared down the fellside. She shivered in her thin dressing-gown. Then she turned and made her way back to the hotel. To her surprise, Jilly was standing in the doorway.

'I came down to see Patrick off,' Jilly told her. 'But then I realised you'd come out, too, and I thought you might like to say your goodbyes alone. Don't worry, darling, he'll be home soon. And then we can talk all about planning your wedding. Patrick tried to tell me yesterday it was all a ploy.' She took in Fliss's dressing-gown and bare feet, her tousled hair and bruised lips, and gave her a warm, happy smile. 'But of course anyone can see that's nonsense. I'm so delighted for you both, I can't tell you.'

Fliss's flushed cheeks turned crimson. It was going to be a long week until Patrick returned.

Funnily enough, as the day went on Fliss discovered that – apart from Jilly – everyone else in the hotel accepted the story that Patrick had invented their engagement to fool the journalist.

'Good for Patrick,' Jean said, as they set the terrace to

rights together later that morning. 'Between you and me she was always a bit of a sneak, that Caroline Morton. She was in my Tom's class at school. She once spilled water on his artwork so she could come first in class. Never forgot that, I haven't. When I read her articles, I just wonder who else she's done over.'

Fliss should have realised a journalist would struggle to escape the events of her childhood in a place like Emmside. Besides, everyone in the hotel thought Pauline's return to the village was far more exciting news than Fliss's pretend engagement. The fact that Johnny was about to become a father was still the hot topic of gossip. When he arrived for work that afternoon, the other members of staff were eager to go over his news all over again and to quiz him all about it.

Fliss was in the canteen, finishing some of the apple tarts left over from the Tudor night, when Johnny walked in. She leapt to her feet.

'Johnny!' She gave him a hug, which he returned with great warmth. Then all the kitchen staff were there, leaning out of the hatch, wanting to know how Pauline was, with Tomasz's great booming voice rising above it all. Fliss had never seen the place so happy. Amazing how the imminent arrival of a baby could make such a difference. She thought of how she'd have to leave all of this behind her when she went back home with her parents, and how she wouldn't be there when Johnny brought his baby to the hotel to show everyone, and she began to feel tearful again.

She tugged on Johnny's sleeve.

'Come and sit down,' she pleaded. 'Tell me all about it.'

Johnny lifted his tray, piled high with food by Tomasz, and brought it over to the table to sit beside her.

'Tomasz must think it's me who's eating for two.' Johnny gave her a wide grin. It was a proper smile for once, and his cheeks were flushed with happiness.

'So,' Fliss said. 'Tell me everything! I thought your aunt said Pauline had a new boyfriend. Is that not true? Is she back to stay? You look like a man who's opened a dustbin and found a million pounds.'

Between mouthfuls of his enormous lunch and many interruptions from Fliss, Johnny pieced together the events for her – how Pauline's aunt had made it all up about Pauline having a new boyfriend, and it was all a lie. Basically, Pauline's aunt was trying to get rid of Johnny, and she'd turned Pauline's head a little. She'd told Pauline she didn't think Johnny was good enough because he was "just a waiter". This drew a gasp from Fliss. For several minutes she let her outrage spill out, and it was quite some time before Johnny was able to get a word in.

'Hold your fire,' he said. He gave a self-deprecating grimace. 'Anyway, she's right. I wasn't good enough.'

Fliss made to start arguing again, but Johnny shook his head.

'I wasn't good enough to be a dad. Before you came here I messed around a lot. All I wanted to do after work was spend time down the pub with my mates. I'm not surprised Pauline left. But someone's told her about you changing the hotel around, about Patrick being back in charge, and how I've started pulling my weight here. And then she got homesick and was googling us and saw the wine-tasting weekends, with my name and photo on it. She said it looked really professional. She started to wonder if maybe I wasn't the waste of space her aunt kept telling her.' His cheeks went a little pink at this, and he prodded at the remains of his lunch. 'Anyway, she's come back to find out. We're not together yet, not officially, but it's a start. And I don't mean to let her go again, not if I can help it. Not back to that aunt of hers, anyway.'

He laid down his cutlery with a look of determination on his face.

'I'm so glad.' Fliss reached over and hugged him again, and then she dabbed at her eyes. 'That's such good news. I really hope everything's going to work out.'

'Thanks.' He gave her a warm smile. 'And anyway, enough about me. What about you and Patrick getting married? You kept that quiet, didn't you?'

Fliss threw him a sidelong look.

'Only kidding.' He burst out laughing. 'Jean told me it was all a hoax on my way in just now. I might have known it. Congratulations on not being engaged. Only an idiot would get married to Patrick.'

He picked up his bowl of apple tart and began tucking in. Fliss should have been glad that everyone at the hotel accepted the engagement as a sham so easily, but in a contrary way, the thought that no one had ever really believed in it was thoroughly disheartening.

She stacked her plates on her tray, her cheerful spirits over Johnny's news fading.

By mid-week, everyone in the hotel had forgotten all about Patrick's engagement announcement, and Fliss was beginning to think he was right to tell her not to worry, and that it would all blow over. That was, until she woke up on Wednesday to find her phone practically alive with texts, tweets and social media messages from all her online friends.

'Wow, you kept that quiet! xx'

'So that's why you ran away to the Lake District – what a hottie! xxx'

'Who knew a guy in a ruff could look so hot? Swit, swoo!'

'When do we get to meet him? And can I be bridesmaid???'

What on earth…? Fliss sat up in bed bleary-eyed, holding her phone at arm's length. A quick flick through her messages brought the answer. She'd been worrying there might be a small story in the Cumberland Herald. That would have been bad enough, but here was a half-page article in the business pages of a national newspaper. The headline ran: "A Marriage Made in Heaven?" Underneath was a photo of herself and Patrick, standing on the terrace in their Tudor outfits, with the fairy lights twinkling behind them. The photo was taken shortly after Patrick had kissed her. There he was, in his black doublet, looking down at her, all dark and mysterious. Fliss's face was tilted up to his, her hands on his shoulders. Patrick's arm was around her waist.

The text underneath was equally arresting, but not in a

good way.

Felicity Everdene is Operations Manager in the Everdene chain of hotels owned by her parents, James and Helen Everdene. The unofficial announcement of her engagement to Patrick Cross, owner of the Cross Hotel – a small family-run business in a quiet village in the Lake District – has come as a surprise to many. Rumours have been running rife in the hospitality industry ever since Felicity took extended leave from her high-profile job some time ago. There has been talk of clashes with her father after a recent acquisition in Stuttgart. Legal proceedings by the German former owners are still ongoing. An extraordinary board meeting has been called for next week, furthering speculation about the future of Everdene Hotels.

And what of the future for the Cross Hotel? Local sources say Patrick Cross may struggle to keep control of his own business once his marriage goes ahead. His future in-laws are certainly a force to be reckoned with. Will the Cross Hotel be yet another small nut to fall under the wheel of the mighty Everdene chain? Watch this space...

Fliss uttered a shocked oath and scrambled to her feet. She'd been helping out behind the bar the night before, as Joanne had taken the night off, and so she'd woken late. She opened her wardrobe and flung on the first set of clothes that came to hand, ran her fingers through her hair and rushed out into the corridor. She had to find Jilly before she read the news or heard it from someone else.

Don't worry, Patrick had said. She repeated his words crossly as she took the stairs two at a time. All very well for him to say. He was out of the country. And in the meantime, Fliss very urgently needed to phone her parents, who would be stunned to read of her impending marriage in a newspaper.

Fliss halted for a second or two, clutching the banister. Something else in the article hit her for the first time. *An extraordinary board meeting?* What was that all about? With her heart racing, she began leaping once more down the stairs.

Jilly was behind her desk, her eyes fixed on her computer screen, her face alight with happy bemusement.

'Oh, you're here, Felicity.' She turned her monitor as Fliss burst in, so that the screen was pointing in Fliss's direction.

'Come and take a look at this. It's absolutely extraordinary.'

So word had spread already. Fliss's heart plummeted. 'I'm so sorry, Jilly,' she panted. 'Patrick told me not to worry about it all before he left. He said nothing would come of it. Honestly, if I'd known anything like this was going to happen –'

'You're sorry? Whatever for, darling? We've got so many bookings coming in, I can hardly keep up with them.'

Fliss glanced at the screen and saw, instead of the newspaper article she'd just read, Jilly had brought up the Cross Hotel's website.

'I didn't understand it at all when I logged on this morning,' Patrick's mother went on. 'There were so many enquiries, I thought people must have confused our hotel with someone else. Then one of the chambermaids told me the Tudor party's gone viral. Isn't that wonderful?'

'Oh, no!' After the newspaper article that morning, anything was possible. Fliss scrambled for her phone, just as it buzzed again in her hand.

"I'm famous!!! Check out the caped crusaders. Haha!! Proper lol-ing!!"

Johnny's exuberant text contained a link to a short video that had appeared on Twitter. Fliss watched the scene unfold in amazement. There was Johnny drawing back his fist, there was a look of startled horror on Cameron's face, and then Patrick and Willy racing to the rescue. The whole video was rendered ten times more melodramatic by the flickering candlelight and the fact that all four of the men were wearing Tudor costume. Patrick looked dashing and a little ruthless in his black cloak as he sprang forward. The shadows playing out over Johnny's angry features made him look all handsome and mysterious. Even Willy was striking in his maroon cap. The only one who looked foolish was Cameron.

Fliss pressed replay and held her phone up for Jilly to see. 'I think this may explain the sudden bookings.'

Patrick's mother put her hand to her mouth. A small giggle escaped her. 'Oh, how dreadful for Cameron. But really, it's his own fault. He'd been goading Johnny all evening. And doesn't

Patrick look terribly stern and heroic? Well this might account for our popularity,' she added brightly, 'but actually, Fliss, I think there's more to it.'

Jilly drew the keyboard towards her and clicked a second tab on her screen. A series of photos flashed up on another social media site. Fliss recognised the name of the photographer who'd been at the party with Caroline Morton. He had an excellent eye for a photo. There was Patrick, looking dark and lordly at the head of the table, and Johnny stalking the room with a mouthwatering selection of dishes on his tray. Another photo showed Fliss in her long, low-cut dress, rushing onto the terrace, and then a further image of Fliss and Patrick locked in a passionate embrace. There were dozens more equally dramatic, and as Jilly clicked through them one by one, Fliss couldn't fail to notice that the photos of either Patrick or Johnny had gained hundreds of likes and comments.

"*Wow, nice! Where is this hotel?*" someone had posted under a photo of Patrick, who was standing on the terrace, legs planted wide apart, arms crossed over his broad chest, looking like some old-fashioned movie heart-throb in a historical romance.

Jilly turned the monitor back round to face her, shaking her head in delight. 'I can't believe how wonderful the response has been. And it's all down to you, Fliss. If it weren't for your Tudor night, none of this would ever have happened. We've had such a flood of interest, we might even have to hire more staff. I know I keep saying this, darling, but I'm so happy about you and Patrick. It's such a *relief* to know you're getting married and that you'll be staying.'

Fliss opened her mouth to tell Jilly yet again that she and Patrick weren't getting married, then closed it with a sigh. Jilly obviously wasn't going to believe the whole engagement thing was a lie until she finally left the hotel forever and went home with her parents.

Her parents! She put a hand to her forehead and let out a cry. 'I haven't told my mum and dad yet about us getting married, and now it's all over the newspapers! I mean, I haven't told them that we're *not* getting married. I have to give them a ring right now.'

Fliss ignored Jilly's bewildered look and darted out of the reception to run back to her room. She didn't want to talk on the terrace and run the risk of people eavesdropping as she was trying to have a private conversation. She launched herself into her bedroom, threw the window wide and hung out of it to dial the number.

Her mother answered on the first ring, almost as though she were expecting her.

'Mum! Have you seen the papers?'

'Yes, I have, darling. And hello to you, too. Or should I say "Congratulations"?'

Fliss breathed out a sigh of relief. Her mother's voice was calm and unhurried. After all her parents' experiences with the press, Fliss should have guessed her mum would never believe anything she read in the papers. Briefly, Fliss explained everything that had happened during the Tudor night, and the journalist's aggressive line of questioning. Her mother took the story of her engagement with a large dose of media salt.

'Well, of course we didn't believe it, Fliss. We didn't see how it could be true, since Jilly told us Patrick wants to give up running the Cross Hotel and go back to Dominica. In fact, she was quite upset about it last time she spoke to me.'

Fliss pressed a hand to her forehead. She felt a stab of that same pain she'd felt the last time she'd thought of Patrick leaving. Everything was such a dismal muddle at the moment – which reminded her. 'There was another strange thing,' she told her mother. 'The newspaper said you'd called an extraordinary board meeting for next week. What's all that about? Did they get that wrong, too?'

There was a small hesitation on the other end of the line. 'Honestly, there's no keeping anything a secret in this business. Your father and I wanted to tell you all about it in person at the weekend. It's nothing to worry about. Just the opposite. It's something we think you're going to be very happy about.'

That was all Fliss could get out of her mother. For the rest of the conversation Helen talked lightly about what they planned to do in the Lakes when they came to visit, how much she was looking forward to seeing Jilly, and about how Minnie wanted to play Pooh-sticks on the bridge, ever since Fliss had told her about it. By the time Fliss ended the call, she was feeling a lot more reassured about her parents' reaction to her "engagement". On the other hand, her mother's talk of Patrick selling the hotel, and all the secrecy around the board meeting, had only succeeded in making her feel even more anxious than ever.

Fliss couldn't wait for the weekend, and Patrick's return.

Patrick

Three days later, Patrick landed at Manchester airport, his spirits lighter than they'd been in years. He was filled with a buzzing excitement that lifted him out of his jet-lag. Everything had gone well in the Caribbean. Better than well – it was perfect. He'd sold his share of the dive school to an old friend of Oscar's. Although sad to say goodbye to Oscar and his family, he had arranged to return for a few weeks every year during the hotel's low season to help out.

Patrick was looking forward to resuming life in the Lake District with more optimism than he would have thought possible only a few weeks before. There were just a couple of problems that niggled at him. Firstly, the visit from Fliss's parents. While he was in Dominica, a few of his friends had emailed him the link to Caroline Morton's article. Her story was supposedly about his engagement to Fliss, but the hints that the Everdene chain was about to swallow up his hotel weren't exactly subtle. He tried to dismiss it as yet more rumour-mongering, but his misgivings were hard to shake off. Still, at least he now had the chance to meet James Everdene himself – something he was looking forward to, in an odd way. Fliss's father seemed a man of contradictions, and he was curious to get to know him.

The other unknown in his mind was Fliss herself. He thought of the offer he was about to make her. It was possible she might turn him down – and what on earth would he do then? He forced himself to concentrate on the motorway ahead of him. By the time he reached Emmside and had begun to climb the fell leading up to the hotel, his optimism was waning and tiredness had begun to take hold. He was driving past the dry stone wall and the view of the lake, thinking of the day he first met Fliss, and the way her smile had burst through his clouded thoughts, when a white Mercedes came shooting down the winding road towards him. He just had time to register the man at the wheel – hair cropped short, sunglasses – and the well-groomed woman beside him as the car flew past.

Patrick checked his rearview mirror and caught the number plate, EVERDENE 1. So Fliss's parents were here already. There was another figure in the car, in the back seat. As they disappeared around the bend he wondered for a moment if it was Fliss, but then he remembered her younger sister Minnie - the owner of the stuffed giraffe.

Patrick carried on up the hill. Once in the car park, he unloaded his case from the boot and carried it through to reception. Sarah was behind the desk, and he greeted her as he walked in.

'Have you seen Fliss?' he said, as he passed the desk. 'I saw her parents driving down to the village just now.'

Sarah shook her head, telling Patrick Fliss's parents had popped to the village to get Jilly some flowers. They'd asked Sarah for directions to the florists'. Sarah hadn't seen either Fliss or Jilly since breakfast.

Patrick thanked her, and made his way up to his rooms. It struck him as odd that the Everdenes had gone out without Fliss. Why not ask Fliss herself to show them where to buy the flowers? He gave a mental shrug. His unease was probably due to tiredness.

A brisk shower and a change of clothes did much to dispel Patrick's jetlag, and an hour later he was seated at his desk with a cup of black coffee at his elbow. He'd arrived too late for lunch, but in any case he didn't feel hungry.

There was a pile of unopened letters on the desk. Patrick

began to sift through the envelopes, putting bills to one side and throwing circulars in the bin. Quite a few of the guests had written to say how much they'd enjoyed the evening – but no card from Cameron, he noted. There was a card from Alison and Guy, thanking him for the great time they'd had at the Tudor night and inviting him round for dinner. *And bring Fliss, too*, Alison wrote. Patrick remembered his engagement announcement and smiled to himself. Alison obviously believed they were a couple. He could just imagine what Fliss would have to say to that, if she found out.

Amongst the bills and thank-you notes was a heavy white envelope from the hotel's accountants in Penrith. Patrick slit it open and drew out the documents enclosed.

"*Dear Patrick,*

First of all, I just wanted to let you know how much my husband and I enjoyed the Tudor evening at the Cross Hotel. The meal was one of the best we've had in a restaurant in a long while. I'm so pleased to see the hotel is in such good hands and going from strength to strength. Congratulations also on your forthcoming wedding. Have you and Felicity set a date?

Patrick's smile faltered. Perhaps Fliss was right. Things were getting out of hand.

My main purpose in writing is to let you know that Cassh-Ex – the firm your father approached for a loan (against my advice, as I told you in our last meeting) – has sold on the hotel's debts. The company who have bought up the debt is called Chisholm Holdings. This means the Cross Hotel is now in debt to Chisholm Holdings. The details are in the enclosed document.

The buying and selling of debts is common in business, as I'm sure you know, but I wanted to let you know as soon as possible. This situation has come out of the blue, and I know nothing about this new company. If Chisholm Holdings decide to call in your debts, it will place the Cross Hotel in a precarious position, unless you have immediate funds for repayment. My advice is to raise the necessary sum and repay as soon as possible.

Please give me a ring at any time if you wish to discuss this matter further."

With a sick feeling, Patrick spread open the document his accountant had forwarded. The words *Chisholm Holdings* headed up the sheet of paper, along with an offshore address for the business, plus the amount of money he now owed them. With the interest accrued in the months since he'd returned home it was a staggering sum. For a couple of seconds his mind went blank at the sight of it. Then he thought of the money he'd raised from the sale of his share of the business in Dominica. It would set his plans back, but repayment was just about do-able if these people at Chisholm Holdings suddenly decided to call in the debt.

Chisholm. The name was familiar, but where from? And then he had it. The blood drained from Patrick's face. He pushed back his chair with a clatter and rose to his feet, the letter scrunched in his hand, just as Johnny gave a tentative knock on the door.

'Christ, I'm glad you're back.' Johnny's eyes were wild in his smooth, handsome face, and his spiky hair stood up in tufts. 'There's been shedloads happening while you were away.' His attention was caught by the document balled up in Patrick's hand. 'And what's that?' he carried on tensely. 'Is it true? Are we being bought out?'

'What do you know? What's going on, Johnny?'

The waiter stepped backwards in the doorway, casting a quick, furtive glance up and down the corridor. He came back inside, saying, in a hushed, conspiratorial tone, 'Fliss's parents are here.'

Patrick's feeling of dread intensified. 'Yes, I know. And?'

'You're not going to believe this, but Fliss's mum and dad spoke to Jilly this morning. They want to buy the hotel and give it to Fliss as a present.'

'*What?* How the hell do you know all this?' It shouldn't have astonished Patrick that gossip travelled like fire through the hotel, but to have all his fears confirmed in this way almost undid him.

'It was Joanne who found out. She was helping serve breakfasts on the terrace and she overheard them talking.

Apparently Jilly went all red. Joanne couldn't help overhearing because they started talking quite loud. Your mum went off somewhere and – '

'And where's Fliss?'

'I'm here.'

She was standing behind Johnny in the doorway, pale and erect, the sound of her approach so quiet Patrick hadn't noticed her arrive. She stepped inside. She was wearing the same blue and white checked dress she'd worn that first day Patrick drove her down to the village. His heart soared at the sight of her. And then he remembered Chisholm Holdings and the sheet of paper, still crushed in his fist. He dropped the document on the table and stood up straight, anger consuming his brief moment of elation.

'What the hell's been going on while I've been away?'

Johnny cast a quick, apprehensive look at the two of them and made his excuses. Patrick barely noticed him leave. Fliss came right into the room to stand in front of his desk. The afternoon sun fell on her dress and her slim hands as she rested them on the chair back.

Patrick pushed the crumpled ball of paper towards her. 'It seems I'm now in debt to a company called Chisholm Holdings,' he said. 'Chisholm's your mother's maiden name. Do you take me for an idiot?'

Fliss flinched a little. Her hands gripped the back of the chair, and Patrick almost relented. Then he remembered everything that had happened, how close he could be to losing his hotel, and his compassion froze.

There was a puzzled frown on Fliss's face. 'What are you talking about?' she said. Almost immediately, she let out a breath, as though the implication had just hit her.

'Oh, very good.' Patrick's voice was clipped and hard. 'So you really had no idea your parents now have a hold on my hotel through a holding company?' He leaned forward, placing his hands on the desk. 'Well, unluckily for you, I've just sold my share in my diving business in Dominica, which means I have enough money to pay off this loan and any others you try to throw at me. So you won't be able to use my debts as leverage to buy my hotel. Nice try.'

Fliss straightened, her blue eyes wide. 'You mean you went to Dominica to sell your business? So you're staying?'

Patrick was thrown off course. Was there actually a glimmer of hope in Fliss's eyes? Then he thought of how differently he'd imagined telling her his news, and his own hopes were swallowed in a tide of bitterness. 'Yes, I'm staying,' he said. 'I'm sorry to disappoint you, but if you want to buy a hotel to play with, you'll have to look elsewhere.'

There was a second or two of silence. Fliss's hands continued to grasp the chair back, her knuckles white.

'I see.' Her voice shook a little, but her eyes had become cold and hard. 'Well, that's certainly a blow that I can't have the Cross Hotel for my new toy. But since I intend leaving anyway, I won't be crying myself to sleep over it.'

'I'm sure you won't let it thwart you. Just like you ignored me when I told you I didn't want to spend money on new curtains. You went ahead and did it, anyway. And do you know the thing that makes me laugh the most? I was going to ask you to stay. To take on the management of the hotel. I'm going to reopen the swimming-pool in the cellar and open up a dive school here at Emmside. You could have had everything you wanted,' he waved the crumpled letter in the air, 'without the need for all this underhand rigmarole.'

Fliss's face could have been carved from marble. Some devil in Patrick wanted to make her feel, to respond with the same heat that was burning him from inside.

He carried on remorselessly, 'You talk about loyalty to your parents. What sort of person stays loyal to someone who acts against a family friend with such despicable ruthlessness?'

If he'd wanted to rouse her, his words had the right effect. Now it was his turn to flinch at the change in her. The cold in her eyes was swept away by glittering heat. She leaned across the table, her face pressed close to his. 'Don't you dare talk to me about loyalty,' she hissed. 'You know nothing about it. I love my parents, and I'll stick by them. I didn't run off to the

Caribbean like you did, at the first sign of trouble. Where was your loyalty then?'

'How dare you? You know nothing about my father.' He stood up straight, glaring down at her. 'And now I think it's best if you leave my office.'

Fliss took a step back. The fire inside her had disappeared as soon as it came. She was never one to stay angry for long, Patrick knew that. What on earth had just happened? Inside, he was shaking, but Fliss took another step away, with a small shake of her head.

'Do you know, Patrick, you're the one who's lost out. It's you who could have had everything you wanted. I'm glad you've found the money to build up your hotel. I wish you every success.'

Her voice broke on the last words and she turned to go. Patrick stood rooted to his desk as her light tread disappeared swiftly down the corridor. Her footsteps died away. When the silence fell he came to his senses. He shot out of the door and into the corridor, but there was no sign of her. He hurried on into the reception and almost knocked Johnny down in his haste. He was about to push past him when Johnny placed a hand on his arm.

'I've been coming to find you, mate,' he said. 'There's a bit of bother on the terrace. I need your help.'

'What?' Patrick shrugged his arm away, his attention fixed on the direction Fliss must have taken. 'Can't you sort it?'

'I've tried. It's Fliss's parents. And her sister. There's a bit of a scene.'

Patrick slapped his hand to his head. 'Oh, for God's sake.'

He turned on his heel and marched through to the lounge and towards the terrace. His first thought as he strode through the glass doors was that the place was busy. Busier than he'd ever seen it. The sun was shining, and every table was full. As soon as he stepped out, it appeared to him that there was a drop in the conversation amongst the guests taking afternoon tea. When Johnny appeared at his shoulder, several people picked up their cameras and began taking photos of the pair of them together. What on earth…? But he didn't have time to work out what was going on because he could see straightaway what Johnny meant about the "bother".

Fliss's parents were sitting at a table by the railing – the one with the best view over the valley, Patrick noted. He recognised James Everdene's cropped head and stocky frame from photos in the business pages. This was the man Patrick had glimpsed at the wheel of the car driving past him at speed on the fellside. He was wearing a dark blue cotton shirt, open at the neck. He had his arm around the waist of the girl standing beside him, whom Patrick took to be Fliss's sister. Minnie had her face turned away from Patrick, but he could see even from this distance that she didn't resemble Fliss. She was taller, with shoulder length dark hair. Her shoulders were slumped, as though she was sulking.

Opposite James Everdene was Fliss's mother. She was wearing a white summer dress, but instead of looking immaculate, as Patrick would have expected of the wealthy Helen Everdene, he could see as he approached the table that her dress was smeared on one shoulder with what seemed to be jam. Her fair hair was coming loose a little from her neat bun. Her eyes were hidden behind her sunglasses, but there was a frown on her brow and her shoulders were stiff with tension. Judging by her daughter's strident voice, it was no wonder Helen Everdene was on edge.

'I want to see Fliss,' Minnie was saying. 'She promised we could go and play Pooh-sticks, so where has she gone?'

The couple at the table next to the Everdenes turned to look daggers at them. Patrick heard the woman mutter, 'People like her shouldn't be allowed into places like this. It spoils it for the rest of us.'

So this was the source of Johnny's trouble. The Everdene's spoiled daughter was causing a scene. Unbelievable. Patrick came to a halt in front of James Everdene, wondering how to introduce himself when all the while he was churning with anger. In the event, he was saved the necessity. Minnie turned a scowling face in his direction.

'Who are you?' she asked.

At the sight of her, Patrick realised he'd grossly misjudged the situation and was immediately filled with remorse. It didn't need much study of Minnie's features for him to gather that Fliss's sister had Down's syndrome.

'Minnie,' her father remonstrated gently. He glanced up at Patrick, his expression full of apology.

Patrick took in Minnie's red, distressed face.

'My name's Patrick,' he told her. He held out his hand. 'I'm a friend of Fliss's, and I live here.'

Minnie hesitated a little before putting her own hand, all sticky with the scones she'd been eating, in his. It was evident she wasn't used to being treated with such adult courtesy by strangers. Her cross humour was forgotten, and she smiled, revealing teeth that were slightly too large for her mouth. Her almond-shaped eyes crinkled at the corners.

Everything Fliss had said about Minnie came back to Patrick – the stuffed giraffe, the dancing at the ballet, the presents of woolly sheep and postcards. All Minnie's childlike enthusiasms made perfect sense.

Patrick said the first thing that came into his head – the thing he said to Oscar's two sons when they were hot and bothered in the Caribbean heat.

'Do you like chocolate ice-cream?'

To his relief, his question had an instant effect. Minnie's eyes lit up. 'Yes, I do!'

'Well, my chef knows how to make a brilliant home-made ice-cream. How would you like to take a look in his kitchen and see if he can get some for you?'

Patrick hoped Tomasz wouldn't be too upset about having his kitchen invaded. He expected a long conversation with the chef on the subject later, but for now, this was an emergency. He glanced over at James Everdene. 'Would that be OK?'

'That would be wonderful.'

'Thank you.' Helen Everdene flashed Patrick a grateful smile. The smile was so like Fliss's, he was momentarily thrown off balance. Then Minnie tugged at his hand, and he turned to lead her in the direction of the kitchen. They chatted companionably as they passed through the lounge about whether Minnie had received her postcards, and what she and her parents had had for their lunch, and the whereabouts of Raffles (apparently a cause of conern). By the time they reached the kitchen, and with the prospect of ice-cream ahead of her, Minnie's fretfulness was forgotten. Fortunately Tomasz was only too happy to indulge any sister of Fliss's, and so Patrick was able to leave Minnie happily ensconced at the chef's large table and make his way back to the Everdenes.

As he stepped out again onto the terrace, some of the guests reached for their phones again to take a photo of him. He wondered if he'd grown another head. The whole day was becoming surreal.

Patrick was just nearing the Everdenes' table when the couple who had been muttering about Minnie motioned for him to come over.

'Well done,' the man told him under his breath.

Patrick looked from him to his companion, puzzled.

The guest cast a surreptitious glance in the direction of Fliss's parents. 'I don't know what they're thinking, bringing kids like that to a place like this. There are special places for that type of child. The parents look like they should know better.'

'I beg your pardon?' Patrick stared down at him.

'You know, bringing handicapped kids to a restaurant. It's not on.'

Patrick's brows drew together. 'If you don't like the clientèle in my hotel, I suggest you leave,' he said coldly.

'What? Hey, now –'

Patrick waved to Johnny. 'Johnny, could you clear these guests' table? They're not happy. Don't bother about bringing them the bill. They're leaving.'

'Well, there's no need – '

'Get your things together,' Patrick told him quietly. 'And don't come back in here again.'

He strode off towards the Everdenes. The look on Fliss's

mother's face told him she must have heard everything.

'I'm sorry,' he told her. 'I can't believe people can still behave like that in this day and age.'

Fliss's mother gave him a smile, the image of Fliss's own. 'Fliss told us how marvellous you are, and I'm beginning to see how right she is. I'm Helen.' She held out a slim hand.

'Good to meet you.' Patrick took her hand in his, surprised at how honestly he meant the words. It was hard to believe that this stressed and anxious woman could be the same person he suspected of trying to oust him out of his own business.

James Everdene stood and pulled out a chair for him. Close up, Patrick could see he was a hard, muscular man who obviously kept himself fit. He took Patrick's hand in a firm grip. 'James,' he said. 'Good to meet you at last. Hope you'll join us. We've a lot to talk about.'

That was an understatement. Patrick sat down, resting his hands on his knees, and waited for James Everdene to begin explaining himself. Fliss's father picked up his sunglasses from the table and began to toy with them. He appeared to be a careful man and was obviously considering how best to begin. In the end, it was Fliss's mother who rushed to speak first.

'Oh, dear, Patrick, we've had a terrible start to our visit. It's no wonder Minnie is so on edge. She does hate it when people don't get on, and there's been so much upset this morning. Dear old Jilly was trying her best to see things from our point of view, but she was terribly worried you'd be very angry and now she's gone off somewhere – we don't know where – and as for Fliss, she's absolutely furious.'

Patrick was feeling all the effects of his long flight, the shock of the news from his accountant, and above all, his distress at rowing with Fliss. His head felt fuzzy, and he could make no sense at all of what Helen was saying. He glanced round, in the vain hope Fliss might appear, but there was no sign of her. He remembered the look on her face as she'd walked away from him. There was a hollow feeling in his chest.

Helen's face was drawn, and James looked grave.

'This must be hard to follow,' James said. 'How about if I start right from the beginning? The thing is, Helen and I came up here to tell Fliss we've decided to retire from the Everdene business. We're starting a gradual process of handing over the reins to the directors next week.'

Patrick eyed Fliss's father, astounded. Of all the ways James could have begun, this was the last thing he'd expected. Retiring from business! It hardly seemed credible. James Everdene *was* the Everdene chain.

'It's Minnie, you see,' Helen explained. 'She's not dealing well with leaving school, and we've talked and talked about it, and in the end we just thought why carry on working when we could spend some time with Minnie ourselves, helping her gain some independence? We have all the money we need. We don't need any more, and Minnie's happiness is precious.'

Patrick glanced at James. He would have sworn Fliss's father must have taken some persuading to retire, but to his surprise James was smiling at his wife in complete agreement. There was a relaxed, contented look to him that Patrick would never have expected before their meeting.

'You understand this is top secret at the moment,' James told him. 'We've called a board meeting for next week, which is when we plan to tell the directors of our decision to stand down. But obviously we had to tell Fliss first, in person. We thought our retirement was the best way forward for all of us as a family. Fliss hasn't been happy working at Everdenes in recent weeks, and when she told us how much she loved your hotel – '

Patrick stiffened.

Helen laid a hand on his arm. 'Oh, she's been raving about being here, Patrick. She'd so love to run her own hotel.'

Patrick clenched his fists. He took a deep breath, forcing his voice to remain cool. 'I can understand why Fliss loves the Cross Hotel. And I understand why she'd love to own it. There's only one problem. I own this hotel, and it isn't for sale. I can't imagine why anyone thought it would be.'

James Everdene had the grace to look a little discomfited at

Patrick's statement. 'Yes, well, perhaps we misunderstood. We had the impression from Fliss that you didn't want to be here. You were talking about getting in a manager and going back to the Caribbean. We thought we were doing you a favour.'

Now it was Patrick's turn to be wrong-footed. It was true that only recently he'd wanted nothing better than to leave Emmside behind him and to persuade his mother to come and live with him in the Caribbean. But things had changed. And Fliss was the person who'd changed them.

Then Patrick remembered the document he'd received that morning. His eyes narrowed on James. 'So why buy up my debts? Did you think I might need some persuasion to sell?'

He gave the word "persuasion" a double-edged emphasis. James Everdene's expression hardened, and for the first time Patrick caught a hint of hard steel beneath the courteous exterior.

'Of course not,' James said. 'What did you suspect? That we'd hang a debt over your head? Did you really think I'd force Helen's friend out of her home?'

'I'd no idea what to think.' Patrick answered. 'Someone buys up my debts without discussing it with me beforehand. With the Everdene chain's reputation, you can forgive me for thinking the worst.'

There was a light of battle in James's eyes. He was about to make some retort, when Helen placed her hand on the table between them.

'Please, you two,' she said. 'We've had enough heated discussion this morning. Patrick, believe us when we say we only meant things for the best. We've got absolutely no intention of holding your debts over your head. On the contrary. We thought by buying them ourselves – before anyone else could do so – we were acting as friends, in the best interest of the Cross Hotel. As long as we hold the debts, no one is going to be chasing you for repayment, and Jilly can breathe a bit easier.'

Patrick took in the earnest look in Helen's expression. It was hard to believe she could be lying – or that she'd play an underhand trick on an old friend. Perhaps, after all, Fliss's parents had genuinely meant to help. It was a shame they'd gone about things in such a clumsy fashion.

Helen was looking at Patrick anxiously, waiting for his reply. He unclenched his hands.

'I see,' he said stiffly. 'Well, I don't enjoy being in debt to anyone. As it happens, I now have the money to repay you.' He dropped his rigid pose and rubbed his forehead wearily, as the honesty of the Everdenes' intentions began to sink in. 'It seems you meant well, but I'm sure you'll understand how I came to take things the wrong way.'

Patrick thought of all the terrible accusations he'd thrown at Fliss that morning and sat up straight. 'My God. I need to find Fliss.'

He leapt to his feet, ignoring the Everdenes' astonished expressions, and was about to race back into the hotel to look for her when he found Tomasz's large form blocking his way.

'I had chocolate *and* strawberry ice cream, and I helped Tomasz with the dishes.' Minnie was holding Tomasz's hand, completely at home with her new friend.

'That's right,' Tomasz said. 'She's a good worker. Loaded the dishwasher no problem and put all our cutlery away. Perhaps we could offer her a job.'

'That's great news,' Patrick said. 'But now I need to find Fliss. I'll be back soon.'

James and Helen exchanged looks, but Patrick had no time to think about their meaning. He darted past Tomasz and found himself the focus of several camera phones wielded by interested guests.

Patrick took the chef's arm and murmured quickly, 'Tomasz, why is everyone taking photos of me? It hasn't stopped since I got here.'

Tomasz chuckled. 'Don't you know? You cut a fine figure in Tudor costume. You need to have a look on social media some time.'

Patrick shook his head. None of it made sense but there was no time to think about it right now. He bade Minnie and her parents a swift farewell and hurried back inside. As he raced through the lounge he came across Jilly, clutching Minnie's stuffed giraffe in her arms and making her way towards the terrace, an anxious look on her face.

'Patrick, there you are. I've been looking for you all over. Have you met Fliss's parents yet? I hope you're not terribly angry. I tried to tell them – '

Patrick caught hold of his mother and kissed her cheek. 'Of course I'm not angry. Well, I was furious at first,' he confessed. 'But now we've had a chat and everything's sorted. I wish they hadn't gone about things in such a high-handed fashion, but they only meant to help. I'm afraid I might have upset Fliss.'

'Oh, Patrick, you have. I don't know what you said to her, but she's very, very upset with you. And she's upset with her parents. She told me she's sick of her father trying to organise her life, and from now on she's working for herself, even if that means starting at the bottom in a hotel kitchen. And she said she was sorry to have to tell me that I'd given birth to an arrogant fathead. Oh dear.' Jilly sank into one of the chairs in the lounge, clutching Raffles to her. 'And now I've got to give Minnie her giraffe back and I'm supposed to tell her Fliss won't be coming back here because she's going away. Minnie's going to be really upset and she'll be getting agitated all over again, and what I'll tell Helen I don't know.'

Patrick heard only one part of his mother's speech and his heart gave a violent lurch. 'Fliss is going away? Did she say where?'

'She wouldn't tell me. Just said she wanted to get away from everyone, and really, I can't blame her.'

Patrick plucked Raffles from his mother's hands. 'Mum, don't worry. I'll find her. Don't say anything to her family yet.' He ran from the room with Raffles under his arm, throwing over his shoulder, 'If she's left, it won't take me long to catch up with her. Not in that old banger.'

Chapter Twenty-Six

Fliss

Fliss hurled the last of her bags into Agnetha's boot and slammed it shut. A couple of bits of rust fell off and lay in flakes on the gravel but Fliss merely strode over them and moved round to the driver's seat. The sound of laughter drifted down from the terrace, which was packed with guests.

She turned her key in the engine. 'Packed with guests,' she told Agnetha in disgust. 'And they're all here because of my Tudor night. And what thanks do I get? I get treated like a child by my own parents and as for that…that pompous *idiot*.'

She reversed jerkily, and Agnetha let out a rumbling grumble. 'Sorry,' Fliss said. 'You're the only one who doesn't let me down, Agnetha. And Minnie,' she added, her conscience hitting her. She felt more than a little guilty at leaving Minnie behind, and tried to banish the thought of how disappointed her sister would be when she found out she'd gone. She hoped the restoration of Raffles would soften the blow, but somehow she doubted it.

She spun the steering-wheel. 'And it's all the fault of that..that stupid, overgrown oaf.'

Agnetha appeared to agree with her. Her engine sounded particularly hoarse as Fliss made her way down the drive of the hotel towards the road. When she stopped to indicate right, Agnetha growled ominously.

Fliss glanced in dismay at the dashboard. 'Come on, Agnetha,' she pleaded. 'We haven't got time for all this. Didn't those mechanics sort you out a few weeks ago?'

She made the turn onto the road winding down the fell to the village. The steep slope downwards proved more to Agnetha's liking, and as Fliss eased her foot off the accelerator the throaty complaining in the engine lessened. At the first tight bend, however, there was a loud bang from under the bonnet, and a cloud of white steam leaked out and drifted past the window. Fliss watched in horrified dismay as the steam continued to rise. It was no use trying to get Agnetha any further. The engine was dangerously overheating. There was nothing for it but to stop in the lay-by where she'd first met Patrick and call the rescue service. Fliss let Agnetha coast down the hill for several agonising minutes. The steam began pouring out to drift up the fellside, and it was a relief when the lay-by came into view.

Once safely off the road, Fliss switched off the engine. Memories of her first day at the Cross Hotel came flooding back – the smell of the gorse and wet leaves, and the sight of Patrick, staring down at the valley.

Agnetha continued to hiss and steam. Fliss put her head in her hands. The momentum of her anger was dissipating now she'd stopped the car, and all she could think of was how she would never see Patrick again. Her limbs were leaden with misery. After sitting for several minutes, feeling an intense dejection, she finally forced herself to open her car door. She stepped outside, her mobile in her hand, and moved over to stand beside the dry stone wall where Patrick had once stood. How full of optimism she'd been when she'd smiled at him that day! Blinking back tears, Fliss brought up the mechanics' number on her screen. No signal. Of course not. She was surrounded by mountains, and everywhere she went in the Lakes it was virtually impossible to make a call, unless she was leaning out of her bedroom window. Fliss toyed with the idea of walking back to the hotel and using their landline, but rejected it immediately. She didn't want to run the risk of bumping into her parents, and she especially didn't want to see Patrick. For a fleeting moment, she wondered what Patrick was doing right at that moment. Probably drinking tea and enjoying the attention of his fans on the terrace, she thought dismally.

There was nothing for it but to walk down to the village. Fliss glanced down at the platform shoes she was wearing and sighed. 'Well, I haven't decided where I'm going yet, but wherever it is, I'll make sure it's a place where there's never, ever going to be a need for me to wear sensible shoes.'

She went back to the car to collect her handbag and find something more suitable for walking in. There was the sound of another vehicle coming down the hill, and for a second her spirits rose. They sank just as quickly when Patrick's Land Rover appeared round the bend and pulled into the lay-by.

For a couple of seconds Fliss toyed with the idea of leaping back into the car and locking all the doors, but she decided that would be childish. Better to act with dignity. She moved back to the dry stone wall and leaned against it, arms folded, trying not to watch Patrick's muscular legs as he swung himself out of the car.

Fliss and Patrick

Patrick took a few steps towards Fliss. She raised one brow in a supercilious fashion, determined not to be the first to speak. Still, it was difficult to remain aloof when Patrick was carrying Raffles under one arm. The stuffed toy seemed to be looking at her reproachfully with its one eye, as though willing her not to be stubborn.

Patrick came to a stop, an uncertain expression on his face, and glanced over at Agnetha.

'Yes, she's broken down,' Fliss said, before he could say anything. 'I'm on my way to fetch the mechanic.'

'Would you like a lift?'

Fliss didn't know what she'd been expecting – perhaps an impassioned apology – but at his cold offer her heart felt like it might finally snap. She couldn't trust her voice to speak. She wished she could throw his offer back in his face, but since that would be childish – and it was a long walk to the garage – she merely nodded once.

'OK,' Patrick said. 'But before I take you down to the

village, I hope you'll please hear me out.'

Fliss waited. This had better be a good apology, or she was definitely walking.

'I'm sorry I spoke to you the way I did,' Patrick said. There was a tremor in his voice as he neared her. 'Your parents' actions came as a massive shock, but that was no excuse for acting as I did. When I got back from the airport, I was ridiculously happy to be back at the hotel. I thought I was finally about to realise all my dreams, and that the future was golden. Like I told you, I've enough money now to begin paying off the hotel's debts, and enough to re-open the swimming-pool and start up a dive school.'

'I'm pleased for you,' Fliss said coldly. 'What difference does that make to me?'

'Please don't make this hard for me.'

Fliss focused on Patrick properly for the first time. His face was haggard. There were dark circles under his eyes, and his voice had broken on his last words. She quelled her sympathy and lifted her chin. 'Why should I make things any easier? You've made it perfectly clear what you think of me.'

'No I haven't. I haven't made it clear at all. I haven't told you how much I love you.'

There was an astonished silence. The wind fluttered a few leaves in the branches overhead, and Agnetha's engine hissed gently.

Patrick took a step closer. 'I've told you what a difference you've made to my mother, and what a change there's been in her since you got here. I've told you about the magic you've worked in the hotel, and how much happier my staff are since you arrived. But I haven't told you how my heart lifts at the sight of you. How it soared that first day you smiled at me when I stood just here.' When Fliss didn't answer, he carried on unsteadily, 'I understand if you don't return my feelings. I hoped perhaps you might….But even if you can't love me as I love you, I hope you'll at least stay. We need you.'

Fliss felt his words seep into her, filling her with a warm, glorious sensation that robbed her of speech. Her lips parted, and her breath came quickly. For a couple of seconds, neither of them said a word. Patrick was rooted to the ground, waiting, his eyes never leaving Fliss for a moment.

Then Fliss said, 'If I stay, can Minnie come and stay with us sometimes?'

Patrick gave a small, shaky laugh. 'Yes, of course. She's already got Tomasz wrapped round her little finger. He wants to give her a job in the kitchen.'

Everything Fliss had dreamed of – the success of the Cross Hotel, a future with Patrick – was about to become reality, but above all else, above everything, his declaration of love made her dizzy with happiness, filling her with an overwhelming joy. She flew forward, throwing her arms around Patrick's neck.

'I'd love to stay.' She heard the thrumming in his chest as she pressed herself closer. 'I'd love to stay more than anything.'

Patrick dropped Raffles unheeded to the ground and lifted her face to his. 'Felicity Everdene,' he said. 'I'm the happiest man in the world.'

And then Patrick was kissing her by the dry stone wall, in exactly the same spot they'd first met, the day Felicity came to the Cross Hotel.

The lake sparkled in the valley below them.

THE END

Thank you so much for taking the time to read *Felicity at the Cross Hotel*. I hope you enjoyed Fliss and Patrick's story. If you did, please consider telling your friends or posting a short review. Word of mouth is an author's best friend, and much appreciated.

If you'd like to get in touch, I'd love to hear from you. I'm the only Helena Fairfax on social media, so you won't have far to look! You can find some stunning photos of the Lake District on my Pinterest page and Instagram, or else get in touch on Facebook, or on my website www.helenafairfax.com.

I look forward to hearing from you!

OTHER BOOKS BY HELENA FAIRFAX

A Way from Heart to Heart

A Year of Light and Shadows (a romantic suspense collection)

The Antique Love

The Silk Romance

ABOUT THE AUTHOR

Helena Fairfax was born in Uganda and came to England as a child. She's grown used to the cold now, and these days she lives in an old Victorian mill town on the edge of the Yorkshire moors. She finds the wild landscape the perfect place to write romantic fiction.

Helena's novels have been shortlisted for several awards, including the Romantic Novelists' Association New Writers' Scheme Award, the Global Ebook Awards, the Exeter Novel Prize, and the I Heart Indie Awards.

When not writing, Helena loves walking the moors with her dog, enjoying the changing seasons and dreaming up her heroes and her happy endings.